THE FEAST MAKERS

BY H. A. CLARKE

THE SCAPEGRACERS TRILOGY

The Scapegracers
The Scratch Daughters
The Feast Makers

THE FEAST MAKERS

H. A. CLARKE

EREWHON

an imprint of Kensington Publishing Corp.

www.erewhonbooks.com

EREWHON BOOKS are published by:

Kensington Publishing Corp.
119 West 40th Street
New York, NY 10018
www.erewhonbooks.com

All Kensington titles, imprints, and distributed lines are available at special quantity discounts for bulk purchases for sales promotions, premiums, fundraising, educational, or institutional use.

Special book excerpts or customized printings can also be created to fit specific needs. For details, write or phone the office of the Kensington sales manager: Kensington Publishing Corp., 119 West 40th Street, New York, NY 10018, attn: Sales Department; phone 1-800-221-2647.

ISBN 978-1-64566-081-1 (hardcover)

First Erewhon hardcover printing: April 2024

10 9 8 7 6 5 4 3 2 1

Printed in the United States of America

Library of Congress Control Number is available upon request.

Electronic edition: ISBN 978-1-64566-082-8

Edited by Diana Pho
Cover art by Anka Lavriv
Cover design by Dana Li and Samira Iravani
Interior design by Dana Li

for the proto-august who
wrote *scapegracers*. cut your
hair, nerd

"Before such an irresistible force 'conspiring kings' will be powerless."—Peter Kropotkin

"Dykefags eat the rich!"—Local dive bar bathroom stall graffiti

THE FEAST MAKERS

FIRST PERSON

Tomorrow was the flocking. Covens from all across the states would be gathering to sift through the recovered specter hoard for the stolen parts of their dead friends. It'd be the most witches I'd ever met in one place, my mother's coven included, and I would sort out my feelings in the morning. Magic and a comfortable crossfade meant I didn't think much about how I'd been waitlisted by two of the three colleges I applied to, or wallow in disappointment about how getting my specter back hadn't instantaneously reversed my mental illness, or that it was "imminently confronting my foundational childhood traumas" o'clock and so on. I walked down a torn-up drive with my friends. It was late on a Friday in mid-March. The five of us shivered in our little outfits, all slathered in scribbled sigils, slaphappy from the pregame, and I loved them, which made this easier. I loved them completely. You've got to lean on what you have.

The warehouse flickered in the dark. From outside, Homo Erectus looked like *Giovanni's Room* flipped inside out. Grime oozed between its jaggedy bricks and drooled in fingers down toward earth. It looked structurally unwell, multiply risky. I'd bet this had been just another factory once upon a time, i.e., in the eighties, that'd choked with the rest of the Rust Belt. Maybe lumber had been pulped here and beaten into flags of paper, or it could've been an auto manufacturing plant, or a steel mill or something. Whatever! It's for mischief, now. Its windows strobed magenta and lime and music slammed inside it. The bass throbbed in the soles of my boots. There wasn't a sign. We traipsed along, Jing leading with bravado in a swishing leopard coat, and as I marched on behind her I wondered vaguely how Shiloh had found out about this place. They'd known themself for all of five months and were already a rave connoisseur, which meant that suddenly I was a rave connoisseur, and that my coven had a reputation beyond the corporate limits of Sycamore Gorge. There were bigger scenes than house parties. My girls were not without ambition.

There was a line. We stomped past it. Waiting dancers eyed us and a vaguely familiar few flashed us scrunchy, unsober smiles. Jing stretched her arms over her head, then relaxed her shoulders, let her leopard coat dip to the small of her back. Yates tucked herself into Daisy's side, and they clung to each other, ran after Jing on synchronized tiptoe, and Shiloh and I edged behind them, all of us within a yard of each other. Particulates in our own little planetoid. Tall girls with little shorts and choppy mullets murmured something about *those witches*.

Hot to be preceded. These days, we held ritual service every time we went out.

As she ran, Daisy unhooked one arm from Yates' waist and produced a bottle of Gatorade from nowhere. She cleared it in one swallow then flipped a Lego between her teeth. Yates mirrored Daze and pulled one hand free to check her phone, then blinked fast, eyes shiny, either from the chill or the fact that it still wasn't Ivy Day, even now, thirty, forty-five seconds since the last time she'd checked her inbox. She'd pulled her curls into two puffs on either side of her head and the spirals of a hangover-proofing sigil sparkled on the nape of her neck. Up front, Jing reapplied her lip gloss. She balanced the kitschy clamshell compact I'd gifted her for Christmas in her palm. It caught the party lights above her, sparkled on her mouth like it'd struck water. Jing snapped the compact shut. She turned to Daisy. Daisy flicked her eyes up and down her, and she crushed her empty plastic bottle and thrust it underfoot, leaned in with a swish of caramel-colored pigtail, and ghosted the edge of her thumb around the corner of Jing's bottom lip. A plummy stain clung to her nail.

"Ugh," Daisy said. She flashed her teeth, expression so bright it was nearly unhinged. Pupils small, still. It'd take a few minutes. "Just heartbreaking."

Shiloh examined their nails. They were meeting up with someone, if I understood their vagaries correctly, and they'd dolled up for it, wore a tiny white tank top, perilously low-slung slacks they'd inherited from Julian, a belt chain borrowed from yours truly, oxblood platform clogs they'd found in the shop. Blotted lip stain, a ghost of blush in the apples of their cheeks. Bone-blond hair, long as their jaw now, smoothed behind their ears with crisscrossed bobby pins. My teeth chattered. Leather sucks for windchill. The shirt I wore beneath, hacked free of its sleeves, didn't help much either. I was cold where my jeans gashed open and cold where my shirt collar dipped. I'd touched up my buzz cut a week ago, and the breeze raked every groove of my skull, pressed on those zigzagged bits where the smaller bones fused together. I sniffed, bounced like a boxer, then pulled my hands out of my pockets and texted them: **You look cute jackass**

Shiloh's pocket lit up. They withdrew their phone in a fluid motion a breath later, frowned at it, then over their shoulder at me, and replied: **ew ilu**

Where's the guy?

inside already

Is he cool?

hes a vegan trotskyist

Does that mean yes or no

bite me

I felt an odd kick of pride that I knew Shi, and that they'd so quickly grown from an extremely evil libertarian nightmare person into a way less evil communist nightmare person. Happy that they could be in the room with the Scapegracers without Daisy hissing now, too. I thought about us coming to save them two months ago only to find them standing in the dirt road's delta with a bag in their fist, speechless, rigid, past tears. I mashed the thought down. I grinned and the dry skin on my lower lip promptly split. It puffed, I tasted like pennies. The night air stung when I took a breath. I was unkissable at baseline, I didn't need the boost. I shoved my phone back in my pocket, then shook my hands out at the wrists, swept one thumb over my opposing palm, and rubbed out some of the tension.

The bouncer said, "Scapegracers?"

Jing said, "That's right."

The bouncer made a face. He asked for Daisy's ID.

Daisy pulled it from thin air and forked it over.

I squeezed my eyes shut, paranoid for a moment that this time, the realfake sigil would flake out on us and we'd be shit out of luck. It was a relatively recent addition to our repertoire. Definitely wouldn't get you through an airport or anything that intense, but it had held up so far in similar circumstances. Fuck, would it be a bummer if it went belly-up on us now! To stand in the cold for nothing! Being known as Scapegracers wasn't a guarantee of getting into places, particularly parties we didn't frequent. This bouncer was a stranger.

He handed back her plastic and waved her through the door.

One by one, my friends melted into the scalding pink darkness. It happened fast. I blinked and suddenly it was just me out here in the cold. Wasn't sure if they were waiting just beyond, or if they'd dispersed and I'd have to wander aimlessly for one thousand years to find them. Alone, I stepped up to the bouncer, who was annoyingly taller than me, and handed him my legal ID.

I hardly looked like that picture now. It was a year old. That version of me had shaggy curls and muddy eyeliner, looked smaller statured, sourer but softer everywhere. No hair meant I had more jaw. I hadn't worn makeup in a month and had the eyebags to prove it. I sniffed, glanced between the bouncer's grip and his screwed-up brow, tried to guess whether he noticed the inconsistencies, or whether he saw through the spell work to my real age, or if he was about to boot me for being the lone non-pretty member of my clique. But then, this was a queer party. Can't imagine most of us looked like our government papers.

He handed me back my ID.

I took a step inside and the world went hot again.

High ceiling, heavy fog, bodies knotted and throbbing to an alien, trilling house beat. There was that smell, the dark tart one that seemed to radiate off LEDs, and it hit the back of my throat and I felt emotional all of a sudden, very in my body, very human and awake. The music pressed on me. Pink mist seethed against my skin, glitter splashed me where dancing melted into moshing. People kissed each other. People drank and looked up at the ceiling, looked through the ceiling and through every tier of stratosphere past heaven with their eyes half shut, their lashes thick and tangled, dripping beads of black mascara. I could feel, I *felt*, there was sensation in my body all around me. My fingertips tingled. My head slightly hurt. I felt good, with strobe lights on the back of my neck I felt like my whole horrible self again, and feeling good made me dizzy. Parties are pocket utopias. Took a while to learn that, but fuck if it wasn't one of the only things I believed with certainty these days. I shook myself. People eddied around me. I nodded to the beat.

Where were my girls? Where'd they wandered off to now?

In my looking I let myself get caught in a current and was swept deeper into the warehouse. I lacked the right vantage to see the far wall from here, assuming that there was a far wall at all and this room didn't yawn on forever, so I wasn't sure contextually how deep into the room I'd gone. A circuit boy in a pup harness smiled at me. A molly-eyed redhead in fishnets jerked a nod my way as they passed. Someone offered me a tab I didn't take, and a flask, and a sticker. The beat changed, felt slower and haughtier, and I followed a girl I thought was Daisy for a while before the girl who absolutely wasn't Daisy vanished and I was suddenly at the edge of a makeshift bar. Radioactive green lanterns swung from hanging chains. People smoked and dripped off each other. The bartender wore a backless dress, and they sported corset piercings down either side of their spine that they'd strung through with bright white shoelaces. I pressed my hip against the bar and focused on breathing. Breathing felt nice. There weren't any open stools, but I didn't particularly need one. I glanced out over the crowd, scanned for Jing's platinum hair, or Yates' ruffled gingham dress, or Daisy's sugarcoated *Looney Tunes* violence energy signature. Far away from me, twisting between throngs of dancers, I thought I spotted Shiloh's arms around a narrow waist, their cheek leaned on a bony shoulder. I gnawed my bottom lip, squeezed my eyes shut for a second. They were overworked. Too much to see. The bartender asked so I got myself water and a sour. I put a twenty on the counter. It must've been enough.

Vision unfocused, I clasped my fist around the cold, wet tin and murmured something like *Thank you you're the best sick piercings uhuh thanks*. I flipped the lid with my thumb. It opened with a hiss. I brought it to my mouth and the taste hurt my teeth. I took a hearty swallow, shut my eyes again.

"Scapegracer?"

I opened one eye just a sliver, peeked between my lashes.

It was a girl. I didn't know her. She was shorter than me even with platforms. She had a curly bob and wore heart-shaped gems below her eyes. I lowered my drink and inclined my head, leaned so I could hear her over the screaming treble, meanwhile swept my free hand over my breast pocket, felt around the place where I'd stashed a few gnarly Polly Pockets for commission hexing purposes. I was rarely without at least one these days. Didn't like to be caught without supplies. I pressed the pad of my index finger over a plastic ankle, barely thicker than a toothpick, and cleared my throat. Both eyes open now, mostly focused, unclouded again. I peered around the crowd over her shoulder. Eyeballed anyone who eyeballed back. "Is he here?"

"No," she said, and then smiled and added something I couldn't hear over the music.

"Speak up," I said. I leaned down a little lower, tip of my nose just above the strap of her dress. It was a milky shimmery bodycon, looked holographic under the flashing lights, soft like a corn snake's belly. Hypnotic. I tongued my gums.

"Do you want to dance?" She smiled at me. One of her hands drifted up and she brushed fingers over my leather lapel, hooked the edge with the zipper teeth. She gave me a little tug.

I took an impassioned swig of my drink then abandoned the rest of it, hoped it hadn't made my hand too cold to the touch. I tried for a smile and faltered, feeling dumb and a little stiff. My head buzzed. My brain was a beehive. My teeth could rattle out of my gums. Whatever face I'd made must've been good enough for her, though. She walked backwards with a fistful of my jacket, and I let her lead me to another corner of the warehouse, nearer to the DJ, a place where there was so much glitter underfoot that it crunched like sand beneath my boots. It was murkier here, saltier. Lots of overlong wrists drifting loosely through the dark.

She tightened her fist, yanked me down a touch, snaked her free arm around the back of my neck. I felt the crook of her elbow against my nape. My gut wrenched like spell work. She moved her hips and I followed her, the bassline went jammy in my bone marrow and made my body feel hollow and when she swayed against my chest I felt a fuse bust in my brain, there were bright lights then nothing. Some central cognitive superego control panel went dark. I grinned like an idiot, then my grin slid off, my eyes shut again. Her temple was warm where it pressed beside my jugular. She said something I didn't quite hear.

I opened my mouth to ask her to repeat it, but instead I went, "What's your name?"

"Lina." (Or Mina? Nina? Sheena? Karina? What?) Then, once again, told me something that did not register in my brain as language. This music was too deep in me. I couldn't hear for shit.

"What was that, sweetheart?"

"I love masculine lesbians."

I fell out of sync with the music for a second. My vision stalled. My throat clapped.

Fingers closed around my hips. I was being pulled backwards, away from this girl, and I blinked and she was gone, swallowed by the ever-churning knot of human people. I whipped my head around but whoever had me was shorter than me, all I could see was red fog. I looked down at the hands on my belt loops then, saw how they were long-fingered, slim-knuckled, with neat sharp nails and maroon papercuts. Gold rings on every knuckle. Jing.

I found it in me to turn around.

She somehow kept her grip on me during my half rotation. She crooked her indexes, hooked them in the loops above my hipbones. The lights bounced off her hair; I couldn't see her eyes beneath her bangs except in flashes. She leaned up on tiptoe, pressed her cheek against mine.

"Where'd you go?" I felt watery and I smiled more earnestly than I hoped she'd catch. I pressed my cheekbone above her ear. No way she could see evidence of goofiness, or any lingering weird. "I was looking for you."

"Daisy's got a hex patron." Jing smiled, I heard it in her tone. "Except she's rolling so I think she'll need backup. Are you game?"

"Yeah," I said. My chest thrummed where she leaned on it. "Where is she?"

"Further back," she said against the hinge of my jaw.

Almost like dancing, her leaning on me this way. She swayed against me. This song felt nice in the soles of my boots.

I felt her lashes. She must've blinked. "Did I spoil your fun?"

"Nah," I said firmly. I didn't know what to do with my hands.

"You let girls drag you anywhere." She pressed her nose against me. For a stupid second I thought she might bite me. "She was cute. Did you get her number?"

"Didn't ask for it." A pulse in my throat just above the place where my specter lived, or at least where I imagined it. My soul ached. I curled my lip, flattened a hand against the small of her back, paused for response. I'd yank it back if she so much as twitched. I'd stuff them in my pockets. I'd gnaw them off, whatever whatever whatever, maybe I was a touch drunker than planned. Should've pregamed less. "Daisy?"

Jing put her weight on me. She wore a candy choker and

the little sugar beads rolled against my collarbone, powder pink and blue. I hadn't worn candy jewelry since I was a kid. I remembered it having a cloying bright taste and getting my wrist sloppy with spit. She strained on tiptoe, brought her mouth beside my daith and said, "Where's the fire? She'll be fine for a second."

Well. Daisy could get into a lot of absolutely ridiculous bullshit in three milliseconds given the chance, and if she needed the two of us it was wild to me that we weren't already across the floor, by her heels, doing whatever was necessary to the point of excess. Jing released my belt. She lifted her hands. They ghosted up the sides of me, waist and ribs and shoulders, up the ridges of my throat, my jawbone, the domes of my temples, the crest of my hairline. She skittered her nails over my crown. Little taps, like a spider's footsteps. They crept down my nape, then traced little zigzags over the one knobby vertebra where neck flowed into back. Like she was spelling something. "You're a fucking dummy, Sideways."

I sucked in a hard breath. "Yes, I am."

"Do you know why?"

What a question.

The hand closed over the back of my neck and she yanked down hard, pulled me until our foreheads flushed together. She was all I could see. "I'm trying to dance with you."

"But Daze—"

"Can wait for like five fucking seconds. As I said." She snorted, rolled her eyes up in her head. Her smirk vanished. She was inscrutable. Also, she was right: there was not a single electrical impulse in the whole of my brain. "Your little e-girl looked like she was having fun. I want a turn. Do I get a turn?"

No thoughts, no thoughts, no thoughts. A weird lick of doubt but I didn't give it language. I would've nodded but couldn't like this, and I couldn't blink either, and the eye contact was cracking some unseen emotional dam and I didn't have any bubblegum to spackle it over. I stepped backwards, unsteadily. The bass barely caught me.

Jing let go of my neck. She spun herself around, tucked her spine against my sternum, reached for my wrists, and crossed them above her navel. She swayed and I folded over her. She was right: I let girls drag me anywhere. I'd let her drag me anywhere. She wouldn't have to drag me, I'd just go.

She pulled her hair to one side and I pressed my nose into the crook of her neck. She rocked on her heels, tucked herself against my chest, thrummed like she was purring. Maybe that was me? Curse dolls folded like Swiss Army knives in my pockets, limbs distending, jostled like clock hands every time Jing moved. I shook a thought off as one arose. I opened my mouth. I saw spots. I bit down on a bead beneath her ear. The snap echoed in my skull. Artificial cherry smacked behind my eyes and against the back of my throat and it occurred to me, hilariously, that this thing tasted vile. I swallowed, scraped my tongue with my teeth. Jing snickered. She cocked her head to the side, stretched her neck. Dracula and Mina. Or Carmilla and Laura?

I gnawed off a second bead.

Something, someone, pulled my gaze up.

Jelly platform sandals and warm brown ankles, ruffled hem, pleats and folds and there was Yates. Yates stood across from us, eyes enormous, fawn lashes batting. Her brows shot up. Her mouth formed a little O. She looked at the two of us like: *Sideways is eating the choker off Jing's throat, okay cool, cute that we do that now, hi ladies, it's me Lila Yates, love you two, do y'all need me to leave you a second, or . . . ?*

I saw her hand hover over her pocket.

If she took a picture I'd put a temporary moratorium on my policy of being mean to most people except for her, hard stop. There would be an exception. Five minutes of awful. She moved her mouth—her jaw dropped, then her lips spread. Sounded out: *Day-zee.*

What about her?

Oh. Right. Daisy was hexing. Jing had come over here to fetch me as backup.

I squeezed my eyes shut, then opened them wide, like that'd manually adjust my inability to focus on anything more concrete than feeling Jing's heartbeat through her little dress and get me up to par. I moved to pull my hands back, but Jing put her nails in my wrists and I froze. She held me still. She took a step toward Yates and pulled me with her, and I felt a bit like a cape, or a big evil backpack.

Yates reached through the fog.

Jing mirrored her, linked pinkies with her.

Yates pulled us, both of us, across the floor.

People looked at us. It felt like plunging frozen hands under a hot faucet. People stared at me when I was just moving through space, at school or in public, with open and unwatered contempt. They stared like they stare at bugs under rocks. But here, in this room, people looked at us because they liked what they saw. I liked the weight of their looking.

Jing felt warm. Her pulse sang against my cheek. I had to remind myself not to get my feet tangled in hers, but my gait was wider, she could lead and I'd keep stepping outside her stride and it'd work forever. Yates held her linked pinkie at eye level, and it looked like she and Jing were making some promise. I wondered if I was implicated in the promise on proximity alone. I wondered if Jing and I looked like an Aristophanes monster like this.

Holy shit. I was gonna kill Daisy Brink for making me know the word "Aristophanes." Where was Daisy Brink?

There, in the darkness, in midair.

Her toes dangled in space, pink platforms drifting like she was treading water. Beaming, dreamy, ecstatic with owl eyes and a grin too wide for her face. Trick of the light but I could've sworn that she looked holographic, like light broke around her head and refracted as a halo. She'd pulled the skinny ribbon from her brow and knotted it around a little doll's ankle. She tilted her head back, dangled it over her open mouth like a bushel of grapes. She whispered against its plastic head with quick flashes of teeth. Her lipstick marred its cheek.

I slid off Jing. I felt like I'd been standing by a bonfire. I moved to her side, Yates found my hand and Jing the other, and we stood around with our knees touching, Daisy suspended between us. Our mouths moved. Muscle memory. Magic stirred and I flushed like it'd kissed me, it rasped over me and snagged me and slipped its hooks deep. I lost sight of Daisy. My body throbbed like it'd been struck. My specter stone pulsed once hard in the well of my throat. It wriggled sometimes, casting like this. I wasn't sure if it'd ever melt into the rest of me, be fully integrated and seamless inside me again. Still: I tasted that salty red taste when I said "Chett" with Jing and Yates, and cold pressure shocked around me like I'd plunged underwater, and my eyes worked, they fixed themselves on Daisy up above me.

She curled her lip and bit the doll.

Its body jerked with phantom life then bloomed with sketchy sigils.

Post-spell exhaustion clapped me. I felt raw and brittle, like the wet had been scraped off my long bones. My lungs flagged. My kneecaps fizzled. The ache struck me and I swayed but didn't fall, because the ache was in my friends, too, and we had just enough left in us to hold each other up. In the back of my head there was hot-pink static, like a sugar high. My sinuses rang. I couldn't focus. Without Scratch in my body, the afterwards was like the old days. It was a good hurt.

Around us there was clapping. There was always clapping, there was always somehow a crowd for this, just rings upon rings of people facing us with their teeth out and their eyes gooey. Two months ago I'd nearly fainted after we'd done six in a row and that crowd had caught me—it was at Dorothy's, maybe, I couldn't quite remember. It felt gorgeous, it was heartbreaking. I felt sick with it. Attention! I would never take cash for magic again, not when magic was caring for people, not when everybody gazed at me and smiled at me, at us, like this in exchange. Christ. Daisy came back to earth and squeezed the curse poppet so tight in her fist I thought it'd pop. Jing leaned in and Yates and I followed her, we all leaned into Daisy, who was laughing, who made me laugh in a fit of sympathetic giddiness. People around us said "Scapegracers, Scapegracers," and I squeezed my eyes shut and burned where their hands touched my back. This felt good, *was* good. I was good! I was alive right now, and here, and whole, or maybe broken in a way I could work with. My friends were here with me, they were devastating and unstoppable and I loved them. God, I loved them. I adore them, even still. We had a few months left before the end. I'd quit thinking for the rest of the night.

My pocket vibrated. Yates threw her arms around Jing's neck and bit her necklace. Daisy took down her hair and buried her hands in it. I wondered idly about Shiloh and I reached for my phone, still vibrating, and glanced at the lit-up screen. My gut flipped. I turned away from my girls, I swiped my thumb across the screen to accept the call and cradled my phone to my cheek but the music was too loud, I shouldered through the crowd and pushed toward an illuminated exit, where beauties smoked in the freezing cold. Long legs in shredded fishnets, glossy platforms, sprays of dead yellow grass. I stepped outside and marched across the cracked asphalt, cigarette smoke curled through the air around me, the sky was purple and orange from factory fumes, my head was pounding and about to burst.

I ground my molars and put her on speaker.

Madeline Kline said, "Sideways?"

White noise in my head. Screeching, crunchy, no thoughts, no words. I sniffed.

"I've got no right to talk to you." She sounded hushed, harsh. "I don't have time to make excuses. They caught me. The Corbies, my old coven, they caught me. They're going to present me at the flocking tomorrow. Decide what's to be done with me."

Breath caught in my teeth. I hissed out slowly. Managed, "What the fuck do you want?"

"Sideways, you were right. I should've asked for your help the first time. I didn't, I hurt you instead, I'm sorry. I'm fucking sorry. Look, they'll kill me. My coven will propose something dire, they're wrathful, and I don't have allies here. I need your help. I need the Scapegracers. They're talking about you four, how high-profile you've become, how you're notorious for just—just *helping* people. Little anarchy altruists. I need the Scapegracers to save me. Fuck my pride, I need *you*. I don't know where they'll be keeping me, but I'll be in the Delacroix, and when my phone dies I'm not going to be able to contact you again, and I don't have any good fucking reason why you should pity me. I'm sorry. Sideways, I'm sorry. Please."

I considered throwing up. I looked out into the woods, the distant cherry lights on a cell-phone tower. I rasped, "Tomorrow?"

"Yes. Sunset at the Delacroix. Can I count on you?"

A family of deer grazed near the edge of the woods. I watched the smallest one bend.

"I hate you," I said. "Yeah. You can count on us."

LAZY DAISY STITCH

The world was ending. It sounded like, CLANG CLANG
CLANG WAKEY WAKEY BEAUTY QUEENS. The
noise rinsed my whole body and I clapped a hand over my
cheek, then my ear because my ear is where the sound comes
in, then my mouth, my seething stomach, my wrenched-up
guts. The floor mashed up against my nose. I parted my lips
and my evil fuzzy tongue flopped out and mopped the hardwood. I cracked one eye. There was blond everywhere. The
hair moved, because Jing moved and it was attached to Jing,
and she shoved the heels of her hands into her eye sockets
and moaned. I saw elbows and knees on the other side of her
body that weren't hers—she'd been lying half on Daisy, who I
assumed was alive, hopefully?

"Good morning, Ms. Stringer," said soft and dulcet Yates
from somewhere above me. I rolled my eyes back in my head,
cringing at the way my own eyelids clung, and beheld her.
She looked so cozy in Daisy's bed. So unrumpled and not
hungover. She wore a bonnet and a satiny nightgown. She'd
stuck her false lashes to the pillowcase like fringy, friendly

caterpillars. She had Daisy's weighted blanket pulled up to her chin, and she folded her hands over the edge so that just her fingers fanned over the fabric. "I hope we didn't get in too late last night and wake you."

Daisy's new bedroom was small, which meant Jing and Daisy and I were crammed together on the floor. I felt pickled. If you gashed me open I'd probably slosh vinegar everywhere. My liver was a fist in my gut. All my organs were fists. They were denser than usual and were going to punch their way out. The walls were pink, violently so, and right now looking at them directly made my jaw hurt. I heaved myself onto my elbows, lifted my chest off the floor, and peered over Jing's body and Daisy's body to the woman in the doorway who'd made a solid fifth of my wardrobe at this point.

Chelsea Stringer stood with a pan in one hand and a metal spoon in another, poised with a commercial-ready smile to bash them together again. The pan looked suspiciously pristine. From the vibe I got, she and Daisy survived mostly on takeout and ashen supermarket vegetable trays. Chelsea looked like Daisy. Startlingly so, I thought, save for the fact that she had a slightly slimmer jaw and a nose bridge free of freckles. She was petite, very pretty in a hypnotically generic way—her eyes were an inscrutable blue/gray/green, her hair was an inscrutable blond/brown/red, her face had been replicated endlessly across network television ad campaigns and department-store catalogues, she could've been any number of white women, picking her out of a lineup would be impossible, there are at least two of her in a crowd at all times—but with that same weird intensity Daisy had, the same shiftiness that made you slightly worry that she'd snap and maul you. Wild to think she was a fashion industry person. Destroyers create. She smiled at us crookedly. "Good morning, little angels. Did you have a fun night out?"

"Yes, ma'am," said Yates with perfect sweetness.

"It's five minutes until noon," Chelsea said. Her voice rasped, sizzled at the edges. "If you don't get up now, it'll be *after*noon. Then you can't have breakfast."

I grimaced. Five hours 'til five and I hadn't told them yet. Should've done it last night but Jing was blackout and Daze was gone and Yates looked so happy for once, last night wasn't the time. When I hung up, I'd stomped back inside and bought another drink and found my girls again, pulled them all close to me, and said nothing about what'd happened outside. Fuck Madeline. I put my thumbs up. My hands hurt. Why did my fucking hands hurt?

"Sure thing," Jing said beside me. She sounded like she'd swallowed sand.

"Daisy?" Chelsea lowered her virgin cookware and took a step forward, pointed a toe, nudged Daisy's calf. Daisy didn't move. Chelsea's smile twitched. She nudged her again, a little more dramatically this time. "Daisy, honey. Wakey-wakey. Good morning, sweetheart. Daisy?"

Jing looked greenish. She cleared her throat and rolled over, curled around Daisy's body, and growled something low and sharp into the nape of her neck. I missed some of it, but through the haze in my brain I thought I caught: *You'll scare her Jesus fucking Christ just twitch or something.*

Daisy swung an elbow back and jabbed Jing in the stomach.

That was enough for Chelsea. She eased, and the air around her head stopped vibrating at such a high intensity, and I thought I saw something cool in her expression, though I'd barely noticed it tensing in the first place. That brawler aura softened up. "There you are. How are you feeling?"

I winced a little in stupid sympathy and peered up at the cracked plaster ceiling. If I had to wager a guess: Daisy felt like hell embodied. Rough shit, being totally depleted of all your dopamine stores. It would be hard convincing her to help Madeline on a good day, but today?

"You ladies can tussle about who gets the shower first while I order pizza." Chelsea rested the spoon in the pot and arranged both on top of Daisy's dresser with a sort of deliberate absentmindedness. "Sideways, are you hungover?"

I blinked at her. Scrubbed my tongue over front teeth, fiddled with the gum in the gap. "It's possible."

"I just would've figured if anybody'd stay sober, it'd be you," she said brightly. "To keep an eye on all your little girlfriends."

"All my little girlfriends," I repeated.

"Because Sideways is just *lousy* with little girlfriends," Daisy hissed against the floorboards. She sat up sharply, waxen-looking, her makeup in dark rivulets beneath her hollow, sunken eyes. Ringlets mashed. She looked like a prom queen that'd been dragged out of a lake. She didn't blink. She made no expression at all. "They're crawling with girlfriends. Like lice."

I lay back down.

"I'll shower first," Yates said. She yawned with one hand fanned politely over her mouth. "Thank you for waking us up, Ms. Stringer."

Chelsea grimaced. "The pizza will be cheese." She blinked, looked around at all of us, then down at Daisy with excruciating sharpness. "You look like your mother."

Daisy squeezed her eyes shut.

Chelsea left the door wide as she left.

A tree frog or something screamed outside. I covered my eyes with my palms and pressed down. I heard rustling; I thought it was Daisy lying back down. Jing didn't move. Eventually, I pulled my hands back over my skull, massaged the fuzz of my buzz cut and said, "They're killing Madeline Kline at the flocking tonight."

Silence sharpened. The air in the room got denser, tighter.

Jing sat up. She looked down at me with surgical intensity. Daisy whipped her head around, glowered over her shoulder. Yates said from above, "Killing her?"

"That was the implication. She asked for our help last night. Called me at the rave." I sniffed.

"Our help. Okay," Jing said. "Fuck. Are we going to do that?"

The ceiling was flat and white and unmoving. It looked like Styrofoam. My heartbeat was going crazy. I was going to puke up my heart. I shrugged, pressed my fingertips deeper into my scalp, and said, "Yeah. We should."

"It would be okay if you didn't want to help her," Yates said softy. "I've got my own thoughts on it, but you get to draw a boundary here if you want. You've done more than your share of helping her already. This doesn't need to be your responsibility."

"I hear you." I screwed my eyes shut, then opened them as wide as they could go. "I don't want her to die. Plus, it's not just me, it's us. She called upon the Scapegracers. That means something to me."

"It means something to me, too." Jing keep looking at me. She steepled her hands together. Said over her shoulder, "Daisy, do you have a rebuttal?"

Daisy kicked her wall. The sound was thin and hollow. She groaned, sat up, crossed her arms over her chest. "I hate her and want her to suffer. That's separate from our coven's work. I'm sick of being bad cop."

"That's all cops," I said. "I'm not going to fight with you."

Daisy took her hair in her fist, twisted it into a bun on the top of her head, and leaned back against her hot-pink wall. "Is the situation that they're going to firing squad her? I don't believe that. What help does she need, exactly?"

"Like, maybe advocacy, but I'm not so sure how good I'd do with that. You're the future attorney, Daze, we can take it on if you're up for it. Otherwise, I don't know, rescue mission.

Girl heist." I took a therapy breath, in through the nose and out through the teeth. "Are we all in?"

"I am," Yates said. "I think it'd mend us. We've frayed over who deserves help before, and I want to repair any lingering fractures, angle us toward a better tomorrow. I don't want us to break over a Shiloh situation again. I don't want us squabbling like that, I frankly wouldn't be able to stand it. Helping Madeline doesn't seem like a question to me. I think we must. Not just for her, but for the Scapegracers. We *do* mean something. We should act like it."

"We literally act like it every day. Last night was us acting like it. Our whole social life has become acting like it, which I'm happy about, for the record. Yuck," Daisy groaned. "Fucking, okay. Okay, sure! Why not! I have terms."

"Let's hear them," Jing said.

"We are not adopting her. She's not invited to parties, she's not gonna be cute with us, she won't be around our scene." Daisy's bun unraveled. It fell across her face. "We aren't forgiving or forgetting. We're helping because we are *professionals*. If she gets even a little bit slick with us, I am literally going to beat her up. I am going to break her teeth. None of you will stop me! You will stand by and let me lobotomize her with my stiletto. You may warn her, but you may not intervene. Cool! Sound fair?"

"Jesus Christ," I said.

"Ew." Yates slid out of bed and stepped over me, padded across the bedroom on tiptoe. She lingered by the door, turned, and faced us. She drew her brows together. "Please don't talk like that. I agree, we're being professional, and if she does something unsafe or threatening I will let you defend us. Okay?"

"Good with me," Jing said. She reached toward me, brushed her nails over my scalp. "We should get ready."

I shut my eyes tight, tried to focus on how her nails felt. Then she got up, and I pressed my hands over my belly, and I made myself think about Madeline Kline. I made myself think about the Pythoness Society, who'd given me my magic, and withheld it just in time for me to meet Scratch. I made myself think about the Honeyeaters. I made myself sit up.

✳

After I'd scrubbed behind my ears and knees and scalded off my taste buds wolfing down a few slices of screaming hot pizza, I checked my phone, and there waited a string of fragmentary texts from one Shiloh Pike.

> **im alive are you alive**

> **i am having the nastiest deja vu**

> **omw home lastnite i felt so sick and so hypervigilant**

> **cant stop thinking about this thing elias**

said to me the last time i saw him. this thing about patience

i had a lot of fun mind it wasn't until after homo erectus, crashed with somebody i met

tell me youre fine

Im fine, I texted back. Were they?

On either side of me, Jing and Yates both picked at their food. Jing looked tired, but not any more so than usual. Maybe a little sour. Magenta denim jumpsuit, lime-green narrow sunglasses, dark circles that she papered over with purple-silver glitter. Yates swung her saddle shoes under the table. Her nails looked like seashells; she tapped them against the side of her cup. Her eyes looked puffy. Across from me, Daisy didn't touch her slice of pizza at all. She hardly even looked at it, or anything specific. Her eyes weren't fixed on this material plane. She drank water slowly, looked more transparent with every mouthful downed. She didn't wear any makeup, a rarity for her, and without her beat she might as well have been made of glass and plastic. I could see teal veins in her face, and the cracks in the wall behind her. She wore one of my hoodies and it shrouded her, ratty hem falling nearly to her knees.

"You should wear your little jackets," said Chelsea, the maker of those little jackets. She sliced her pizza slice into increasingly intricate jigsaw pieces. She drank orange juice from a champagne flute into which she'd thrust a mini umbrella and a sabered pair of olives. They looked like eyes. Memories. "If you're going out all serious. Keep rank."

"Cute," said Yates affirmatively. She glumly slid her phone over to Jing, murmured something about her bias, who was also being cute, apparently. "Thank you for letting us stay over."

"Oh, of course." Chelsea yawned. She stacked her pizza bits. It looked perversely like a little person. Or maybe my brain defaulted to spotting curse poppets? "Will you be coming over again tonight?"

"I'm taking Sunday to study and spend time with my family," Yates said.

Jing and I looked at each other.

"We'll let you know," said Jing.

"Yeah," I said. In the back of my head: *Crawling with girlfriends like lice.* I didn't even have lice. I wasn't crawling with jack shit. PTSD doesn't crawl. Jackets don't crawl. Mr. Scratch was at home under my pillow as a happy little notebook, he certainly wasn't crawling on me now. I hadn't a single girlfriend to my name. Which like—that is totally fine, whatever, I totally don't need a girlfriend, who would when they've got the power of friendship or whatever the fuck.

"We're gonna be late if we don't get our asses on the road." Jing pulled a hand through her fringe. "We ready?"

I stood up instead of answering, jerked a nod in Chelsea's direction that she didn't seem to notice. It was a small apartment, sparsely furnished, with a sort of open, rough-edged unfinished vibe that made the surfaces all feel colder than they really were. Clammy. Fleshy salmon insulation blushed where the wall peeled back. Dress forms hovered in the corner of my vision, spotted with pins and raw twists of gauze. Sycamore Gorge was apparently a hell of a place to find a two-bedroom with a six-month lease on short notice. It'd taken Chelsea a month and a half to find this place. She'd initially planned to take Daisy with her back to her place in Harlem, but Daisy had had a full-on tectonic meltdown at the notion of leaving and they'd abandoned the idea. She wouldn't be staying with her father. She wouldn't be out of Sycamore Gorge until she graduated. She would've kept couch surfing between Jing's place, and Yates', and mine, but the thought of Daisy being without an official mailing address gave Chelsea a meltdown of her own, so here we are.

I was in my leather, the jacket that had been my dad's before me. It was patched and studded and battered to hell. It felt safe. I tied the Scapegracers jacket around my hips for cohesion's sake and nobody objected. I crossed the room, swayed the meat of my upper arm against the doorframe, waited for my coven to get up and going. I hadn't scoured off the malaise in the shower. Most of the hot water had been gone by then, so. I shut my eyes. I breathed, and once I noticed that I breathed I couldn't forget it. I had to pump my lungs on purpose. In out in out in out. Annoying.

I heard the chairs screech.

My girls brushed past me. One pair of shoes, a softer soled second, then a third. The third paused by the doorway.

Fingertips brushed over the back of my wrist, nails ruffled the spray of little dark hairs there. I opened one eye.

Jing jerked her chin. "Are you good, Sideways?"

I bit the inside of my bottom lip, tore off a stray bit of skin and winced when it stung, like an idiot. I furrowed my brow. I twinged where she touched me. It felt like after a spell died, after the world-changing effect but still in tight proximity with mouth foam and fried electric nerves. I nodded, righted myself. "Yeah." I glanced once behind me at Chelsea on her phone, then glanced at Jing, at my reflection in the sparkles underneath her eyes. "You driving?"

"I am." She didn't pull her hand back. She looked at me, I could feel her looking at me. I wanted to squirm but didn't dare. Jing tilted her chin up, looked me head-on. "What do you want to happen to her?"

For a second I fritzed and thought we were talking about me in third person. I blinked. I swallowed spit. "Madeline?"

Her eyes narrowed a touch like, *Yeah duh who else.*

"I don't know," I said.

"Are you not still pissed at her?"

"Fuck Madeline." I eyed the ceiling fan. It was stationary, had an eldritch Y2K energy signature that set me on edge. Lilac dust caked the top of each blade. If they turned it on, it'd be like a bruisy blizzard. A total war upon my allergies, too. "Pissed isn't right. I don't think about her enough to be pissed at her." Was that true?

"Can you promise me something?" Her sunglasses slid down her nose, dangled by the hooks around the curve of her ears. She didn't blink. She'd saw my head in two if she kept looking at me like that. "Look at me."

I looked at her.

"In my eyes."

Darkest eyes in the world.

"The Pythoness Society is going to be at the flocking, or some of them anyway. I know they're the women who sent you your *Vade Mecvm Magici*. I remember the letters you showed me. I know you're gonna meet them for the first time in T-minus ninety minutes, and I'm sure they're going to immediately adore you and kiss your Docs and promise you the moon, if they're smart. You're a brilliant witch, Sideways. They're going to want you. If you want them back, fine. I won't blame you, and I won't be bitter, I won't resent you if you go with them. Just promise if you're going to go, you'll give me a heads-up. Pull me aside and tell me. Not a text. Face-to-face, like this. Can you do that for me?"

Her shins braced against mine. Her sneakers interlaced between my boots. If she stood any closer, if she touched me, she could've shrugged me on and worn me. She stared at me. Her jaw was set.

I pushed her sunglasses up with the back of one knuckle.

"I'm not going anywhere." The words came up thickly. I shook my head. "You're crazy if you think I'm going anywhere without you." Without you? I amended: "Without the Scapegracers. You're my coven. I intend to act like it."

"You better." She bounced and she was shorter suddenly. Had she been standing on tiptoe? Thoughts came to me,

45

woozy red ones, but I stamped them out. I put my hands in my pockets, ground my molars together, wasn't sure if I was allowed to look away yet, or if that was something I even wanted. *Allowed.* What, it wasn't like Jing was the boss of me, now was it? "Do you feel ready?"

"Yeah," I said. I thought about asking her if she did, but Jing wouldn't ever admit it if she didn't. I cleared my throat. Clawed around my head for something to say. It was so quiet in here now that it was only me. I missed Mr. Scratch. He's happier now, he so prefers being book-shaped, but my skull was a ringing pit without him. I was bottomless nothing. Nothing, emphasis bottomless. Maybe I did want a girlfriend. I coughed, and this time managed to actually clear the phlegm cobwebs. "Did you finish the book?"

"Nearly," she said. Her expression changed. She smiled a little, then screwed her brows up, gave me a little shove. "I'm trying to savor it. You can just get your own, you know."

"I know." I shrugged. She'd given me a book back when we weren't cool. When I'd swallowed my specter, it'd given me a drop of attention span back, just enough for me to find a nice stretch of floor and read for a few hours. Jing's marginalia practice was fucking extensive. The book was swollen with notes and tabs, her underlining, her cramped notes, her charting scenes and characters and thematic arcs, hissing when characters she didn't like spoke, drawing little hearts and stars beside particularly romantic or violent passages. Nerdy Jing was a rarity. I think even Yates and Daisy didn't know the extent of it. When she'd given me the handle of her fanfiction blog last month, we made an actual blood oath with actual blood that I wouldn't tell a soul about it. I felt lucky, I guess. It was a hell of a thing to share. Anyway, I'd told her, and she'd given me another book that I tore through about a month after the first one, and as much as I wanted her current fixation, there was a part of me that was resistant to the notion of getting a copy Jing hadn't touched yet. They were *our* books. Part of their magic was in the sharing of them. They wouldn't be the same without her editorial touch. I shook my head, pulled a hand out of my pocket, and smoothed it down the back of my skull like she'd done last night. "I'd just rather mooch, that's all."

"So be it," she said. She released me, then strode out the door and down the stairs without a backwards glance. I heard her car chirp as she unlocked it, heard her shout something at Yates and Daisy, heard the slamming of car doors and an engine's overblown pop song revving.

I stood there for a second and rubbed my wrist.

Behind me, Chelsea snickered and said: "Catch up with your little girlfriends."

So I did.

THREE

THE FINAL HOUSE PARTY

I called Madeline four times in the car and got nothing. We pulled over for me to briefly panic in a cow field, cooled me down enough to get back on the road, and almost had a plan by the time we approached the Victorian mammoth. The extent of it was this: cool and normal. Case the house, get our hands on an operational itinerary, find Madeline, smuggle her out, and advocate for her after the fact. It would be so silly, trying to make like we hadn't done it. If we were truly high-profile, we would be the obvious suspects. So! Discretion, not in the cards. Efficiency was the move. Speed and accuracy. What could go wrong?

Dead ahead the Delacroix House exploded upwards and outwards in intricate gingerbread frills. Old snow clung to it, and icicles long as my femurs. Colored lights bled through the windows. Irises clawed through gray slush on the lawn below. It was ostensibly closed for business today, but the look of it said otherwise—people teemed on the long porch in long fur coats and cowboy boots, smoking and bickering and embracing one another. It felt like a music festival or an artist's funeral. Even from this distance I could hear acrid laughter, drunken singing, weeping, and blunt-edged threats. Jing pulled into the lot, cut the music, and eased into one of the last available spots in a sea of variously glossy dark or rust-fucked cars.

"Sideways," Jing said. She leaned back, caught my eye. Her brows twitched inwards. "Did you know there were that many witches in the continental US?"

I had no head for guessing numbers. Surely, these people could've filled the Homo Erectus warehouse. Glimpses made my teeth hurt—hobble skirts and safety pins through nose bridges, garter belts and boiler suits, boas and bolo ties, a bathtub's worth of pomade, heavy metal jewelry and animal bones on strings, a mirage of strangers that felt like people I'd already met. Intergenerational queer community I had, and beloved witches my age, but seeing scores of older witches plucked some chord in my gut. We grew up. Who'd have thunk it. "No," I said. "Stick close." Admittedly a moot point in this crowd—there were scores of showy femmes here, but they trended hard toward goth and milf. My coven brought the only pastels along with them. Avenging angel Bratz dolls in a sea of Elviras and Morticias would be easy to spot. Funny to think I might be the only one of us who blended in. I scraped my tongue with my teeth.

We got out of the car. Daisy pulled up her hood, took off without us, and Jing swore and locked up and stomped after her. Yates lingered. She smoothed her satin jacket. She said, "If we get separated, we'll meet back at the car."

"Sure." I frowned. "What's wrong?"

"It just feels heavy. Like we're about to make adult choices. I don't know if that makes sense." She worried her thumb over her zipper. "Everything is so tense right now. The future feels close. Do you ever feel superstitious?"

I braced an elbow on Jing's car, stepped between her and the witch crowd. There was something spooky about the suggestion. I'd been the witch of Sycamore Gorge for years. She and I shared that title and a book devil now. What's more superstitious than that? "How do you mean?"

"Like you've got an itchy feeling. A bad hunch." Yates looked through me, past me. I thought for a moment that she might cry. "I've asked Scratch about it. I know you know this, just—I need to talk this through. There's cosmic energy, which flows everywhere, and everyone feels it. Concentrated violence and habit hardens it, makes and maintains the architecture of power, and those of us who chafe against that structure grow specters, and because we've grown specters, we can touch the still-fluid currents of cosmic energy and knead it according to our desires. There's a current, is my point. Mr. Scratch says that some witches are more sensitive to it than others. Not like, stronger casters, I mean, some witches can feel magic's current more. Like getting achy with the weather. You know how skittish I can be around some of this stuff. I think I feel it—more intensely than you three. I'm not a scaredy-cat. I am always on edge because I can *feel* it. I can feel when it's thicker, I can feel when it's faster. I was attracted to Levi at that Halloween party because he had it. It was stolen, so it was duller, but he had it. I was scared of you because you had more."

I frowned. Unease kicked in me. I believed her, and following that logic, this many witches in one spot seemed like a headache waiting to happen. That didn't seem quite it, though. I thought about Shiloh's bad feeling. "Okay. What are you feeling now that's got you worried?"

"I feel like we shouldn't be here." She zipped up her jacket to her chin, thrust her hands in her pockets, bounced once on her heels. "Not us like the Scapegracers. I mean like, *all of us.* I just feel so sick."

"Like we shouldn't be gathering for the specter stones?" I craned my neck, tried to meet her gaze. "Lila, hey. Are you okay?"

"I'm not so sure." Her eyes were still fixed on something invisible to me, something just beyond my collarbone. "It's good that we're gathering. Assembly is great, I don't want to cast doubt on it, even with the troublesome Madeline piece. I mean, *here.* At the Delacroix House. I don't have anything concrete, and maybe this isn't cosmic sensitivity, maybe this is just straight-up anxiety! I'm all wound up for normal reasons, too. I don't know."

"No, I trust your intuition. We'll keep our eyes out. If something's wrong, we tell each other immediately, and we figure out who here is trustworthy and we tell them, too. How's that?" I bent my knees, put my face in front of hers.

She glanced up at me from under her lashes. She looked sharp.

"We should catch up with Jing and Daisy," she said. She took my elbow in her hands. "Let's go."

I swallowed a lump and straightened my back, started toward the Delacroix. I tried to imagine magic eddying around its frosted spires, like the northern lights or oil floating on water. When Scratch lived inside me, I'd seen the rare glimpse of where he was from, what he'd originally been. It was hard to remember how beholding it felt. It was a slosh of light in my memory. Like a moving bruise.

I brought my focus down.

There was a crowd amassing on the lot before the long porch walk. There'd been people before, but they had a different vibe now. Bees swarming rather than simply chilling in the meadow flats. Shoulders came together, bundled leather and velvet and thick ancient wool, and I felt in my gut that somebody was about to get fucked up. I didn't see Jing or Daze. I braced for the worst. I tilted my head back, tried to peer over some of the shorter people, but everybody was wearing platforms and all I saw were the backs of bowed heads. People circled. The witch ring was at least three bodies thick in every direction and completely blocked the stairs. I pushed through, tried to clear space for Yates and me, and managed to get us in view of the clearing.

Two dudes lurched in the circle's center.

The beefier of the two, blue-haired and bearded, yanked his shirt up over his stomach. He dripped tattoos. The whole cosmos flexed down his belly. He curled his lip, reached two fingers under his binder, fished something out—a long rectangle, the length of his palm—and tripped his thumb over some subtle button. The blade flashed into midair. Its metal looked milk-colored. The tip danced in space.

Simultaneously, a weasel reared his longboard back. He was hatchet-faced, murderous—there was a cut under his left eye that muddied his lank yellow hair, smeared his already ruined eyeliner—and the way he looked at the bigger guy told me that he'd follow through. This was not a man who tapped out. Weasel would absolutely splash Blue Boy's brains all over the steps, so help him god.

The onlooking witches seemed . . . amused? Intrigued? Annoyed? Exasperated? They smoked spliffs and cloves and did not move to intervene. A woman with fabulous enormous Dolly Parton hair was recording on her phone.

"Andy, honey." A tall woman across from us folded her hands over her heart. She wore red leather gloves and a neat button-down, had her hair in lacquered jet-black finger waves. A tattoo across her cheek read *HOLY SHE*. God, be still my beating heart. She stared daggers into the back of the blue guy's head. "Quit while you're ahead."

"I've got a Corbie to pluck," Andy barked.

"Fuck you," the scrawny one spat back. The veins in his eyes looked like bunches of licorice. His eyes looked like water balloons or flash grenades. They were too big for his long skinny knife face. He white-knuckled his longboard, which was, on second glance, painted with a broomstick along its wheelbase, which felt so stupid and *extremely* cool to me, and jerked his head back, leered up at Andy with an expression I'd never seen in real life. Anime deathmatch face. It made the air vibrate. "Fuck you, you insipid, *presumptuous* little fascist *fucker*."

"You're calling me a fascist? Me? Pull your head out of your ass, Dominick." Andy spun the knife's handle around one finger and caught it in one fluid motion, then traced it in the air, connected invisible dots between Dominick's pierced brow down to the line of his long, pinched mouth. "I will shred you. Don't think I won't."

"Boys!"

Both of them snapped their heads up.

A worn and weary somebody shouldered through the far side of the ring. Salt-and-pepper crew cut, white shirt and workpants, steel-toed boots, slim earrings. Short and proud and fat. Maybe mid-fifties? Early sixties? I was terrible at adult ages. Crusty old dyke, by any rate. Hypnotically androgynous. The witch looked between the two of them, then at Dominick with sudden diamond-splitting intensity, took a few strides to the left and said, "When I passed by you, and saw you polluted in your own blood, I said unto you when you were in your blood, *live*."

The cut on Dominick's cheek zipped itself up neatly. He looked stricken. He blinked like he was smothering tears. He glanced at the caster, murmured something too low for me to hear.

The caster dismissed him with a huff. "We'll have enough to fight about later. Stop tussling. Dominick, and . . ." Eyes flicked up, fixed on—me? I swam with gooseflesh. "You. Baby butch. Come help me set up."

I stood very still, slack-jawed.

Yates whispered into my neck, "Case the house! That's part of the plan."

Through my teeth: "What about you?"

"I'll find Jing and Daisy!"

"I'm not leaving you alone—"

She pushed me into the clearing where the fight had broken out, and when I whipped my head around, Lila Yates was gone. Fresh nerves and my hangover sloshed together. I looked back, and the old butch was waiting. The blue-haired man, Andy, was gone with *HOLY SHE*. The weasel, apparently Dominick, remained.

Dominick pulled a face. I couldn't tell if he was a rough nineteen-year-old or a baby-faced thirtysomething. As I made my way toward the butch, he tucked his longboard under one arm, a horrible frown on his horrible mouth.

We followed the butch together in silence for a moment. The quiet itched.

God, cool and normal was a terrible plan! I sucked so fucking hard at both of those things! I needed intel, ASAP. I cleared my throat and tried: "Who's . . ."

"Blair. She's in the Anti-Edonist Union. They're based in a holler south of here." Dominick spoke with a reedy, nasal drawl, barely loud enough for me to hear. He didn't look at me when he spoke. He looked grayish. I picked up my pace a touch, strode onward at Blair's heels. On the porch, women with broad sun hats and dark sunglasses floated a foot above their wicker armchairs. They drank

Bloody Marys and openly gossiped about everyone who walked by. Their heads turned as we passed. Blair's shoulders tensed. Dominick looked contemptuously at his shoes. I thought I heard one of the floating women say: "There goes the firing squad."

I missed Mr. Scratch. I wanted to know if he could articulate the rancor going on. Did the Honeyeaters flock when a safe house called? Did they get along swimmingly with their peers, feel something like, I don't know, solidarity with their fellow witches? Women supporting women? No?

Inside the Delacroix was calamity. Workers in white tie ferried objects back and forth, some of which (folding chairs, folding tables, tablecloths, stacks of plates, cutlery) made sense, others (a ball python, a bouquet of swords, milk crates stuffed with books, fireworks, a disco ball) less so. I thought I saw Maurice Delacroix himself conducting traffic, his back to the neon display lights over the lush, rich wallpaper, but he was gone in a blink. Jacques and Pearl, a musician and a server respectively, both sat on a low staircase in matching velvet suits and morosely passed each other a handle of Fireball, which they drank straight.

Jacques made eye contact with me.

I tried for a smile and wasn't sure if it landed.

Blair led Dominick and me through a set of doors I hadn't been through before, and the world on the other side was bottle-green and damasked with tall ceilings and seaglass chandeliers. There were framed mirrors and raised hanging surfaces that'd been shrouded with white sheets. I wondered what was under them. I decided quickly that it was none of my business. At the room's head, maybe twelve paces ahead of me, a fireplace yawned. It looked like a lion's mouth, carved teeth and eyes and mane that spiraled outward into the deep green wallpaper. Two iron loops twisted through either side of the hearth's upper lip like angel bites. A poker rested in those loops. A low fire twitched below.

The floor was clear aside from a mass of folding chairs that quickly piled against a side wall. Blair crossed the floor with an easy stride. Real butch swagger, a showy confidence tempered in hurt and harshness. I wondered if I'd ever walk like that. She picked up a stack of four-ish chairs and glanced over her shoulder at us, or at Dominick, rather. "Here?"

He winced. "Good a place as any."

I said, "Sorry, what?"

Blair looked at me, then. "D'you know why you're here?"

"To help set up," I said, feeling ridiculous.

A smile tugged at the corners of her mouth. "Which coven are you with, sugar?"

Dominick, suddenly interested in the fact that I was alive, turned to look at me. He searched me. There was a seriousness in his evaluation that I didn't strictly appreciate. I wondered abstractly if Andy would've bodied him if the fight had gone uninterrupted.

"I'm—"

"Eloise!"

My government name clapped me up the backside of my head. I spun around, mouth open.

A woman leaned against the doorframe. She looked maybe Julian's age, had a silver streak in the dark waves above her brow. She wore a slim knee-length dress and thin gold chains. She was, inexplicably, familiar to me. She smiled at me with jarring, disarming warmth. Without looking at her, I felt Blair's body language shift behind me. I wasn't sure if she was breathing.

The woman crossed the room. Her heels clacked and echoed in the back of my skull. The closer she came, the thinner the world stretched around her. The room accordioned, and it felt like with every stride, she stayed in place, and the room rolled underneath her until she suddenly stood close to me. *Very* close to me, closer than I'd stand next to anybody who wasn't a Scapegracer or maybe Shiloh, and despite being shorter than me, she filled my vision to my periphery. She smiled wider; it made her eyes crinkle. She took me by the shoulders and appraised me, looked me up and down, then pulled me into a quick, tight hug.

My brain made a sound like a teakettle.

The woman leaned back. She said, "You're so tall."

"Yes," I said, stunned.

She laughed. "In my head, you're still little. I haven't seen you since you were a little girl. Kindergarten, I think. Look at you now! You look so like Lenora, but—but you've docked your fluffy ears and tail." She reached toward my buzz cut but stopped just short of touching me. "Have you been getting into fights?"

There was a car crash in my head. My pulse rammed in my hard palate. "What?" I shook my head, pulled a face, braced myself for the sharp, reactionary anger that usually took me whenever anybody reminded me that I'd been a little kid at all. The anger didn't come. Something softer and worse did instead. I bit my tongue. I looked down at the chains on her neck, little herringbone snakes, and my gut kicked and I wanted to cry, which made me want to pry the chairs from Blair's hands and hurl them against the hanging mirrors, or maybe crawl into that fireplace and bury my body in the coals.

"You called me Auntie Lupe then. Don't you remember?" Her smile faltered for a millisecond, but only just. She shook her head. "It was a long time ago. You can get to know me now, as a woman. I've been looking forward to meeting you. We've got a lot to discuss."

I wasn't sure if there was anything I'd like to discuss with her. I wasn't sure if I was a woman. Lesbian and Scapegracer were my principal identifiers and that second one was being called into question. My stomach hurt. Bad thoughts swirled. If you knew me when I was little, if you knew my mother, where the fuck were you when I was in foster care? I am alive because you sent a spell book, but couldn't you have sent a little lunch money, too?

"I'm helping Blair set up," I said stiffly.

"Oh," Lupe said. She blinked, then craned her neck, peered over my shoulder. "Hello, Blair."

Blair said, "Hello, Guadalupe."

"It's been a while. You haven't been to any parties in ages." Lupe's eyes sparkled with something. Maybe loathing? Something stickier than loathing. It made my skin prickle. "I hadn't expected you to come. You look well."

"The Anti-Edonists always heed the call toward flocking." Blair sounded raw, exhausted. There was a pang in her voice, the weight of some shared history, but I couldn't parse it, I wanted my bones to flatten and to slip through the floorboards and dissolve into the ground water. A Pythoness approached me and mentioned my mother to me and had the audacity to carry on small talk over my shoulder? Or was this not small talk. Man, I was supposed to be saving Madeline! Blair said, softer this time: "It's good to see you."

"It's nearly time." Dominick's voice scissored through the tense adult lesbian staring, and I jerked my attention back on him. He looked grave. When he spoke, he barely moved his lips at all. It didn't even look like he was breathing. "Finish up without me. I'm going to go get her."

Her.

My mouth opened and I said: "Madeline?"

His snapped his eyes at me. The red veins sparkled. His expression shifted in some indiscernible way. He took a few steps nearer to me. His hair, long as his collarbones, swished forward and hid the edges of his face. "Are you Sideways Pike?"

I jerked my chin down and didn't blink.

He stood toe to toe with me all of a sudden. It made

Lupe back up a little, and I slapped down any embers of feeling I might've had about that one way or the other. I leveled with Dominick. My pulse hammered.

Dominick inclined his head and said to me: "Thank you, and I'm sorry. You'll have your justice soon."

I opened my mouth to retort, *I've got my justice, I think.* Nothing came out.

In a whirl Delacroix staff pushed through us and descended on the chair stack. Lots of elegant lines and stiff, pomade-burnished hair. I blinked and Dominick was gone, vanished into the fray, and Blair had peeled off with the stream to help. Chairs formed half rings around the fireplace, recalled makeshift church pews. They looked like ribs. There was an aisle down the middle, and people moved with eerie synchronicity up and down it as they slammed down chairs beside chairs. I turned to Lupe, but she was halfway across the room, talking to Maurice Delacroix, who looked worn to the bone. His cheekbones broke the light.

He nodded at me, waved two fingers, checked a pocket watch.

I blinked again and the room filled with witches. They smelled like perfume and tobacco and leather and poppers. They streamed around me, took places among the newly assembled rows, spoke animatedly about heaven knows what. Someone must have put on a record—there was a thin crackle then a whirl of rough, honey-thick blues. Someone with a sense of humor, or evil, unforgivable irony. This was Madeline's song.

Hands on my back. Hands above my left elbow, a forehead against my right sleeve.

"There you are! Ohmygod, learn to answer your phone."

"Where are we supposed to sit? These chairs look so bad. My thighs hate vinyl."

"Are you okay? You look like you saw a ghost."

I squeezed my eyes shut as tightly as I could, and the reunited Scapegracers pushed me down the aisle. We kept going and going. I thought for a second that they'd march us directly into the hearth. When I opened my eyes we'd somehow managed not to stomp into the fire, and we lingered before the front row, which was as vacant as the head of a classroom on the first day of term. Jing and Daisy and Yates arranged me in a chair, or maybe I sat on my own, and the three of them arranged themselves beside me. My head swam. Daisy, still dead eyed, was somehow half on top of me. Her nose pressed my neck.

"We can't find her," Daisy hissed. "There are literally no exits that aren't crammed with people. Not to be the fire-safety freak, but if Madeline pulls a Christmas, that'd suck so much."

"What is up with the setup?" Jing put an arm around my shoulders, craned her neck to scan the crowd. "I feel like we're about to watch community theater."

"I think it's starting," Yates said.

"Yeah," I said. "It's starting."

PROTECT ME FROM WHAT I WANT

Madeline walked down the aisle. Chin up, shoulders squared, patent leather brogues breaking the light. Dominick and two witches I didn't recognize trailed behind her, hard and gloomy, but I couldn't look at them. I couldn't look away from her. She'd grown her hair out since she sawed it off—sawed mine, too, I'd been in her hands at the time—and had slicked it back. She looked hollow, sallow. Her eyes hung half-shut and the lids looked bruised. Lips chapped. She wore a suit and it made her look like she'd been cut from construction paper with dull scissors—long, too angular, more exaggerated than organic life ought to be. The air around her head shimmered. The way all the attention fixed on her sizzled the edges of my vision. It was too intense. It hurt my teeth.

Madeline strode up to the fire's lip, put her toes on the pearly hearth tiles. She paused, rolled her shoulders, about-faced. She didn't look at any of us. She fixed her gaze on some indeterminate speck in heaven like a dancer spotting a turn. She knelt without blinking. Her trousers looked impossibly black against the floor. She put her hands in the air, wrists by either temple, and didn't resist when Dominick and some stranger took those wrists and extended them. I watched, awestruck and nauseous, as they wound chains around her wrists and the mantel's hooks above her. Heavy chains, something you could use to lash a gate. Little sigils painted up the length of every other jump link. They padlocked the chains in tandem, spat some minor incantation, and the fire behind her jumped up with a shock of violet light.

Not cool, not normal. Nobody was doing the plan.

Madeline curled her lip. She lifted her gaze and her lashes brushed her black slashes of brow. Her expression was inscrutable—I wanted to say she looked tired, but she didn't. Something scorched in her. Maybe there was some part of me that had splintered off my specter and lodged in her throat forever, but I swore for a moment that I felt a rush of white-hot fury that was not of my own making. It burned. I scraped my tongue with my teeth and wanted to break something with my hands. Her hands maybe. On second thought, maybe this rage was mine. When she'd said she'd hurt me because she was afraid of her coven's retribution, I hadn't believed it could be this bad. Witches were against power. This felt just like it.

Madeline gave her chains an experimental tug. They didn't give. She jerked her head to the left, locked eyes with the witch who wasn't Dominick and said in her low, raw voice: "Is it time?"

The stranger witch nodded.

Madeline snorted, then resumed her neutral position, head forward, gaze blank. "My name is Madeline Kline. I was a Sister Corbie once, but not anymore. I am here because a witchfinder yanked the specter from my neck, and to avenge myself I took another witch's specter, and I used it to burn a witchfinder child alive. Because I am uncovened, I've asked for any determinations of justice"—a mirthless smirk flickered then died—"to be made by the full present flock. I defend myself, as per usual. You've got an hour to question me, a forum will be held, and I will be dealt with according to consensus." She hardly spoke above her breath. I felt bitter cold and shifted, pulled my jacket closer around me, Daisy closer to my chest.

She hadn't said my name. I'd expected her to say it. Why wasn't she looking at us?

Someone behind me said, "That's not quite the whole story, is it, dove? I've heard that you were intimate with that witchfinder who took your magic from you. That spell they use for their violence requires the witch's consent. You must've agreed to it. You know him well. Is that true?"

Clipped murmurs filled the air. Immediate derision, both for the concept and the question, impatience and curiosity and the peaks of clashing displeasure.

"He was my boyfriend," Madeline said. "I was stupid. He attacked me."

"Did you know he was a witchfinder when you were together?" A different voice, maybe sympathetic.

"I didn't know when it started." Madeline's lip twitched. "Things happened pretty fast after I found out."

"She's a kid," said one of the women who'd been floating on the porch. "I cannot believe we're pressing a vulnerable girl about her involvement with people who actively seek out vulnerable girls for destruction."

"Witchfinders take out entire covens once they find one witch," a woman reclining beside Lupe said. "Her misstep could've led to the death of every single Sister Corbie, the seizing of their specters and their book devil. I'm not interested in blaming Kline for the violence done to her, but the stakes cannot go unstressed."

Took the mood down a touch. Jing shifted beside me, unsettled Daisy, who put her elbow in my gut. I winced but allowed it. I didn't have it in me to move. If I moved I might break some dam in my head and the feelings would slosh out of my nose and spill all over the floor.

"I didn't know," Madeline said again. She looked waxy. "I thought he was just a boy when we met. My fucking mistake."

"I'd say so," someone from behind me added. I assumed they were sneering. Had that nasal edge.

"You didn't come to us for help." Maurice Delacroix. He wasn't where I could see him but I knew his voice. "You were surrounded by people who would've helped you. You worked here. You performed here, in this house, and had all of my resources at your disposal, not to mention your own coven. You didn't call upon your community. Why?"

"I don't know," Madeline said curtly.

"I think you do," he replied.

She grimaced. The tail of it flipped and went smile-shaped. "You heard Tonya. Levi Chantry is an unforgivable offense. I knew how the Corbies would act when they found out and I was right. Why the fuck would I think you'd be different?"

Dominick's jaw twitched.

"I literally don't know why we're talking about this. They hurt Madeline. Scary and bad! That's not what's pressing, here," said Daisy from my lap. Then, in a louder voice: "Why did you pick Sideways?"

My gut twisted. My veins clapped shut and my body went frigid and I died violently in every dimension then slammed back like a rubber band. I seethed all over. I wanted to push Daisy Brink off my lap so hard she'd bowl into Madeline and make a strike sound, bowling alley victory display screen in midair and everything. I put an arm around her waist and pulled her a little closer to me instead.

Madeline shot her eyes at us, beseechingly.

"Well?" Daisy prodded. "Spit it out. Why Sideways Pike?"

Her silence stretched a moment longer. "Because she was there."

Daisy tensed like she was going to spring. I closed my arm around her tighter. She strained on my lap like the crook of my elbow was a leash. Out of the corner of my eye I saw Jing reach for her, saw her put a warning hand on her scabbed-up kneecap.

Yates said: "Could you talk about the Christmas party? Could you tell me your intentions? I can understand retribution for what was done to you, and as a preventative measure to protect girls like us who Levi and his family might find in the future. Dozens and dozens of people you didn't know nearly died as well."

"I just wanted the Chantrys dead."

"You locked all the doors and started a fire," Jing said.

"Couldn't have them slipping out, now could I?"

"Dozens of people," Yates repeated, but Madeline shifted and she fell silent.

Into the back of Daisy's neck, I breathed, "I promised her we'd save her."

"Hush," Daisy growled. "Trust the process."

Madeline's face had flashed a bloodless, horrible lavender color. A few strands of jet-black hair sprang from her pompadour and fell across her face like cracks. "The spell was for killing Chantrys. That's all. I didn't mean for the house to catch fire. I refuse to apologize for going after witchfinders."

"The spell didn't work because you were casting with Sideways' magic," Jing said. "It didn't work and you nearly fucked up and killed everybody, us included."

"That," Dominick hissed, "is the problem."

Madeline whipped her head around to look at him. He leaned against the wall beside the fireplace, bony shoulder shoved up against the bottle-green wallpaper, a vein throbbing in the spoon of his temple. He and Madeline didn't look alike. Still, whatever passed between them read with a tension that skewed domestic—he felt like her big brother, or an uncle maybe. Their expressions were nearly the same.

Dominick took a step away from the wall. "You aren't ours anymore. This isn't our call. But I bring to my sisters," he said, darting his eyes over the witch assemblage, "*this*. Madeline endangered me and all my elders. She put our lives and our book, a book that's been among the Sisters Corbie for four centuries, in jeopardy, and hid our peril from us. She lied to us. I'd forgive that—she's young and has her reasons to be mistrustful, and with full knowledge of the situation we could've banded together and stood against the threat. The problem is, Madeline didn't just endanger herself and every Corbie by extension. Madeline fraternized with a witchfinder and became one."

Madeline's face turned.

"After Levi Chantry stole your specter," Dominick said, fully facing us now, face turned from her though he addressed her directly, "you stalked around for *months* searching for unaffiliated witches. You knew dozens of witches in community, you worked *here*, you had coven mates. You were looking for someone alone. You needed someone vulnerable, inexperienced, and without the protection and guidance of a dedicated book devil. If you went after me, the other Corbies would've skewered you for it, and you're smart. You'd never go after somebody who knows you well enough to know when you're conning. Fucking hell, Madeline. You got close to her. This happened at a house party. You went to a house party and used witchfinder magic to rob a girl of her specter so that you could use it." Dominick's eyes flashed. "I don't believe you. I don't believe that you didn't know that Levi Chantry was a witchfinder, because you knew how to hunt like him. You're a grifter and a liar. You're a witchfinder. You know their trade."

Concord snapped. People talked over each other, erupted into side conversations and hissing, snarling spills of discourse. A few witches stood, then half of them did. Jing twisted in her seat and said something brisk to a witch behind her. Yates looked at the ceiling beseechingly. Daisy cracked a laugh.

Madeline locked eyes with me. Something in her look muffled the rising fever pitch.

"Jesus H., settle down." Blair clapped her hands and the arguing tapered to a quick-paced, prickly murmuring. She stood up, kneaded her hands. She looked mournful, I thought. Sober, solemn. Shadows hung off the lines in her face. "We need to talk about the Chantry boy. He was fourteen. We can talk about retribution and violence some other time, your aim to kill the witchfinding family is not what troubles me. The only life lost that night was the youngest." Blair shut her eyes, brows in a knot. "A child is dead, Kline. A witch killed a witchfinder's son with magic she stole by that family's teachings. There will be repercussions for this. I doubt they'll just fall on you."

Daisy put her nails in my wrist. I let go of her, but she squeezed harder, leaned back against my chest. I could only half-see Blair from around Daisy's head. Her shoulders tensed. I wondered for a horrifying moment if she was going to cry. I wasn't sure what I'd do if she did. I wasn't sure what I was going to do in general. I put my arms back around Daisy and wished for a moment that she was heavier. I could barely feel her. She was hardly enough to anchor me to earth.

"I don't have a question in this." Blair sighed. She dropped her hand and reached to rub one of her shoulders, hand under her jacket. "You made choices and we will share the burden of their consequence."

"I can't take it back," Madeline said. She said it tonelessly but with conviction and my skin crawled. She hadn't looked away from me. I wondered if this was part of some spell. The purple fire behind her flashed higher and I thought about Jing's basement and being magic-drunk and drunk-drunk and Madeline's glowstick halo cracking on her forehead, how the candy-bright trickling had made her look holographic, how I'd had such an instant and all-consuming crush on her that I didn't ask a single question. "None of you have done a single fucking thing about witchfinders. Nobody does. Complicity is not moral high ground. Letting them pick people off isn't moral high ground. I used their tactics because they worked." She shook her head. More fringe sprang loose from its sculpted arc. The chains clinked, and it occurred to me with a jaggedy start that they looked like they hurt, that her skin was a pinched white around the metal's edges. "You won't get penitence out of me. Do your worst."

"So be it." Dominick tossed his head back. "You used

witchfinder tactics because they worked. Your words. Witches observing, I think Madeline Kline shouldn't have her specter inside her. I think that she's a danger to every witch alive. That's the method she'd use, and it's what I propose. Tonight, we look through the specters recovered from the witchfinders, and we will pull this rock from between Kline's jaws and keep it here, in the Delacroix House, with the burned devils in urns and the living devil archives. This ends here."

Daisy tensed in my lap but I could hardly feel it because I could hardly feel anything at all, now. A cold rinsed me and my body went screaming numb.

Dominick looked down at Madeline, kneeling before the fire with her arms wrenched back, and he inclined his head, said something that I shouldn't've have heard, that was out of earshot and therefore impossible, but cut around my head all the same. He tucked a lock of sallow blond hair behind his ring-heavy ear and said to her, voice small and brittle: "My worst is yours, little sister. I'm sorry. Death to traitors. See you in hell."

Madeline closed her eyes. She squared her shoulders, swayed her hips forward, loosened her arms so that her pose of confinement looked comfortable, some model contortion, not a gallows slouch. Anne Boleyn stretching her neck out so her killer can get her with a single smooth whack. I could see all the veins in her. She looked poisoned. The tension fell out of her mouth. She looked at me and said, "I knew I'd never grow up."

Some fuse blew in my head. I pushed Daisy onto Jing and I stood up, suddenly my height felt cartoonish, I was Alice in Wonderland and I'd fill the whole house. I turned my back to Madeline and I stared at my fancified elders. "Isn't anybody going to ask *me* what the fuck I think should happen?"

Lots of blinking. Clearly, most of the people in this room had no idea who I was.

"I'm Sideways Pike," I said. "I'm a Scapegracer. She took my—it was my—I'm the one she robbed. I'm also the person who smuggled the specters out of the Chantry house." The energy shifted in the room, and suddenly I was an understudy onstage and everybody was looking at me, so I picked a face in the crowd, some stranger with long eyelashes, and spoke just to them. "I know Madeline fucked up. Believe me, I do. I refuse to believe that pulling her specter out solves anything. It doesn't fix that month of my life, it won't unkill the Chantry kid. It might kill her. I have my specter back now. I risked my life breaking into the Chantry house to recover hers. It is outright insane to me that we're seriously considering wounding her like a witchfinder would. Literally what would that accomplish?"

Dominick watched me carefully. He said, "What would you propose?"

The plan! Be so fucking cool! "Letting her go." I looked at my coven, who looked thrilled. I looked at a different stranger. "Chett-hexing her."

"Chett-hexing her," Dominick repeated incredulously.

"Yeah." I looked over the audience, which was also what the audience was doing.

Someone offered in a loud whisper, "They're the ones who curse people in clubs, no?"

"The one with the accounts," someone said.

"Does anyone else have anything to ask of Miss Kline?" It was Maurice, in the back. He sounded strained. "If not, we should adjourn to the parlor."

Everyone started talking. They stood and made for the door in one great wave, like everybody was eager not to look at Madeline anymore, or desperate to scream at each other unobstructed. I felt furious. Furious. My blood beat through me in mean, sour punches. There were hands on me, Scapegracer hands, Jing and Yates on my upper arms, Daisy around the back of my neck. Daisy, right—I put an arm around Daisy and crushed her to me. I tucked her cheek in the hollow of my throat, and imagined that my specter throbbing by her ear was still inside of Madeline, even just splinters of it. I thought as crisply as I could muster: *You're not going to die here, Madeline Kline.*

Kline thought back with old Scratch clarity: *I won't if you do something about it.*

"Sideways," Jing said in my ear. "You sure?"

"She hasn't said shit," Daisy hissed.

"She thinks loudly," Yates said. "I agree. We stick to the plan."

"Nobody is being cool at all," Daisy pressed.

"Yeah, well," I said. I rested my chin on the top of her head. "Fuck this noise. We're busting her out anyway."

"Literally shut the fuck up, they'll hear you," Jing whispered. She squeezed my arm. "All in?"

"All in," said Yates. She had that oracle of Delphi look again and I prayed uselessly to the cosmic current itself that maybe it could calm down so that she could relax and feel at peace and look less creepy. "Are we going to just wait for everybody to leave? Everybody might not leave."

"Nah," said Jing. "We're getting reinforcements."

Daisy bounced on her tiptoes in such a way that she turned all four of us on an axis. Somehow, we were all facing chained-up Madeline Kline, who was staring miserably at the floor in front of her, like a dog in a kennel commercial. I was going to hyperventilate if we didn't do something active right fucking now.

Daisy said, "Chill here for five minutes, 'kay?"

Madeline looked up at us. She blinked. She rattled her chains.

"Great!" Daisy said, and with a power she alone possessed, she herded us into the hallway.

FIVE

GLORY BE TO SHOPLIFTERS

Jacques and Pearl met us under the stairs. I wasn't sure which fucking stairs these were, there were so many staircases in the Delacroix House and I was increasingly convinced that a blueprint of this building would be less a set of logical, physically feasible rectangles and instead a layer cake of shifting curlicue labyrinth squiggles, but as much as this stretch of house was moored to the material plane this spot was near the kitchens, I think. It was dark; the red felted wallpaper had a brown coolness like old blood. There were ambient knife sounds and a heavy rosemary smell hung over everything. Low chatter. Workers blustered nearby with trays of grimoires and finger food. Just out of sight, kitty-corner with the six of us huddling, people discussed Madeline and what would soon be done to her. I felt like Macbeth before the dinner with Duncan or some shit. I missed crew. Who was that kid? Sideways of before, rest in pieces.

Yates leaned in toward the reinforcements. "Thank you for this," she said. "I thought you'd understand and have good hearts about the matter at hand."

"Maurice could fire us," Pearl said flatly, "but our asses are not on the line here."

"Yours are," Jacques added. He looked, if I read him right, somewhere caught between livid and unspeakably sad. He was a delicately built boy, one of the prettier people I'd ever met, I think. He cupped a hand over the back of his neck. "Madeline is not my friend anymore. I wish her well far away from here. I've never seen a flock this dense, not for anything so serious, and I think that means they're afraid. Later tonight they're sifting through the specter stones you found. It's ugly to me that they're willing to add another to the pile."

"Hard not to be edgy when we all might straight up die," Pearl said. They adjusted a rhinestoned strap that seemed too delicate to hold up the glimmering mass of their dress. The fabric looked like smashed glass. I wanted to grab it, to knead it between my thumb and the hook of my forefinger. I didn't, but I put the edge of my sleeve in my mouth and sucked to shut myself up before I said something to that effect. Pearl smiled. Their eyes lit up with weird white spots. Light catching their contacts, but it could've been magic. I shivered. "Literally, imminently we could all die, and that's on baby Madeline, *so*. You wanna save her? That's on you—I mean, she witchfound you, so it's your business if you wanna be the bigger person, but I can't abide it myself."

"But you wouldn't snitch," Jing said, warning. She brought down her brows in a V.

"No." Pearl looked at Jacques, then at the staircase's belly above us. "I'm not going to ruin your scheme or whatever. My help will be minimal, but you'll still get it."

"Thank you," Yates said. She put a hand on Daisy's elbow.

Daisy looked like death.

"We won't all die," Jacques said. He leaned back against the wall and looked between the four of us. "The Chantry family might seek retribution, sure, but they're one family, and we're a mass of exceptionally powerful witches. They're not stupid. We outnumber them."

"Mm," said Pearl.

"Still," Jacques said, ignoring them, "you'll need to be careful. I know you know, but seriously. You run the risk of alienating yourselves from Maurice and his network by doing this. It would be catastrophically dangerous for your coven to be all alone right now."

Pearl mouthed, *coven.*

"*Coven,*" Daisy repeated with ancient, sizzling venom and a smile.

"For now," Pearl said. They sighed, touched Jacques' shoulder, communicated something imperceptible to me with a glance. Then they looked at me, specifically me. They wore colored contacts in a flat candy-apple green. I thought about medical supplies. I thought about bleeding out and then tried to stop thinking. They said, "She's going to be alone for a good thirty minutes. I overheard Dominick talking to Maurice—he needs to call the other Corbies and debate particulars, something like that, and Maurice wants her space respected in the interim. She'll be in that room still. It's locked for everybody but staff, because nothing is locked for staff. Whatever you're going to do, you'll need to do it fast, because Dominick is a mean son of a bitch and I wouldn't tangle with the Corbies for the life of me."

"I'll take you," Jacques said. He frowned, then said, "I'll do that much for her. Get her out of here. May she flourish a thousand miles from me."

"You're nicer than me," Daisy said.

"Many people are," said Yates. "Thank you again, really."

Jing murmured into the back of my neck, "You're being quiet. What's up?"

I sucked in a hard breath, startled by Jing's closeness but less than I could've been. I knew her energy signature or her perfume or whatever. Her nearness had a particular feeling. I cocked my head in her direction and squeezed my eyes shut. An absolute miracle that my irises didn't pop under the pressure. "Trying not to emotionally process anything."

Jing snorted. She pressed her forehead between my shoulder blades, then drew herself up, became Jing the Lead Girl again. She flipped her hair over her shoulder. "Do it to it."

Jacques nodded. He set off, strode between Yates and Daisy without a look back, and I took off after him. Someone slipped a hand into mine—Yates, felt like Yates—and I squeezed it, made myself breathe as we started down a hallway so chock-full of oil paintings it looked staged. Daisy and Jing were just behind me, silent but prickling.

From behind our heads as we descended, Pearl's dry cough: "Sayonara, fuckers."

Dodging people was impossible. There were potential onlookers everywhere. People screaming at each other and throwing little fruit cubes and sobbing hysterically and making out, reclining on armchairs and pacing up and down the hallway, someone kneeling, someone dragging someone by the wrist, someone adjusting someone's dress, the crowd was cacophonous, and I couldn't have kept track if I tried. Itchy ripples of other people's magic crawled like static. General ripples of their intensity for each other, too, not that feelings were neatly separable from magic. It must have been some pre-Scapegracers power, the fact that we were continuously seen and even smiled at but not caught. Jing and Yates and Daisy had so much social sway by virtue of being the three of them. They walked in lockstep and something unlocked in the hindbrain of everyone around them: *These girls are existentially cooler than I, and meaner, and prettier, and it's a delight for them to traipse around near me and do whatever they'd like.* Girls should get whatever they want. Nobody questioned us. A few people waved.

Didn't question me, either. Watched me with wary recognition from earlier, but I was theirs, and besides, I imagine I was tough to think about. Cowards.

I gave Yates' hand another squeeze.

Jacques led us around a twist, a turn, took us through a statue gallery where giant marble women lounged in hard gossamer and ate fake dangling grapes, down a carpeted ramp, through double doors, and suddenly we stood outside the room we'd been in before, the worst room in the whole Delacroix House. I felt seven emotions at once and acknowledged none of them. They sloshed around and curdled in my fingertips. I missed Mr. Scratch. I wanted to hit something. I wanted to see a mirror so I could jump out of my body and sucker punch myself. I clenched my core, jerked my chin up, took a breath.

Jacques said a little prayer and touched the doorknob. Despite all the background chatter, I heard it unlock with a crisp, cold click. He pulled it open a sliver, then lifted his head, glanced skywards, like he could look through the rafters and read etchings of heaven above. "There," he said. "Good luck."

I nodded at him, tried for a smile and faltered. Mostly I just stuck out my teeth.

He slipped out of sight and was gone.

Jing opened the door a crack, just wide enough for my shoulders. I stepped through the gap and pulled Yates with me. Daisy fell close behind us, then Jing at the end, closing the door with a dollar bill wedged between the tongue and its reciprocal locking mechanism—a cartoonish sleight of hand that worked, miraculously enough. We stood in the green room without outside eyes on us. I bristled all over. Gooseflesh crawled.

I looked toward the hearth.

Madeline rasped, "Took you long enough."

"Way to be grateful, you treasonous bitch." Daisy spat on the floor. "If I had it my way, I'd kneel on your throat and pour glitter in your nose. Sideways chose to save you out of the goodness of their heart. Be nice to them!"

"Be cool," said Jing to everyone.

Yates said, "Glitter in her nose?"

I shook myself. My head felt so empty without Mr. Scratch inside it. Bowl sans goldfish, coffin sans vampire, whatever. My blood roiled. Endorphins fizzled around my ears. My endocrine system was a shook-up bottle of Coke. The rib rows of chairs were empty now, pushed askew, and I felt a perverse shock of nostalgia for the crumbling sunken church in the woods where I'd found sleeping Shiloh. Felt like pews. They weren't pews though, because if this were a church, Madeline would be Christ, and holy shit that was hilarious. Absolutely hilarious.

The fire behind her corkscrewed in a high, screaming violet. I wondered if that meant she was nervous.

If she was, it didn't show in her face.

Madeline didn't lift her jaw. She just looked at me with an upward roll of her eyes. Backlit like this, she looked frightening. I tried—I don't fucking know, telepathy or whatever—and thought, *Do you know what spell they used on the chains?*

Madeline shivered. Her nose twitched. *It's a Sisters Corbie special. It's just a placeholder that prevents secondary spells from being cast on an object. I can't hex them off, and neither can you. What are you doing?*

Reverse mind reading, I don't know, don't worry about it. Does it hurt?

Yes.

Could we position you to make it hurt less?

You could get me down. She made a face. *I want a ciga-rette. Could you get me a cigarette?*

Projecting thoughts like this wasn't comfortable. It felt like concentrating too hard on a logic puzzle. I sucked at logic puzzles. I looked her over like, *Does it look like I have cigarettes on me*, but quickly saw that *she* did. They were tucked in her breast pocket. I walked up to her, tried to smother a weird thrill in my gut, and I reached two fin-gers for her breast pocket, slipped them in the dark gap of fabric, and scissored my fingers shut around the laminated plastic I found there. I pulled upwards in a smooth, slow motion. It'd be what Jing would do, I thought. I held the box by its lid for a moment, dangled it between index and middle finger, and reached a free hand into my pocket, dug around for my lighter. I found it, withdrew it, and fished out a skinny little poison stick. Dropped the box on the floor after that. I cocked my head back, looked down my nose at her, waved the cigarette in a lazy figure eight. Rubbed it in a little.

Madeline looked greenish.

I asked, "Yeah?"

She answered, sounding pinched: "Yeah."

I flipped the cigarette around, offered a bit of fool's gold paper.

She inclined her head and put her lips around it.

I lit it for her. She lugged in a gracious, noxious breath. The cherry bounced. Ash flecked from it like snow or dead skin. Something changed in Madeline's face. There was color in her cheeks. Miraculous what having a soul could do for one's complexion, I guess.

Daisy said behind me, "Are you kidding me?"

I puffed up a little. Said, "We can't get the chains off with magic. Jing, do you have bolt cutters in your car?"

Jing waved her hands in the air. She gestured at the lighter, mimed taking a drag with a peace sign, and made a throaty little sound at me. "No," she said, "I don't have *bolt cutters* in my *car.*"

Madeline blew out slow. Smoke curled around the hollows of her cheeks. Smoking cigarettes was vile and like atrociously nineties for my tastes, but damn if she didn't look cool. No fair.

Yates let out a little gasp. "We're on ground level, right?"

"Yes," Madeline said against the back of my fingers. She looked—*looked*—at Yates. I felt a stab of jealousy at that look. I wasn't sure about the jealousy's direction. My stomach hurt. "Why?"

"There's a garden outside," Yates said. She said it with revelatory excitement. I wasn't following.

Neither was Daisy, apparently. "What about it?"

"Wouldn't that mean there's a toolshed? There is topiary here. Topiary would imply big shears for pruning animals out of big fuzzy trees." Yates thrummed. "If we got a pair of garden shears, do you think we could cut through the chain?"

"Cut through the chain," Jing repeated.

Madeline's eyes flashed. She smiled—really smiled, with horrible, unforgivable debonair—at Yates. "With that attitude. There is a shed. Should be just to the north." She cocked her head to the left like she was indicating a direction. I wouldn't know. I had zero true north. My compass was just my furious fuckoff knot of homosexuality ever alive and fuming inside me. Madeline said, "The window should be open. If you can climb out of it, you could get into the shed without a hitch. It should be just a specter lock, it should open for any of you. Most doors here are specter locks. Whatever. This could work."

Yates beamed.

Good enough for Daisy Brink. She lurched toward the far wall, caught a chair in her fist somewhere along the way, and dragged it up against the wall. It made a horrible sound, like she'd scruffed a mechanical piglet. She climbed up onto it, gave the window an upwards yank, and a cold wind swirled in around us and tossed Jing's hair around. Daisy sniffed. She glared down at Jing and Yates and me. There wasn't any of her usual fizzy brightness in her. She was a grisly sort of pale. "Jing and Yates with me. We'll be back in a jiffy."

"Shouldn't one of us stay back and cover Sideways in case this goes belly-up?" Jing folded her arms over her chest. I had the sense that this was more Socratic than confrontational, but she did have a certain tone that made crossing her terrifying, and this tone was that.

Daisy, however, was without a lick of serotonin anywhere in her body and therefore was past fear and well into some primordial affective sink that put her less in the category of girl and more in the category of swamp monster. She curled her lip into a nasty little smile, blinked twice, and said with all the vocal fry in the world, "We need to let Sideways be alone with Madeline so that they can discreetly change their mind and murder her real quick. Come on!"

Madeline coughed.

Jing snorted. She touched Yates' elbow, and the two of them bolted after Daisy. Daisy stood, jumped from the chair, and oversaw Yates' shimmy out of the window, boosted Jing after her, and with her cheerleader's wisdom having done its work, she clambered up again herself. She shot a glance over her shoulder at us before she disappeared on the other side of the wall. She mouthed: *Be cool!*

"Charming friends," Madeline said once she was gone.

All the air snuffed out of the room. Alone with her—I hadn't been since it happened.

"Don't talk about my friends," I said. Another suck and the cigarette was all but gone. I dropped it, crushed it into the carpet under my heel. Sorry to Maurice. "Don't hit on them, either."

"Was that your girlfriend?"

"I swear to fucking god."

Madeline leaned her head back. She rolled it to the left, then the right, vertebrae popping, then came back to center. Her eyes fell shut. It occurred to me after an ugly moment that she'd shut them because tears were swelling along her lash line. A dart ghosted between her brows. She squeezed her eyes tighter. None of the tears fell, they clung to her lashes like beads. She sounded raw. "Sideways," she said.

My throat clapped. I shook off naming feelings and knelt for some reason. Maybe to be on eye level with her? My body moved with more animal purpose than my brain could account for. "Hey," I said. "You're going to be fine."

She cried like a boy.

I didn't know what to tell her. I didn't forgive her. Scar tissue doesn't dissolve once you point at it. I leaned forward, leaned closer than I should, pressed my forehead against her forehead and stared at her point-blank. Her lashes could've tangled with mine. "Do you miss me?" I curled my hands into fists then shook them loose again. "My specter. That part of me. Do you miss having me around inside you?"

Madeline shuddered. A vein flared at the edge of her jaw. "I miss," she said thickly, "that you hurt all the time. I've never had *you*, Sideways. Just your ache."

"That's most of me," I snapped. There was a tremor in my fingertips. What was I doing? Why couldn't I shut up? "You miss that I *hurt*?"

"I was all but dead. You stung every waking minute of every day. You made it hurt to swallow. Talking hurt. Breathing hurt. Some nights I didn't sleep because you just stung and stung and never let up." Her breath hitched. She smiled a little. It wasn't how she smiled at Yates. "You were the only thing I could feel at all."

I choked. I bluescreened.

I kissed her. Madeline bit me, she pulled my bottom lip between her teeth and pressed against me, shoved her ribs against mine, breastbone to breastbone, thigh to thigh to thigh to thigh. I put hands around the back of her neck, fit my thumbs behind her ears, in the hollow hinges of her jaw. The chains rattled in their rings; she must've yanked them. I kissed her harder. She put her tongue between my teeth, and I wondered if I tasted how my specter tasted. If she remembered how it tasted.

In the back of my head, her voice: *I do. It does.*

There was a screech and three low thuds.

"Scissors," Yates said with jarring, giddy brightness. "We found the scissors!"

I flew back, fell flat on my ass. Tore my eyes off Madeline—she was blushing, Madeline was *blushing*, and I was going to die—and looked at my Scapegracers, who were making some show of looking back. Daisy looked aghast. Yates had the garden shears, and she crossed the room with buoyant briskness, opening and closing the tool as she went with a nervous *snip snip snip*. Jing looked—tense. I'd been expecting condescension or pity maybe, or hilarity, but not tension.

Yates lifted the shears. She put the chain in their beak, screwed her face up, and they cut through smooth as butter. Too easy. Nonsensically easy. The blades had a pearly blue sheen to them. Funny how Yates' good heart was more than enough. Magic was so funny. Imagine trying to riddle out a science for this shit.

The chains slipped off the rings and clattered to the floor.

Madeline's arms dropped like lead. She let out a thin sound of pain. Selfishly, ridiculously, the sound made me think about me. I tingled all over, felt a poison ivy zingy evil itchiness. I shook myself. I wanted to dissolve. I got my feet underneath me, turned to ask Yates about the big kick-ass scissors she'd found, about the magic she'd just thrown around without even having realized it, about her glowing, immeasurable power.

Dominick said from behind us, "You've got to be fucking kidding me."

The five of us bolted like deer.

STICKS AND STONES MIGHT BREAK MY BONES

Ducking behind Jing's cherry-red convertible like a bunch of shitty cartoon spies, knees popping, inches from the oil-slicked asphalt, the five of us panted and tried and failed to think. We'd run like hell and scrambled out that window, my knee stung about it, I must've banged it on something. They didn't pursue us the same way. Maybe it was a dignity thing. Like, technically this was still according to the plan, but when everything was mortally terrifying, actionable next steps felt so obscure. My head swam. My bottom lip felt swollen, raw where she'd bitten me, and I sucked on it and stared at my hands to keep myself from glancing over the hood at the house.

"Why haven't they chased us out here?" Daisy snapped at Madeline.

Madeline just looked at her. After a moment she said, "Dominick's a smoker. He doesn't run."

"You're a smoker, but whatever. Let's not wait for him to walk," said Jing, whose expression was still blurry and

ominously indistinct and made me feel like I'd broken something, though I wasn't sure what the something could be. She
flicked her eyes between us, then leaned close, whispered
something in Yates' ear that made Yates shudder and press
her fingertips to the hollow of her neck. Jing looked at Madeline. "Do you have a place to go?"

Madeline pulled a face.

"I think we're in the right." Yates frowned.

"How sweet," Daisy sneered, rubbing her eyes with both
fists.

"No. I think we're right." Yates scrunched her brow. "I
want to stay. I want to hold ground in this."

"Can we talk in the car?" The asphalt between my palms
looked blacker than it should, like it was made of water. I
could smack through it if I wanted. "We need to move."

"Agreed," Madeline said.

"Shut the fuck up," Daisy said.

"Agreed," said Jing. She stood, unlocked her car with a starburst flash of headlights—how the little techno *chirp chirp*
was so loud was beyond me, but it made my skull hurt and I
flinched from it—and yanked open the door. "Everybody in."

"No," Yates said. She spoke with a firmness. "This is
wrong, and we're in the right, and I want to look everyone in
the eye and tell them so. I'm staying. I'm going to convince
them not to follow you."

Madeline's expression changed beside me, but I couldn't
bear to look.

Jing stared down at her from the driver's seat. She looked

stunned, her frozen weirdness smudged over with open shock, and then she shut her eyes and faced the steering wheel and leaned the back of her neck against the headrest. Every hair on her head looked crystalline against the leather. "I'm not leaving you alone. Are you serious about this?"

Madeline rounded the car, slid in shotgun, slammed the door behind her like a punctuation mark. She jolted her head up with a snap, fixed on something beyond the rearview mirror, then slammed one hand on the dashboard and said, "Now, for the love of god, we need to move *now*."

Yates bounced once on the balls of her feet. "Yes," she said. "I am."

"Shit," Jing said. She twisted the key in the ignition, revved the engine a few times, brows in a knot. She stared where Madeline stared. I saw her flick the tip of her tongue between her teeth. "Fine. Daisy, stay with her." An order. "We will be back here ASAP, hear me?"

Over top of the car, I could see the steady amassing of witches on the porch, distant faces grim and pinched. They watched us. I felt their eyes on me like bugs. The crowd thickened. Peels of witches pulled away from the central cluster, started their procession down the walk. I swayed against the car and sucked in a hard, cold breath. "We're really splitting up?"

"Yeah." Daisy put an arm around Yates' waist. It was a gesture that fell somewhere between bodyguard and boyfriend. "I can hold them off. You with us or them, Pike?"

I couldn't think. I wanted Mr. Scratch. He would've picked for me if I panicked.

Why the fuck had I left him at home?

I rounded the car. The faces on the porch had definition now. I set my jaw, jerked open the passenger's side door, and seized a fistful of Madeline's shirt.

Madeline's lip curled like, *the fuck?*

I hauled her up and thrust her over the gearshift. Her eyes popped wide and she kicked out but not before her shoulders struck the backseat, arms a mess on either side of her, heels up near the headrests. She clambered upright. I grimaced, sat down where she'd been, and pulled the door closed beside me. I scrubbed a hand over my head. The buzz felt like sable. "Let's move."

"Call me fucking immediately if you think you're in imminent danger," Jing hissed out the window. Low light fell through the windshield and made her hair catch like fire. She locked eyes with Yates. "We'll be back soon. Keep a choke chain on Daze."

"She'll be good, she won't need one." Yates' eyes sparkled. "Good luck!"

Daisy spat on the gravel beside her feet.

Jing gave her a curt nod. She pulled out fast then, whipped the car around with roller-coaster fuck-off carelessness, and zipped out of the lot with acceleration that she hadn't practiced legally. I glanced at the speedometer and my stomach flipped. Dread kicked around my head, and shimmering, nauseous elation. I coughed and it twisted into something like cackling. I braced a hand against the glove box.

Jing's lips moved. She muttered something to herself,

something terse and needle-sharp, the same thing over and over again. Air warped around her head. Light refracted in ways it shouldn't. She swayed forward, glitchy phantom halo sizzling, and pulled one hand off the steering wheel and pressed it to the back of her mouth. She put it back. She rounded a corner.

The lipstick stain she left glowed at the edges.

It was a sigil. Her kiss had made a sigil just below her knuckles.

I balked at her. I flattened against the car door and just looked at her, tried to fit all of her in my brain at once. She was too much to take in. I smiled wider. The air felt cold on my teeth. "Was that a spell? Did you just cast a fucking spell, Jing?"

"Keeping people off my back," she snapped. Her eyes flashed up, matte black and livid, and she locked eyes with Madeline in the rearview for a split second before she looked back at the road. "Where am I going, Kline? Talk fast."

"South. I've got people over state lines." Madeline shifted on the seats behind me but I didn't want to look at her. I was busy staring at the magic on Jing's hand. Madeline spoke curtly and I knew, somehow, that she was lying. She wasn't positive, anyway. I felt it in my gut. I blamed telepathy. "If you get me a few miles past Sycamore Gorge I'll be fine. I can make my own way from there."

Jing flared her nostrils a touch, rolled her neck, her shoulders. She sped a little faster. Trees melted, looked like feathers on folds of endless wings. The sun sank lower and made the pavement shiver. Felt like racing down an angel's spine. The car might burst into literal flames. I wondered about the spell she'd cast, and about the incantation she'd whispered too low for me to parse. I had cotton mouth somehow. I gnawed on the meat of my tongue. I said, "What people, Madeline?"

The car made sounds underneath me, all around me. It turned my bones taffy sticky and made me want to die. No music, just the high whine of Jing speeding and asphalt tripping underneath us. My bottom lip had a salty taste. Wild that the swelling hadn't gone down. Madeline didn't say jack shit and Jing looked like she was ignoring us or trying. I peeled my eyes off the lipstick-stain sigil and glanced in the rearview. I opened my mouth to repeat myself.

Madeline made a face that shut me up for a second. She pulled one of her knees to her chest. She put a hand in her hair, sculpted the pompadour back, and every strand looked glassy against her long fingers. She looked at nothing, eyes unfocused, mouth in a tight line. "I've done this before. I know what I'm doing."

"Not what I asked."

"Sideways," Jing said. A warning. Didn't know for what.

"I'm not keen on the thought of you being homeless with Dominick on your heels," I said. I mean, it was true, I wasn't. The thought made me feel sick. I might be sick any second now. My blood ran sour. All cars go to hell. "This is fucked."

Madeline looked grayscale. She kneaded her hands together.

"You know this crowd better than we do. Yates and Daisy are fine, right?" Jing glanced at the rearview again, and through some power more ancient than magic, pulled Madeline's attention out of the twelfth dimension and dragged it back to earth. Jing's expression was lethal. That look used to scare the shit out of me. Still did. "No harm will come to them while I haul your poisonous hide out of Sycamore Gorge, understand?"

"They'll be fine," Madeline said, convincing nobody. "I don't think harm would come to them. Not real harm."

Jing glanced at the road, then back at her. "If something happens to either of them, I'll kill you. Know that."

Madeline inclined her head. "The pretty one. What's her name?"

We hit a bump and I fantasized wildly about it having been me.

"Yates," I said. "You're talking about Yates. Lila Yates."

"Don't talk about Yates," Jing said. She clucked her tongue. "Sideways. Put on some music, would you?"

I felt around for the aux cord. The wire was clammy; its texture skeeved me out for some reason. I flipped my phone over in my palm, tried to conceive of music that'd make any of this tolerable as I punched in my password, and then my eyes fixed on the unread calls and bam! Endorphins screaming all at once.

Shiloh had called me five times and texted only once: **i need to talk to u asap**

"Fuck," I said aloud.

"Is it—"

"It's Shi," I said. I shook myself, returned the call. My phone felt grimy on my cheek. Bile pinged at the back of my tongue, but nothing came of it. I squeezed my eyes shut. Something must be wrong with Jing's suspension, it was making me feel worse than usual, and I was firm on blaming the object before I blamed myself. The phone rang and rang. Each tone flashed across the back of my eyelids with a little purple burst. I got their machine, which was without prerecorded message. Inbox full. I pulled my phone back to dial again but before my thumb hit the glass, they were calling me and I fumbled to receive it.

Against my temple and far away, Shiloh said: "Where are you? Are you still at the Delacroix?"

"What is it?" Jing inclined her head beside me, lipstick-sigil hand tensing on the steering wheel, wisps of platinum swishing from behind her ear across her cheekbone.

I shook my head, shoved my temple against the rattling window beside me, which was a fucking mistake. My guts seized. The crooks of my fingers screamed, and I made myself ease up on my phone before I snapped it vertically like a graham cracker. "I'll be back soon. Daze and Yates are there. Why, what's up? Are you okay? Is Julian—"

"I saw Tatum Jenkins' car on Elm Street."

My head was a hornet's nest. Just crawling buzzing awful.

No complex cognition, no abstract thought, just noise noise noise. I gritted my teeth and said ungently, "I don't know who the fuck that is, Shi."

"Tatum Jenkins is a witchfinder," they said. "An evil piece of work. You don't get it, Sideways, my blood family, as far as Brethren went we were moderates, we believed in compromises, but the Jenkins family isn't like that, they're fucking unhinged and—"

"Slow down," I said, "breathe. What? What exactly are you trying to tell me, here?"

"Tatum wouldn't just hang around Sycamore Gorge for the hell of it, Sideways. He's here for a reason, I'm sure of it. I've got a rancid feeling about this, and I'm worried about you four. The Jenkins family doesn't believe in leaning on systems alone to eradicate witchcraft, they just hunt. They make trophy sport of it. I . . . one of the witches that I . . . I did with them. I'm not screwing around, I need you to be extremely careful, okay?" Their voice kept cracking. It was all breath and no music, just hushed, crackling consonants, and I got the sense that this had been full-on panic a few minutes prior. "I have a really bad theory and I need to know you are fine."

"Theory," I said. I couldn't say anything else. I thought about Yates' weird feeling from earlier and felt out of my mind. I crawled all over. "Tell me about your theory, Shiloh."

"Who are you talking to?" Madeline said, a little loudly. She sounded suspicious. "Did I hear *Brethren?*"

"Shut *up*, Madeline," I barked.

"Wait, is Addie in the car with you?" Shiloh's voice cracked. "Is she—"

"Jesus fucking Christ. Yes, she's here with me, we just busted her out of witch jail." I pulled the phone away from my cheek and put it on speaker, then twisted around, jabbed a corner of it against Madeline's shin.

Madeline said, "Who the fuck are you talking to?"

I took the phone off speaker and pulled it back to my cheek. "Theory."

Shiloh was quiet on the other end of the line.

"Shi."

Nothing.

"Shi, talk to me. You're freaking me out. Speak up."

"Does she know about me?"

"Nope. Hasn't come up. Ex-family ex-friend theory."

They laughed. It came out staccato, brittle. "Remember how y'all killed my baby brother?"

My heart slammed against my teeth.

"I think that he might be here for a memorial."

Molars against ventricles, again, again. My organs all yo-yo'd inside me.

"We'll be safe at the Delacroix. There are lots of us there. Safety in numbers." I silently thanked personified sky entropy that Yates and Daisy were still there. I shook my head, tried to steel myself. "I'll keep myself sharp, okay? I'll be careful. I promise."

"Sideways," Jing breathed.

"Don't do spell work frivolously right now. Not without like, extensive protective warding or something. Nothing flashy, okay?" Shiloh sounded distant. I thought they might be pacing. "For the love of god, please be careful."

"Beg fucking pardon?" Harsher than I'd intended. "Listen, you've got no position to lecture me about when I can and can't use magic."

"*Tatum puts out jinxes,*" they hissed. "Mimics galore and trip-wire jinxes, Sideways, please please please tell me you'll be—"

Lavender fire burst out of the sigil on Jing's hand and the world glitched in jaggedy vertical slices. The light was everywhere, it flooded the car and pressed on me with a warm, watery pressure. It felt like Jing. It smelled like her, salty sweet like her sweat through her perfume, and it was all over me, and for an infinite splintering millisecond I felt nothing but a shock of warmth. The shape of her kiss mark blazed between us. It seared my eyes like I'd looked dead-on at a naked lightbulb. Wherever I looked the kiss mark followed, arcane, lovely, violently girly and brimming, overflowing, with never-ending purple light.

The car pitched hard.

We spiraled left.

My head lit up in screaming bright orange. Vision flat and burning, lungs clapped against the folds of my belly so hard I thought they'd snap loose, hilarious, freefall pain coursed alive and electric in my face and neck and shoulders. I gasped. My tongue felt slippery. Was I choking?

Air didn't pull in through my teeth. I swam suspended in a thick, hot nothing, and I knew that I was dying, but then someone touched my back and I blinked and saw the livid green spiderweb that was Jing's windshield. There was a line dividing it vertically. That was new. Did I have a piece of glass in my mouth? My eyes fixed, and the line took on three-dimensional form; it was symmetrical, pocked with staples, gravy-brown, deeply boring. We'd hit a telephone pole. I couldn't breathe through my nose. In a giddy rush it occurred to me that in fact I did not have a chunk of windshield in my mouth, and that the hard, sharp-edged thing was a tooth. One of my front teeth balanced on my tongue like a party pill. It was not in its gum cubby. Fuck. Bummer. I opened my lips a crack and thick blood oozed, fuck it was everywhere, it was all over my face and my lap and the dashboard I'd slammed my face on, just everywhere. It clung thick to my eyelashes. Wasn't sure how it'd gotten up there. If I rolled my eyes up, I could see the big sparkly strawberry gobs against the light. Nausea roiled once, hard. Did that mean I had a concussion? It'd better fucking not.

Beside me Jing Gao screamed bloody murder. Specifically, when I started listening she was going, *SIDEWAYS SIDEWAYS OH MY GOD SIDEWAYS PLEASE FUCKING MOVE OH MY GOD SIDEWAYS SIDEWAYS SIDEWAYS BABY PLEASE.*

The purple light was gone. It's fun to observe shit like that. Magic, man.

I spat my tooth into my palm.

The screaming stopped. Hands on my shoulder now, feather light but with immeasurable intensity, giving me the gentlest of shakes. I grimaced. Grimacing stung, because my bottom lip was fucked. Split, I'd guess. Must've bitten it pretty hard before my tooth gave up on me. Blood fell clean out of my mouth, out of my nose, and onto my cupped hand. Thick worms of clotty blackish blood. That had not been on purpose. Blood was not really stoppable at this point. I might flood the car and drown Jing and Madeline.

Jing and Madeline.

Jing had been yelling.

I squeezed my eyes shut, kept them clenched for the length of an inhale, then opened them. I looked to my left. My neck was stiffer than necks usually were and this motion wasn't well supported. I looked mostly with my eyes.

"Sideways," Jing said. Her makeup made dark arcs around the curves of her cheeks. Had she been crying? I didn't care for that at all. That felt wrong. She leaned forward, eyes flashing and dauntingly waterier than I'd ever seen them, and gasped, "Are you alright? Talk to me."

I tried to smile. It hurt immediately and more blood fell out of my face and onto Jing's sleeve, which made her wince, which made me wince in turn. I searched for language. Surely there was language inside of me, still. My linguistic capacity was not stored in my front teeth, cool as that'd be, and I needed to say something, say anything, because Jing had been crying and I realized that I might have looked fully dead there for a moment. She might've thought I had snapped my neck. It was a cold, clammy thought. My throat cloyed. Blood slicked down the back of it and made my insides fold. I searched her face for a moment, like speech might live there instead, and was comforted by the fact that her face didn't look broken, or even super bruised. Sweat made her bangs stringy, pasted them against her brow. She flushed a deep red. That hooked something out of me. I leaned in, body screaming, and said thickly: "Did you call me baby?"

"I hate you," she said. Her brows shot up. She shook her head, and a lopsided grin broke over her. Another inky tear fell. I watched it run down her jaw with mild horror. "You're the fucking worst."

"My tooth came out." I sounded funny. "I sound funny."

"You look funny." Her brows twitched. More tears, they left cracks in her makeup, and I felt less shackled to earth after each. "You look like hell."

"That tracks." I leaned closer, said with all the firmness I could muster: "I'm alright, see? It's alright. I'm okay." I brought up my free hand, the one without a tooth in it, and circled my thumb over her left cheekbone. "No tears."

She leaned her ear against my bloody, wet palm.

"We are so fucked." That didn't come out of Jing's mouth. My sweet purgatory shattered. I managed to move my neck enough to peer down into the backseat, hand still on Jing's cheek, and beheld a thoroughly un-pompadoured Madeline Kline.

Madeline looked like the soothsayer who told Julius Caesar to get fucked. Huge eyes, ashen, gaunt and ghastly, unsettlingly earnest. Her hair fell across her face. She stared at something indistinct, and then that something turned into me.

We held eye contact for a quick ugly forever.

She tore her gaze off me, kicked open the door, and slithered out of the car. I heard her soles thud against the pavement. She left the door ajar in her wake.

I turned my attention back on Jing and blinked, which freckled her with little ruby specks, and said: "We should follow her."

Jing said, "I don't know if you should get out of the car."

"I'm okay," I said. My voice was pitched oddly. Pinched sounding. I thought that potentially my nose was broken. My nose had been questionable before and a deviated septum wasn't going to improve things. That'd suck later when I had time or capacity to really think. For now, my head was a slurry of television static and white-hot globs of ache. I didn't know what to do with my tooth. For lack of better impulse, I put it in my pocket. I reached for the car door, gave it a limp, sorry tug. "I'll be okay."

Jing sucked in a hard breath. She looked at me a long moment and then she got out, passed around the front of the car. The broken windshield cracked her like a kaleido-scope. Jing looked nice all psychedelic. My neck felt sticky. I felt like I'd bitten the head off a honey bear and all the honey had sloshed down my front and it was the single most grimy feeling on earth. I felt disgusting. Jing made her way around the pole and appeared beside my window, and she opened the door for me, peered down at my face with open, brittle concern. She spoke crisply, without blinking. "Can I help you up?"

Was I the girl in the bottom of the pool, now? The dead little baby deer dyke?

My pride disagreed, but it was overpowered by some gut wisdom that moved my mouth for me. "Yeah," I said. I poked my tongue up into the fabulous screaming hole where my front tooth should be. "Thanks, yeah."

She leaned over me. Her blond hair fell along the line of her cheek and brushed my chest, sopped up some of the red there. It clung like paint. My stomach went sour. She reached down, movements careful and rabbity, and unbuckled me, manually guided the straps so that they did not touch my body as they receded back into their above-hanging plastic slit. She took a step back. "One foot out, come on."

One foot out. That worked! Foot on pavement.

Jing nodded and touched my arm.

I twisted. My vision also twisted with a moment's delay, which was exciting. I glanced at her—she spun, still warbled and aglow with hallucinogenic angel squiggles, which I knew she did not have intellectually but emotionally couldn't process as abnormal—and pulled my weight up, balanced my pelvis over femurs over bottle caps over whatever was inside of calves. The sunset screamed at me. Heaven was excruciatingly pink, a snarling, hungry, evil pink, and it pressed down on my shoulders and pulled

more blood out of my face. I didn't move but did a pirou-
ette. I slammed a hand on the car. Jing put a hand on the
middle of my back, said my name a few times like it was
some minor incantation. I inclined my head and opened
my mouth. It was like upending a pudding cup. Dark red
splattered between my boots in a single, viscous mass. I
hoped I hadn't coughed up my soul. That would suck a
lot. Jing didn't jump back, which I guess I had anticipated
somehow. She leaned in, pulled me closer, just enough to
hold some of my weight. I worried about crushing her. I
worried about her body getting mashed under the horror
show that was me.

"Steady," she breathed.

"Mm-hmm." I grimaced, took a step or two forward.
That worked, feet worked, body suspended and attached to
feet seemed to be doing as they ought. Progress. I reached
out one arm and hovered it in midair above her shoulders,
worried for a moment about touching her, about staining
her clothing.

She lifted on tiptoe and shrugged me on like a jacket.
"After Madeline, yes?"

"Yes," I said.

She steered me toward Madeline.

Madeline was only a few yards away from us. She stood
at the edge of the road beside a ditch about as deep as a
bathtub, and I felt a smidgeon grateful that Jing's car had
decided to eat shit on the pole instead. Crows jumped
around to my left, beaks scissoring at the downed wires

on either side of Jing's crunched-up hood, and they cawed, they just kept cawing their incessant *Caw caw caw I'm a bird what's up* bullshit antics, and it was so loud that I thought I might shatter. I swayed against Jing. She bore my weight more than I thought she could. Later I'd apologize, or maybe just thank her.

We came nearer to Madeline, shadowed against the violent pink sky and the chalky blue-black road. She peered down, face pale, lips pulled tight over her teeth. The ditch was hemmed with tawny dead grass, looked like cheap plastic hide on a hideous pair of boots, and it was not immediately apparent to me why the sight made Madeline look so wan.

We pulled ourselves beside her, peered down with her, beheld what she beheld.

Six raccoons at the bottom of the ditch. They looked like planks in a stretch of railroad. All belly up, with their feet stretched above their heads and toward the tips of their stripy lemur tails, stomachs as long as possible. Mouths like stingrays. Fur parted and rippling subtly in the breeze. They lay on top of the blackish gunky snow and something soft. Evenly spaced. The soft thing they rested on, I thought it was a coat initially, but three blinks later and I saw the hooves and fluffy knub of tail. Horizontally stretched beneath them was a deer skin, head retained, peppered with bead-sized flies. Marker stains peeked from under the raccoons. Sigil work, I thought. Unthoughtful, lazy sigil work.

"Tatum Jenkins' car," I mumbled.

Jing looked at me.

Madeline, fixed to the spot, did not.

"To think I could've died because of some guy with a name like Tatum."

SEVEN

IMBALANCED HUMORS

I lay on the hood of Jing's car with my phone against my cheek. The pink bled into gooey purple above me. Jing and Madeline were arguing mostly through a series of complex unfathomable glances. Telepathy was contagious. I felt like absolute hell. I did not call an ambulance because I was ambiently petrified of how much it'd cost my fathers, and I was not dead anyway. I could deal with an ugly mug. Mug didn't have much going for it as it stood initially. The ringing stopped. I called again. I closed my eyes and shivered.

"Sideways?"

"Took you long enough." Voice still funny. Could've stood to be funnier, frankly.

"What's wrong?"

"You sound like a narc when you're nervous, Shiloh."

"Sideways," they repeated, this time a little lower. I sensed, despite my lack of accessible reference points, that this was older sibling voice.

"Tatum Jenkins trip-wire charm or whatever," I said.

They were quiet, must've shifted their mic around,

must've done something muffled and rustling. Sure did hate that sound! All sounds were bad. Everything was low-grade agony. "Where are you?"

"On top of Jing's car." Hadn't been what they meant. "Side of the road somewhere, I can send you my location. Shi," I started, wheels not turning so much as skittering wildly at the same rate as the language leaving my mouth, "I need you to take Boris' car and come by and pick us up."

Jing and Madeline looked up at me.

I had not discussed this with them, or with myself as a matter of fact.

I continued. "I need you to bring the Scratch Book. You've gotta take me and Jing to the Delacroix, and you've gotta take Madeline wherever she needs to go, 'kay?"

More silence. A more staticky one. For a moment I thought they'd say no. Then, with a concern that was slightly too weird and tender for my liking: "Are you okay?"

"Um." I squeezed my tongue tip into the tooth hole again, poked my lip up with it. Still bleeding but less flamboy-antly, I'd say. Sort of congealed and half-assed bleeding now. Grosser, thicker, grimier. I felt like a slug's gut. "Would say I am less than peachy."

"Are you by the trip line?"

I squinted one eye at the ditch that held the absolute nightmare pile of dead little dudes. Made me want to cry and also throw up and also laugh so hard I eviscerated myself. I wondered how long it'd take for those crows to go nosh on the raccoons. I wasn't sure if I wanted them to leave them be or wanted them to down them like Jell-O shots so that they weren't arranged like that anymore. "Affirmative."

"Are you hurt?"

"Hmm." A fly landed on the bridge of my nose. I just sort of let it happen. "Yeah."

They took a beat. "Do you want me to tell Boris and Julian?"

"Whoa, ma'am. Abso-fucking-lutely not." My tone did not match the ache in my face. I sounded, to my ear, congested but over-casual. Sort of a stoner's slowed tempo drawl. "Julian will have a straight-up panic attack, please don't. It's cool. Be cool. That's the theme of the day."

"Are Jing and Addie okay?"

They'd started arguing again. Then, spectacularly, Madeline jumped in the evil terrible roadkill ditch and crouched out of sight. Jing hissed something at her but nodded. My blood had started to dry in her hair. It crusted milky brown. Jing whispered again, and then Madeline straightened up with, much to my dismay, a raccoon in her hands. She held it upside down. Its tail fell over her wrist. She shook it once hard, like she was rooting for loose change, and I thought for a fleeting moment that I'd actually knocked something vital out of place in my brain and was experiencing the world's worst hallucinations. Madeline flipped the raccoon back over. I watched her steel herself, square those athlete shoulders of hers, and set her jaw before she pried open the raccoon's mouth with two fingers. Its stiff pink tongue peeked up between its teeth. She pushed a finger past it, fished around inside its mouth. Then she tossed the raccoon down, shook out her hand, and said just loudly enough for me to hear her, "It'll go faster if you help a little, princess."

Jing sneered something impressively mean. I missed half the words in it but the half I received were enough to curdle cream. Then, to my horror and admiration, Jing leaped down in the ditch beside Madeline and picked up a raccoon, which she held away from her at arm's length.

Madeline knelt to get another. This one was chunkier.

"Jing and Madeline," I said to Shiloh, "are not dead."

They made a thin sound, and then said curtly, "I'll be there soon."

"Cool." I swiped my thumb, and they were gone.

I turned my location on and wondered idly if whichever government agency or social media marketing robot was currently watching me thought I looked like absolute shit. I sent Shi my location and set my phone facedown on my stomach. It was cold and felt heavier than a phone should feel. I peered down my nose at my ex and my—and at Jing in the death trench and said, just loud enough to scatter the crows: "You're fingering the dead animals for what reason exactly?"

"Mimics." Madeline thrust a raccoon corpse away from herself, looked askance at her raccoon-contaminated hands. "Witchfinder homing device. If they planted one, it'll catch your girlfriend's magical signature here, and she'll be wandering down the side of the road at three in the morning right into some Vineyard Vines bastard's holy hands."

"Oh!" Me, bloody by the poolside, overlooking the Chantry kid jamboree. Shiloh pre-Shiloh. Shiloh's dead brother. All that glass in my knees. "I'm familiar."

"Like this?" Jing thwacked a set of hoary jaws against her palm and out popped a marble swirling with a rich, creamy lilac light. It looked wet in her hand, glistened slightly. It could've been the moon. Jing made a face. She looked at it like it was a house centipede in a cup.

"That'd be it." Madeline swayed close to her, put her brow near her brow, squinted at the evil marble. "Keep that with you."

"I don't want to be walking down the road at three a.m. into the hands of some Vineyards Vines bastard," Jing said tightly. She rubbed the mimic on her sleeve, then, thrillingly, tucked it in her bra for safekeeping. "If I smash it with a hammer, will I die?"

Madeline frowned. "I think you'll be fine, sweetheart. Just keep it close."

Sweetheart. Sweetheart. She was not allowed to say "sweetheart" like that to Jing.

Jing could've died and I could've died and Madeline could've died in a car outside of Sycamore Gorge corporation limits. None of us would've graduated. I crackled with blood, still. I felt soaked. My bones weren't red anymore. Sad white celery bones, all their proud red sluiced out of my jacked-up awful open face. I put my feet up, braced my boots against the telephone pole that'd sucker punched us earlier. I tried to think about Yates and Daisy and then decided I was fine with the delusion that Daisy could keep the both of them safe, at least for a while. I decided despite evidence to the contrary that none of the Delacroix House witches would bring harm upon them, and I decided that it was going to be alright, that tonight it would rain, that these loser puff clouds would move aside for a jacked purple thunderstorm. It could roll over this spot with strobe lights and distortion like a floating eldritch noise show and rattle the earth with endless meaty bullet-shell droplets that'd scour my gore muck off the pavement and seep it into the earth where it'd vanish, reassimilate with Eden or some oil spill or whatever, and help sprout new dandelions come morning. I kept my phone balanced on my stomach. I decided that next time I checked it there'd be an acceptance with a scholarship waiting behind the glass that I'd never have to worry about because I'd never grow up. I would be suspended in amber forever. Last night forever and ever. Dancing with my Scapegracers until the cosmos stop spinning. Madeline never called.

Madeline and Jing were talking. They had a hushed, hard tone. Weirdly wistful.

I thought they might've been talking about me but that could've just been wishful ideations. I was good at wishful ideations. I watched the clouds move in fast gnarly spirals, too soft to hold a shape, and watched the sky just behind get leached of the last bits of pink. It would be a sooty gray nighttime. Almost the color of Daisy's magic.

For sure I had a concussion.

Oh, for sure.

Clouds bent and Madeline barked the coldest laugh I'd ever heard, and I wondered what the joke had been. Me, maybe. That'd be reasonable. I gave the tip of my nose an experimental dab with the inside of one wrist, and new pain drenched me. I sputtered, turned my head to the side, and spat red over the car's red hood. Jing loved this car. She loved this car so much. What a tragedy that a Tatum had done this. What a tragedy that it'd happened at all. No good deed yadda yadda. My ears rang. I hoped the bruise on my brain was cool colors, at least. Heather yellow and swamp-monster green and lipstick-kiss deep red, something like that.

Why must bodies be sacks for pain?

Headlights flooded everything. I cringed so hard that I thought my facial features might crumple in on themselves. Light sucked. I hated light so much. Who gave light the right to be so acidic? I threw an arm across my face, elbow over my nose bridge, and strung together a thread of threats. Whoever was making headlights happen, I would stuff them in a barrel and push it down a hill. I'd drill holes in the bottom of all their cups. I'd ghost their girlfriend. I'd steal their dog. I'd break their nose. I'd break their nose worse than I'd broken mine on the dashboard. I'd make them swallow my tooth.

The light wasn't going away. It hadn't rolled down the road away from us.

Was I about to be abducted by aliens?

Could they at least be hot big-tiddy aliens?

"Jesus H."

That wasn't a hot big-tiddy alien voice. I moved my arm off my face despite every nerve fiber in my body screaming to the contrary and looked up, and across the way from me, halfway between my sorry ass and Madeline and Jing, was Shiloh Pike. They wore a crisp blouse, a creamy blazer, dark pleated slacks. They weren't looking at me. Their jaw, illuminated by the horrible headlights, was angled toward Madeline. I couldn't see their face. Nausea hit me. I hadn't thought this part through.

Madeline stood stock-still. I didn't think she was breathing.

Jing took a step back. She edged around them, came nearer to me, but her eyes didn't leave their shoulders and the tension strung between them. She approached the hood of her car. She stood before me, beside the pole. She put her hands on my ankles and squeezed them, still looking over her shoulder.

I looked over her shoulder as well.

Neither of them moved. No blinking, no intake of air. The wind died down, because the pathetic fallacy is real and happens with great fury I think. Then, Madeline broke it. She tore a hand back through her hair, scraped it against her skull, and said just loud enough for me to hear: "You're—"

"Shiloh, now." They rocked their head back, revealed the line of their throat. Hands turned out, palms empty, facing her. "Shiloh Pike."

Something shifted in Madeline's face. Her brows darted up. She looked stricken.

"It's good to see you," Shi said.

"You did it," she said.

"I did," they said.

"Pike, like Sideways?"

"They saved my life."

I squirmed on the hood and Jing squeezed my ankles again, anchored me.

"I hate you," she said. Then, more urgently, "I hate you and I was going to kill you."

"That's fair." They inclined their head. "Are you going to do it now?"

A vein in Madeline's jaw twinged. She swayed back; her face lost the light and shadows obscured her, I couldn't see the look on her face. Her hands stirred the air beside her thighs. Fingers twitching.

Shiloh put their hands in their pockets.

Madeline took a step forward, then several. She ran at them. Her strides were enormous, she cut through the space and suddenly had her hands in their blazer. She held them at arm's length. They were the same height, their chins parallel. She curled her lip and snarled something prelinguistic and anguished, she shook her head, then pulled them toward her. She pressed her face into their shoulder. Their shoulders heaved, and I thought she'd either coughed or sobbed once, hard.

Shiloh leaned into it. They leaned their cheek against her temple, bowled their shoulders in, but kept their hands to themself. They murmured something that was none of my business. Retroactive concern flickered through me, nerves about whether Shiloh and Madeline should be around each other, if they would feel comfortable with her knowing them as they are now, if she'd already known, if she'd kill them on the spot, if the world would end, et cetera, but these things melted off my brain fast. I averted my gaze. I felt like a voyeur. I looked up at Jing instead.

She'd been looking at me.

I tried to smile.

She made a face that I thought probably meant, *Holy shit you look rough.* Or maybe she was worried? I nudged one toe against her belly, gave her a little push, smiled with more intention. Poked my tongue through the hole and waggled it at her.

She smiled for half a second before she wrinkled her nose.

I felt a little warmer. A little proud.

"Sideways," Shiloh said.

I pulled my eyes off Jing somehow and looked up at them. They looked down at me with a cool look, solemn and measured, concerned in a way that read bizarrely professorial if not parental. They reached into their enormous breast pocket. They withdrew a marbled, warbled book.

Mr. Scratch, sweet Mr. Scratch.

They handed the book to Jing.

"Do you need an ambulance?" As soon as Jing had pulled the Scratch Book from their hand, they reached down and brushed their fingertips against the line of my lapel. Nails tripping on the zipper teeth. "You look a mess."

"You look a mess," I repeated in a whiny immature squeaky version of their voice.

They flicked their eyes up at the sky, steeled themself, and looked back down at me. "Do you need help getting into the car?"

"I can help them," Jing said before I could say something ridiculous.

Shiloh gave her a curt nod. They turned on their heel, paused to tuck their hair behind their ear, and clipped back to their car. Or, I guess, Boris' car. A glance in that direction revealed Madeline already in the passenger's seat, looking openly distraught in a way that I wasn't ready to accept. I wasn't going to throw her over the armrests again. I was not sure I could do that without making my brain into bangers and mash, anyway.

I sat up.

My vision bobbed up after me.

Jing released my ankles and moved to hook an arm around my middle. She helped pull me off the hood, oriented me toward the car, guided me as I lumbered in the direction of Boris' backseat. Boris would be chill with this, I determined. It was vaguely possible that Shiloh had asked him rather than temporarily stealing his car outright, because Shiloh's hero worship of my dad made them ceaselessly deferent, plus they were sooooo polite. Jing opened the door for me, watched as I stuffed myself inside. I'd been sicker and more delirious in this car before. This was fine. Everything was totally fine.

Jing sat beside me.

I slumped over and put my head in her lap.

"We fucked up the Vineyard Vines dead animal spell," Jing said. She held the Scratch Book in one hand, which I liked because being near it brought me a profound and unshakable calm, and rested the other on my neck just below my ear, which, whoa man. Shit. Holy fuck. "Am I safe to cast?"

"I wouldn't yet." Shiloh turned the car around. The machine-over-pavement vibrations were not my favorite. "It should be alright, but I wouldn't test it, not here. Give it a song or two."

Madeline rested her temple on the window.

I looked up at Jing. I tried to put a thought in my mouth that was Yates and Daisy shaped. I'd put my phone in my pocket at some point, which I knew because it was jabbing me, but I didn't have it in me to check it. I had no idea what I should say. I reached up one dirty finger and twined it around a dirty lock of her hair, just the tip, the place that'd sopped up some of me. "I made you gross."

"I was already gross," she said. She rubbed her thumb at the hinge of my jaw in little circles. That shut me up. She opened the Scratch Book, and I could just see loving tendrils of ink flutter around across the page and greet her. It welled around her fingertips, the places she held it open. She paused. "Does anybody have a pen?"

Madeline shook her head or jerked her chin at least.

"There's probably a pen or five in the floorboards," I mumbled against the fabric on her thigh. I wasn't sure if she heard me. Also possible: she did hear me but wasn't sure how she was going to find one of those pens while I was lying on her like this. I mean, she could lean over me? There would be worse things.

After a moment's deliberation, Jing brought the book near her face. She scraped a smeared mascara bead off her cheek, one I'd missed. The ink bled into the paper pulp and started swirling, and she rested the book on her knees in front of me, murmured something quick and repetitive as the car turned a corner, pulled her saline-makeup-Scratch solution into long shapes across the page. Her face flushed, glittered around the edges with magic-casting radio static. She inhaled through her teeth. She looked at me. "Roll onto your back."

Hmm. I rolled onto my back. Knees toward the ceiling, toes against the door, my nape up against the fullest part of her thigh. When she breathed, her belly brushed against my ear and made me feel homesick. I tried for a smile again.

She put the open book on my face.

Ink sloshed from the book's living core through her sigil into my skin. Globs of it, acrid and chilly, slippery like slugs or still-living oysters, squiggling and worming through my pores, through my ruined sinuses, my crunched bone, my eye jelly, the licorice ropes of my optic nerves into my big bad sea-sponge brain. The blood taste metal became ink taste. Tart carbon sharpness in the lining of my throat, in the lymph nodes under my jaw, under my tongue, between my cheeks and remaining teeth. The ink swirled around. Car wash inside my face. I gasped, but I could breathe. Lungs riled then chilled. Blood flowed, so did god-smack cherry-red spectral vitality. Some dented part of me undented. Vast swaths of caked gore flecked off and were consumed by the book. The pulp felt smoother against my cheeks, well-nourished. Reality focused.

I wanted to cry.

"Thank you," I mumbled.

Where is your tooth! You had a tooth! Sideways, there should be a tooth here! Please do not break your face. I love you, my sweetest darling. I would rather your face not be inside out. You made Jing cry, also. That is distressing. This is not ideal. Where is your tooth!

The words washed over me like they had when Mr. Scratch was inside me, but I felt each letter traced across my forehead as the words flew in some odd acrobatic attempt to maintain his textuality. He wriggled around impatiently. He spelled "tooth" a few more times.

I pawed around my sides, reached into my pocket, and realized with a flip of nausea that the pocket I'd put my phone in was the tooth pocket. My phone felt very wet. It was a blood phone now. I avoided touching the blood phone and withdrew the no-good gravel shard, held it in my hand, slightly unsure what to do with it. Should I pop it in my mouth like a mint?

Yes, popping your tooth into your mouth will make it easier for me to glue it down.

"Glue" was an interesting verb.

It's for sticking. I am being very contemporary. I am a fresh handsome book. This is me being stylish. I use verbs like "to glue" now when I am doing medicine.

I snaked my hand under the book tent and put my tooth in my mouth.

Wow, it was remarkable how much I hated putting a knocked-out tooth back inside my mouth. It was definitely in the top ten worst things I'd ever put in my mouth, I thought. More than one of those things had been at Mr. Scratch's behest. Numbly, I thought, *Are you going to eat my tooth?*

No, you use your tooth for eating. It looks delicious but it is not for me. If you find extra teeth, it'd be my pleasure to eat them, but I wouldn't eat any part of you that you need, know this well. Tempt me not with this one. Could you please put this tooth where it is supposed to go? Root side to the meat if you please?

It took some tongue finagling and a perilous fear that I'd fuck up and swallow it. Still, I held the tooth against its gum, which hurt but not how I'd braced for it to hurt. More an annoying flashy ache than proper pain. I waited.

He globbed down through my gums and lassoed the errant bone. He lugged it upwards, nestled it in the pink to which it belonged, gushed around with an intense, eyeball-dissolving thickness that made me paranoid about asphyxiation. I blinked and the swelling went down. I gave the tooth an experimental shove with my tongue tip. It wiggled a little but was definitely attached. Also, it was even farther apart from its twin than it had been before. Miles apart. He'd doubled my gap. You could hang a hammock in my teeth now.

You're at the Delacroix. What a horrible place. I truly hate this place. You should go upstairs and knock over all the other urns. They would hate that. They could not hate it as much as I hate them. Your brain has unbruised and your nose is less broken, salty sweet Sideways. Jing's spell worked well. Be grateful for it and her. I am beat. I am going to be book-shaped. Thank you for the delicious blood. Be quick.

I pulled him off my face and closed him, rested him on my chest. Mr. Scratch hadn't sucked the blood from Jing's hair and the horror of it hit me full-on now, rattled something in me, made my throat feel mushed and sour. The car kept running, and a quick glance out the window told me that Shiloh hadn't pulled into the parking lot and was stalling just beyond instead. Madeline tapped one foot. Shi's music lulled softly, soothing bedroom pop I'd never have liked if it wasn't for them. They played this song a lot. I knew the words. I glanced up at Jing again. I cleared my throat. Residual gore muck slimed the roof of my mouth.

Jing broke into a grin. She didn't hold it long, but the second she'd struck it lit up in my head. Jesus, she had a disarming smile. It made being filthy and busted in the back of my father's car feel like something on an ancient wall in gilt and egg tempera. Jing was beautiful. She looked less nervous, looked like something stiff and prickly left her, even if it came back next inhale. She drew her brows together and said without a lick of irony: "God, I love magic."

I bit down before I could riff off that.

"If you're going to go, get going," Madeline said.

Stupidest move in the world, I brought my body upright. Sitting didn't make my guts flip. Lights had lowered outside, the sun was all but gone, and neons blazed in the Delacroix House's far windows. Looking at the colors didn't hurt. Jing opened her door and stepped out of the car, and closing it behind her didn't icepick my ears. I breathed a moment, tried to push chemicals back through my body. I leaned forward, pressed my head to the back of Shiloh's headrest. I bit my lip. Mr. Scratch hadn't fixed it, or maybe it was psychosomatic, but it still felt swollen from where Madeline had bitten me. I squeezed my eyes shut, tucked the Scratch Book against my belly under my shirt, and said aloud: "Are you gonna be alright?"

Shiloh paused. They tilted their head to the side, cheek against the leather, and made a thin sound in their throat. "I'm not the one I'm worried about."

"We can hold our own, you know," I said.

"Don't underestimate the obstinacy of these people," Madeline said.

I glanced at her.

She jerked her chin in the air, closed her hands around her upper arms, caught between looking tough and looking scared. She was staring at the Delacroix House. She didn't look grief-stricken. Something left of that—resentful? No. She swept her tongue over the curtain of her gums and made a single, punctuated *ha*. "Covens are held together with trauma bonds and ritual theatrics, Sideways. They're not going to make the *right* move, they're going to make the move that works best with whatever story they're telling to make themselves feel better. If I'm not a villain, that means nuance might exist, heaven forbid. They'll pick what's dramatic and vindicating and can be performed with great spectacle. Optics over justice, routine over change. Just the cheapest contrivance of catharsis. God, to think I needed them." She smiled a little. Nothing on her face changed. "That house is crammed with desperately wounded people who only feel important when they've convinced themselves that it's poetic, whatever's happening to them. The Sisters Corbie thought it was poetic when they saved me and they love playing vengeance, but it's playacting, it's all playacting. I don't believe any of them. Neither should you. If you and the Scapegracers are genuinely interested in magic for helping people, you don't belong here. I'd take your girls and go, if I were you. Get far the fuck away from this mess."

I considered for a moment. Less her words and more the cosmos at large and how it currently felt sweaty and crawly all around me. I tucked my shirt in. I squeezed my belt until the leather made my palms itch. I pulled back, sat upright. "When you were me, you did do a lot of running away, yeah." I huffed. "Text me if the world ends, Shi, okay?"

They inclined their head.

I climbed out of the car and chased after Jing, who'd made it halfway across the parking lot. I heard the car pull out, heard their near–golden ratio U-turn and the purr as they vanished down the road, and then everything got quiet. No birds, no reedy tree sounds, the bugs were dead still, traffic was gone. My body made sound and that was all. I stomped on purpose just for something percussive. I picked up my pace.

Even bloody, Jing's head glowed in the dark. Ignis fatuus, a will-o'-the-wisp. North star in *wretched* and *girl*. I'd follow her anywhere I think.

Christ. Fuck.

The poetry in my head was getting worse and worse. This was getting out of hand and I needed to cut it out. I needed to get it together and focus on what mattered, which was getting to Yates and Daisy, who both existed but god knows in what condition. I steeled myself. I caught up with her.

She had her face back on, the unflinching brutal homecoming court one. Chin up, shoulders back, knives in her eyes and so on. She didn't look at me when she shot her hand out. She caught me around my wrist, then tripped her nails down my palm, interlaced her fingers with mine.

Holding hands didn't mean anything, I reminded myself. It was critical to remember that we held hands all the time. Magic loves making gay little bitches hold hands. We were gay little magic bitches and so much of our time now was just sitting in a circle, clasped like this, doing our spells and being best friends who are strictly platonic for sure. Holding hands let power flow. Bodies touching meant they could be one body for the purpose of channeling entropic wildness. Links on a chain. We had to touch. How were we supposed to survive whatever might come next if my hand wasn't on her, if hers wasn't on me?

My toe banged the flat vertical face of the first step up onto the walkway.

Pain went off in cartoon sparkles behind my eyes.

"Watch your step, dummy," she said.

"Bite me," I mumbled. You'd think that after breaking my face open that stubbing my toe would hurt less by contrast, but no, it hurt an unreasonable amount and I wanted to be a major baby about it and everything. I stuck my chest out, grit my molars. I let her pull me up the rest of the steps.

"It's a good sign that they haven't texted you," Jing said as we neared the front door. There was a slice of hot light underneath, and the low notes of some jazzy pop standard circa nineteen-whatever. It was the song that Madeline had covered here. Funny in a sick, unfunny way. Jing shifted her weight. Her brows came together. "Yates likes giving thorough reports. If you haven't gotten one, there's nothing to say. We might be in and out of here soon."

I wondered if I should ask about how we'd be getting out of here now that her car, our ride, was a spitball on the side of a woody country barely-road without streetlamps or hope of fast retrieval. My brain clicked on the more important thing after that.

I didn't know if Yates hadn't texted me.

I hadn't checked my phone since I called Shi, and that'd been a while ago.

I took my phone—still wet, why must it still be wet—from my pocket, held it near my opposing hip, the one that wasn't near Jing's hand in mine. There sure were notifications waiting on my lock screen. I inconspicuously unlocked it, tried to convince Jing and myself and the universe that I was just checking some terrible app or whatever.

Yates had tried to call me seven times.

As Jing reached for the door, she called me an eighth.

EIGHT

GLUTTON FOR PUNISHMENT

The foyer was witchless. It felt chill in that grandiose, solemn vaudeville way it usually felt during business hours. The earlier calamitous mingling had made the building seem bigger, the walls less like a hard structure and more like a bunch of curtains. It was a fancy restaurant with an art gallery again. A goddamned bistro.

Jing whipped her head around and meanwhile into my phone I said, "Hey."

"Jesus be thanked, I thought you wouldn't answer." Yates spoke high in her register, sounded more sibilant than she usually did. Was she whispering? I shivered. The Scratch Book soaked cold sweat off my skin. "Where are you? Are you okay?"

"We're here, we're in the house. Foyer, like the please-wait-to-be-seated-type area." I bounced on my toes. "And you? Where are you and Daze?"

"Dinner," she hissed.

There was so much blood in Jing's hair. "Beg pardon?"

"Dinner, we're at the big witch dinner, and Sideways I

am so stressed that I might actually have a stroke. I need you to come here right now. Right this moment, alright? Main dining room, like the space with the stage where Madeline used to perform. Please come quick. They keep asking for you."

Whatever I'd been bracing for her to say, this had not been it. Zero time for relief that Yates wasn't in some literal damsel trap. I got the sense that *I* was about to be the damsel. Fuck was I not a fan of that. I cleared my throat and jerked down my chin, and when it occurred to me that this was a phone call and she couldn't see my affirmation I said, "I'll be there soon."

"Good," she said, then hung up on me.

I put my phone down.

Jing looked at me. Her brows steepled. I fought off the memory of what it'd looked like when she'd been crying.

"They're having dinner. The flocking is having a formal dinner in the actual restaurant portion of the house," I pieced out, processing each syllable only as it left my mouth. "Yates is stressed about it." Left off the part where they were asking for me because I didn't want to process those specific syllables. Those ones sucked. "So, she's not dead is what I'm saying."

"And Daisy?"

"She didn't mention Daisy. Just assumed she was alive."

"Never assume." Jing rolled her eyes but froze mid-eye-roll. She brought her gaze down my chest and back up. I squirmed a little. I couldn't place if she looked repulsed or fond. She said, "We are filthy with blood."

"I thought Mr. Scratch ate it off my face," I said.

Jing curled her lip. "What the fuck, that's disgusting. Not what I asked him to do to your face. Anyway, no, not all of it. You still look like *Texas Chainsaw Massacre*. Not Leatherface. The hot boomer Final Girl in the jumpsuit."

"Oh." I frowned. "She *was* hot, yeah."

"We can't walk into a formal dinner with tensions so high looking like piglets escaped from a butcher shop, Sideways." She swayed her weight from foot to foot, like a boxer. Her forehead creased. She was squeezing my hand to powder, though I doubted it was on purpose.

Still, I squeezed it back. "Hey," I said. "It would be pretty metal to just waltz in and maintain the plan. Nobody's cooler than nonchalantly blood-splattered queers, I'd say."

Her mouth twitched.

Progress. I shook my head, tried to manually toggle new thoughts. Something must've clinked in the right way. Little pinball lights went off. "Restroom first, we wash up before we walk in. Really fast, five minutes tops."

Jing nodded. It eased a little tension out of her face, like clearing an Etch A Sketch. Bottom lip softer.

I pulled her in the restroom's direction, and after a few strides she'd caught herself and was leading me again. I smiled to myself. Maybe I'd be good at this, at being stupid and sturdy enough for her to remain composed. Jing was so elegant. She had such terrifying, wonderful poise, and I could safeguard it by annoying her enough that she forgot that she was scared. That seemed like a good secondary life's purpose besides my coven's work and all.

She pulled me through an open doorway and the lighting changed. The glitzy art-deco fish-scale wallpaper gave way to broad swaths of glass. Floor-to-ceiling mirrors, like a ballet studio might have. The mirrors looked greenish where the edges joined. Glossy black floor, glossy black ceiling. There were stalls that I assumed were empty, except for a far set, which was occupied by at least two people. I heard their shifting and their breathing, low harsh laughter, high airy sighs. None of my business.

We leaned over one of the seashell sinks.

Jing had been, as always, correct. My darling spell book had not eaten all my blood. I looked like a dry riverbed. Head wounds are so extravagant, and for what? I loomed nearer to the mirror, tried to ignore the fact that it was angled ever so slightly, and that it revealed the mirror wall behind us and created infinite parallel mirror universes with endless Jings and Sidewayses, bloody and disgusting, grimacing at themselves. Her little dark pink jumpsuit caked with gore forever. I sniffed. "It was bad, earlier. The crash, I mean."

"It was bad," she confirmed. "Over now."

"Fuck witchfinders." I reached for a knob beside the faucet, unsure of how else to proceed. "I don't want to ever make you feel like that again."

Jing watched me while I wet my fingers. The dry blood loosened, flowed off me like watercolors. Made a showy spiral as it curled its way down the sink. I washed my hands, kneaded suds into the lines of me, under my skinny sliver of nails, the backs of my knuckles, the seam of my sleeve. I splashed water on my face, then. Bowed my head over the porcelain and scrubbed my nose with the heels of my hands, scraped the grime off my chin and my neck. It came off in big ribbony flakes like rust. It was satisfying in a way I didn't care to unpack. I splashed my scalp, chased my hands down the nape of my neck, then I pulled my head up a touch, locked eyes with the nearest externalized me. That bastard looked back without blinking. Still off somehow, but less overtly, appallingly bad. My nose had a fun little dent that hadn't been there before. My bottom lip looked overfull. My teeth were insane.

I straightened up, tore loose a paper towel—thick, creamy paper, handled more like fabric than wood pulp—and dragged it down my mug. It came loose with a bit of color. Better than nothing. I crumpled it, tossed it in the bin's direction, and glanced at Jing.

Still looking at me. I don't think she'd stopped that entire time.

"Enjoying the show?"

Something dangerous flickered in her look. Warning. What gives?

I rocked back on my heels, put my hands behind my head. I jerked my chin down. A gob of water I'd missed fell from my cheek to my collar. "You okay in there?"

"Yeah," she said. Her tone felt weird on my ear, distant. Her mouth drew taut, then her neck, then the line of her shoulders. She pulled her eyes off me, then, looked at the mirrored wall instead. She made a face. One finger drifted up, tapped the place above her reflection's blood-dipped hair. "I thought you died."

"So much for that," I said, trying to sound stupid. I gave her a big goofy grin, with bad teeth and everything. Waggled my brows. Did my best impression of every cartoon villain at once.

She glanced at me, or my reflection rather, for a split second before flickering back to her hair and her collarbone. The light hit the glitter under her eyes funny. I don't think my antics registered. Her pallor was freaking me out. "I crashed my car into a telephone pole, and you broke your head open on my dashboard and went still for a solid three minutes. It was three minutes. You didn't move," she said, overenunciating every syllable, "for three fucking minutes." She sounded furious. Anybody who speaks so slowly must be furious. The fury didn't radiate toward me. It stuck around her, clung to her. She parted her lips. Trying to make herself breathe, I think. "It was a long time."

I blinked. It had not felt like three minutes. My brain stem emitted a low-frequency screeching sound and tried to process what that might've meant, and what her energy meant now, and whether she'd spared me permanent damage with whatever sigil she'd drawn in the backseat. I thought too much. My brain was spent. My spine, wiser, sent my hands out, had me pull another paper towel from its silver hook and fold it long ways.

Jing spoke a little louder. "I'd been speeding. We were going eighty-five."

I nodded. No more thinking, just an acknowledgment that I'd heard her. I twisted the knob again, tested my thumb under the water. The stream broke into glitter around the edge of my nail. I waited like that, waiting for her to speak, for the water to feel warm.

"I thought I killed you, Sideways."

"Hmm." I wet the paper and shut the water off. I turned away from the mirror and looked at her, the flesh her, corporeal and real across from me. She was shaking. My brows screwed up in a knot. "You didn't kill me. I'm right here."

Jing's jaw clenched. She flushed, I didn't think I'd ever seen her flush before. Blotchy red spots bloomed under her eyes. Her mouth got tighter. I realized, with considerable awe, that she might cry again. I did not possess the faculties to handle shit if she cried again. That'd be the end of me. We'd be goners.

"Hey." I took a step toward her, caught the tip of my forefinger under her chin. I tilted her head up, brought her focus back up on me. Real live obnoxious me, not imaginary dead me. God, her eyes could've filled the room. Jing's eyes were barely reflective usually, almost matte. Pupil and iris nearly indistinguishable. They devoured all surrounding light. Teary as she was now, I could see myself in them, and I didn't care for it. When I look at her, she's all I want to see. I inclined my head, brought my nose nearer hers, spoke a little lower in my throat. Thought that might be softer. I wanted to be softer for her. "I'm right here, alright? If you kill me, it'll be with your hands behind the drugstore like god intended. I'm okay. It's okay. Now, are you gonna let me wash the blood out of your hair, or not?"

She bit her lip. Trying to keep it still, I think.

"That a yes?"

"Yes," she whispered, just an edge to her exhale.

"Good girl," I said. I dropped her chin and lifted a lock of hair off her jaw, folded the paper around it. Rubbed my thumb into the hook of my forefinger. I tugged downward, and the hair looked—well, still off-color, but more blood-tinged than clumped with the stuff. I moved to another section. All the thoughts fell out of my head. Just a matter of being gentle for once in my life. This wasn't so bad. I could be good at this.

The girl in the far stall gasped, "Mercy, mercy."

Jing snorted and her mouth went lopsided.

You know what? Chaos be praised. I was glad I was sharing this moment with randy anonymous witches. It felt like a club's bathroom, and god knows I've spent a lot of quality time in those. I leaned back, looked her over. Her jumpsuit was bloody in a way that I didn't think paper towels could fix. My clothes probably also were, but I had goth powers and it didn't show on my solid wall of black fabric like it did on her magenta. Blood pooled on the denim's face like nail polish. She wasn't wearing her Scapegracers jacket. Neither was I, I realized only now. I hadn't remembered her taking hers off. Mine must've just slipped off my hips. Maybe they were in her car? I stared for a moment. "Do you want my leather?"

She looked down at herself, then up at me. "Yeah, I want your leather."

I shrugged it off and draped it over her shoulders.

Something kicked in my gut.

"You'd be a good punk, Jing."

"I'm good at everything," she said stiffly. She shook her head, and there it was again, her steely femme composure. She slipped her arms into the sleeves. The leather reached her knuckles. I had a feeling or five about that. Leather made her jumpsuit read different, made the glitter smeared under her eyes look purposefully fucked up. She looked like a pop star. She bounced on her heels once, eyed me. Specifically, she eyed my arms. I'd excised the sleeves from this T-shirt at some point because muscle tees are gayer, I don't know don't ask me, but now I felt naked. Her eyes fixed on a place below a string of moles, the spot below my bicep where I'd gotten bored about a month back and given myself a stick-and-poke sigil. It was for grace. Thank you, Scratch. She clicked her tongue, finally looked me in the face again. "Let's go rescue Yatesy and Daze, alright?"

I smiled a little. Out of the corner of my eye, my exponential reflection's tooth gap looked cartoonish. It was the Mariana Trench. Chasm between Scylla and Charybdis–type tooth gap. Daisy *fucking* Brink! Right, Daisy Brink. "Yeah. Sounds like a plan."

She strode out into the serpentine hall that'd spill us back into the main foyer, and I kept close at her heels, hands shoved in my back pockets, gooseflesh down my arms. A reel of people strolled past us; a gorgeous fat girl in a clingy velvet dress, skulking trad goths with wide splashes of black hair, a man with more piercing than lip who caught my eye as I brushed past him. His bejeweled mouth twisted.

"Godspeed, Sideways," he said.

I opened my mouth to say something, but then he was gone.

Foyer. Just Jing and me.

She was already nearly at the doorway. She'd waited for me, but I got the sense that she was pretending that wasn't the case. I shook myself off. Seeing her felt grounding enough. This would be fine. We'd find our girls and we'd either put out fires or we'd ditch. And we'd be so cool! Go Scapegracers.

I came near her side, and we walked into the dining room together.

I'd never seen it so packed. The room's dimensions seemed different than they usually did, hollowed out, distended. Odd alcoves had been carved into the walls, honeycomb style. The art flowed from the far anti-geometric corners, crawled onto the ceilings, all the rich red and cream faggy masterpieces this house accumulated feeling more like a living collective slime mold than a series of individuated frame-bound canvases. Candles burned everywhere. Streaming femur church candles, sometimes as many as six on each table, and clustered on columns, smoking from crystal chandeliers. Translucent silk curtains divided some of the tables. They moved like spindrift, compelled by some unseen breeze. Maybe breath?

Certainly there were enough bodies in this room to make a tide of it. If this were a jar of gumballs and there was a cash prize for stupid guessing, I'd put it at maybe a hundred-some witches, a hundred fifty max. Less than this afternoon in statistical terms, but their presences had come out after dark, and the density made them all feel enormous and impossibly multifarious. High tide for vibes. I didn't understand how the floor could withstand the weight of them. I didn't know how we hadn't broken the mantle and crashed into the earth's pith. The witches were a marvel of texture and light. Colors glanced off them, whirled and refracted with phantasmic prism brightness. I wasn't sure if I super believed in auras, but every person in this room had their own gravitational sphere, that much was undeniable. Their outlines hung in the air when they moved. Olibanum must be burning somewhere. It melted through the feasting smells, the game and golden fat, smoked pepper, rosemary, dark wine, and bright harsh greens. Knives tripped on porcelain, long nails skittered down glass stems, wingback armchairs wheezed. Whispering, low laughter. Inexplicable undulating light wandered around the middle of the room.

On the stage a girl sang. I didn't recognize her. She looked softer, icier than Madeline. Platinum hair to her hipbones, crimson backless dress. Sugary soprano. All breath. She sang something winding and repetitive about love and its absence, and behind her Jacques' fingers fluttered over his saxophone's neck. He played with his eyes closed, his brows drawn. The pianist I didn't recognize looked like he might cry. I knew the song, I think some pop indie artist Yates liked had covered it at some point, and the almost-familiarity made my head spin. All of me was spinning. I braced my hand against my stomach, pressed the Scratch Book close to me. It felt like a breastplate. Why did I need a breastplate?

I was in a place I belonged, and boy, I was so underdressed.

"I saw Daisy just now," Jing hissed in my ear.

I jolted, snapped my head around. Witches sprawling everywhere, cackling over their carved-up dinners, kissing, crying. I drank in everything. Surely Daze and Yates wouldn't be hard to spot. God, there were so many women. A woman with twin braids so long she'd rested them on the table like a briefcase popped olives into her mouth. A woman reclined on another woman, the two of them mouthing the love song lyrics with startling synchronicity, their lipstick preternaturally red. A woman putting out her clove on another woman's tongue, the screaming orange cinders shivering, sifting, coalescing into a spare, angular glyph across the muscle's face. A woman reading a romance novel. A woman twirling her butterfly knife over her knuckles to impress a woman that rested her chin on her hands. My gaze pinballed. I felt woozy. My knees, fathoms below me, had an interesting new unsteadiness. My bone marrow was suddenly marshmallow fluff. I hoped that I was handsome. I hoped that somebody, literally anybody, loved me. I loved everybody. I felt so high.

I blinked and turned to tell Jing something obvious, but she was not beside me anymore. I whipped my head around, hunting for her flash of bleach brightness, but I kept finding different people, all strangers, never my girl. I looked between witches in profile. I took a few steps forward, wove between tables, swiveled my head back and forth. I couldn't see her. I couldn't see any of my Scapegracers. The music abraded my arms. I felt a knock of déjà vu, not for any time I'd been in the Delacroix House before, I think, but for some carnival I'd visited with my mother as a child. This felt like a big top. I rasped my nails up and down my opposing forearms. A table I passed sang along with great passion, and I found myself mouthing the words as well, grinning stupidly, ambiently terrified of everything and nothing at once. I caught a glimpse of a wall that seemed new, and it was too molded to be rectangular. One corner wrenched up like a glob of paint slashed through with a hairpin. Some sunken part of my brain provided *Lambert quadrilateral.* The recollection did not help. I had no idea what the fuck those words in that order meant. My head was melting down my neck and over my shoulders like the candles all around me, it was coughing up empty signs that signified nothing, just confetti and light. I was wading through a veritable wheat field of candles and my head genuinely was going to not exist anymore. I was ooze. The love song ended. Everybody clapped.

"Pike?"

I stopped and turned my head.

It was the adult lesbian, the Anti-Edonist Union witch who'd helped set up earlier. The one who'd broken up the fight between Dominick and Andy and recognized me as another butch, as being like her. Blair. She'd donned a navy sport coat with its collar flipped up and hung a silver cross around her neck. She looked grim, but not unkind. She inclined her head, brought her cheek near my cheek, and spoke barely loud enough to be heard over the next song's dawning. "Are you alright?"

"I'm looking for my friend," I said.

"I see." She paused, shifted her weight. "I saw a girl with the Star Thieves. Petite, pigtails, silver satin jacket. One of yours?"

My throat clapped. I nodded, struggled to speak for a moment. "Daisy, yeah. That sounds like my friend Daisy."

"I could take you over there if you'd like," she said. Another pause. "Lot of people have been talking about you, Pike. Do you know why?"

I squeezed my eyes shut. I shook my head.

"You're a Pythoness legacy who's not a proper Pythoness pledge. It's going around that you snuck upstairs and broke a vase to make your own book from dead ink. You sanctified your own coven. Madeline Kline took your specter from you, and you lived for a month without your specter, and you robbed a witchfinder family of their hoard in that time. Your coven has made itself known to your local community. Everyone here knows you by name. You've made a public practice of your hexwork. And now, you've freed the girl who stole from you before she could receive punishment for the crime she did unto you."

Hmm. I swayed a little, rubbed the corner of my mouth with the back of my wrist.

"Is any of that untrue?"

"It's not how I'd put it," I said.

Blair's brow creased. Her tone softened. "You're awfully popular."

Oh?

Awfully popular?

Wow, *popular*. Glinda and Elphaba shit. Wild. Those two should've been girlfriends, huh? Head still melting, now at record-breaking pace. Being popular wasn't being loved and it shouldn't matter anymore but holy hell was that still something that made my heart feel drunk. My Scapegracer fantasies always folded me into the sequined crust of femme-y popularity, and in those fantasies I either had no body and floated beside them in the abstract, or I was in a make-believe body that moved through space differently than mine ever would or could. I was a Popular Girl. Their friendship, invaluable, had not changed how incompatible I am with either of those things. But this? This was novel and I was strung out enough for it to feel *good*. Witch popular, dyke popular. Eyes on me. Like, finally, I was being beheld by people who knew what they were looking at. My name was in people's mouths. I had a reputation and it shrouded me, floated in front of me before I walked into a room. Only for a second did I think about clubbing last night and that girl who'd asked me to dance with her. She had asked me because I was a Scapegracer and because I was masculine. Was that not popularity? Didn't I already have this? Prudent lines of inquiry that I abandoned as soon as they arose.

I Whack-A-Mole'd them. I only wanted to bask. Maybe I was still concussed.

She caught my line of sight when she shifted. That brought me back down, just enough to listen. She had beautiful crow's-feet. I liked the way they draped. Focused on that to avoid eye contact. I had the unexplainable feeling that if I looked at her dead-on, I would burst into tears. "I want you to be very careful, sweetheart."

I put my tongue in my tooth gap. "We're plenty careful. Blair, can I ask you something?"

She crossed her arms and inclined her head.

"Are there going to be consequences for smuggling Madeline out of here?"

"You know what? That depends." She took a glance around, said, "Miss Yates and Miss Brink did an awful good job convincing Maurice not to disinherit you from the flock. Put it out of your mind, for now. When consequences come, they'll name themselves. Now. You girls were present when Madeline killed that witchfinder boy, weren't you?"

Was that where this was headed? There was something slimy in my windpipe. It was getting tough to breathe. "Yes, ma'am." Present, and participant. I remembered Shiloh's voice pitching in my phone, remembered *Remember how y'all killed my baby brother?* and felt a reactionary kick, like, it wasn't our fault. We were trying to save everybody. Maybe, if we hadn't lifted up the house, the firefighters would've plucked him from the rubble still kicking, but we didn't have a better option at the time. I never let myself think too hard about it. I'd tried to bring it up with Shi, but they never wanted to talk about it. They told me once, one of those nights where they camped out in my room, that it didn't stop them loving me. That we did what had to be done. Was that true?

Blair sucked in hard. "It's going to be dangerous for you girls. The Brethren will assume your responsibility."

"Figured," I said vaguely.

"Do you want to join the Pythoness Society?"

"No," I said. No question. My hands felt numb.

"That seemed the case. That in mind," Blair said, "folks are discussing where else you might land. They're discussing whether the whole of the Scapegracers should join a single coven, or if different girls should split off based on their own strengths and virtues. Lila Yates would make a fine Pythoness in your stead, Lupe's taken a shine to her. Jing Gao would make for a brilliant Dagger Heart or a Crimsonist. Daisy Brink could go with the Star Thieves, like her mother before her. People bicker over you. Placing bets. Most money's on Madeline Kline's vacant seat among the Sisters Corbie. Of course, you'd be welcome among the Anti-Edonists, if you'd like. It'd mean a life of blessing strike funds and cursing cops, but that doesn't seem too far from your wheelhouse."

The numb in my hands shot up the rest of my body. I couldn't feel my lips or my toes.

"Sideways," Blair said.

"I'm not leaving my coven. I've got a coven."

She folded her hands. "I admire that, but you've got to think carefully about this."

"I have to find my friends," I said, and I peeled away from her side, marched in a random direction deeper into the thick of the dining room. The love song got louder and louder. It pounded on me. The room warped, distorted. I squeezed my eyes shut, opened them wide. I rubbed my wrist at the edges of my eyes, tried to mash the tears down. I wasn't sad. I was in a post-emotional state of livid raw exhaustion. I felt more animal than normal. Everything smelled delicious, which was somehow so hilarious. I hadn't eaten in hours. I was so hungry. I felt faint all at once. I wondered how much blood I'd lost earlier. I wanted to go home.

"This song is for the Scapegracers," the soprano breathed over the mic.

I stopped dead.

The lights felt darker, pinker.

I wrapped my arms around my stomach and threw my head back, gaped up at the ceiling. I couldn't make out any details on the canvases above me. The paint looked wet. If it dripped on my face and shoulders I don't think that'd faze me. The girl started singing and it broke my heart. I didn't know her. What gave her the right? I staggered forward and felt aware all at once that I was *popular*, that people all around me were excited to see me, watched me with great interest. People showed me their teeth, yellow stained white tinging blue, and waved their fingers at me with great admiration or maybe malice. They mouthed things at me that I couldn't parse. Happy things, claiming praise. We think you're so cool. We want you so very much. We've got a theory or five about you. We want to know everything about you. The you abstracted in our hearts will live on forever so long as you're here. We love you, Sideways Pike. Look at you go!

I fell forward. It was just taking another step, but I kept expecting my chin to smack the rug. It never did. I cut forward, kept walking, viscerally aware of the fact that I was onstage somehow. This was so much easier when I'd been Lady Macbeth. A lie, one that didn't work on me even as I thought it. I'd been a terrible Lady Macbeth. I'm an unconvincing lady. The unsex-me bit was all I could manage. Nobody believed that I was in love.

I brought my head down, looked around again. It was a terrible feeling.

Then, a glimmer. I spotted Lila Yates.

She sat beside Lupe and a fistful of women in sleek black cocktail dresses. She smiled at the stage, said something serenely that made the women laugh. The candlelight caught on her lashes. She looked so tired. She leaned her cheek against her palm. I don't think that she saw me standing there. Too many spinning plates for that.

I set my jaw and closed the distance.

There weren't any empty chairs at Yates' table. I trudged up beside it, beside where Yates sat. Language rattled around my chest cavity. Head felt murky. I stretched out a hand, ghosted one finger across the tablecloth beside her hand and said, "Lila."

She looked up and her eyes shot wide, and without a beat she tossed her arms around my waist and pressed her face against me, cheek against my belly, against the Scratch Book. She held me like that for a long moment. My throat clamped shut. I rested a hand on her shoulder and worried for a moment that when she released me, I'd collapse.

"Eloise," Lupe said. She beamed at me, waved a hand at the women around her. "Welcome home."

I swallowed thickly, swept my thumb over Yates' shoulder blade. I said just loud enough for her to hear: "Are you alright? Where's Daisy?"

"Diplomacy," she breathed with a note of pain. "I am still doing it. How about you, are you okay? Where have you been?"

"There was an accident. I'm okay now. I'll explain later," I said. My gaze fell on the table, which was a mistake. The meal hadn't been finished. Meat glistened on bone. Red fruit gleamed like hunks of ruby. There was grain on a nearby plate that could've filled a treasure chest. The soprano hit a chorus and one of the Pythonesses hummed merrily along. I decided I didn't trust Blair. "Are they sending anybody after Madeline?"

"Daisy and I convinced them to hold off until they consulted you specifically." Yates peered up at me, nose around where I imagined my spleen lived. "Are you sure you're alright? I worried, we both worried. You two were gone a long time."

"I'm sorry I made you worry. I should've called you. It wasn't fair to keep you and Daisy out of sync with what was happening. You'll get a full report," I said in what I hoped was an assuring tone. I was beyond thinking of something quippy. If I kept smelling food I might regress and kill something. Come to think of it, a bit of old-school violence sounded profoundly cathartic right now. I wondered where Dominick was lurking. I bet I could get that guy to hit me. "Thank you for holding things down here." Less thank you for "consult me specifically," but holy shit, that was outside my current realm of comprehension. I couldn't process the implications of that right now.

"Sit, sit," said Lupe.

Someone made like they were going to stand up to fetch a chair, but before they could manage, Yates pulled me into the chair with her. She arranged herself halfway in my lap, thighs over my thighs for the sake of fitting us both. Mercifully, this particular wingback curved in such a way that it hid my face a little, at least if I sank back into it. I let out a thin sound through my teeth. Sitting felt fantastic. Proximity to Yates felt fantastic. I was so fucking tired.

"Have you eaten?" Yates said into my neck. She dangled off me, and I put one arm around her to make sure she wouldn't slip. She was so warm it made my head spin. Quieter, hushed with a conspiratorial sweetness: "I had so many appetizers that I can barely touch dinner. Witches love charcuterie and tiny little sandwiches."

"You are the best girl in the whole wide world. Lila Yates, I could kiss you." God. God. It came out in some strangled middle between a gasp and a growl.

Yates huffed a breath and batted her lashes. She twisted

on my lap, fanned one hand over my sternum, and she swayed her weight against me, pinned our spell book between our bellies. She touched my cheek. She kissed my open mouth. Shock clapped. Yates kissed me, she was kissing me, I couldn't move. I didn't dare. She kissed me so softly, sweet and slow and melting deep, and she flicked her tongue over my bottom lip and smiled against me, and I'd never breathe again. Lila Yates was kissing me. Then, she wasn't. She nestled against me, yawned like a cat. Toyed with the neckline of my terrible sleeveless T-shirt. "Just do it next time."

I looked down at her plate and could not remember how to make my hands work.

"Today has been one of the longest days of my life, I think. Feels like that anyway. I think it's this place, it's unmooring. That cosmic current feeling is so hectic, it feels like something's building, and it gets in my head, you know? It makes me think in poetry. Line breaks in normal thoughts. Earlier I thought I saw an angel, but it was dust in my eye. I'm so tired, Sideways." I felt her lashes brush my neck. She got bolder when she was drunk, more affectionate, and I wasn't sure if her magic sensitivities would be secret when she was sober. I sucked in. It was hard. "I'm really proud of us. They're trying to poach me, but know that being a Scapegracer makes me such a happy girl. I'm so blessed that you and Daze and Jing are my best friends, that I've got Scratch to watch over me. Even with the horrible weather and college coming, I'm a happy girl. Do you want some wine? I've had a lot of wine."

"I'm glad you're happy. You deserve to feel happy. We

should keep our voices down." My head spun. No words in here, that was my limit. My lips buzzed. I gnawed my tongue, then something animal took over in my brain and I leaned forward, seized the fork with the hand I didn't have on Lila, and tore into her dinner. I wasn't sure what I was eating, not that it mattered. It was warm in my mouth, and rich, and studded with crystalline salt. Heartbreaking stuff. I wolfed it down and glided over the absolute devastation of her kissing me then telling me she was proud of me while I was sitting next to my dead mother's friends whom I had every intention of rejecting wholesale despite the eight-year-old in my head screaming contrariwise with great speed. I barely chewed. If I choked, I choked. So be it. I'd dodged death once today. This was platonic. She and I, we were platonic.

"You're a gem, Sideways." She rested her cheek against the meat of my arm. "You'll be a great girlfriend for somebody someday."

I froze with the fork between my lips. I couldn't taste the food on my tongue. I made myself chew, swallow. "You, too," I breathed. "We just gotta make it to someday."

NINE

DEGREES OF SEPARATION

I was about to shatter. I could tell. I could feel it, the edge of my spiritual force field getting incrementally more fragile. It was thinner than mica. Mohs of the Mohs scale could not comprehend how scrapeable my patience had become. I looked at my empty plate, which was Yates' empty plate, and locked eyes with my ghostly reflection in the porcelain. I held its gaze. I dared it to move before I did.

"The Society is two hundred years old. We've got a legacy of grandeur, ingenuity, and grace. We've never lost a witch to a witchfinder," some Pythoness explained to me over her salad. "Not a single one. We're the solitary practitioner's haven, a network of strong, independent women that pull on each other's unique talents to ensure that everyone in our fold can be autonomous and free. You know, I don't think another coven here could say that they've never lost a witch to witchfinders. Do you think so, Lupe?"

She made a little humming sound in her throat. "We'd be the only ones, yes."

"Exactly," the first Pythoness said. She'd made the mistake

of introducing herself to me while I was in the throes of gorging and sadness. I did not know her name and I couldn't bring myself to assign her one in my head. I put a hand on the Scratch Book, the shape of which had gone miraculously unremarked upon, and felt grateful for a moment that Mr. Scratch wasn't in my head anymore and couldn't hear brags like that. Yates wasn't on me anymore, she'd migrated to perch on the chair's arm with a daintiness that shouldn't be possible, and I felt cold without her. I felt ambiently but palpably protective of her. These witches better keep their thoughts in their heads. The Pythoness leaned forward. "I'm sure you've read about the Founders—the Pythoness Founders have a little biography in one of the early volumes of the *Vade Mecvm*, right?"

"Not in the first two," I said.

"Hmm, really?" She cracked a laugh. "I ought to go back over those. Anyway, they were dedicated to the idea that witches were at their best and strongest in unity from a distance. Smaller targets moving faster. I mean, we get together for the sake of sharing ideas and mutual aid, maybe a few rounds of drinks, but we're not bound by region or trade. I mean, the Anti-Edonists are just a glorified union. You can't be a Dagger Heart unless you live with their commune. The Crimsonists all live in the same apartment complex. It's smothering, and does it provide any real protection? Apparently not!"

"My mom was a Pythoness, yeah?" I flicked my eyes up, looked her over.

She smiled like she was selling me mouthwash. "Lenora Pike, yes indeed. I never had the privilege of knowing her, but you knew her, right, Marissa?"

The Pythoness beside her made a face.

"I knew her," Lupe said. "She was brilliant. Quick as a whip."

"Being a Pythoness didn't seem to work out too well for her." I wiggled my jaw. "Seeing as she died at thirty-four."

Yates shifted. She touched my arm and I stiffened, so she dropped it.

"Eloise, what happened to your mother was a horrible accident. I am so sorry." Lupe flattened her hands on the table. The pink light glinted off her rings. She looked genuine, sounded legitimately torn up about it, but that was not doing much for me right now. "Some things are beyond our power. I wish I could change the past. I wish I could make things brighter for you. You are so young, and you've lived through more than your share of heartbreak. What I can do is offer you a chance for a better future."

"I'm not interested in splitting up my coven. I'm already spoken for. If you'd found me a year ago, I would've been thrilled, but you waited until after I found my people," I said. "I don't know what to tell you."

"Well, you're all going off to college, aren't you? Are you going to the same school?"

"What?"

"Lila told me that she expects to matriculate to Yale, where her parents met. Are you planning on going to Yale as well?"

Yates squirmed. She hadn't heard back yet, I knew that much.

As for me?

"No. Hilarious, no," I said. "I'm not going to an Ivy."

"So, you'll be separating from your coven in a manner of months." Lupe's eyes sparkled. "Your power is strong when you're together with your book devil, I'm sure about that. It's commendable. You're an inspiring group of young women. Also, all of you are targets and there are very powerful men who will want to see your end. Even if you didn't have history with witchfinders, they'd come for you. They are exceptional hunters. Do you have plans for how to keep yourselves safe under those circumstances? Have you decided which of you will be taking the grimoire? Whichever three girls are left without it will be at a considerable disadvantage unless you've come up with some strategy."

I wasn't sure why they hadn't snuffed us yet. I was reluctant to bring up the lack of Brethren in our lives to Shiloh, because they flinched when I brought it up, but I got the sense that *they* got the sense that if they hadn't snatched us up, it wasn't an inability thing. It was a timing thing. I thought about the memorial for David. I pushed the thought aside. A candle melted so low to the table that I thought it'd catch the cloth on fire. It didn't, not yet. It just spread like spilled milk.

"Your concern is sweet," Yates said when I didn't break the silence. I wondered if people who didn't know her as well would notice the tipsy glide between words. She leaned forward, hands clasped, and smiled with shining, unsober dimples. "It seems so absolute, that's all. If I was in danger, would I need to be yours for you to come and save me? Sideways came and saved me before I was theirs. You know," she said with a little cat yawn, "I don't see why we couldn't be comrades in this. Your impulse to break up my little clique and grab the broken pieces comes from a place of care, and I think that's lovely, but we're so smart, and it's the future now. I think there's a real chance for intercoven solidarity here! Shouldn't that be the goal? If I am in danger at school next year, can I rest assured that the nearest Pythoness would come to my aid not because we share the same book devil, but because we are both witches?"

The one called Marissa murmured behind her wineglass, "Maybe she should be sitting at the Anti-Edonist table."

Beside her, a stringy witch replied, "I don't think that table knows about femininity. They'd think she's lost."

"Don't," Lupe said thinly. "Not tonight."

I wanted to break my plate. "Yeah," I said, in a heavy-handed attempt to back Yates up. "Shouldn't you be willing to help on the general principle that we don't want witches dead? You don't want more dead witches, do you?"

"Of course not," Lupe said. She looked irritated. I wasn't sure if it was because of Yates and me or because of the whisper-shouting women on her left. "What an awful thing to say."

A fourth Pythoness said, "So! Sideways—you prefer to be called Sideways, right?"

I eyed her.

"Where do *you* plan on going to college?"

I continued to eye her.

"You know, there's a grant fund that we keep within the Society. We believe that it's vitally important for our women to have access to whatever resources they need, so we make a point to pool together an allotted amount of money every year. College is enrichment. If you were a Pythoness, we could probably help you a considerable amount."

That gnawed at something. I smothered the something, bashed ghost fists on the something until it shut the fuck up and yielded to me. I refused to consider it. They were waving bribes in front of me. I wasn't having it. Surely, I wasn't so easily bought. "Generous." I smiled. "I hope you find a Pythoness girl who needs it."

Lupe whispered something in Marissa's ear.

Yates beamed. "Hi, Jing."

I whipped my head up, scanned back and forth until I saw what Yates was seeing. Maybe five tables over, a cluster of witches had congregated to chat, and among them was a head of blond hair and a studded leather jacket. I caught the edge of a patch that read BURN BARONS NOT OIL. My heart kicked. Yates must've felt it, she shifted and perched on the arm of the chair, and once she no longer touched me I stood up unceremoniously, bumped the table with my hipbone as I arose, and edged my way around the Pythonesses. Yates followed me, I heard her excuse us both, but I refused to let Jing slip from my line of sight lest she vanish forever in the witch sea. I wouldn't so much as blink. I leaned forward, pushed myself deeper into the dining room. I shouldered through a few cliques and thought little of it. Yates reached out to brush her knuckles against mine, and I caught her hand and pulled her along with me. She kept up with my stride, matched me as I rounded the final table between me and Jing Gao.

There she was. We'd found her, I'd found her.

"Hey," I hissed. It came out harsher than I'd planned. Nerves were just fried, was all.

Jing looked up. Her eyes fixed on me. She shoved the martini glass she'd been holding aside, into the hands of a witch who clearly hadn't been expecting it, and threw an arm around my neck. She lifted on tiptoe, pressed her nose into the hinge of my jaw and breathed, "Jesus fucking Christ, why didn't you answer your texts? I've been looking for you."

Breathing felt good. It was paradoxically much easier and exponentially harder to do that when she was this close. I leaned my cheekbone against her temple and peered down the length of her back, wondered whether I should reciprocate the crushing. My jacket just hung off her, barely touched her frame, and that made my stomach hurt. I blinked. Oh. My jacket.

"It's because my phone is in your pocket," I said.

She broke into a laugh. "Of course it is, ugh. Look, one of the Anti-Edonists is a mechanic and offered to rescue and unfuck my car, but it sure as hell isn't happening tonight. We're going to have to think of a different way to get out of here."

"Right." So, Shiloh. Dad or Dad or Shiloh. Cool. "Where's Daisy?"

Jing pulled a face. "She's with Golddiggers Incorporated."

"Beg fucking pardon?"

"Here's the thing," Yates said. She still held my hand, and she stepped in closer to my side, made this situation into more of a group hug. "A lot of the political orchestration was before dinner started. Daisy went full Cicero, it was so extremely adorable, I am like, so proud of her. She's such a wonderful girl. Anyway, the Pythonesses approached me because they liked me, I think. There's been a lot of scheming to absorb us or split us, and they've apparently been telling people that I'd be a good match. I am not impressed. Daisy—" Yates glanced around, like she was checking if the cosmic coast was clear, then dipped her chin and whispered loudly, "Daisy approached the Star Thieves and mentioned her mother and I think it went over poorly. Things got tense. It was asymmetrical, shall we say, with the response the Pythoness Society had to seeing you, Sideways. I think Maurice spoke to one of the women in the group? Like, gave them a little order to play nice. That's why they offered Daisy a spot at their dinner table. Daisy knows that."

One of Jing's eyes fluttered back in her head. She rocked her heels back down to earth, but kept one arm hooked around my neck as she said, "I tried to hang around with them for five minutes and that was too long. They are possibly the most insufferable people I've ever met in my life. Ever. They are the most evil crop of brunchgoers that exists."

"Brunchgoing witches," I repeated. It was weird, hearing them take this tone about any girls, period. Usually we are very pro—evil girl. I wonder what they'd done. It must've been severe.

"Uh-huh. Daisy is holding her own. She's put up with people like that before. I asked her if she wanted me to rescue her, and she told me no." Jing closed her eyes for a moment, brows in a V. "I'm going to try again after the next song."

I nodded, scrubbed my tongue over my gums. "When are we getting out of here?"

"You're going to need to talk to the Corbies," Yates said.

"Goody." I grimaced. "To be clear, I'm explaining why the death penalty is shitty, yes?"

"Essentially." Yates smiled faintly. "Look, if I could manage, so can you."

"You are a saint," I said.

"I am just a girl, and I am exhausted." She put her hands in her pockets. "I worry about Daisy. I think she's been skipping therapy again."

"Her therapist is such a fucking asshole." Jing shrugged. "We'll go over en masse and be hot and intimidating, that'll wear the Star Thieves down some. They could use a healthy ego knock."

"The bloody clothes oughta help with that." I snorted, then winced at myself. I blew out through my teeth. God, the gap was weird. "Can you hand me my phone? I want to see if Shiloh's going to be around to pick us up or if we're going to have to plan something elaborate and stupid."

"Sure thing," she said. She reached her hand into my pocket and her face dropped. "God, did you just pour blood in here? The lining is soggy."

"Blood?" Yates balked. "Excuse me, blood?"

"Phone," I repeated.

Jing shook her head. She pulled it out, handed it over. I dropped Yates' hand to receive.

"So, blood," Yates said. She sounded crisper. Disgust is a great way to sober up. "There was blood in the pocket? There is blood on your clothes? What happened exactly? Tell me right now or I will lose my mind."

"Okay, so," Jing started.

I rubbed my phone on my jeans and unlocked it. Shiloh, I needed to text Shiloh. I had so very little battery left. Phone charging sigil, that was going to be a thing I'd make as soon as we got home. Bullshit, I'd make it tomorrow. When I got home I was going to crumble into sawdust and whine until my dad made me hot cocoa. I fumbled around with my thumb, opened my messages, then saw the notification.

Email notification.

"Oh, my goodness," Yates gasped with a hand at her mouth.

"Right? And then," Jing continued, expression grim. She pulled her arm off my neck for the sake of waving her hands, pantomimed shaking a raccoon corpse.

Little tap of my fingertip and it was open.

The header of the artsy weirdo tiny liberal arts school that Boris had attended flashed bottle green across my screen.

The spit in my mouth went icy. It was hard to focus. Nausea hit.

"Please say you didn't," Yates said.

"Lila, I wouldn't lie to you," Jing said. "You know we did."

> Dear Eloise M. Pike,
> Congratulations! I am delighted to offer you admission . . .

I read again,

> Congratulations! I am delighted to offer you admission . . .

A third time, and then I read onward. I was sizzling, my veins were neon electric, I read through an entire body paragraph that held no content and blathered warmly about the school and the fact that it was a school, I flicked my eyes up to the email's opening and back down, I opened my mouth to tell my Scapegracers and then I read the last paragraph.

I'd been awarded a scholarship. From what I understand, everyone is offered a scholarship, because the school is bananas fuck-off expensive, we're talking $50K a year, and Boris had assured me that he and all his friends had received scholarships that shaved off two-thirds of that at the very least. I looked at my scholarship. I looked at the numbers that trailed behind that snake-impaled dollar sign.

My scholarship was $10K.

Four years would be $160K, that's before room and board and books and whatever.

My dragon hoard inheritance, the money I'd had waiting for me that my mother had left for this purpose, would barely cover my first year's tuition. That'd felt like so much money a month or two ago.

I said something flimsy. I wasn't sure if it was language that left my mouth. I didn't say it loud enough for it to be discernible even if it had been. Shoved my phone in my pocket, turned on my heel, slipped between a few people lingering to our right. My back was to the soprano, going on about love again, this time with the sparkling reassurance that it must exist even though she'd lost it. I wove between slim shoulders, around the perimeter of a table filled with kissing people, then a table where two women took turns burning bits of broccoli rabe with the knobby candle centerpieces. I walked faster. I closed the distance between myself and the door. I wasn't sure if Jing and Yates had noticed yet, and if they had, I'd at least have a few seconds' advantage.

Through the doorway, into the foyer. There was a couple kissing in the foyer, up against the wall, hands on thighs, et cetera. I'd go outside. I staggered to the door, thirsty for a breath of cold air, but when I yanked the knob back I beheld a flock of smokers on the patio, lounging against the porch railing, ribbons of smoke spilling from their mouths and corkscrewing up toward the moon. I gasped, took a bracing step backwards.

I locked eyes with Dominick.

He took a drag and rasped, "There you are."

Nope. No. No.

All my horror education failed me. I whirled around and bolted back inside, took a turn I hadn't made before, then another, and a third. Walls flew by with jewel-toned paper. Suits of armor with big axes and glints of sword, long tapestries, painted busts, odd taxidermy. It flew past me. I took a sharp turn, the room forked, and I went left then up a marble staircase. The carpet runner looked feathered. I was stomping up ten thousand peacock tails. At the top of the stairs, there was a landing, then a single doorless arch. Above it a sign read LOUIS ROOM.

I went in the godforsaken Louis Room.

Turns out the room was a gallery exhibit. Greek-looking statuary loomed along the parallel side of the room like ghosts in sheets, missing limbs, missing eyes. Gods, I guess. I don't know. The far wall was covered with gnarled hunks of white rock. Bits of rock had shapes I recognized—a length of finger, a chunk of nose, a curl of hair, jagged genital knots—but most didn't. In the dark it frightened me, but not enough to make me leave. There was a double-sided bench in the room's center, and I ran for its far side, collapsed across its face.

I lay there for a second in the cold, quiet dark. I pulled a withering breath in, and in, and in. I covered my face with my hands. I waited for something, I didn't know what, to happen. Nothing did. The sob broke out of me and I bent, my body screwed into a fishhook, knees near my sternum, Scratch

Book pinned between myself and myself. I cried hard. It felt like coughing something up. I dry-retched, I shook all over. I kneaded the heels of my hands against my eyes, but they kept spilling. I thought I might be sick. I thought I might be dying. I couldn't think.

"Lights. On or off?"

I couldn't place the voice. My memory leaked out of my ears. "Fuck you," I heaved. I rolled away, faced the rock collage. "Off."

I heard the approach. Soft soles, sneakers maybe. Worn boots. The footsteps came quietly, scuffed a little. The other side of the bench whined. Whoever it was, they'd sat.

We hovered in silence.

I kept crying, but I cut the sound. Holdover skill from foster care. Eventually, when it was clear I couldn't wait them out, I rolled onto my back and blinked up at the ceiling, or at least where the darkness got harder. Tears rolled into my ears. Awful. I didn't have sleeves to wipe them. I grimaced and said thickly, "What do you want?"

"We need to talk," said the person who I understood with sinking horror was definitely fucking Dominick. "So let's talk."

"I am," I spat, "occupied."

"Tough." His tone was inscrutable, which was to say it didn't sound malicious. He sounded—pensive? Apprehensive? Thoughtful, dare I even consider it? It sounded high in his register, more air than phonation. I wondered vaguely if he was gay. "I won't draw this out."

"I'm not going to tell you where Madeline is," I said. "I don't even know, so don't try any shit. Get it?"

He made a reedy sound in his throat. "Chivalrous."

"Comes with the territory."

"Tell me about the Chett hex."

I hiccupped. I wanted to get off this bench and kick it until it snapped. "My coven hexes people who hurt girls such that if they try to hurt girls again, they suffer."

"I'm into that." Dominick paused. "I think violence gets the point across. There are covens here that forbid offensive magic, it abrades their sense of propriety. They're *good* witches who do *good* magic, like moral high ground is meaningful when people are hunting us for sport. We bash back, we defend our own, and when one of us hurts one of us, we stomp them out immediately."

"Ripping her specter out means she can't get better." I did agree with that first bit. I mashed my phlegmy face against the bench.

"I like you, Pike." He was so quiet I almost missed him over the sound of my own breath. "Madeline was my sister once. I'm ashamed of her, and what she did to you. I think she needs to be punished before this flock because I think everybody here should be fucking terrified of what happens to witches who attack witches. I have zero qualms being the supervillain if it prevents what happened to you from happening again. I should've asked you. For that much, I'm sorry. It was harm done against you. You should've had the first say. I've asked around about that hex of yours. It sounds pretty fucking gnarly. Hell of a community service to offer, kid."

I mashed my face harder.

"When you ran off with Madeline, there was talk about cutting you off from the flock. I think that's stupid. It's also stupid to leave Madeline unpunished. If your coven puts a Chett hex on her, we're square. Your turn. Talk."

I did not know how to talk. I heard him twist around though, heard his denim rustle against the hardwood, the jingle and scrape of his belt chain against his keys. I had the suspicion that he was going to keep talking if I didn't. I couldn't deal with that. I'd hit the upper limit of acceptable stimuli an hour ago. I opened my mouth to cuss aimless circles around him, but what came out was another, even uglier sob, and that kept him quiet.

Some while later, I managed sound. What came out wasn't a speech. I pulled myself upright, sat like a human person, wrapped my arms around my stomach and said: "I want to throw myself down the stairs."

"Don't." He coughed. "Why?"

"I don't think I'm going to go to college."

"What?"

"All my friends are going off to college after we graduate but I'm going to be stuck right here because I fucked up and I didn't get a good scholarship so I won't be able to afford to go to this school. It's the only school that accepted me. I don't know what I'm supposed to do. I'm so stupid. I ruined everything. Like I was depressed for a fucking semester and failed two classes and now my life is ruined. I don't know how to tell my dads. They're going to be so disappointed in me. I'm so, *stupid*—"

He stood up abruptly.

I thought for a moment that I'd scared him off, this time by accident.

I hadn't. Dominick rounded the bench and stood in front of me, maybe two yards back. He sat on the ground there, elbows resting on his knobby knees, ankles crossed, one hand on his opposing wrist. He stared at me, unblinking. "Sideways."

"What?"

"Shut up. Fuck college."

"*What?*"

"Sucks if you wanted it and now it's gone, or gone for this year anyway, but the fact remains. Fuck college. Dropping out of college was the best thing I've ever done. Among the best things. What, did you want to be a doctor or a lawyer, some shit like that?"

"No."

"I thought not." He leaned forward, eyes burning. "Fuck. College. You didn't fuck anything up. If you still care in a year, try again in a year, but listen when I say this: you are a witch, you've got a network of people who will help you, and you absolutely do not need to bleed debt forever to get a degree unless you really, *really* want one. It's a class barrier, that's it. If you want to go to learn, join a reading group. If you want to party, party. If you can tolerate the absolute shitshow that is dealing with witch personalities, I am confident you can get work with any of the bastards downstairs. You're going to be absolutely fucking fine. Chill out, don't be self-destructive. Do you understand me?"

Dominick was so annoying. I wanted to kick him. I tugged a fistful of my shirt and shrugged, shredded the skin of my lip with my bottom teeth. The Scratch Book jabbed at me. I pulled it out, set it in my lap, and said more quietly than I would've liked, "I just don't know what I'm going to do now."

"Me neither. That's life." He huffed a breath, cocked his head back. "That your grimoire?"

"Yeah," I managed. I was about to really dive off the cliff. Full-on mental breakdown wipeout. I took a deep breath, tried to pitch my voice down and barely managed. "We call it the Scratch Book."

"Cool," he said. "Can I see it? I won't open it. Just like the feel of these things."

I made a face, but motion sounded good, and this was a new thing to think about. A thing I liked without stakes. That was something. "Be gentle. He'll bite you if you give him bad vibes."

"A wakeful book devil." His nostrils flared once. "Ours doesn't talk much. She's aloof. Most of them are. I think she's addressed me personally all of twice and I've known her for a decade now." He reached out his palms. "Let's see him, then."

I shifted, took the book in my hands. I squeezed it. The edges pressed against my palms, and the sensation was grounding, cut through some of the feverish numbness that'd swept me. I could've sworn the book pushed back against my hands. It felt like a headbutt from a cat. I extended my elbows, offered this awful weasel man a glimpse of my spell book, my fresh gills.

He took it carefully. He had a lighter hand than I'd expected, graceful, deliberate movements. It didn't mesh with the skateboard violence I'd seen on our first encounter. Dominick held the Scratch Book in his hands. He traced his fingertips over its alligator ridges, the dips and folds. "It looks like a composition book."

"It was once, before Mr. Scratch."

"Mr. Scratch," he repeated. It put a huge, lopsided smile on his face, which was bizarre, because it turned out Dominick looked like a totally different dude when he smiled. All his ghastly knife gauntness became angular and interesting. He wasn't handsome, nor was he pretty, but he was striking like this. He examined the Scratch Book's spine, its headband of my hair, its sprayed edges—edges which had not been sprayed the last time I looked at it, which meant that those edges were red with the blood he'd sucked out of my face this afternoon. "That's a cute name for a devil if ever there was one. Is he cool?"

"Yeah," I sniffed. "He's cool."

He took a deep breath, looked up from the book and square at my face. "How old are you, Sideways?"

"Eighteen," I said with a frown. "Why?"

"I'm a piercer. That's my job. I've got a slate of guest positions at studios all over the place from June until December, and then I'll be in Detroit for a month or two." He furrowed his brows. "You're fucking annoying but everyone is. You're a nice enough kid. I like that you smuggled a criminal out of death row, even if I think that was stupid and kind of hate you for it. Look, I can't promise it'll pay much, but if you can't think of something you'd rather do before June, I'd be willing to take you on as an apprentice if you'd be into that. You can get paid to stab people. That seems like your vibe."

Bam, the wall I'd been building brick by brick came crashing down. I was crying again, crying hard with ugly abandon. I dragged my forearm over my face, coughed a few times, flailed around for some grip on my emotional equilibrium but couldn't find purchase. My stomach hurt.

Dominick looked stricken. I got the sense that he wasn't good with feelings as such.

I shook my head and took the Scratch Book from his hands, shoved it back under my shirt, and pressed it there while I caught my breath. I shook my head, swallowed some snot. "No, like," I heaved, "it so *totally* is my vibe."

"Offer rescinded if you cry all the time," he said. "Ugh."

My diaphragm kicked and a laugh cut out of me. It didn't sound too much different from the sobbing, I think, but it made me smile and that felt novel. "You are such a fucking dickhead."

"That's common knowledge," he said. "Ask anyone."

I took a measured breath. "Why were you fighting Andy on the porch with a skateboard earlier?"

"You make it sound like Clue." He shrugged. "I love to fight and hate that guy."

"Why?"

"He's a tankie." He yawned. "Least favorite Dagger Heart. Said some statist shit, implied that we'd be stronger as a witch collective if we established a firm hierarchy of responsibility. Fighting's part of flocking. It's tradition. Let's go downstairs, alright? I'm done being in this room."

"Yeah," I said. I slid off the bench. "This room fucking sucks."

A REAL PIECE OF WORK

A ghost lurked at the bottom of the staircase. Hood drawn, arms crossed, shoulders shifting ceaselessly under that mercury-colored jacket. "Sideways," the ghost called with resonant vocal fry. "Do you know we've been looking for you for like, twenty fucking minutes? Screw you, I'm going to eat you, don't vanish like that."

Thank goodness, holy shit.

"Daisy," I said. My lungs cleared. I bounded down the stairs four at a time and caught her at the bottom, pulled her into a strangle hug. She was practically teddy bear–sized. Good for emotional support. I crushed her, tucked my chin over the top of her head, and took a few slow belly breaths.

She tolerated the hug. It was clear that she wasn't jazzed about it but was willing to put up with it for my sake. She looked rough in a different way than she had this morning, veiny and twitchy, without her evil glow. She squirmed in my arms after a moment, so I released her, and she shot up three steps and jabbed a finger at Dominick. "You," she snarled.

"Me," he repeated.

I caught her by the scruff of her—my—hoodie. "We worked it out, it's fine," I said. My voice sounded horrible. I swallowed, cleared my throat, tried to speak low enough that it wasn't as excruciatingly obvious that I'd been crying. It probably showed on my face, but I couldn't do anything about that. "Don't kill him."

"I thought killing him was the plan! That'd be the cool thing to do!" She thrashed her shoulders, yanked herself out of my grip, and shrugged her shoulders against the wall. She pouted like a kid, eyes rolling, brows in a tight knot, but the look on her face was a little too grim for me to discount it. "If I can't kill Madeline and I can't kill this guy, what am I supposed to do? Calm down? Grow up."

"I missed you," I said. "You're like if a Chihuahua was a person." I scrubbed a hand over my face, flinched to find it still wet. "We're going to Chett Madeline. That's the agreement."

Daisy bounced on the balls of her feet. "Damn right."

"Where are Yates and Jing? If I have to wander around this house again looking for them, I—"

"We're here," Yates said from behind me. I glanced over my shoulder. Jing and Yates lingered in the hallway behind us, shadowed and still glamorous despite all odds. Jing had pulled her hair back off her neck, twisted it into a tight bun. Yates worried her hands together. "If everything is alright, Maurice asked me to bring you back to the dining room. There's going to be an announcement, I think." She lifted her gaze a little, looked between Daisy and me up at Dominick. "You, too."

"Is it news about her?"

Vague. I glanced between the two of them, too worn out to guess anything elaborate.

"He didn't say what it was about," Yates said. "It sounded important, though."

I grimaced, braced myself like I was waiting for a gut punch. I counted backwards in my head. The numbers ticked down, and when I struck one, I nodded at Yates and Jing and followed them back through the house. It washed over me. I wondered how workers here ever got used to it.

Back in the dining room, I jabbed my thumbs below my tear ducts and tried to find five things I could see and five things I could feel and five things I could hear, like the video app talk therapists said. I gave up quickly. The crowd felt weird, but a different weird than dinner. Antsy. Half of the witches around us looked variously restless, bored, or at the right level of intoxication to start making flamboyantly stupid decisions. The other half looked straight ahead. Grave faces, merriment stripped off with acetone. A few of the grim ones murmured to their friends, and those friends flipped, passed the somber along. Solemnity rippled across the flock. We sat at our own table off to the left of the stage. None of us said anything.

The band was gone, and Maurice Delacroix walked across the stage alone. He stopped beside the microphone and lifted his chin. It was like he'd clapped his hands. Chatter died. Without music, the room felt cavernous and overwhelmingly large. It was like being in a warehouse, or a giant's mouth. Maurice surveyed us all, then spoke. "It's been a long day and I don't want to keep you. Rarely do we all gather like this. It pains me that we do so only when we've got a tragedy to untangle. The matter of Madeline Kline has been settled between the Sisters Corbie and Scapegracers covens, and anyone with something further to say should seek an audience with them. Our matter is this. A specter hoard was uncovered at a local witchfinder den. The Scapegracers coven recovered those specters and brought them here, where they've been held by my house until such time as we could all be present to determine what will be done with them. I am inclined to leave identifiable specter stones up to their coven's jurisdiction, and to hold the remainder here in the Delacroix House archives.

"I am here to tell you this—I had come to believe that every person to whom those stones belonged had died. I was wrong. We've heard word from Molly McNeal, a solitary hedge witch who has described to me the torture she endured at the Chantry family's hands. The speculation that's been circulating today is largely true. McNeal is alive, and she has expressed her desire to come to the Delacroix House and recover the soul that was stolen from her nearly three years ago."

I sucked in a hard breath. Three years.

Beside me, Jing whispered: "So one of Shiloh's, then."

Nausea flipped and I shoved my palm against my chin, forced my mouth shut.

"We had been unaware of McNeal before today. As such, she was not invited to flock. I thank the Anti-Edonists for having informed me of her existence, and for the Corbie scryer who helped us locate her whereabouts and contact her this evening."

Meager applause floated around the room, a few drunken cheers. It died down fast. There was a tightness stretched over us, an itchiness, and it made the hair on my arms prickle. The whole room crawled with gooseflesh. Finding the woman with her soul torn out wasn't exactly reason for jubilation.

One of Shiloh's. God, it kept ringing in my head.

Maurice steepled his slender dark fingers. He held them under his chin and was silent for a beat, looked over all of us again. He could've been a conductor overseeing his symphony. He pulled our attention taut. He lowered his hands. He said, "Molly McNeal's organ is in that pile, and none of us will touch them until she can. We will not squabble over her soul. I evoke every power of this house in that determination—not one of us will take a specter from that store until she has seen them and found herself. The consequences for anything else will be immediate and dire. Am I understood?"

Silence, but movement. Glasses were raised and chins were dropped in affirmation.

"Good." Maurice squared his shoulders. "Molly McNeal cannot be here until this coming Saturday, a week from today. She cannot come sooner. It's been discussed. I invite you all to reconvene here at that time, or if the travel would prove difficult, rooms can be provided upstairs. Thank you all, adieu, good night."

He stepped back and calamity broke out throughout the crowd behind us. Some people were clearly furious and made sure everyone immediately around them knew. Others seemed resigned to the delay, or else so seriously affected by the update that they looked outright murderous whenever someone suggested the wait would be inconvenient. A sad-eyed someone, my hero, rolled and lit up in the middle of the room. One witch pushed another witch. Lupe followed Blair out of the room, both looking openly distraught.

The Scapegracers just sat there for a moment. They looked at me. I looked at the ceiling.

I slid down the chair. My heels skidded over the Persian rug, my ass slipped off the edge and dangled in space, legs straight, spine curved like a waning crescent moon. My chin was level with the table's edge. I was ready for this day to end.

"Scapegracers," said Maurice, who was suddenly standing at the table's side. He had his partner with him, a man called Jupiter, and he checked his watch before he leaned forward, peered down at my quickly sinking body. "Sideways."

"Mr. Delacroix," I said.

"About Madeline," he said.

"What about her."

"Dominick told me that the Sisters Corbie retracts its claim on Madeline's fate. I accept the retraction, but know that the responsibility of handling her now falls on you. This house suspends its grace from her, and we expect never to see her here again. If she harms another witch, I will expect your coven to handle it personally, lest the Scapegracers be held accountable. You would also be suspended from our grace. I would not recommend being without and outside us."

"I think that sounds reasonable," Yates said.

Daisy whispered something in Jing's ear. Jing frowned, waved a hand at Yates, who waved her hand back, which made Jing look between Maurice and Jupiter with an expression of stern satisfaction. Jing and Yates looked at me. Daisy picked dirt from under her nail with a toothpick.

"Well," I said after a moment, even lower now. "I think you can count on me to kick her ass into the next dimension if she does what she did to me again, yeah."

"Good, I thought as much. I expect you worked things out with Dominick?"

"Does anyone ever truly work things out with Dominick?" Jupiter added with an edge that suggested history.

"Yeah," I said. "I have, I think."

"Excellent." Maurice checked his watch again. He and Jupiter conferred about something in quick, low tones. Maurice ghosted a kiss over Jupiter's temple, then turned back to us. "Will you be needing rooms tonight?"

"I want to go home," came out of my mouth before I could stop it and think of a more adult-sounding thing to say. I sank a little further. The tip of my nose dipped beneath the table. My boots jutted well between Yates' ankles across from me. Thank god this corduroy upholstery had grip.

"Thank you," Yates said.

"We appreciate it," Jing added.

"We're gonna need a ride." Daisy yawned behind a hoodie paw. "There's that."

"Hmm." In a fluid, dancelike motion, Jupiter snaked a

hand out and caught a passing witch above the elbow, held them fast. "Andy, sweetheart. Did you come in the van?"

"Uh." Andy smiled a little warily. "Yeah. D'you need me to pick something up for you?"

"I need you to make a delivery," Jupiter said with a smile.

*

Andy was a pretty good sport about it, I'd say. Reacted better than I would've given that he'd been asked to carpool a bunch of shitty grouchy traumatized high schoolers who lived an hour away when he'd clearly been on his way upstairs to crash. His van was enormous and seemed remarkably 1970s, and the inside had been carved to death, Sharpied and nail polished and sigiled with park bench love and density. It had marvelously tacky leopard-print seating. Aside from a few water bottles and a silvery leg that I assumed was part of a drum kit, it was cleaner than I'd expected. Nobody spoke much on the way home, directions aside. He'd played music that I'd liked, and maybe Jing liked, because I'd successfully dragged her into my sludge metal hell. He noticed when I had a minor car-related freakout twenty minutes in and pulled into a gas station, where he'd gone inside and bought me a Coke, and turned a blind eye to Daisy stuffing a small bag of Doritos up her sleeve. He dropped Jing off first, which made me sad in a way I couldn't parse, then Yates, then dead-eyed Daze. When I was the last person left, he turned the music down, cleared his throat.

"So, you're Sideways."

"Uh-huh."

"It was cool that you caught Kline yourself and let her go yourself. Inanna is super impressed with your coven. If ever you all need help, reach out. Bashing back is our whole shtick." He shot me a smile in the rearview mirror. "You okay?"

"I get carsick." Simplification seemed the move. "Long day."

"You're telling me." He shook his head. "Being around other covens for a week is going to be a *lot* for all of us. Feel lucky that you're local. Speaking of, is there anything to do around here?"

"Drink." I yawned. "I mean, there's a gay bar and a few like, rave type things, if that's your scene. The Delacroix House is as cool as it comes. I don't know how to one-up that. I mean, do you like antiquing?"

"You seem a bit young for bars." His brows shot up. "Witches as a class love weird old shit. You should see the Anti-Edonists' safe house. It's like a museum."

"Well, you're in luck. Turn here."

He turned here.

There it was in all its glory: ROTHSCHILD & PIKE, my midwestern Elysium. I unbuckled as the van pulled to a stop and swallowed a flash of bile, pressed my palm against the van's tacky door. "Voilà," I said. "Best antique shop on earth. They've sold some pieces to Maurice, actually. Part of why the Delacroix is cool is because my dads are."

That's a thing I got to say because right now they were not in earshot.

"Your dads own this shop," he repeated. "Cool. Fuck it, okay, I'll spread the word. There's a gay bar and a gay-owned witch-approved antique shop. This is gonna be one hell of a week."

"Welcome to Sycamore Gorge." I nodded, pawed for the door handle. "Say, what's the time?"

"Quarter til ten," he said.

That felt both radically early and unforgivably late. How was I so wrecked at ten on a Saturday night? This time last week, my evening was just getting started. The Scapegracers would say out until like, six in the morning sometimes, mischief willing. Fuck, being old was going to suck. "Thanks for the ride," I said, opening the door.

"No problem," he said.

One foot on the pavement, and I glanced over my shoulder. "Hey, can I ask you a question?"

"Shoot."

"Your fight with Dominick, earlier."

He slammed his head back against the headboard and stared up at the van's slashed-up roof. "What about it?"

"Is he like, bad news? He's not a serial killer or anything like that, yeah?" I blinked. "Are you a tankie?"

Andy made a strangled sound. He broke into a grin, rubbed his hands over his eyes. "Oh, fuck me. Okay. Here's the thing: I don't remember what we were really fighting about, but the thing about witch infighting and leftist infighting is that it's all the same infighting. I straight up could not tell you what we were arguing about. We are all very possessive of our niche opinions. Plus, Dominick seeks out conflict. He is the most self-righteous, condescending, belligerent jackass I've ever met. Think what would happen if a cartoon wizard decided to ruin everything by transfiguring a prickly pear into a dehydrated Satanist skater boy. That's him. He's just a wretched ex-twink, Sideways. Anyway, he's that intense all the time, he never unclenches, but he's not a bad guy. He's a good organizer and a good caster. You learn to think it's charming."

I put both soles on the asphalt. "Right. Thanks."

"See you in a week," Andy said.

I shut the door, the van rolled out, and I was alone on the sidewalk. Cold air felt good in my lungs, felt clean. The silence felt good. Fuck, I'd been way too overstimulated. I wanted to lie facedown on the floor of my bedroom and shut down. I'd tell my dads about college some other time. The morning, maybe. I wasn't ready to let them down. I couldn't handle that tonight. Maybe Shiloh would be out, and I wouldn't have to bring up what was happening on Saturday or breach the topic of witchfinding with them yet. I needed tonight to be simple from here on out. I needed not to make friction with the people who loved me. I couldn't afford for them to stop.

I unlocked the shop's door, relocked it behind me.

I waded through the creamy darkness with my eyes half shut.

The shapes of my dads' shop in the dark pulled some of the grief off me. The silhouettes made noble monster shapes, those ever-shifting assemblages of mannequins and parasols and Martian globes and surgical straws flowing together with odd, chimeric harmony. The air smelled golden, like resin and tobacco, mass market paperbacks, shafts of light. I fit here. Nothing expected anything of me here. I moved through the shop without flipping a switch in perfect thoughtless peace. I knew where to step, where to sway my head to avoid being sideswiped by wayward taxidermy. I knew who I was, which was to say, I was finally smart enough to not be a person with the burden of a personality, bullshit problems, aspirations and philosophies and whatever the fuck. I was an animal body slumping to the apartment door. I unlocked it, relocked it behind me, simple mechanical motions, and I trudged up the stairs with one palm flush against the wall. The paper dragged against my skin, felt nice. Everything would be fine.

I opened the door at the top of the stairs and stepped into clementine-colored lamplight. Home smell walloped me. I pitched forward against a wall, pressed my forehead next to a picture of dumb little eight-year-old me without any front teeth, and shut my eyes.

It was not silent.

There was conversation being had.

A war jolted to life between the big ugly lobes of my brain: investigate or lie facedown right here in the hallway and sleep immediately. The second option seemed much sexier. But also, fuck, I ought to tell Dad and Dad that I was home safe, right?

I resented my own inclination toward being a good kid for them.

I peered down at the floor between my feet and whispered, "Soon baby," then kept walking, one arm slung over my stomach, mushing the Scratch Book against my abdomen like it'd keep me upright.

If my sonar capabilities were even slightly functional, the sound was emanating from the living room. Which, like. Duh, where else would audible conversations be had in this apartment? I rolled my shoulders, fantasized about sticking my head under the kitchen tap and drinking water right from the spigot for a few minutes, and trudged down the hall into the living room with Julian's and Boris' names already half-formed in my mouth.

I rounded the corner and my eyes almost popped out of my head.

Four people sat around the coffee table. Julian perched in an armchair, beaky and sleepy-eyed in an elbow-patch sweater, and Boris sprawled on the floor beside him in jeans and a white undershirt, one knee pulled under his chin, his slick back shiny to the point of being reflective. On the couch, beside Shiloh, was Madeline fucking Kline. She had Schnitzel the bastard tabby cat in her arms like a human baby. It looked like she'd been crying.

There were cards in their hands and cards on the table.

They were playing rummy. Motherfucking rummy.

Madeline looked avoidantly at the ceiling.

Shiloh looked avoidantly at their cards.

Dad and Dad were having a side conversation about best restoration practices and acknowledged my entering only with a polite nod and smile, as their antique stool talk was apparently all-consuming.

If I didn't scream it'd just burst out of my ears like teakettle steam. I stared daggers at Shiloh, who was loudly not looking at me, and tried to beam a giant flaming question mark into their mind. I was about to have an honest to god temper tantrum. I was about to become a werewolf. I was going to eat my family and jump out a window and run into the woods and never be seen again. I stared down Madeline fucking Kline. Madeline Kline! Holding Julian's cat! Playing rummy with my dads! I shook my head, unable to process. "Are you winning?"

"Julian's winning," Boris said. "Want me to deal you in?"

"No," I said. I walked past them, ducked into the kitchen, numbly went through our cabinet and got myself a glass. I slammed it down. I got our water filter from the fridge and poured myself a glass. I downed it. The living room, adjacent and extremely within earshot, was silent, light furniture chatting aside. I poured myself a second glass. I walked back into the living room, startled to find that Madeline Kline was *still there*. I stood across from the coffee table and sipped my water. I tried to incinerate the rummy cards with my mind. It didn't work.

Boris paused mid-furniture remark, glanced my way. "Did you chip your tooth?"

Madeline and Shiloh were making such a show of not looking at me that I thought they might physically seize up. Schnitzel was purring like an overheated electrical appliance. He kneaded his white paws against Madeline's sternum, tipped his head back, shoved his whiskers against her cheek. He never got cuddly with me. Traitor.

"No," I said again. "My teeth are normal."

"Is that blood on your trousers?"

"It's fake. We were filming a movie," I plucked from nowhere. Boris looked at me hard but didn't press. It was something we'd do, after all. We'd made little *Ghastly* parodies semiregularly. I would give Scratch these clothes as soon as I'd pulled them off. Let him suck them clean.

"I'd love to see the movie. I'll manage if it's scary." Julian yawned. He put down his hand and waved his hands over all the hearts he'd gathered. "I just can't justify mixing stains like that. I like my walnuts a healthy ash blond, and I'll be damned if we put a walnut stool in the shop and pass it off as mahogany. I'm a man of integrity."

Boris hummed, scrubbed a hand over his mouth. "What am I, then? A liar?"

"You are my moral counterpoint. Order and entropy. Our marriage provides universal balance." Julian touched Boris' shoulder. He glanced at Shiloh and Madeline. "I'm stunned that we are not boring you. We can leave you kids to do something that isn't rummy."

Shiloh coughed into their sleeve. "Always a pleasure," they said thinly.

"Didn't know you were having friends over, Shi," I said. "If you'd texted me, I would've brought snacks." That was a lie. If they'd texted me I would've blacked out and who knows where we'd be.

Shiloh used to be an adept stoic. When they first came here, their expression hardly ever changed, their tone never varied, and their mood was all but a mystery. Either they'd gotten softer, or I'd grown to know them better, but it seemed crystal clear to me that Shiloh was downright mortified. Mortified and intractable. They looked at me and I knew that there'd be no fighting them on this. Their eerie blue eyes flashed. They said, "Madeline's staying the night. I took it up with Boris and Julian."

They got to ask my dads for things. They got to go over my head like this, because this was their house, too. The anger I felt didn't account for that. I was undergoing my werewolfication. My skin was starting to split.

I wasn't sure what to do.

"Boris," I said. I looked away from Shiloh before I said something I'd regret.

Dad glanced up at me, still shuffling, gave me a smile.

"Can I borrow you?" The water jumped in my glass. My hand must be shaking. "My room."

The smile fell, but his eyes stayed crinkled. Wordlessly, Boris stood up, stretched his arms over his head. The tattoos on his arms were faded; he'd gotten most of them in bars, and I focused on them instead of how completely I was melting down. Anchors and flowers, real old-school stuff. I wondered if he'd ever want to get something matching with me. I couldn't hold the thought in place. Warm ideas kept slipping into panic.

He jerked his head toward my room, and I took off as slowly and as coolly as I could. I stuck to the plan. When I trudged down the hall, I didn't kick anything, and I didn't slam the door. I flipped on my light and sat on my bed.

Boris leaned against my doorframe. He lifted his brows.

"Dad," I said.

"Mm-hmm?"

"I'm not going to college," I said. "Not next year, at least."

Boris considered. He didn't blink. "May I sit?"

"Yeah." I pulled my knees to my chest and tried not to hyperventilate. I'd almost died today. I could've never seen him again. Ugh, I hated thinking about shit like that. I like being reckless but I hate consequences. "I've been offered a piercing apprenticeship. Even if I don't take it, I'll work a year or two first, I think. I could work here, or maybe," I searched my ceiling, "I can get a job with one of your friends. Be a PA or something. Get a trade. I don't know."

"Slow down," he said. He sat on the foot of my bed, hands on his knees. He had paint on his knuckles. "You don't want to go to school this year?"

"Yeah," I said. "Not this year."

"Alright. Piercing, that sounds like something you'd be good at," Boris said. "You've got the right temperament for it. You're good at keeping people calm and you've got a good material sense, and an artistic eye. No tremors. Look, all's well with me. College isn't going anywhere. If you want it later, you know where to find it." Boris cracked a smile. "Would you give me a nose ring?"

"Yeah." I pressed my head against his shoulder. "Is Julian going to cry?"

"About this? No. He dropped out of his own program, I'll remind you. He wants you to be happy. It's all that really matters to him and me, alright?" Boris clapped my back. "You look really tired."

"I'm really, really tired," I said. "I can't remember being this tired."

"You should sleep, then. Nothing more to do tonight." He kissed the top of my head. "Get some shut-eye. You can deal with the girl you hate in the morning."

"I don't hate her," I protested as he stood up. I waved my hands in the air, like that'd convince him. I kicked off my boots. "It's just—"

"You hate her alright." He flipped my light switch. "See you tomorrow, kiddo."

ELEVEN

THE MOST IMPORTANT MEAL
OF THE DAY

Banging on my head. Actually, knocking on my door, but it might as well have been fists on my big nose. I mashed the heel of my hand over my ear and ground at it, tried to snuff out the sound like burning paper, but unluckily for me, that's not how sound works. I lay there, still buttery with sleep, and wondered why the knocking didn't just kill me outright. Nothing was killing me outright these days. I was getting sick of it. My tongue had a caterpillar texture against the roof of my mouth.

"Sideways. May I come in?"

I did not figure out who had spoken. At this stage of consciousness, I radically did not care. Anyone would've been the wrong answer. I put my face under my pillow, recoiled when my cheek hit the Scratch Book's cover. It had not occurred to me that it would be where I'd put it. Object permanence was such a bore. Witches should be exempted from that shit.

"Sideways."

I made an ugly zombie sound.

Silence, with intention.

"Fine," I said into my mattress. Slightly louder: "What d'you want?"

My door opened, then shut. Soft little clicks. Then, a voice that was now undeniably attached to Shiloh said to me, "We need to talk about Madeline."

My eyes shot open. I stared into the flat, stiff darkness of my headboard. Slowly, bones creaking, I twisted in bed and sat upright. My pillow fell to the wayside and I did not move to retrieve it. I blinked at Shiloh, my face scrunched, and yanked a fistful of my shirt up, scrubbed my tongue with the cotton. My eyes focused. Allergy crust flaked off from between my lashes.

Shiloh wore their pajamas still. That meant it was probably the real morning, like 9:00 or 10:00 a.m., something abominably reasonable. They did not share my penchant for hypersomnia. They were a real live morning person. In their silky cream pajama set, they could've been some sort of obnoxious lovely chirping bird. Hair tucked behind their ears, a healthy post–skincare regimen glow to their face, their mouth in a firm line. They held a mug in their hands. The mug was shaped like a cartoon character circa 1960-something. Steam curled from it in mesmerizing dragon-breath gusts.

They nodded, or jutted their chin up more like. "For you."

"You've brought me coffee to discuss having brought my mortal enemy into my home," I said. "A bribe. You've brought me a bribe."

"Yes." They paused. "Would you rather I drink it?"

I groaned, lurching forward unwillingly. Animal brain beat out pride. "God, fuck. Fine. Yes. Give the coffee to me."

They crossed the room with as much grace as one could cross my room—I lived in a jungle whose undergrowth was an impenetrable field of tangled black sweatshirts—and paused beside my bed, held out the mug without changing their expression. I admired their grip strength. Shiloh held the mug with only their index finger hooked around the handle like a trigger, the rest of their fingers folded, knuckles braced against the ceramic cartoon tail.

I grabbed it around the belly and burned my palms immediately. So be it. I brought the mug to my lips and knocked back some scalding black heaven, then took a rattling breath, peered over my bribe at my insidious sibling. I sniffed. Cognition was starting and I knew once it got rolling, it'd be bleak. I nodded at the foot of my bed. "Sit. You're making me nervous."

They sat. They smoothed the silky fabric over their knees, pressed down on a wrinkle with a hint of a frown. "I will text you next time."

"That's a way to start. Damn." I blinked, taken aback. "Asking forgiveness rather than permission usually involves asking for forgiveness. Are we bypassing that part?"

"I am not sorry. It would be an empty gesture, asking you for forgiveness. I respect you too much for that." They lifted their chin and looked regal in a way that made me want to push them off the bed. "Every proper hotel in a three-mile radius is fully booked for some godforsaken reason and I happened to have space I could provide here. This is my home, yes?"

I glowered, took another sip. I liked this blend. "Yeah, yeah, it's your home, I get it. I get it, I do." Still hated it. Not the "this is their home" part. The other part. I pulled a long breath in through flared nostrils, pushed it out between my trench teeth. "Does she not want to kill you now?"

"Oh, no. I think she very much wants to kill me." They paused. "We had a talk. A long talk, I drove her around for an hour or two before it became incredibly clear that she didn't have anywhere to go. I did not love my few days of homelessness, shall we say. I care about her. I had this, you gave me this, and it would be impossible to live with myself and not share it."

I coughed. "She's sparing you because she liked your compassion?"

"She killed my brother." Something flashed in their face and they looked away from me, poured their attention over a spot on my wall instead. "I do not entirely feel compassion."

I squeezed the mug against my chest.

They took a moment. The veins in their eyes stood out with startling clarity, made their Easter egg–blue irises look scary in a way I thought I'd gotten used to by now. They shook their head. Their hair fell from behind their ears, feathered across their face. "I'm a killer and I've got killers for friends. It's all very dramatic." They smiled a little, looked weary. "I don't know, Sideways. I've done inexorably terrible things, and people I love who did not love me were pun-ished for it by people I love. It's such a mess. You know, it's his birthday this weekend? David's, I mean. He—he would've turned fifteen."

I nodded. I didn't know what to say.

"It doesn't bode well." They swallowed, lifted their gaze, focused now on the seam where my wall met my ceiling. "You could've died yesterday because Tatum came to town because my brother died because of Madeline. Because of Levi. Because of me."

"A lot of leaping." I grit my molars. "Let's just blame Tatum for that one."

"Contextualizing helps me intellectualize my feelings away. Sideways, I'm going to get my hunch out of the way. Is that alright?"

"Let's hear it."

"The Scapegracers are not subtle. There are fan accounts about you. You're deservedly famous. It's not hard to find the parties we attend, my family absolutely could if they so desired, and Elias could decide they're illegal, break them up with his boys, and book all of us whenever he'd like. He hasn't. The quiet keeps stretching. I've been thinking about the night David died."

We didn't talk about that much. I scratched a zit on my neck and counted backwards in my head.

"My family came home. Levi and Abel were deranged, dead exhausted and jumpy, and my—Elias—was beside him-self. He collapsed in the foyer. Mother went to him. She and

I had been arguing, she was trying to convince me to stay, but when Elias staggered in, it broke. She stood over him, and my brothers explained to her what had happened to David. They wanted to go back and kill you, Sideways. They wanted to do it that night. Not the witchfinder way. With rifles. But Mother told them to be patient. She made some calls. She came back upstairs, and she told me that I could leave, but that if I left, I wouldn't be hers anymore. I asked her if she was going to hurt me. She told me to be patient. Then she left me, and I packed a bag, and I ran. I stayed in the church for a few hours, I didn't sleep, it was cold. When it was daylight and they hadn't come for me, I started walking back here. Back home. That's when you and the Scapegracers found me."

"Shiloh, I'm so—"

"Spare me. I don't need or want a sorry. The piece that worries me, here, is patience. You four didn't see the Brethren around for two months. That doesn't mean they didn't see you. Witchfinders aren't reckless. They bide their time. They've got enough power that they can afford to be strategic. I might be paranoid, I might be piecing together a puzzle that isn't real, it might be that my family has spared you while they nursed their grief, not because they're planning something big. Tatum showing up makes me *worry.*"

My ears rang. I rubbed my hands together, like I could squeeze the anxiety out. I could taste my own heartbeat. It was sour. "I'll tell the girls. It's . . . I hadn't thought much about the quiet. I've been trying so hard not to think. Are you okay?"

"No. I'm fine, though." They examined the edge of a perfectly buffed nail. "Are you okay?"

"We'll see." I nudged their side with my toe. "Madeline's here. Tell me about that." Convenient, actually, if I was going to Chett her, but I wasn't done being unfair yet. Paranoia squirmed around in my gut. I missed Scratch inside me.

"Yes." They huffed, almost smiled. "She's asleep. She snuck out at maybe five or six, but she must've changed her mind. Came back around eight when I was getting up."

I grimaced into my coffee. I considered throwing up. "Can we go back to talking about Tatum Jenkins?"

"Ugh." They resumed their ceiling staring and leaned back on their elbows, made an obtuse angle of themself. Look at that! I was a font of math facts. I'd done my homework without cheating for the first time in months the other day and it'd made a genius out of me. That college that'd broken my heart was missing out. Shiloh said, "Tatum is the worst person I've ever met."

I frowned. Shiloh had met a lot of shit-tier people.

"The second time I went hunting, it was just with him and none of my brothers." They lolled their head back, stretched out their throat. "He thinks it's fun. You know, among the Brethren, we were considered moderates? The man who I used to call my father thinks he's helping people. I believe that he genuinely believes that. The Jenkins family, less so. They're openly contemptuous of witches. They're punishing people. They're inflicting harm on purpose because they think witches deserve to suffer. They've got *reach* to see to that suffering, too. Tatum's dad is a senator."

I watched the steam curl off my coffee. Senator Jenkins. "Holy shit. Wait, like the smarmy meme evangelical? Sleeps with interns, spews conspiracies out of the side of his mouth?"

Shiloh grimaced. They pulled a hand through their hair. "That'd be the one, yes. Tatum's angling to go into politics as well. He'll inherit his father's district. I would be sincerely shocked if he didn't. They burn specters to pull odds in their favor. He's"—they paused—"I don't know if I've met many people who are so eagerly cruel as Tatum. He and Abel have been best friends since they were born, so I've known him all my life, and he's just—different. Brethren witchfinders aren't kind people, but Sideways, it's a cult. There are degrees of nicety among even the most indoctrinated people. Tatum Jenkins is *vicious*."

"The Jenkinses are the people who do their animal viscera scrying with endangered animals, right?" I recalled with vivid clarity the open stag in the Chantry homestead basement. Guts in a bucket, chest like a mouth. I tried to imagine some *Dead Poets Society* prick kneeling over a zebra that'd been pried wide like that. A wave of queasiness rocked me. I shuddered, scooted backwards into my pillow stack. "Goddamn it."

They grinned. It was an ugly, rueful look. It looked painful. "If we're conceptualizing witchfinding as murder, or at least grievous injury, Tatum's owed a steep shitty true crime docuseries, shall we say. He hunts all the time. Once a month, maybe, since I was fourteen or so—he was sixteen then. He'd show me the specters. He'd keep them wrapped up in a bandanna in his breast pocket so that he could pull them out and show me." They blinked. "He gave me the scar on my face."

There was something about the look in their eye. Real pain, the ugly marring stuff. I couldn't bear it.

"I want to kill him," I said. I sat up a little straighter. "I want to go full Daisy Brink on this guy. I'm serious."

Their grin dropped. "Promise me you won't go looking for him. Sideways, he's dangerous. If I'm right, he'll be around all week, and I— *He could've killed you last night.* Jesus H. Christ, do you know how much blood there was?"

"I was mercifully concussed and kind of beyond comprehending the amount of blood beyond 'some,'" I said. "How did he even find that many raccoons?"

"He's a good hunter." They paused. "Do you know how witchfinding magic works?"

"Mr. Scratch didn't want to teach me," I said. "How?"

They swiped their tongue over their front teeth. "I know you know some of this, but still, for emphasis: energy, whatever we want to call it, is everywhere. It's like air. It's been shaped and calcified into hierarchal structures by human hands across history, let's call that power, and witchfinders tend to fit extremely well into that structure. Witchfinders and their kind made it for themselves. Witches don't fit into that structure. Witch magic flows through the specter, which is a callus that forms when someone experiences a rupture in their life that disjoints them from that power, or when they've built those calluses their whole life because the structure itself is traumatizing. The friction makes for magic. That's why it hurts so much to use. It makes your body sick. It's also why, if you ask anybody I grew up around, magic is evil. If it was meant to happen, it wouldn't hurt." They snickered. "Pretty rich. Exercise should be evil, then. Whatever. Anyway. Witchfinders aren't chafing against power and they can't stir up cosmic energy with that chafing and bring it through their body as magic. So, what's the evil logic, here?"

I shook my head, took a sip.

"Make that pain some other place. Steal it from something else." The whites of their eyes got redder. "If you know how to do it, it's easy to find little alive things and kill them for sake of making a rupture point. If you're good at it, you can just terrorize people and use what comes of that. What Levi did to Yates? The mimic he made in the pool? He scared her on purpose. He made her fear for her physical well-being, maybe her life, so that he could generate a spark to find Addie."

The coffee went cold in my mouth. I couldn't swallow.

"There's a witchfinding spell for immobilization. If Yates couldn't move, that's why." They sniffed. "Tatum does it wrong on purpose."

"Wrong," I repeated.

Shiloh cleared their throat. "The spell only lasts an hour or two. It puts a person under, makes them fall asleep so that they can hold still long enough to actually charge a mimic, or whatever other spell is being cast. That's how everyone who isn't Tatum uses it, that is. Tatum scrambled a clause in the incantation. It immobilizes you, but it keeps you awake. It feels like your blood circulation being cut off all over. Stings like that. I know because he used it on me to charge a mimic once."

I put the coffee on my bedside table. "Come over here."

They crawled in my direction, tucked themself against the headboard beside me, pulled one knee to their chest, and hugged their arms around it. They worried a little snag in a seam by their kneecap.

"Can I hug you?"

They nodded vaguely.

I slung an arm around their shoulder. We stared at the same stretch of wall and I dug around for something I could say that'd make things less awful. I failed. "I need to tell you something. It will make things worse."

"You couldn't make things worse."

"Somebody with a missing specter is coming by the Delacroix House to sift through the store we found," I said. "She'll arrive this weekend."

They tensed all over. They did not breathe.

"Shi?"

"I was wrong," they whispered, voice hoarse. "You made things so much worse."

"How's that going to square with . . ." I stumbled, "with this weekend?"

"With David's birthday?"

"Yeah."

"God, it could be bleak." They rocked their forehead

against their knee and I thought for a moment that they might get sick. They screwed their eyes shut, twisted their mouth into a hard, white line. "Is it going to be the full crowd? All the witches who were around yesterday, I mean? The patience piece is getting grimmer, Sideways."

"I think it will be most of them, yes. Maurice isn't letting anybody sort through the specters we recovered until she's gone through them herself, and I got the sense that most of them will stick around for that." I didn't unhook my arm from around their shoulders. "Her name is Molly. Is she one of yours?"

"I don't know." They exhaled with a hiss. "I don't remember. I never—I was not particularly concerned with names back then. Maybe. Probably. Might as well have been, even if she wasn't." They turned their head and looked at me. "She's the only person alive with a specter in that pile, then."

"Yes," I said.

"So those other people died," they said. "I killed someone."

"Yes," I said. "You did."

Shiloh took a moment. Their eyes unfocused. Eventually they said, "I don't believe in hell. If it were real, it'd be a cop-out. It'd abdicate responsibility in life for sake of some promised unseen punishment later that'd fix nothing. It'd fix nothing. Hell is masturbatory egotistical nonsense. Hell is incarceration, hell is a rhetorical trap, hell is an excuse," they said faintly, "and I'd sign myself up in an instant."

"Hell is real," I said weakly. "I've seen the ads."

Their shoulders shook. I wasn't sure if they were laughing

or crying. I wasn't sure if I felt bad for them, but I certainly felt bad writ large. I pulled my evil sibling close to me, and they rested their head on my shoulder and gasped there, and I leaned my cheekbone against their brow bone and watched slats of light fall across my wardrobe. I reached over them, took the coffee back up, and choked down another sip. It was tepid now, but I'd burned off my taste buds and that would have to be fine. "So does Madeline live here now? Say no challenge."

They cleared their throat and didn't look at me. "I don't think she will, not permanently. Not like how I live here. We talked a long time last night. I don't think you should be privy to most of it."

"Fine by me," I said.

"Right. Well." They took a breath. "I'm going to give her my trust."

"Your trust?"

"My money. I've got a trust fund. I checked, it's still there. I thought it wouldn't be. Inconvenient side effect of waiting until I was eighteen to disown me, I guess. Would've been lovely if I'd had known that and could've used it to, I don't know, sleep in a hotel instead of a condemned moldy chapel. Anyway. It's not—I mean, it was meant to be my college fund and something to help with rent for a year or two. Petite bourgeoisie money. Ugly, I know."

"The fact that you say shit like petite bourgeoisie now." I frowned. "I've got my mom's life insurance money. I get it. Weird little pockets of miasmic cash privilege."

"Mm-hmm," they said, skating over the fact that they'd

been an entire libertarian when I'd met them. "Anyway, I've got a very good scholarship. Full tuition, room and board. I'm just looking at book expenses. So, I'm going to give her my money is the point. She's going to take it and go far away. Addie is the most resourceful person I've ever met. She'll make it out there. I don't think she's planning on going to college yet. She's got most of an associate degree, community college stuff she did the past two years. You know how East High kids are. Anyway. I imagine she'll be here until I figure out the best way to wire things over, and then she'll be gone."

I whistled a low note. "Fuck, Shi."

"I know." They frowned. "This week is going to be bizarre. I seriously doubt my family would start anything with so many witches consolidated in one spot, they're smart enough to guess how those numbers would play out. Still. Awful."

"Yeah," I said. "Yeah, I think you're probably right about that."

"The trial. You snuck her out of there. Why'd you do that?"

"She asked me to help her."

"You are an exceptional person, Sideways."

"Do not start, I will eject you from my room if you start."

"Alright." They straightened up a little, leaned into my arm. "Is the witch community still cool with you after you smuggled their prisoner out before they could cosplay being my ex-brothers?"

"Fuck." I coughed. "Mostly, I think. I'm on thin ice. Shi, can you do something for me?"

"I can try," they said.

"Can you show me a picture of Tatum Jenkins?"

They jerked their head in my direction. Their nose brushed my cheek in the swing. "Sideways Eloise Marie Rothschild Pike, I swear on all things holy, if you so much as think about going after this guy, I'm going to—"

"Chill. Chill, I have zero plans of tracking this guy down, okay? I just want to know what the guy looks like. How am I supposed to defend myself if I don't have an image in my head of what I ought to avoid?"

Shiloh made a quiet, anguished sound in their throat. They felt around their chest and produced their phone from their pocket, unlocked it. Their hair fell in their face again. It looked nice all fucked up like that, I thought. Ruffled made the baby blond look more textural, less wispy flat. "Lucky you, he didn't block me on Instagram after I went private." They curled their lip. "Sideways, I cannot express to you the degree to which I hate this fucking guy."

"He broke my face, so. Same," I said. Not to mention the absolute horror show of every other thing I hated him for, which I could not even inwardly mention without wolfing out. "Show me the bastard."

They turned their phone around and waved their fingertips around the perimeter of its screen. "The bastard."

There he was. Tatum Jenkins reclined on a sailboat in board shorts and a polo, its collar turned up to the wind. He was lean and tanned, sandy hair tousled, smiling with unnerving hospital tile–white teeth, and I had the immediate sense that this picture was subliminally selling me something—shoes, maybe, or a general department-store sale. He had the edge of a tattoo on one bicep, what looked like a cross and a time. Or a date? "Sixteen-thirty," I read aloud, squinting.

"Judges 16:30." Shiloh rubbed the bridge of their nose. "Death of Samson."

"That means nothing to me, I've gotta say."

"Never change," they groaned. "Would it mean something to you if I told you that he's got Psalm 109 on his calf?"

"Absolutely not."

"You've lived a charmed life, Sideways Pike."

"I literally was neglected in foster care because my mom was hit by a train when I was eight."

"Holy shit. Holy shit, god, I'm sorry, that's awful." They flinched, shook their head. "I didn't know. I retract earlier statement about your life being charmed." A beat. "It *is* charmed in the sense of it being magic. Magic charms."

"Turns out I hate you, actually."

"That's reasonable."

"I've got a hunch." I sat up a little straighter, lugged my arm over their head. It'd been losing a touch of circulation. Pins and needles. I shook it out, flexed, scowled, scratched an acne bump on the back of my neck. "Could you hand me the *VMM*? The second volume. Thicker."

They shot me a bewildered look.

"The old spell book." I'd almost called it my old spell book. They'd want them back soon, the Pythonesses. God,

I wanted to cry. "Should be to your left in the circle on the floor."

"I know," they said. "I just didn't think you'd ever want me to touch it."

"I shouldn't even be touching it." Felt like acid in my mouth, admitting that. I forced a toothy smirk on, gnawed on my vile unbrushed tongue. "Pass it to me, would you?"

They looked me over, then complied. Shiloh had long limbs. They didn't even have to get up to fetch it. They rested the book in my lap, and I flipped the pheasant-claw clasp, pushed it open, smothered the kid part of my mind that still felt seen and held and beloved by this book, or its first installment anyway. I had Mr. Scratch. I had my own book. This one had given to me what it could give to me and I was grateful and angry and whatever. Thoughts for another time. I shoved the book in Shiloh's direction and leaned over, flipped to a would-be blank page that read, SPECTER.

"Touch that," I said.

"The page?"

"Uh-huh."

They lifted a hand and suspended it in the air for a moment. They looked at the word, then at their own fingertips, the space between the two. They looked at me. They lowered their hand, brushed the pad of their thumb over the S's bottom hook.

The word bled minty green.

SAME MISTAKES

When Jing texted me, Shiloh had been lying facedown on the floor for upwards of an hour. I nudged them with a toe sometimes, gently beaned the back of their head with the kitschy Halloween stuffed animals that peppered my bedspread, but they did little by means of acknowledgment. A big-eyed mummy lay on its side in the middle of their back, a ratty owl in a wizard's hat near their left elbow, a candy-corn snake across the back of their knees. They did not move at all. Their hair splayed around their head like petals on an upturned daisy, overbright in contrast with the black T-shirt overgrowth they'd laid themself upon. If the stuffed animals didn't rise and fall, I would've thought that they had experienced some cardiac event and died.

"You could say I witchfound you," I said as I closed the *VMM*. "The tables have turned."

Shiloh made a wounded animal sound.

"Being a witch is very cool. Do you feel cool?"

"I am having a crisis."

"All cool people are in crisis."

Silence again. It was like talking to a mossy log. I leaned my elbows on my knees and peered down at them, gave them another nudge. "You are not nearly as pumped about your newfound access to magic as I thought you might be." I hadn't thought much, actually, in any direction about this. It hadn't occurred to me until they'd brought up Tatum how likely it'd be, them having a specter of their own. I got the sense that it was complicated because, yeah, history and so on, but still. Was there not an initial spark of all-consuming joy upon the discovery of one's own magic? They'd come around, I told myself. I covered the *VMM* with a pillow so that I wouldn't have to look at it and could avoid a crisis of my own, and that's when I got the notifications from Curse Daddy.

hey good afternoon bitch. are u working rn?

Nah we're closed today why

can u meet me at ice cream gasoline in 15

Yeah totally wait are you ok

ya bb im ok lol

"Ice cream gasoline" meant a gas station about two blocks from here. It was always open and barely staffed, and the Scapegracers and I had committed many a misdemeanor there, and I held a perverse fondness for it as a meeting place now. Small towns, man. I stood up, peeled a flannel off a rung of my footboard and shouldered it on over the shirt I'd slept in. "Changing," I said aloud. "Ass warning."

Shiloh made a quiet sound and did not lift their head.

I kicked off my sleep sweats, jerked on a pair of jeans. Grommet belt, wallet, wallet chain, second wallet chain, carabiner, mismatched socks with holes and relative cleanliness, beanie, leather jacket—I ran through a mental list of things I might need and couldn't come up with anything else.

"On the wardrobe," Shiloh said into my floor.

"What?"

"You are wearing the shirt you slept in. Gross. Wardrobe."

"You're wearing the shirt you slept in," I murmured in a squeaky, mean little juvenile *nah nah* voice under my breath, then peered around once, unsure initially of what they'd asked me to find.

There was a parcel on the wardrobe. Something wrapped in tissue paper, rather.

"Did I miss my birthday?"

"Did you?"

"Nah." I frowned. Summer birthday. My brain was oozing out of my each and every pore. I took up the mystery object, unwrapped it, and shook out yet another black T-shirt. It said something in veiny illegible lightning letters and across its breast, two monsters—busty ladies from the waist up, enormous millipedes from the hips down—stabbed claymores through one another's hearts. "Aw, what the fuck." I hugged it to my chest. "This is so sweet, thank you."

"One of the DJs at Homo Erectus makes these." They shifted their head just enough to reveal one eye and turn it up on me, a shock of blue against their pasty face and my goth polyester oil slick. "Thought you'd like it."

"You thought right." I shucked off all my top layers, pulled the new shirt over my head, then tugged back on the flannel and the jacket, smoothed my hands down my front. The jacket was lined with studs, so smoothing didn't really do shit, but the gesture felt consolidating. I hunted around for a pair of work boots, the sturdy ones for hauling furniture. "I'm going out."

"I gathered that."

"Are you gonna be cool having your witch crisis without me for a few hours?"

"Will you be gone hours?"

"No idea, but you know."

"I should be," they said, "alive."

"Madeline isn't allowed in my room while I'm out. Or while I'm in. Just keep her out of my shit, okay?" I laced up, double-knotted. These boots were steel-toed and they made me feel like a giant, which was cool. I stood up, rolled my shoulders back, shoved my hands into my pockets. Weird little bits and bobs in there, a thimble for sewing patches, loose coins, a bottle cap or two. Little dolls for impromptu hexing. A cicada husk. An unwrapped lozenge that I hoped hadn't already been in my mouth. I sniffed, cracked my neck to the side, popped the big knobby vertebrae that fused my nape to my shoulders. "Hey, I'm proud of you. Seriously. Welcome to the team."

They made a low sound.

I stepped over them and waded through my room wreck, closed the door behind me when I left. Down the hall, down the stairs. I passed Boris on the way down, and he flashed me a quick smile, murmured something incoherent about my shirt. He had his phone tucked between his cheek and his shoulder. I think he was allergic to the prospect of any sort of headphones/AirPods/accessory for listening situation. I waved two fingers, crossed into the shop, through the shop, and out of the shop into the open Sycamore Gorge air. It tasted green and wet and sweet, a cloying, mushy spring flavor that I didn't particularly like but would miss when it was gone.

I set off down the street.

I hadn't lived in this town my entire life. I wasn't born here. The decade I'd been steeped in it had marked me, though, in ways of which I wasn't always proud. Every step outside was a contradiction of hypervigilance and ease—I knew everything, recognized and anticipated every weed in the sidewalk cracks, every notch in the building facades, the bent-up syringes, the candy wrappers, the dalmatian spots of ancient gum, and I knew everyone, and everyone knew me. I might not know their name, but I damn well knew their face. Might know where they worked, or who their kid might be. They knew me because I was the queer daughter of the queer antique dealers. My difference was socially established, and even if it wasn't, I was easy to spot. My butchness was a beacon. I was a big gay lighthouse for violences big and small. A *big* gay lighthouse. Quarrel with me and see what happens.

It was a decent day, warmer than yesterday had been. Grayish, shadowless. I had no idea what time it was and didn't care to pull out my phone and check. I stomped through curls of dirty snow and over rainbow slick puddles. I nodded at someone who waved at me, a shop patron who might've been a lunch lady back in middle school. I petted a dog attached to a guy who worked concessions at Daisy's football games. Good dog, too. Square-headed silly pit bull with a goofy, pinkish smile. Wish I were a square-headed silly pit bull with a goofy, pinkish smile. I'd really been fucked over with the whole human bit.

I crossed the street, kicked a bottle, trudged some more, crossed another street.

The gas station hummed. Its signage flickered erratically, like a twitching eye. No cars in the lot, but the lights, as ever, were on inside. Flyers for lost cats, youth groups, and yard sales papered the windows, and the fluorescence that bled through them took on a yellowish tint. I walked between the skeletal gas pumps, managed not to trip on the curb, and pulled open the door.

Bell chimes. I glanced around and didn't spot Jing, which meant I'd definitely beat her here. She was hard to miss. Still, I wandered up and down the snack aisles under the pretext of looking for her, eyeballed the ghastly canned beer in the coolers, the metallic sacks of salt and grease, dried fruits, powdered donuts, rectangles that claimed a right to sandwichhood. Hot dogs rolled on dungeon bars. Coffee burned in the bottom of a pot. I'd made all the rounds that felt defensible, trudged around toward the counter.

A wall of ice cream separated me from the man who separated me from the wall of assorted tobacco products. The man wore a pinstriped smock. He looked like hell, just unspeakably miserable. Knew him from somewhere, because that was inevitable, but I couldn't place it now. White spots of pressure bloomed on either side of his mouth. Rather than greeting me, he stared at my chest. I wondered if I should feel weird about that.

"I didn't see you at the show," he said eventually.

"Oh." I glanced down at the hot killer millipede babes. "Were you at Homo Erectus?"

"Bless you." The guy didn't blink. It occurred to me that I'd seen him around at parties—farm parties, not Scapegracer parties. This guy might've been someone's older brother. "Do you want something?"

"Medium black cherry malt." I cleared my throat. "Uh, thanks."

"Okay." He turned away from me and gathered the required components of black cherry malt making. I frankly wasn't sure what a malt tasted like, or what that word meant. When I ordered for myself, I usually just got a bowl of whatever the special happened to be, or chocolate barring that.

He put something in a blender. My eyes glazed over, and I thought about Shiloh's specter, and what would've happened if I hadn't been the one to think up that possibility. I wondered if the Chantry family would pull a specter out of their own kid. If there were conversion therapy torture camps for Brethren witch kids.

The guy turned back around and put the malt on the counter between us.

I pulled a few bills out of my wallet and handed them over. "Keep the change," I said.

Bell chimes.

I looked over my shoulder and there was Jing Gao in a screaming red windbreaker. She wore it open over a white dress, her hair in twin French braids, her earlobes heavy with dangly stars, a bandanna around her neck. She had a backpack with her, not her school one. This one was plasticky and mummified with stickers. She used it for overnights, and once to sneak candles into a dance club. She smiled when she saw me. Made eyes at the malt. "Without me?"

"For you," I said. I swept it off the counter and offered it to her. "What's up?"

"You got me a malt," she said.

I brandished it like a knife.

Her smile warped a little, got wider, then she forced it off and donned something in the vein of seriousness. "Don't mind if I do," she said, and took it from me. "Step outside with me?"

"Alright." I put my hands back in my pockets.

She led me back out the doors, and I followed with my heartbeat fluttering in my teeth. It was unseasonably warm, I thought. Low forties, maybe into the fifties. A little too much for my layers, but chill enough that I wondered about Jing's legs. Broadly, I wondered about them. I shook my head like that'd cool all the rampant wondering.

She took me around the building's edge, to the back where its wall faced a line of barren trees. Names and scribbles were etched in the concrete. Jing lingered under a string of arrow hearts. Emerald bottle shards glittered underfoot, but the glass aside, she was the only thing that broke the bleak gray monotony. She put the straw in her mouth. Her seriousness fractured. "Is this black cherry?"

I shrugged affirmatively.

She shook her head. "You remembered. That's hot."

I made a face like that pit bull had earlier.

"Alright. On to business." She took a thoughtful sip. "I don't trust the Delacroix witches as a whole. Individually, sure, but the vibes were exceptionally weird to me last night. I love that place, but some of the covens—some of them rubbed me the wrong way, and I've got no idea what to make of them. Cool people but like, to what end."

"That's about where I'm at."

"I feel weird about the idea of giving them a rundown of everything going on with us."

"What's going on with us?"

"The Chantry family, I guess. Whoever set that witch trap." She shook her head. "I want people to be safe, and people should know the extent of the threat. I think what I'm saying is, I'm not sure if we should share about Shiloh."

"That's up to Shi, I think—but I'm inclined to agree with you." I scuffed my toe in the gravel. "They've got a specter. Don't know if they'd do anything differently now that they've found that out."

"They do?" She tilted her head to the side. "What color is it?"

"Minty," I said.

"Cute." She rotated her wrist and the paper straw traced hypnotic circles in the air. "I wonder how many people have specters and never find out about it. I'd wager the numbers are steep." She furrowed her brow. "I wanted to ask you something about Shi, actually."

"Yeah?"

"They know how witchfinding magic works, don't they?"

"They do," I said. I shifted my weight, eyed a few birds on a distant wayward elm branch. Meaty, slumped-over birds. Turkey vultures or something of that ilk. "Why?"

"I want them to shut off my mimic." She reached into her dress and withdrew it, held it between her middle and ring finger in the space beside her jaw. It'd be so innocuous looking if I didn't know what it was, what it'd been made to do. A bead, a marble, nothing significant. "I've been thinking about where I want to hide it, and every idea feels gross. I don't want it in my room. I don't want it in my house. I was an inch from going out in the woods and burying it, or smashing it up with a hammer, but I'm afraid of accidentally setting it off somehow. I don't know. I'm definitely overthinking it, but I'd sleep better if it stopped existing, point-blank. It's a liability. If you took this home and showed it to Shiloh, would they be able to turn it off?"

I sucked in a breath and held it for a count. "Yes," I hissed on the exhale. "I'm pretty sure they'd be able to do that. We'll destroy it."

"Good," she said. She stretched her hand forward, and I mirrored her, cupped my hand for her. She dropped the mimic in my palm. I curled my fist around it. It was warm against my skin. My head was on fire. I put it in my jacket pocket and stared at the cigarette butts on the ground between our feet. She took a half step nearer to me. "Sideways."

"Mm-hmm?"

"I've got something else."

I swallowed thickly, looked up at her without lifting my chin. My eyelashes feathered the edge of my vision. She tucked her malt under the crook of her arm, pinned it to her rib cage, and pulled her backpack around her side. She unzipped it. Fluidly, she reached into the bag, and out came a thick, fresh book. It was a novel petaled with sticky notes. The latest book in our two-person book club.

"I finished last night," she said. "I couldn't sleep. I was so wired, so I just stayed up and read the last half in one shot. I cried like a kid." She smiled a little, flicked her eyes from the cover to me and back down again. "Tell me how you're feeling when you finish, okay?"

"Of course," I said. I took it in my hands and held it delicately, like it could feel how I handled it. Rubbed a thumb down its spine. I wished I'd brought a bag to carry it, settled on tucking it in my inside breast pocket for now. It was some feat that the pocket could manage it. This book was massive. I accepted that it fit out of some act of minor spontaneous magic. I buttoned my jacket up, hugged it against my ribs. "Thanks."

"This is a look," she said, looking me up and down.

"What, book lump is good?"

"The whole ensemble." She pursed her lips, considered me, then felt around her neck. She hooked her bandanna with a finger, searched for its knot, and with a twist of one knuckle it was undone. She took a step closer to me. She lifted up on tiptoe, slipped it around my neck, tied a knot at the hollow of my throat. "There. Some color."

I twisted the bandanna around, pulled its wide section up over my nose, waggled my brows at her. "Do I look like a bandit?"

She tugged it back down. "You always look like a bandit."

"I'll take that as a compliment."

"It was intended as one." She huffed a sigh. "I'm due for a family dinner in T-minus twenty minutes. I've got to get my ass across town on foot, so I should get going."

"Yeah," I said. I flattened my hand over the bandanna, pressed it against my throat. "I'll see you tomorrow?"

"You will." She snickered, thrust her hands in her windbreaker's pockets. "See you." She walked around me at that, slipped from sight.

I stood stock-still for a moment after she was gone. I pulled the bandanna up over my nose again, shoved my shoulder blades back against the wall. It smelled like her perfume and the sweet salt of her sweat. I squeezed my eyes shut and tried to live in it for a moment, in the weight of her book on my chest, in the fabric's texture where it rubbed the seam of my ears and my jaw. No thoughts. No worry or higher comprehension. I shivered a little, but I wasn't cold. I felt like I was melting. I was a crayon on a sidewalk in July.

I shoved myself off the wall. This was too much, whatever I was feeling, to bring back home straightaway. I needed to walk it off, and when some of the nervous energy was gone, I'd go home and curl up and devour this book in one sitting, assuming Shiloh wasn't on fire and Madeline wasn't on fire and so on. I wanted to know what happened that made Jing cry. She'd annotated the other books she'd let me borrow, and I wondered if she'd marked where it'd happened. It was still a horrible thought, her crying. Walk it off, walk it off, walk it off.

I took off in the opposite direction Jing had left in, slumped around the gas station's perimeter. My head was brimming, I didn't move with much intention. This was motion for motion's sake. I only stopped at the front side of the gas station because of the muscle car there. There hadn't been a muscle car there before. Maybe a stupid thought, as

cars showing up at a gas station was hardly cause for concern, but this car was *weird*. It was ostentatious in a way that
drew attention to itself, sculpted-looking, its paint job uncannily white and clean. It wasn't parked at a pump, but pulled
into one of the ill-conceived parking slots, and left running.
License plate from a state over.

I hung around for a moment, just to see. Just for a peek.
I thought it'd be funny to get a glimpse of what asshole corresponded to this evil ugly wealthmobile. It'd be an anecdote
to torture Julian with later. He couldn't stand muscle cars,
had some aesthetic objection that he'd contorted into a moral
one. Even better if I could describe a wayward nouveau riche
grandpa or a red-faced teenager for spice.

The door opened with a shrill chime sound.

A boy stepped onto the curb with a six-pack dangling
from one finger. Bronzy, indescribably American Eagle–
looking boy. He wore sunglasses for no discernible reason,
a sweatshirt over his button-down, a pair of salmon shorts.
The air around his head warped a little, like his head bruised
space as it moved through it. I'd never seen him before, I
thought. Also, maybe, I had. There was a tattoo below his
knee, a twist of script. I thought I saw, *Let this be the reward
of mine adversaries from the Lord.*

I cleared my throat, cocked my head to the side. Jing's
bandanna stayed put across the bridge of my nose, hugged
the line of my scar. I took half a step nearer to him. I dropped
my voice and said, "Tatum?"

The boy looked up, glanced around with an earnest expression of, *Huh what?*

I took a step closer, then another. "Tatum Jenkins?"

He turned to face me and curled his lip, expression bored, mouth slack. "Do I know you?"

Rage took me. It foamed in my veins and skimmed over my vision. White-hot Pop Rocks rage.

Oh, buddy. You fucking will.

THIRTEEN

NAKED HEROES ON URNS

His beer bottles shattered on the curb like drops of rain.

I had him by the back of the sweatshirt. He looked strong, but he was my height and hadn't seen it coming somehow, despite the visual cues to the contrary. Maybe Tatum Jenkins wasn't a guy who was used to real live threats. His mistake, whatever. Be smarter next time. I hauled him around the building's edge, back to the place Jing had taken me. There weren't cameras back there. No sight lines with other buildings, only visible from the road at odd angles. I could get unlucky, but I wasn't feeling unlucky right now. Boy, I sure was *feeling*.

He'd almost killed me. This fucker had almost killed me. He'd almost killed Jing, and godforsaken Madeline, and he'd done it indiscriminately. We would've been arbitrary girl deaths. Belt notches, if that.

And *Shiloh*.

I thought about the look on Shiloh's face. The scar on Shiloh's face.

Rancid sugar rush sparkles gushed up and down the

lengths of my arms. I buzzed all over. Marrow thrummed. My pulse beat in my teeth. Tatum's feet worked, and I knew that once he caught himself he'd turn on me, that he'd be as hard as me. He would not fall to the earth like a rock and start moaning. He would not be another Austin Grass.

He caught gravel with one foot and whirled. He went livid, wound himself back. He was going to hit me, or maybe hurl his whole body at me. He'd crush me with momentum like that.

I still had him by the back of his neck.

I jerked to the left and pushed him along, put my weight behind his swing. I closed my fist in the fabric. I slammed his face against the brick.

His sunglasses snapped. It made a horrible sound, worse somehow than the crunch and the wheeze. They must've been expensive. The glass was heavy, didn't shatter when the frame gave out. It jutted down in one blunt piece. It sliced open his cheekbone. Red fell fast. It spilled down the side of his face, splashed his sweatshirt, made ugly Rorschach splatters on the wall. He shuddered hard, opened his mouth, and gasped. I must've knocked the wind from him. His tongue lolled, looked weird and blotched with purple like a chow chow's. It brushed brick. "You fucking bastard," he managed.

Bastard. Did he think I was a man?

Rage foamed in me again and I slammed my boot into his ankle, shoved downward with the hand at the back of his neck. He left a smear. It was thick and dark and smelled like money. I wanted him on the ground. I wanted his face in the dirt, I wanted my sole on the back of his neck, I chanted something in the back of my head that was harsher, rougher than magic. Frenetic broken nothing. Something Shi had said, something about hell. Well, I'll be damned. I agreed with Shiloh, I didn't think hell was real, but fuck if I wouldn't give Tatum Jenkins an immersive simulation. I grit my molars, my gut boiled. I threw him to the earth and drove my boot into his rib cage.

He thrashed hard, sputtered like a carp. Veins flared in his face. His lips vanished, and he snarled, spat bloody bubbles on the dead blond grass. He clawed at the dirt, searched for purchase. "Ease up on me," he hissed, "I swear to god—"

"Fuck you," I dripped. I stepped on his wrist.

He coughed, an awful, ragged sound. "My wallet."

I blinked.

"My wallet is in my back pocket," he heaved. "Just take it."

Huh, look at that. He thought he was getting mugged. Something animal squirmed in my stomach. I looked him over, this mess of a witchfinder under my heel, and I scowled under the bandanna.

Ask and you shall receive, I guess.

I crouched down and made for it. Oxblood leather. I tugged it out of his pocket and held it with two fingers, shoved it down my neckline with a feeling of odd satisfaction.

Tatum rolled his head to the side and flashed his teeth at me.

He torqued. His leg struck out, swept my feet out from under me, knocked me off the grass and his wrist. The ground flew up around my face. My vision clapped. Instinct carried me and I rolled, tried to cover my belly, tried to get my knees under my chest. He slammed his knee in my gut before I could manage. A gasp knocked out of me. I kicked, wrenched myself to the left, got myself out from under his shin but fuck he was fast, and heavier than he had any right to be. He scrambled over me, fell over me, slammed his forearm across my clavicle and pressed so hard my breathing hitched. He oozed on me. Blood fell out of his face and drenched Jing's bandanna. God, I was a terrible friend.

"You're dead," he breathed. He grinned at me, leered at me, ribs heaving under his pale sweatshirt. His eyes looked enormous, an impossible searing lime green, and they pressed out of his skull and bulged at my face. They looked overripe and gooey. If he shook his head, they'd *shlunk* out of his face and burst on my forehead like the yolks on over-easy eggs. "I am going to obliterate you, get it? I am going to break you and break the broken pieces of you, and I'm going to stuff your slime in the trunk of my car, and I'm going to feed it to my hunting dogs. You will be a stain when I'm done with you. You won't exist anymore."

My brain frothed. I saw glitter and white-hot starbursts. I opened my mouth and said with a conjured Daisy Brink affectation: "You're really fucking ugly."

He panted. His expression was stuck on his face. "What?"

I slammed my forehead against his forehead.

His eyes rolled around in his skull.

I wrenched my hips left, heaved him right, pushed all my weight against him and pitched him off me enough to get myself out from under him. Our legs tangled; I yanked mine loose. Something throbbed around my ankle, but I shoved recognition of that out of my head. He clapped his hands down my chest, clawed at my jacket, clambered for fistfuls that the studs made impossible to grasp. He pulled at me, tore at me. The book banged against my sternum. He hooked his fingers in the pockets, ripped his nails around the buttons. He snarled and I got my boot under his diaphragm and shoved hard.

He stumbled backwards. He caught himself in the grass, but it took a second, and I just needed a second.

I bolted. I peeled out of there, made for the tree line. I heard him, I knew he wasn't far back. He was after me. He was on my tail. The turkey vultures swooped around between naked branches over my head. I crashed through dead overgrowth and vicious little green vines, I lurched between birch trees that sloughed bark like bandages, I braced for the incline. The ground got steeper underfoot. The angle sloped hard. I ducked under a low-hanging branch, sidestepped an abandoned bottle, made my way down to the creek bed.

He was after me. I knew it in my hindbrain, I felt it. He was close by me. I could smell him, the wet copper muck I'd made of his face and the cologne he wore, something cloying with musk and vetiver and gushy cut melon. It clung in the back of my throat. The creek wound its way through the trees, cut a shallow bank out of the earth. It was runoff. Dirty water, smoky translucent specked with poisonous grayish flecks, stuff I'd played in as a kid. Rocks jutted like tusks. I pressed forward, boots in the water. There was a concrete pipe up ahead. Drainage culvert. It rose from the water like a mouth. Four foot tall, maybe, walls as thick as my hand was wide. It ran under a road and opened on the other side, spilled into more space like this, a strip of dubious water that ran behind a strip of apartment buildings and a laundromat to cut between more trees.

I didn't look behind me. I had faith in universal entropy just enough.

I dropped to a crouch and trudged into the dark.

Sound cut. There was only a glimmer of light at the far end. Something scurried, a possum maybe, a feral cat, a monster, who gives a fuck. My boots broke the water, and the splash sound was skull splitting. The ceiling dripped and I chose not to question why. My pulse hammered. I was sick with it, sick on myself. I breathed through my teeth, mouth open, eyes darting in the dark. The tunnel accordioned out in front of me. It kept going. It hadn't felt nearly this long when I was a kid. I hadn't had to crouch when I was a kid. The squirmy thing moved past me to the right, disturbed the water, sloshed my ankle. I made a sound but swallowed it with the bile. Crouching made my body scream. The concrete smelled slimy above me. I didn't want to touch it. I grimaced; it peeled up into a grin. I pressed forward and forward and forward. Nothing hurt. My brain was a chemical factory. It was a firework warehouse in a dry summer. I felt giddy. I had his wallet. I had the bastard's wallet. I'd mugged Tatum Jenkins, I'd hurt the man who'd hurt my loved ones. He wanted to feed me to his dogs.

I stepped out into the sunlight and sucked in a fresh double lungful of air. Air was colder over here. I'd come up somewhere that felt different, intrinsically different. The sky flushed maroon. It looked like a spill of chocolate milk. My feet were freezing, my socks were soaked. I climbed up, climbed out of the bank. The patches of woodland spread up like wings on either side of me. Steep was my only option. The inclines were ridiculous, just funhouse levels of silly and horrific. I lunged up one. I caught a sapling in my fist and pulled myself up with it. The roots whined. My wet boots weren't finding purchase on the dry leaves. The ground was too dead for this. I needed a tangle of weeds, needed something green and leggy to pull myself along. I needed spikes. I coughed up a laugh. I wasn't sure when I'd blinked last and my eyes burned. My vision went glassy, and I saw too much of the world at once with overwhelming panoramic clarity. I felt like a gyroscope. I was so nauseous I thought I might collapse. I clawed my way up a little higher, the dead flora gave way into a patch of slippery fossil-studded rocks and I nearly slipped and died but didn't, I nearly split my skull but didn't. I hauled myself up higher still. I could see something constructed. There was a low chain-link fence above me. It was the most beautiful thing in the world.

I put my fingers through the wires and vaulted. I scrambled up the side and slammed myself down on the lawn beyond it with one breath. My lungs clapped when I landed. My mouth popped open. I panted, seethed all over. I felt the magic bleed out of me—or was adrenaline not magic? Whatever it was, my righteous zinging bio-glitter was leaving me and I wasn't sure how much further I could press on like this. I rolled onto my hands and knees, dry retched, made my lungs work. I imagined my lungs filling up like water balloons, imagined that oxygen was something that I'd be able to see as it sloshed in and out of my mouth. My stomach burned. Jing's book felt like an anchor and it'd tear me through the earth's crust. It was a fucking miracle it was still on me. Must really want to be read. That was hilarious for some reason. I laughed again and it made my sides hurt.

I waited for a sign of him. I pressed my forehead against the grass, it needled against my scalp, but I couldn't pick out discernible sounds. Bird sounds, distant car sounds, but no human sounds. Bad news for me if the turkey vultures had found me on the other side of this tunnel, if they'd followed me all this way. I was dead meat.

Couldn't hear him, though.

This was stupid. He was a hunter. Shiloh said he was a good hunter. He was good at hunting animals and he was good at hunting women. Why did I think I would be able to hear him? Why did I think I'd be able to see this bastard coming?

Why did I attack him in the first place?

All this growing up I'd done, and I was still doomed to be me. Violence felt like me. Wrath was a second home to me and it quickened through my body and I hated myself and felt horribly nostalgic at once. I loved the way this felt. I loved feeling so much. I hated myself. I was scared sick. I hoped it'd leave a scar. I hoped he'd carry around what I'd done to him forever. What a thought, that he'd killed god knows how many witches and all I'd done to him is fuck up his Ken doll face. How staggeringly inadequate. I'd fixed nothing. Could get myself killed over nothing.

I pushed myself up. I was kneeling now. I peered down into the ravine, but I didn't see him there. I wondered if he'd given up and turned back in the pipe. I wondered if he'd followed me in at all.

I looked opposite the woods and familiarity hit me. I knew this place and not like how I knew every place in this godforsaken town. I stood up. My knees were wet, and the balmy forty-five felt bitter all at once. My hands ached. Fingertips slightly swollen. I hadn't even hit him! I lumbered toward the set of apartment complexes. They were all identical, a hideous office building facsimile of a Tudor style, white faces cut with dark wood, roofs high, materials garishly synthetic. I staggered between two of them, wheezing, dizzy.

I passed the third when I realized why I recognized these. Chelsea and Daisy lived in one of these.

But holy mother of fuck—which?

I fumbled around my chest, then up and down my thighs.

My phone was on me, thank god. I felt its shape. I pulled it from its pocket ditch, turned it over on my palm. I'd cracked the screen. A glitch rainbow starburst bled out from the spot I'd shattered it, but the edges of the home screen were still intact, and when I dragged my thumb over the glass it still unlocked. I couldn't make out my contacts well. I felt clumsy, too big for my body. I had an exciting new tremor and fine motor control was beyond me. I managed to pull up a contact that was hers, I hoped. I pressed call. Daisy never had her ringer on. My chances were slim to none.

It rang and rang.

Breathing ached. I took a few steps forward without intention beyond putting a few more stitches of distance between me and the creek. I couldn't feel my toes. I worked the muscles in my face, stretched my expression out just to prove to myself that I still could.

She didn't pick up.

I called again. More ringing, internal and external.

There was a miserable picnic table that'd been painted in the fall without consideration of what water did to unsealed pigment, and only grime-slicked rust curls of blue clung to it now. The wood looked soft around its bolts. I jumped up onto it, it whined beneath me, and I spun around once, scanned for him. I kept bracing for his bloody sweatshirt to materialize between those Tudor apartment buildings. People would see it if we made a scene here. If I killed him here that'd be the end of me, but if I didn't kill him here that'd be the end of me. I tried to think and hit a block. Strategy evaded me. The script in my head was pre-human and livid. There was no plan. If he came here I'd jump on him. What had I done?

She didn't pick up.

Numb and mechanical, I moved to call her a third time. Incoming call cut me off. I couldn't see who was calling, the shatter obscured their contact details, but I picked up on nerves alone and shoved my phone to my ear.

"What gives, Sideways? Why are you calling me? I am painting my goddamned nails."

"I'm outside," I said. My voice sounded funny. It was too high and all air.

"What?"

"Daisy, I'm outside, are you home please say you're fucking home I need—"

"Wait, wait." I heard rustling, movement. It was her, but even with the phone static as material reassurance the shuffling made my skin crawl, made me stare back at the woods again with my pulse in my teeth. He was back there. He was somewhere in there, somewhere down the slope. "I can see you. I'll be right down."

"Can I come in?"

"Our buzzer's broken, just wait—"

"Quickly, Daze."

"Okay, okay, Jesus, chill out."

I bounced on my toes. My teeth chattered and I hugged one arm around my stomach, shoved the book into my belly. A squirrel leaped from one tree to another, skittered up and down the trunk, and I watched it then silently screamed at myself for watching it and not the ground. If he was coming up, he was being slow about it. Or intentional, he might be purposefully drawing this out, he might be biding time for some reason beyond my comprehension. I tasted sour in the back of my throat. My knees creaked underneath me. I wondered if I was going to faint.

A door opened and snapped my attention up.

Daisy lingered in the doorway. She was backlit, looked ghoulish and unspeakably pretty in a tennis skirt and a clingy sky blue crop top, her cardigan—my cardigan—long enough to brush her thighs. She had her fingers splayed, moved her hands in front of her in that slow, alien *I'm trying not to fuck up my polish* way. She yawned, then jerked her head, indicated the void space behind her. Her satin headband shined under the fluorescence. I couldn't tell what color it was supposed to be. It stole pigment like a crow's feather did. "You coming in or not?"

I stepped off the picnic table, yanked the bandanna down over my nose. It was stiff, held its shape. His blood felt fudgey. My stomach roiled. I made haste across the communal yard, stepped into the building, and told myself as Daisy let the door drop that this meant I was safer, that he wouldn't be able to get me here.

I wasn't sure if that was true. I wasn't sure if I believed myself.

Lucky for me, I was beyond surface analysis of absolutely anything and couldn't interrogate myself to death. Daisy turned and started her ascent up the stairs, and I followed her in silence. I tried to make my footsteps match her stride, tried to deaden the sound of my own stomping by overlaying it with hers. I held my breath. I tried to imagine my blood thickening, slowing down, cooling to molasses. I willed the violence to leave me. I was running low on will.

FOURTEEN

GAL PALS

I stepped inside. I was still shaking. I reeked of blood, and it was worse somehow by virtue of not being mine. I curled my hands tight, then shook them loose, but that did nothing for the tremor. I grinned again. It might've been a weird pre-mortem cadaveric spasm more than an expression that corresponded with any kind of feeling. I wasn't sure what I was feeling, if I was even feeling at all. Thawing, maybe.

"Hiya," said Chelsea from the living room. She had her hands on the waist of some dress form, pinched pleats into muslin with her fingers. She held pins in her lips. Her hair looked a mess. The lamps weren't enough to make the room properly bright, and she was more illuminated by the television screen in front of her than the fixture overhead. She was watching some David Lynch movie. A girl in the box was singing softly on a stage. Chelsea didn't look up from her dress form. She warped the fabric over the limbless belly and frowned.

"Come on," Daisy said. She took my wrist and pulled me

through the kitchen, led me into her room and slammed the door shut behind us.

The pink scalded me. Psychological association rather than actual material sensorium, but her bedroom tasted like artificial strawberries. It was saccharine, illness inducing, abrasive and soothing at once. She had a pink beaded curtain for a closet door, a pox of gel stickers up and down her bed frame's legs. She'd thumbtacked a long rope of fairy lights in a pentagram on her wall. There were wrappers on the floor, indiscernible twists of plastic trash, crumpled papers, crushed flowers, discarded rompers, and lacy bralettes. Her lipstick collection spilled across an old Hollywood vanity, which supposedly doubled as a desk, not that Daisy had probably ever used a desk in her damn life. No posters on the walls, but many taped on the ceiling. She'd bought a bunch of old skin mags off my dads and had had a hell of a time tearing out the centerfolds.

I leaned against the door, made myself just breathe, just be. Her room was a sensory nightmare and I relished it. It felt like her. I drank in her acid energy and tucked my hands in my armpits. I slid down the door, skidded onto my ass, legs stretched in front of me, boots sprouting up and out. My face twitched, I felt its jerky little movements but couldn't find it in me to stop it.

Daisy flopped backwards on her bed. She kicked her feet up on the wall, twined her hands around the footboard, rolled her cheek to the side to look at me. She batted her lashes, drawled, "So did you murder Jing?"

I blinked, shook myself. "What?"

"That's her bandanna." She shot a slow smile at me. "There's blood all over it. Did you kill Jing Gao?"

"I—"

"Because so we're clear, if you did, I've got to kill you next. I will tie you to a log splitter and saw you down the middle like in the old-school cartoons." She yawned. "Lesbians snapping and killing each other is so Hays Code. Cliché as all hell. Ew. Pass." A pause. "That's how you know that Clytemnestra was gay. She killed Cassandra. Homoeroticism!"

"What the fuck are you talking about?"

"I'm trying to make you smile, jackass." She stuck out her tongue. "You're such a bore. I'm charming when I'm nerdy. Anyway, why are you covered in blood? Did you get in a fight?"

I clamped my temples between my hands. "Yeah. I got in a fight."

"That's hot." She rolled to fully face me, combed a hand through her hair. It spilled off the bed, feathered over her pearlescent sheets. Her friendship bracelets clattered. One of them, nearest her elbow, read SIDEWAYS. God, she was so cool. I wanted to hyperventilate. Daisy flashed her teeth at me. "You don't look too fucked up. Did you kill him? It was a boy, right?"

"It was a boy," I mumbled. I worried my bottom lip between my teeth. "He didn't get me too bad, I think. Might be some bruises."

"I love bruises." She stuck one of her legs straight up in the air, jabbed a finger at a dark green splotch on her thigh. "Remember when I fell off the lunch table? When I was dancing on it to that Lesley Gore song last week? This was from that."

I manually nodded my head, moved it with my palms. "Yeah." She'd twirled around in circles, kicked over milk cartons, performed a whole routine before she got caught and landed her detention sentence. They let her off easy, just two days. How she hadn't been suspended was beyond me. She would've been a hell of a theater kid. I smiled a little, hissed an exhale through my teeth. "That ruled."

"Lesley Gore was a lesbian." She dropped her leg, tucked one hand under her cheek. "Did you know that?"

"No," I said. It kept the smile on. God was I wired. "I didn't."

"I adore her." She rolled again, this time onto her stomach, and rested her chin in her hands, swam her toes through the air in lazy figure eights. It felt practiced. She flashed her dimples. "So, tell me about this fight. Anybody I know?"

"I hope not." I didn't know why I was being hesitant about this. I cleared my throat, braced myself to say his name, but I was leery about pronouncing it. I thought I might get sick on it. I stuffed my hand down my shirt, fished his wallet out of my sports bra, and tossed it Daisy's way. "I think I really fucked up, Daisy."

She caught it one-handed and lit up for a moment, alive with unfettered, undiluted glee. "Oh my god. Oh, my fucking god, you mugged somebody!" She thumbed the wallet open, swept out his driver's license and glowered over it, gloating like she'd done it herself. Her brows shot up. She snapped her attention back to me. "You mugged somebody named *Tatum Jenkins?*"

"Uh-huh."

"Did you Chett him? Boy, we totally could've called it the Tatum hex. What a name."

Holy shit. Holy shit, I'm a witch. I do witchcraft. Like, most of my time is devoted to binding harm-doers from doing harm. This is my whole lifestyle. "It didn't even occur to me. I mean, like. I just got so mad. I was too mad to think."

She beamed, cradled her cheek in one hand, used the other to fan herself with his ID. Then she got a look at my face. "Was it self-defense? Did he hurt you?"

"No," I pieced out. "No, he didn't even see me coming. I'd never spoken to him before. He—he's a witchfinder, he's hurt plenty of other people. Shiloh. He hurt Shiloh. That was most of it, I think. I mean, he'd hurt me if he could, but—"

"You jumped a witchfinder and just beat the shit out of him?"

I sniffed. "I left a mark, I guess."

"You know, that means he probably had no clue you were a witch. That means he might not go after you." She flicked his ID across her room. It clattered against her vanity, knocked over a few seemingly identical peachy nude lipsticks. "Are you okay?"

Maybe he will. Maybe he's patient. "I feel fucking insane."

"Join the club." She screwed her face up, then scooted a little, patted the space beside her. "Come over here, would you?"

I slumped forward obediently. Knees hit the carpet, palms unlatched from my skull, and with some unseen celestial guidance I managed to put my feet underneath me and walk across her floor. My boots looked bizarre against her pastel patchwork carpet. I was the wrong genre. I lingered by her bedside, unsure of where I should put my hands.

"Sit," she said.

I sat. I faced away from her, stared at the door, imagined the knob shaking.

My beanie slipped backwards off my head.

I patted down my scalp. "I was wearing that, you know."

"And now you're not." She tugged my jacket collar. "If you're gonna hide out in my room, at least pretend like you're comfortable here."

I unzipped the jacket. Pulling it off felt like shucking armor. My body tingled, floated. I half folded, half crumpled the jacket, the book inside it, and my flannel, and dropped the parcel I'd made on the floor. Leaned down and untied my boots before she asked it of me. I toed them off, then tucked my hands between my thighs.

"I wish I could've been there. I love a good fight. I would've been *right* there, in it with you. I would've clawed his eyes out. I mean it," she said. "I would've helped you hide the body."

"He's still alive," I said.

"Not in my daydream scenario he isn't."

I looked at her over my shoulder. I had some retort, but I lost it. She'd crept closer, was all but curled around me now. She twirled my beanie around her fingertip, had an odd, pouty look on her face. I cleared my throat. "What are you doing?"

"What does it look like?"

"Beats me," I said.

"Sideways, you are dense as hell sometimes."

"Often. I am dense at rest."

Daisy made a show of sighing. She tossed my beanie over onto her bedside table, reared back on her knees, perched on her heels so that she and I were at eye level. I always forgot how short she was. Daisy's presence could've busted a stadium wide. Bizarre for that to be so physically compressed. Chaos diamond. She folded her hair over her shoulder, caught one lock and twisted it around her knuckle. "Do you think I'm pretty?"

"Yes." I chewed my tongue. "Everyone thinks you're pretty."

She leaned forward, put her weight in her fingertips, sank them deep into the bed. She didn't blink. I could've counted her eyelashes, she was so close. "But do you?"

"I think you're pretty, Daze."

She seized me around the shirt collar and tipped me over. The back of my head hit something downy and skinned with silk. My throat constricted. Her hands loosened, pressed on either of my shoulders, pushed me hard into the mattress. In my head, she submerged me and I drowned in all the satin, was consumed by it. I tried to swallow but couldn't. Daisy crawled onto my chest and I saw spots. She tipped her head down. Her hair swished around my jaw. Something about her expression put hooks in me, made old pain fresh.

"Daisy—"

"God. It's always *daisydaisydaisy.* They really landed me with the worst name on earth," she said. "I was damned to be infantilized my whole life. Fucked up, if you ask me. I'd say I took it in stride, though! I'm a good flower." The corners of her mouth twitched. "You can pluck all my petals and go, 'She loves me, she loves me not.' Ain't that cute?"

I opened my mouth and shut it.

"Do you think I'm scary, Sideways?"

"Absolutely terrifying."

"That's why I like you so much. I am an extremely uninspired person to crush on. Most people, when they have a crush on me, it's just that they like the archetype. I'm a cheerleader. I'm petite and I've got good skin. I'm bitchy. Everybody likes that and it bores me to death because they're not really into me. I'm good cultural capital. I'm adorable. Now that everybody knows I'm gay, though, I'm screwed. Which is to say, I'm not screwed. I don't know how to hook girls with the girly thing. Girls know how it works. They see what I'm doing, and it doesn't impress them, I think. You, though. You've never treated me like that. You treat me like a peer. Like we're equals."

I breathed, "I am not sure where you're going with this."

"I'm not going anywhere. I'm lost. Come find me." She curled her lip. "Do you want me?"

"Want you for what?"

"Jesus Christ, Sideways." Hands made fists again, and she yanked me off the bed, pulled me up until our noses touched. She looked at me dead-on. "Do you *want* me?"

My brows shot up. I couldn't move, didn't dare breathe.

"I want you," she said. No mean little smile, no winking and shoulder shimmying. She sounded deadly serious. She dropped her voice. "You know, I wanted to *be* you when we met. You let people think you were ugly and violent and scary. You told people to call you Sideways, you all but named yourself off a custom homophobic slur. You didn't lie, or hide, or defang yourself. You've never baby-voiced your way out of a situation. I wanted to be you. I wanted to wear your skin. I thought you were hideous and disgusting and I hated you and I thought you were so, so fucking cool. So dreamy." Her hands crept around my collar, hooked the back of my neck. "Everybody was scared of you and you never hit on me back."

"I thought you were straight," I said.

"That's because you're stupid. We've been over this. I've been tugging your pigtails for longer than we've been friends, dummy." She hissed a breath. "You're my dream butch. Are you kidding me? You come over because you kicked the life out of an absolute creep dressed like a fucking horror movie slasher, and you're so gorgeous and I—don't you want me? You can do whatever you want to me if you want me."

"Daisy."

"Sideways."

Delicately, tremor not all gone, I rested a hand between her shoulder blades. I forced myself to hold her gaze. No hiding. I rasped, "Are you okay?"

She froze. "That's not an answer."

"So, no." I tapped my thumb on one of her vertebrae. "It's cool, you don't have to be."

"Is this because you're in love with Jing?" Her expression flickered. She breathed harder, her back flared under my hand. "You're in love with her, aren't you? Is that why she gave you her bandanna?"

I sucked in a breath.

"Figures. I mean, good. That makes sense, you've got excellent taste, and Jing's the best. Just one of the absolute best people I've ever met. You *should* be in love with her. I would hate you if you weren't in love with her." She looked stricken. The blood left her face, and she grinned wider than her face could accommodate. She looked like the Cheshire cat. She looked like she was going to shatter. "Nobody's in love with me."

"That's not—"

She yanked me forward, nails in my nape, and kissed me. She kissed deeper than I'd expected, hungry and desperate, unspeakably sweet. She poured herself onto me, smothered me. She put her tongue between my teeth. She bit my bottom lip, quicker but sharper than Madeline had, then pressed a flurry of soft little kisses up and down my jaw.

One hand dropped from my neck and caught a fistful of my shirt. She tugged it, untucked it. It drifted away from my belt. The strawberry air of her bedroom felt chilly on the exposed skin of my lower back, prickled gooseflesh down the base of my spine. She kissed behind my ear. She shifted in my lap, arched her back, wound her hips over mine. She moved and my insides went liquid. Her hair fell around my shoulder. My head swam. My eyes wouldn't focus. She put her mouth on my jugular and a sound came out of me, low and raw from the seat of my throat.

"Daze," I gasped. "I—"

"Don't lie to me," she said. "Don't you dare."

"I wouldn't." I shook my head. Both of my arms were around her waist now, I wasn't sure how that'd happened, but I held her, and I told myself that I had to be gentle or I'd crush her even though I knew that impossibly she was as strong as me. "I love you, Daisy. Yates and Jing, do you think they don't love you, too? Do you think Chelsea doesn't love you?"

"Chelsea doesn't have a choice, she's blood," she spat. She'd frozen midmotion, her nose in my neck, her hands balled in fists at my back.

"We both know blood's not love."

She didn't protest. Her father's presence hung in the air but neither of us acknowledged it. She put her mouth beside my larynx and was silent a moment, held her frame perfectly still. She was sucking a bruise, I think. I didn't mind that. I cocked my head to the side, gave her more room.

"So, what's up?"

"I don't want us to split up. I don't want to graduate. None of us are going to the same colleges. We probably won't even be in the same states. I haven't been without Jing for more than a week since we found my mom. Yates too, once we had her. They're my girls. *You're* my *butch*. This Scapegracers thing," she whispered, "I really really need it. I'm not ready for us to not be together. I never thought much about what would happen if I lived through the end of my senior year, not seriously. I've said I want to be a prosecutor, and I still want it, but it's not real. It's a silly little power trip daydream. This is real." She pressed her face into my shoulder. "I'm scared, Sideways."

"You and me both." I held her tighter, rocked us a little. Shut my eyes. "I'm scared, too."

"I don't want to grow up. I hate this town and I hate most of what's happened to me here, and I'd love the chance to never come back, but you're here. When I think about not being where you are, I can't breathe. When I'm around you and Jing and Yates, I want to be around."

"I'm really glad you're around. I'm really, really fucking glad."

"God." She shook and I pretended I didn't notice. She'd hate it if I noticed. "You don't need to worry about me, I'm not a quitter. Hey, did you know my mom quit being a Star Thief before she kicked it? Apparently she got born again and ditched all her witch friends, and that was it. It was like a month before it happened. She must've said some nasty things to them, that coven was not pleased to see me. They'd left her choker in the Delacroix for a reason. It's because they didn't want it. They didn't love her anymore. Me neither, frankly."

I made myself swallow. I stroked her hair, for her sake and for mine. "Yeah?"

"Yeah."

"I do worry about you."

"Why? What's there to worry about?"

"I mean." I wrapped a lock around my middle finger. "Sometimes when we party you look miserable."

"Figures. I am miserable, on and off. Who isn't? We're coming of age into global climate cataclysm and the government wants people like me to die and I'm about to be torn away from my friends because apparently I need to take a chemistry class before I'm allowed to punish abusers for a living. My brain sucks. I've done my best to be everything morality plays have told me not to be and I haven't been cathartically murdered for it yet. I'm a lesbian but I've only fucked boys. I'm really good at that and I'll never do it again so that's a huge waste of my résumé-building time. I'm extremely hot but the lesbian I've got a world-ending crush on doesn't love me back. My dad hates me. He just bought his twenty-two-year-old girlfriend a little dog. I don't have a little dog. If I did I'd name him Godzilla."

I made a strangled sound. "Jesus, Daisy."

"What? It'd be a cute name for a little dog." She huffed. "Am I being too heavy?"

I sighed, squeezed her. "No. I can bear the weight. It's a lot and I hate that it's a lot, and I guess that it's just that you make me sound—weird. I really do love you. I wasn't lying."

"You love me as a friend."

"Holy fuck, yes. Are you kidding me?" I shook my head. "I don't think you realize how existentially stoked I am that you're my friend. I'm so, so fucking glad you're my friend. I love you to pieces, Daisy. I love you desperately. Please never stop being my friend."

She grunted. "You're stuck with me. I'm like a lamprey."

"You're the coolest little lesbian lamprey."

"I would be the biggest lamprey ever, actually. Usually, those fuckers are little. Like, banana-sized or something." She shook harder. The collar of my T-shirt felt damp. "Fuck, I made this all about me. Sorry."

I wasn't sure if I'd ever heard her apologize earnestly before. "It's cool," I said. I leaned my head against hers. "You have effectively wound me down. I was way too keyed up when I got here. Heart rate is normal and non-concerning, now. Thank you."

"You really didn't think to hex him?"

"Nope."

"We've got his ID." She hiccupped. "We could make him something custom. Something a little stronger than a Chett hex. Just you and me, permanently damaging a terrible man together. We can get tacos delivered. How's that sound?" Then, quieter: "I want you to stay over a little while longer. It doesn't need to be all night or anything, I get that there's school in the morning. I just . . . I want you to be here, I guess. Whatever. I don't know."

"I'll get tacos if you're buying." I brushed my lips over her temple.

"I love you, too," she said.

I opened my eyes, glanced up at the ceiling. It was truly miraculous how many skin mag posters she'd managed to fit up there. A smile tugged at me and I didn't fight it. "I know."

"Ugh, I hate feelings. This is so gay."

"Daisy. We were having a moment."

"If I don't ruin things, it's not me, it's a doppelgänger and you should kill it." She squirmed so I opened my arms, let go of her. She slithered off my lap, stood on the floor. I shivered in the wake of her. She was a space heater of a human. All that evil pressed into such a little body generated a lot of warmth. She trudged over to her vanity, toyed with a few of her friendship bracelets as she walked. They made a clicking sound. As she reached for Tatum Jenkins' driver's license, she looked in her mirror, locked eyes with me. "I was right, though. Wasn't I?"

"Right about what?" I pulled one knee to my chest and contemplated whether I should separate my flannel from my jacket. It was slightly colder than felt comfortable in here. All the hair stood up on my arms.

Daisy plucked up the plastic card and tested it between her fingers, bending it as far as it'd go without snapping. Her lips moved in parallel with the license, dipped between a concentrated frown, icy neutrality, and an impish, malefic grin.

She glanced up at me, tapped the ID against her temple. Her eye makeup was heavy under her eyes now, muddy and wet. Her mouth was an angry pink blur. "You look a mess, just so you know. This lipstick is *not* transfer-proof. It looks like you got sucker punched square in the mouth. Anyway. Was I right that you're in love with Jing? Love-love?"

My jaw went slack.

"Well? Speak the fuck up, Pike. Inquiring mes want to know."

I opened my mouth and shut it. She was right. It did look like I'd been hit.

"So, I'm right," she said.

I didn't blink, didn't breathe. I just nodded my head, a quick downward drop of my chin, and a shiver.

"Knew it." She stuck her tongue out. "Could've just said that. Now, pull up the menu, would you? Not that I need it, I want that chicken avo one, you know which one. Onward. Tatum Jenkins. I'm thinking we make it so that he can't remember how to read and every time he smiles one tooth falls out."

"Brutal," I said. "You're fucking brutal, Daze."

"Yep," she said. "That's why I'm your favorite."

FIFTEEN

WICKED WEST HIGH

Time melted. We cursed that driver's license, Daisy and I, then Chelsea drove me home and I crawled into my bed and slept until the screeching started. I had phantasmic nightmares that I can't remember. Julian made Shiloh and Madeline and me omelets, which we ate around the table in unbroken silence, aside from Madeline's mumbled thanks. Madeline wore Shiloh's clothes, which fit her oddly. She didn't meet my gaze and vanished back into Shiloh's room before I could think of something to say to her. I'd hex her in the evening. I'd tell Shiloh when I could bear it. Julian drove me to school, Boris drove Shiloh to their weird awful Christian private school, Madeline remained in my home and did whatever it was she did during the day. She had online classes, maybe. I don't know. I didn't ask.

Sheridan and Monique gave me a cookie they'd baked, which was sweet of them. Mickey-Dick attempted to sell me various pharmaceuticals I think he might've stolen from his dad. A new kid tripped in the hallway and just stayed on the floor, and everybody sort of assumed he'd had a seizure, but no. He just hadn't found the will to get back up. All of this was before the first bell. I lingered by my locker with the cookie in my teeth, and the overhead lights made the air look filmy, like there was a burned milk skin over everything. I lugged out a textbook or two, a functionally useless laptop-adjacent rectangle that the school made us keep on hand, the Scratch Book, and Jing's fiction. I felt grateful for a moment that my devastating exhaustion and my raw nerves canceled each other out enough for me to move through space mostly without thoughts. I wandered in the direction of class. I was awake enough to nod back at people, to manage something like a reciprocal smile when necessary, even a single, corny wink at Alexis Nguyen when she flashed her new navel piercing at me. I could do this. I could manage the class thing.

I took a step into my first-period class and my kneecaps went rubbery on me. My head fizzled, my tongue was too big to fit between my jaws, my guts wrenched up and I thought I'd heave. The malaise was gnarly and it pinged around me like a swarm of gnats. I felt bad. This felt bad.

The whole choreography of the classroom was silly as shit. The tidy rows of fused chairs and pathetic desk wedges felt ridiculous, the lesson plan that'd been scrawled on the board seemed arbitrary and without discernible point, everybody looked miserable, and this teacher was not one of those rare special teachers that I guess I'd had who cared about changing lives or whatever. This dude was a coach for some sports team who had to do this in addition to baseball. He was barking at a guy whom I didn't particularly care for because that guy had the audacity to put his head on the desk with his hood up, and I felt an immediate kick of fury on this kid's behalf. *That* woke me up. The kid looked past miserable. He looked like he was floating around in transcendent numbness. It was like, 7:00 a.m. Literally he was just tired.

What was the point of any of this? I wasn't going to college, so what was the aim here? What was I supposed to get out of this particular hell theater? What life skills were available to be absorbed? Was I quicker or kinder for being here? More resourceful? More resilient? No. I entertained a lurid fantasy of climbing out of the window and wandering into the adjacent cornfield, all pale dead stalks and chunks of ice, and walking until I couldn't walk anymore. I imagined myself collapsing and somebody finding my body and thinking I was a weird mushroom. I imagined myself anywhere else, doing anything else, doing magic in the Delacroix, or that abandoned house where Madeline had torn the soul from my throat, or selling bone-and-ebony armoires to glamorous strangers on the floor of Dad and Dad's shop. I imagined myself in the public library, cotton-mouthed and without a drop of stress, pulling titles off shelves just to gather trivia facts. I thought about clubbing. I thought about open deer in the Chantry family mansion.

What an elaborate waste of my time.

I sat at my desk. The bar was too close to my body for my liking. It'd be cool if they weren't all the same size. It would be additionally cool if there was like, adequate surface space. The evil lacquered chicken wing I had to work with hardly accommodated the mechanical computerish rectangle, much less all my other stuff. Laptop situation be damned. I just opened the Scratch Book and pretended I was jotting down notes off the board.

The Scratch Book hummed under my fingertips. I didn't flip the pages; they flowed like feathers on an extending wing and the texture of their edges as they brushed the meat of my fingertips felt exquisite. It felt good, and I was grateful for a moment that I was a human person with a body who got to do this. That was a good thing about this classroom: it offered a flat surface I could put my book on, and light by which to read. So, points for that.

My friends had left so many little notes in this book. Their spell work and incantation lyrics, sure, but little doodles and lovestruck bullying curled their way along the margins, punctuated passages about charms and curses we'd made together. Jing had written a list of pop stars she thought had specters, and Yates had drawn little stars beside the names she agreed with and frowny faces beside ones she found unlikely. Daisy speculated whether various sex acts could generate magic because "void" and "friction." Yates and Mr. Scratch had fielded a serious conversation about the legitimacy of potion making, and whether she could cook a meal with intention and incantation and produce a magic effect upon ingesting it (Scratch seemed convinced). Lots of astrology arguments that'd warped into lunar calendar–specific spells, few of which had any utilitarian purpose, many of which looked and felt quite cool. There was a spell we had that, should you whisper "Jupiter said you bit her so you're bitter" four times under a waning gibbous moon, your legs would shave themselves. The actual process was horrifying. Hair writhing free of follicles was a gruesome sight to behold. I didn't really care about shaving my legs, or anything else for that manner, but I'd definitely done the spell just for the thrill of seeing stop-motion worms in real life. I flipped through iterations of the Chett hex, the twister spell, our ID charm, our spell to keep water cold, our spell to heal blisters, levitation, falling slowly. After a page where Mr. Scratch had explained to us that he wasn't going to make us a hangover spell due to thinking maybe we should feel hungover sometimes, then proceeded to show us anyway, there was a list that I hadn't thought much of before now. It was fragments. Jing had written down lines of poetry she liked, and after each she scrawled a bit of analysis—how each fragment felt in her mouth when she read it aloud, the feelings produced, the flavor, the cadence, the relationship between the sounds in each syllable, how we could model chants in each fragment's wake.

Ostensibly, I'd read these before. There wasn't a bit of this book I didn't know by heart, even with it growing all the time. I just hadn't mulled over this bit. It was brilliant. Jing was brilliant. Exacting and inquisitive and analytical and romantic, level-headed about beautiful things even as she clearly adored them. I'd never really read much poetry, not of my own volition, but I made myself go back over the lines she'd pulled, made myself murmur them under my breath. I wanted to feel their magic out. I wanted to weigh them on my tongue. I made a note to myself to pursue the poets in search engines and libraries later, the ones I recognized and the ones I didn't alike. I'd fall down rabbit holes. I'd read them and learn about them and have something valuable to say about them. I could ask her questions about them that'd impress her. I'd learn something.

I knew she wrote fanfiction and elaborate essays that she posted on blogs under pseudonyms, but did she write poetry? Would she let me read it if she did? I might not get it, maybe not in an intellectual sense, but I'd feel it, I was sure of that. Chewing what she'd written in Scratch ink, I felt it, I felt the language move in my body like magic moved, because maybe those things were inseparable, and maybe Daisy was right. Maybe she'd been right about me.

I wanted Jing to write poetry about me, is what I wanted. Or think of me when she read it, or think of me in general. I wanted to be somebody on her mind.

Fuck. Regroup.

I traced out the spell I'd made with Daisy the night previous on a blank page. I'd hand it over to Daisy at lunch, because the incantation had been her doing and it'd been vile and required her little heart dot *i*'s for full effect, I thought, but I could at least get the sigil down while it was still fresh. Turns out defacing IDs: extremely fun. I put down the angry zigzags that comprised this glyph, made the lines thick, showy, and brutal. Mr. Scratch purred under my pen tip. He devoured the ink I laid down and replaced it with himself, remarked along the margins: *This is not a very gentle thing to do to a person.*

He isn't a gentle person.

Past a Chett?

It didn't feel right at the time.

Perhaps that's so. These are gruesome angles you've drawn here. You and my dearest Daisy both, you're reminding me of an old Honeyeater of mine. She had a spell that caught beards on fire.

That sounds fucking incredible, holy shit. Could you show me?

I will always show you things I know.

Still, I appreciate it when you show me Honeyeater things. I know it can be really hard.

It can be. He twisted around in serpentine curls, a motion I read as being pensive. *I've been thinking about them often. I've been thinking about how they would have liked you. I love my daughters. I have the proudest pages in all the world.*

I cracked a smile, put my chin on one fist. I traced with a fingertip, *I miss you being in my head sometimes, you know that?*

You were a good familiar! I would like to never be in your head again because your head is extremely warm and uncomfortable, but I do love you and will cherish my Sideways sinew time forever and always. Why were you sad? When you sat, you seemed extraordinarily sad.

I was sad because high school feels pointless.

It is teaching you how to be a citizen. That is a point. It is perhaps a bad one; there are complaints to be raised. However, it also gives you time to talk to me and that makes me happy because I love to correspond with my foremost darling and pupil. Do you like poetry now?

I think I have a crush on poetry.

If you write poetry a love letter please do it in me. It will be more romantic if it is made of book devil than it would be if it was made garishly and unkindly with a ballpoint pen. Anyway, I think you should read your book.

I stared for a moment. My ears felt hot.

Slowly, with intention: *What do you mean?*

She gave you a book and I think you should read it. There are bits in there.

Bits, I repeated.

Of me. Unless that is a secret! In which case, I am definitely not in any notes in the book at all. I am only here. I am Scratch the singular, notorious for being only right here and nowhere else at all.

Heat spread. It was no longer just my ears. I pulled my sweater up, covered my nose and sank in my chair, which could not really accommodate my sinking. My feet dipped dangerously into the dude in front of me's territory. I cleared my throat, moved to press a phrase into the Scratch Book's pulp with the edge of my thumbnail, but the bell rang and everybody rose around me so I stood up, too, shut the Scratch Book, gathered it with the rest of my stuff. My feelings did not stay contained within his binding. They dripped out and splashed all over the place. I felt giddy and wanted to do something unforgivable. I wanted to lie on the floor in the middle of the hallway. I wanted to eat a bouquet like it was a flamboyant salad. I wanted to—fuck, I was having extremely gay daydreams and suddenly I'd missed my turn, was in the wrong corridor. I backtracked. There weren't enough people in the hallway for things to be chill.

I was late to my next class.

The teacher within said class said something to the effect of, *You're late to this, your next class. What gives?*

I said something to the effect of, *I dunno man, I simply was not on time.*

He threatened detention but didn't follow through, the weenie.

I sat unpunished by anything but circumstance. I put my stuff down. My lungs worked like I'd been running and I thought about Jing Gao.

A PowerPoint flickered across the front of the room and I opened my computational alligator mouth. The girl sitting diagonally from me, an absolute hero, was watching an extremely violent nineties anime. Blood splashed across the screen in magnificent arching geysers. Two desks down from her, somebody was placing a delivery order. I wasn't sure how they planned on getting the pizza into the building, but damn if I didn't admire the process. Very anchovy-heavy order. Just beside the would-be pizza-recipient, someone had a messenger app open on their screen and was sending picture after picture of the expensive cars that'd suddenly taken up residence all over Sycamore Gorge, seizing all the free parking and generally making life miserable. The composite energy of the room's inhabitants, the structure itself, and the day that flowed within it felt better than it had before. I felt better. I felt foolish and buzzed all over.

I opened the novel under my desk and started reading.

I read and read and then the bell rang.

I gathered my shit, I moved with the flock, I sat down at yet another desk, I opened the book and read. My head swam. I felt heavy with story, rich and delightfully seasick. Jing's marginalia would put medieval monks to shame. I read breathlessly, with a big noxious grin on my mouth I kept trying to smother lest it get me caught. I carved through a hundred some pages before the bell rang yet again, and that marked my lunch period. I shook myself. First time in a long time, I wished class had lasted just a little longer. I wanted more time to just sit and read. I liked these other lezzies. Fictional lezzies were real pieces of work. Feelings everywhere, big fuck-off magic, world-ending stakes on their shoulders all the time. That sounded exhausting. I ate it up. I wandered toward lunch with that grin still on my face, chin up, shoulders back, gut glowing with a sensation not unlike time plunged in a grimoire.

My Scapegracers would be at lunch.

Acceptable reason to get myself to stop reading, I guess.

I strolled along the sad teen throng, threw nods at people, waved two fingers and what have you. Weird, how many people looked at me now. Not glowered at me or smirked at me or sneered and rolled their eyes, but just looked at me like, hey, that's a person I know.

There were people who didn't look at me, of course.

They were afraid of being Chett. There was a misunderstanding that had spread about the Chett hex, I gathered. One prong of it punished gazes with intent to do harm, but for those we'd bound with it, it could easily be misconstrued as "you will be in a world of hurt if you look in a Scapegracer's direction." Wouldn't be the case if they looked at us and were chill the whole time! But, hey. If it works.

People we hadn't deemed Chett but probably should deem Chett made a point not to look at me. There had been too many (read: four) instances of guys collapsing in the hallway because they looked at one of us askance. The avoidance still felt new. I was so used to people ogling me, so used to being the spectacle that was being tall and broad and gender nonconforming and alternative, and the pronounced refusal to look was both invigorating and also unsettling in ways I wasn't really ready to unpack. Like, I was very used to being sneered at and did I exist without sneers? Totally, but it felt weird and different. Whatever. Whatever.

I thought about characters who I wanted to be kissing and wondered if Jing had written about them kissing and if Jing wrote about kissing the way she herself would like to be kissed. So many questions and only one me.

There was a crowd gathered around my lunch table. In fact, as I trekked into the cafeteria it struck me that so many people had gathered around my table that I could not see the physical structure of the table, or of the girls who sat around it properly. Odd assortment of people, too. I knew some of these people well—Sheridan was there, and Alexis, and a girl on the field hockey team who was also apparently gay because the entire school was undergoing a giant homo metamorphosis—and some people casually in a Scapegracer party capacity, but there were some people brushing elbows with my named peers who wouldn't ever make it on the invite list. The energy wafting off them felt giddy, apprehensive, positive in a hungry sort of way. I was reminded of the turkey vultures from yesterday.

That reminder made one of my ribs hurt and I pushed aside thoughts about what that might mean for my bodily wellness and longevity. Concern later! Fuck that noise, boring and stressful at once. I wanted to eat. I stood behind the crowd, cleared my throat, and felt a bolt of annoyance when they didn't automatically get the hint and scatter. Bullshit that telepathy only worked with Madeline Kline. I took some guy by the shoulder and pushed him to the left, square into a varsity volleyball girl with whom I'd been in several group projects.

The guy jerked his head up at me. He looked stricken.

My group telepathy kicked in.

The crowd parted. It opened and I took a few hearty steps in my lunch table's direction, and there beheld across the flat blue table my Scapegracers holding hands. A shiver rocked me, my follicles zinged. My insides churned and turned tart. I grinned, rubbed the back of my neck, imagined for a wild moment that I could feel the endorphins clattering under my skin like glass beads in a shaken bag. I knew this one. This one was classic. Yates and Daisy and Jing were levitating something.

Levitating what?

I glanced up, then higher, and circling near the rafters like a sad escapee birthday balloon was somebody's backpack. It bounced off the ceiling. Its straps dangled slack. The bag was full and grayish, had a manatee look about it as it bobbed high over our heads.

I brought my eyes back down and opened my mouth to address my coven, but before I could, my attention was intercepted by a spectacularly morose-looking Austin. He stood at the foot of our lunch table with his head tipped back. He frowned. All the theatrical displays of hypermasculine belligerence I'd come to expect out of him were gone, suspended by the greater mortal anguish of being faced with magic. The most popular girls in school were holding his shit over his head and he couldn't do anything about it, other than maybe jump pathetically with his hands up? This was a goddess-clique-versus-pesky-ant situation. He was out of his depth.

They'd been friends, once.

He was still popular, still beloved by many for reasons beyond my comprehension.

I wasn't sure what had brought this on but it dug my dimples out.

"Cool," I said. "Inside blimp."

Yates glanced up at me, beamed and batted her lovely long lashes, then glanced back around at Jing and Daisy and communicated something with the power of her gaze.

The three of them chanted in tandem, "Float skyward, drift high, float skyward, drift high," and then on unseen cue with heartbreaking ease unclasped their bejeweled hands. Yates fanned hers over her heart. Daisy cracked her knuckles. Jing covered a yawn that revealed her long sharp teeth.

The bag plummeted from the rafters. I watched it fall in awe. I had never seen a backpack fall from such a height. It dropped through space with tremendous speed and smoothness of motion. Gravity! Very majestic. The descent was silent but in my heart, the whistling sound rustled my scruff of hair, billowed my jacket back off my waist.

Austin Grass' bag hit the floor two yards away from us with a crunch.

Austin made a sound like he'd been hit.

Literally that was the sound he'd made when I'd hit him.

People freaked the fuck out. The crowd dispersed, rushed the backpack or returned to their respective tables, erupted into laughter and gushed excitement, muddled fear and praise. One of Austin's boys collected him and steered him toward the carnage. Undoubtedly his school-sanctioned pseudo-laptop was in that bag, and I did not imagine that those devices were built to withstand the asteroid treatment.

"I love you guys." I sat, shoved my elbows on the table, shoved my jaw into my cupped and waiting hands. Some thought gnawed, some thought shaped like *patience*, but I looked at the three of them and I couldn't sustain the paranoia. "You guys are the best."

Yates patted her curls, speared a few green beans on the end of her pink plastic fork. "Thank you for your support. I love us, too."

"He didn't start some shit, did he?" I rubbed the corner of my mouth. "If so, you let him off easy."

"No," said Jing. She blotted her bloody-plum lipstick with a napkin. I did my best not to think all that much about that. "Didn't, actually."

"Nuh-uh," Daisy agreed. She'd begun the process of braiding her hair, and I felt her phantom fingertips down the back of my head. Only thing I missed about long hair. "He was minding his own business."

"Unfortunately, the stress of impending Ivy Day has worn away at my better nature and now," Yates breathed, "I just want to be mean to boys all of the time."

"Fate determined that we should just punish Austin for being alive," Jing said.

"Three fates, three bitches, et cetera." Daisy wrinkled her nose. "Sorry we didn't wait around for you, but also like, you were slow as hell getting here."

"No worries. You've got my full permission to bully Austin at your leisure whenever you so desire," I said. I sat, pulled forth my lunch canister, said a little prayer of thanks that Julian was so consistently amazing. There was some sort of couscous situation in this canister. I wasn't sure what was going on but whatever it was, I was on board. I took up my spoon and shifted, took a slow breath. "Are you feeling okay, Yates?"

"Hmm?" She made big eyes at me, fork in mouth.

"About proximity to Ivy Day."

"*Hmm.*" She rested her fork beside her vegetables, folded her hands together. "Well, it is in forty-eight hours and I am on the verge of losing my entire mind. I've called off work but fully intend to be in the shop just vibing. I want to sit in the section with all the jewelry and wear a pill hat with a little veil and one of those enormous mink coats and listen to several hours of ASMR. I have stress bullet journaling to do."

"That should be totally fine, yeah." I swallowed some couscous. "Do you want me to ask Julian and Boris for you?"

"I already did but thank you." She blinked. "Any remarks from the three of you or can I debrief about the status of my K-pop boys?"

"I found a knife in the locker room. Like a kitchen knife. One of those big murder boys." Daisy frowned. "A cleaver? A cleaver. I found it, like, wedged between two lockers, so that's something."

"Oooh," Jing said with genuine interest. "Slasher shit. Did you keep it?"

"Duh, absolutely yes. It is in my purse right now as I live and breathe." To prove it Daisy plunked her purse on the table, shoved it in Jing's direction.

Jing opened it, glanced inside. Her brows darted up, which made me smile for some reason. "Well, fuck me sideways. You're right. That's a cleaver. Your appraisal, sir?"

The open purse was tilted my way.

A cleaver glinted inside.

I whistled through my teeth. "Big knife. Looks well fed. More than seven USD but less than five hundred, to be reasonable."

Jing nodded, satisfied, then pushed the purse back in Daisy's direction. She shook a hand through her hair, hypnotically wavy today, tripped her fingertips along her scalp above her ear. I watched her knuckles. The couscous in my mouth went still. "My mom wants to take us prom dress shopping, which might be contentious, because I imagine that's Chelsea territory."

"Damn right," Daisy said.

"Chelsea doesn't really make menswear, does she?" Yates tilted her head to the side. "She struck me as a ready-to-wear gowns and feminine separates person."

"Yeah, I guess." Daisy blinked. "Prom dresses are that."

"Sideways," Yates said.

"Sup?"

"Do you want to wear a dress or a tux to prom?"

Prom. That word evoked eldritch dread. "I mean, I wore a tux to homecoming."

"How about that, then?" Yates raised a brow. "What if we picked out a tux for Sideways and went shoe shopping? Doesn't step on Chelsea's toes, and means I get to spend time with Mrs. Gao."

Jing flicked her eyes at me. "They like the same sitcoms. I don't get it."

"Shondaland forever," Yates said. "Settled?"

"Settled," Jing said.

Daisy shrugged.

Tux shopping. Four-person tux shopping for a me tux. Christ. Fuck it. "Sure."

"Good," Yates said. She touched my wrist. "Do you have remarks?"

"Uh." Might as well. I rubbed one thumb into my temple and said, "I'm pretty sure I'm gonna take a year to work instead of going to college in the fall. Maybe I will next year, I don't know. I was offered a piercing apprenticeship, so I'll be doing that, I guess."

The mood dropped and jumped at the same time. Everything flipped and remained at stasis. I examined the composition of Julian's couscous dish and said a little prayer that this wouldn't make me a loser again and break everything and unravel months of love and trust in an instant.

"Damn," said Jing. "That's hot."

"Yeah," said Daisy.

"I like that," Yates said. "Academia is a toxic mess anyway. I get that I have fully bought into this scheme, but it's a scheme nevertheless, and I'm proud of you for finding an alternative that might be more fulfilling for you."

"Thanks," I said. My mouth wobbled so I stuffed it.

"Now," Yates pressed. "Last words? Last chance."

"We're good," Jing said. "Bring us the news."

Yates nodded gravely. She pressed her hands to the table, and with the poise of some Homer singing an epic that would determine the course of history forever, Yates explained to us what the matter was with her choir of K-pop boys.

SIXTEEN

HIDE-AND-GO-SEEK

The rest of Monday was water through my hands. Shiloh and Madeline were scarce and both of my fathers were legitimately busy, having sold a set of authentic midcentury chairs for an exorbitant sum of money to some minor celebrity with family two counties over. I went upstairs, took an hour-long shower and scrubbed off my upper layer of skin, feigned my homework, and read a hundred some pages before I passed out.

Tuesday morning, I ran into Madeline on the way down the stairs. It was early, I was going to fetch something for Boris that he'd left on the checkout counter and wanted to look at, and I'd thought that moving my bones might do me some amount of good. I hadn't turned on the lights. I'd let memory guide my steps, ghosted one palm over the wall as I descended more for the feeling than as a brace, and nearly fell to paralysis or death when I knocked shoulders with her.

She paused on the steps. Hovered in place where we had collided. We stood in silence, neither of us moving, a horrible murky tension in my lungs when I dared to breathe in. Breathing out was harder. The tension didn't want to expel.

"Out late?"

She shifted her weight but said nothing.

"Weird day to be—"

"Sideways," she said. I couldn't see her face beyond the raw shapes her bones made in the dark, the planes of her cheekbones, her nose bridge, her brow line, the swell of her chin. Her eye sockets were gone. Her hair, free of product, bled into the surrounding shadows and made it seem like her head lacked edges. She was a ghost face with drifting adjoining hands, no middle. "We need to talk."

"Now?" It was five thirty in the morning. It was not even morning. Some nights, this would still be yesterday. I tongued my gums. "Fine. Talk."

"You haven't thrown me out."

"Correct," I said. "You're Shiloh's problem. You're not mine to throw."

She snickered. It was a cold, small, quiet sound. "I would say I'm very much your problem, actually."

"You and Maurice Delacroix both. Everybody expects me to Chett-hex you. It's what I offered to Dominick instead of hurting you like you hurt me. Probably, I will. I Chetted Shiloh and they're literally fine, don't worry about it. Still. You're not my problem. You hurt me once and you won't again," I said with a confidence I lacked. "You haven't apologized. Is this you apologizing? On my steps at the crack of dawn? Can we do this tonight?"

"I haven't apologized because I'm not sorry. I'm not equipped to be sorry for what I did without my specter. It was cruel and at the time I thought it was necessary." She must have shifted again. The step cried under her feet. "I'm sorry that that's when I met you."

"Piss-poor timing, meeting you when you were looking for victims."

"Yes." A long pause that made me too aware of myself, of the sounds my living body made, my lungs in their bone casing, the pores in my skin skimming against clothes. "You saved Shiloh even though Shiloh helped kidnap you. Shiloh was going to do to you what Levi did to me, and you saved them. You didn't even know they were them, yet. Yes?"

I gnawed a strip of skin off my bottom lip.

"I don't understand why you did that. I don't understand how you could've taken a person who did that to you into your home, given them access to your space and your time. You shared your name and your life with them. You drew sigils on them to protect them from their family. I don't fucking get it. I would never do something like that. What a nightmare," she rasped. "You've let me in your space. Me, after what I've done to you. What a *nightmare*."

"What's your point?"

"I fucked up is my point. I thought you were some hobbyist. Your coven devotes itself to actually helping people, it's the only coven I can think of that actually gives a fuck about people outside of its confines. You do magic to protect people or entertain them, and I tore your fucking soul out, and you kept doing it. You didn't even slow down."

"Madeline."

"I'm not finished." She leaned closer to me. I felt her breath on my cheek. Her voice was low and harsh and honeyed. It was unmooring. I made myself keep my jaw level, made myself look straight ahead. "I'm furious with myself. I've mangled just about every area of my life, and you could've been something good inside of it. You could've been a good person for me. If I'd met you with my specter inside me, I would've been a damn good girlfriend to you, Sideways. I mean that. I would've taken good care of you."

My gut dropped.

"One of those girls has got to be in love with you. My money's on the one who gave us a ride. You should've seen her face when we crashed. It was grief like in the movies." Madeline made a sound in the base of her throat. "She's hot, and a competent spell caster to boot. Jing, right? She's the one who threw that party, the one where I met you. Or if not her, one of the other two, or any of the countless girls in whatever withered histrionic wreck of a witchcraft community exists. There are girls who must absolutely adore you, and I hope when they do, they do right by you. I hope that they do better than me."

My hands shook so I shoved them in my pockets. "You and me both."

"I miss you."

"You what?"

"Being near you, being in your space, it's made me miss your specter. It's fucked up to say it, but I thought you'd want to know. I've missed the way you used to sting."

"I hope you miss it forever," I said. I rocked back on my heels. "May you miss me hurting for the rest of your life, Kline."

Something fizzled in the air.

A creak came out of her mouth. I wondered if it was a laugh. "You're gonna hex me like a shitty ex-boyfriend."

"Mm-hmm. Are you going to let me?"

"Sounds like it. I'll come to your room tonight and we'll see it done."

"Where are you going to go?" I shut my eyes, which changed nothing. I still saw the bones of her face. They'd been burned onto my corneas like I'd looked head-on at a naked lightbulb. She was a purple splotch on the backs of my eyelids. I wondered what she'd look like with her Chett choker. "I know that Shiloh's giving you their trust fund. Tell me you're going somewhere with it."

"California, I think."

I thought about her singing onstage, her hands over a mic stand, the look she'd held on her face. California was a lofty and seemingly impossible goal for somebody from around here. It was less a place and more an abstraction of glamour and wealth and tremulous heat. There were palm trees there. I'd never seen a palm tree in real life. I'd never seen an ocean. All these things seemed wrong and off for anybody who stewed in Sycamore Gorge miasma all their life, but not for Madeline Kline. Madeline Kline could make it in LA. She had magic to grease the wheels, real stuff to wedge her in among the tricks. She was tall and spare and haunting. Madeline could leave the Midwest and *make* it. She could be in movies. It'd be a way for her to haunt me forever even with substantial distance between us.

"That'd suit you," I said. "They like lying. You like lying. You'll fit in."

"You're such a bastard." She sounded like she was smiling. She whistled a breath through her teeth. "I'm still arranging things, but I'll be gone before you know it. I'll never darken your doorway again."

"Shiloh will miss you," I said.

"That's their problem."

I reached a hand into the darkness and curled it. It felt like leather, what I'd grabbed—less like mine and more like a letter jacket. I made a fist and brought it close, but I hardly had to yank her. I think she had the same idea. Madeline leaned in as I pulled her, and she cast one hand around the side of my neck, clasped the place she'd put the sigil, the place where she'd maimed me. We pressed our lips together. It was chaste but it echoed. It sank through me like a splash of ice water. I held the moment, held her jacket in my fist, held the kiss just long enough for whatever ancient magic to take root.

Pact made, I released her. We walked away from each other, me down into the depths of my fathers' shop, her up into the warmth of my home. I didn't look over my shoulder. I felt something in the territory of ease.

*

School happened. I had a nosebleed directly onto a math test. At lunch we found a cricket in the nuggets.

*

I went home and worked the counter for a few hours. I bombarded Yates with the worst possible memes as was my duty as her friend. I entertained a vivid fantasy of myself as a twentysomething, home from a shift where I'd consensually stabbed then adorned somebody's navel, smoking on the couch of a girl who loved me. I went upstairs.

Madeline came into my room, I marked a doll, I marked her throat, and she left. In her head I thought, *Are you sure?* and in mine, she thought, *Don't think in my head.* It was cold and quick, professional. No small talk. I gave her the iteration of the hex I'd given Shiloh, but I did it from the foot of my bed, not touching her, not meeting her eye. When she was gone, I lay on my bed, and decided I was done suffering over her. My neck fluttered cold, a mirror of the hex, the last dregs of our bad connection flaring up. I wondered if it'd work. I hoped I'd never fuck up in a way that meant I'd find out. She left my bedroom, and I thought about the fact that she'd agreed to the spell, like I'd agreed, and I felt something near forgiveness. Not it, something else. I touched my pillow where she'd rested her cheek while I worked. I'd keep her doll.

I put it in my closet, then crawled back into bed, flipped my pillow over.

I got Jing's book and read.

Hours dripped. My papercuts felt citric bright.

I messaged Jing, **Oh my god?**

Jing messaged back, **have you finished? what do you think?**

So I went, **Not yet, but I'm close and I'm nervous there is not enough page space left for everything to be good and chill lol**

So she went, **no worries, it's a lot but it ends alright i promise. i've got another story lined up when this one's done if you want it**

Of course I want it, I sent her. **I'd read anything you sent me now I think.**

＊

Wednesday morning, Yates skipped school. I was texting Daisy and Jing. I texted flagrantly and wantonly in class well within my teacher's eyeline because I was beyond caring about repercussions and the matter at hand was too important. This temporary group chat was called the war room. I could only access it with my laptop, because texting with my cracked-up phone sucked, and that meant I was running around the hallways computer-first. The war room was our strategy pit to discuss the split-timeline possibilities—what happens if yes, and what happens if no. We kept wigging each other out with the prospect of no. What if we were jinxing it? We asked Mr. Scratch about whether jinxing existed, and he responded with a loopy anecdote about how once when he was living inside of a cat he'd made a sigil that was vaguely shaped like a shrimp and his Honeyeater daughters had fed him shrimp later that day. This did not help.

We all asked each other if she'd texted any of us with updates. Updates wouldn't come for like, hours, but nevertheless we compulsively checked her social media stories in case something was suddenly different, or she was posting sad song lyrics, or anything like that. We sent a slew of memes and unrelated texts to open up avenues for her to vent, if need be, but she didn't open any of our messages. We considered, in a shameful moment of panic, texting either Dr. Yates or Dr. Yates, but thought better of it. Jing texted her brother, Akeem. He sent back a picture of his dorm rabbit, along with, **She'll be okay.**

Lunch without Yates was bizarre. She never played hooky. She was only gone if she was sick, and that meant we were all sick. At our alien Yatesless table, we looked between each other, and the elaborate meal the three of us had conspired to cook in our separate homes: brownies from Daisy, an elaborately sliced fruit salad that would've shamed Edible Arrangements out of existence from Jing, a plate of noodles that Julian had helped me make that she'd once remarked was delicious. All of us had two-second panic attacks. We were bringing a meal over to her place after school. Mandatory.

We would scale the walls like Romeo and shove the dishes through her window if need be. No texts.

What if something had happened?

What if this was the timeline when the answer was no?

School swept past, the day ended. We didn't leave school, we loitered around the gymnasium like little freaks, bickering about what to do. Should we just go over? Should we call her? We were already well into double, triple, quadruple texting. Some things were gauche. But gauche in the name of a friend's wellness is totally fine, right?

Daisy and I were coping with the tension by scraping gum off the bleachers with our IDs and flinging the grayish-pinkish wads at each other when Jing's phone went off, which was perplexing because the whole battle room group chat was here together, so how any of us could be calling her was a medical miracle. Then we wondered if it was a spam call about warranty or insurance or some adult problem. We snipped and whispered and cussed at each other, and then Jing stopped reading and actually glanced at her phone and her eyes went enormous and she wait, "Wait, shit."

Daisy and I looked at each other and went, "Wait, shit."

Jing closed her book and thunked it on the box of fancy flower-shaped fruit. She cradled her phone to her ear.

Crying sounds.

Fuck.

I was going to make crying sounds.

Daisy shook her head, her expression caught between disbelief and grave offense.

"Yates, baby," Jing said into her phone. "Baby, I can't understand you, I—where are you? We'll come to you, just say the word."

"Did she—"

Jing shot Daisy a look of pure venom and cut the sound she was making as she made it.

My knees turned rubbery beneath me.

"Okay," Jing purred. "Okay, I hear you. We'll be right there, alright? You hold still, we're on our way." She hung up. She looked between the two of us.

"Is—"

"Does this mean—"

"She's home," Jing said. "No details, just location."

"Results, then?" I shook my head.

"Unclear. I'm bracing," Jing said.

"Those bastards," Daisy hissed.

"Hold that until you know she wants it." Jing squared her shoulders. "Come on, let's go."

The three of us gathered our shit. We marched down the hall in lockstep, a feat considering that one of my strides usually equaled two of Daisy's. Daze and I both flanked Jing, and I took my breathing cues from her, tried to match my emotional metabolism to hers. Jing was firm, unflinching, stern, unswervingly compassionate. This was the Jing I'd fallen in love with the morning after that party.

I tried to be like her.

We got in Jing's car, we went to Castle Yates, I hyperventilated the whole time, just this time not for me.

Jing killed the music and twisted the key.

Yates sat in the emergent blondish grass on the side of her house. Crocuses bloomed around her. She had her knees pulled to her chest, her arms thrown over them, her face buried in the nest of her limbs. Her shoulders shook. Her skirt spilled around her like an overturned pom-pom.

"Oh, Lila," Jing breathed.

We all got out of the car.

Yates looked up. She sniffed, worried her lips together. Her eyes had a puffy, red flush to them. She'd been crying hard. She was crying still. She looked between the three of us and hiccupped. In the evening light, her baby-blue nail polish looked silver.

"Gosh, Yatesy," Daisy said.

My brain glitched. My mouth opened and out of it came, "How are you hanging in there?"

Jing and Daisy both looked at me like, *Jesus fucking fuck, Sideways, use some context clues maybe?*

Yates blinked. She rubbed her eyes, a dimple on her chin and between her brows. She huffed a breath, made a little O between her lips, shuddered once hard. She looked at me. She whispered, "I'm hanging in there."

"I'm so sorry, Lila," said Jing. "Want us to get you inside? We brought treats."

Yates shook her head.

"I'm going to eat the admissions boards," said Daisy.

She shook her head again. "Guys, no."

"No?"

She held her fingers together, pressed her hands against her cheeks. "I got into four."

"Four Ivies," the three of us said in tandem.

Yates cried harder.

We descended on her. Jing and Daisy beat me to it, but they're fucking tiny and I could fit my wingspan around them both, and I squeezed Yates through them both with abandon. Yates sobbed, and I also maybe sobbed. I wasn't sure why I was sobbing. It flowed and flowed. I put my knees in the dirt and squeezed her. I felt the worms underneath us rejoice.

"You are so brilliant," said Jing. "I'm so proud of you. So, so incredibly proud of you, baby. You are fucking unstoppable. You are the most amazing girl I know."

"Why are we crying? This is fantastic," said Daisy.

I just kept sobbing.

"Because, because," she hiccupped, her nose in my elbow, somehow. "Because now, I'm going to have to pick."

✳

I came home and the shop was bustling.

The shop is extremely cool, but most of our revenue came from my dads coordinating with people privately. They were good at finding eccentric gays with means who like to fill their lives with unusual objects. Relatively little of our income was in-store browsing. Absolutely wild, then, for it to be absolutely jam-packed.

I walked inside and looked around, lost for a moment.

Human bodies were obscuring all my weird-stuff chimeras. The shapes were different. People were moving stuff around. Picking things up, looking them over. Showing other people the things they'd found. A person with a lime-green undercut showed a person dressed head to toe in black ruffles a globe that had been labeled with pre–European colonial nation names. A person who wore a slinky backless dress as though that was a casual and terribly nonconsequential thing to wear on a Wednesday afternoon looked through our selection of parasols. An adult butch in a denim boilersuit perused a few old science-fiction periodicals.

Wait, I knew that butch.

That butch was Blair.

Holy shit, the shop was brimming with witches.

My worlds were colliding.

We were way understaffed for this.

I weaved my way through the crowd, nodded and smiled where appropriate, said hello back to the people who greeted me by name. My head buzzed. When I finally crossed to the counter, fate struck me square in the chest.

Both of my fathers stood behind the counter.

In front of the counter, the elegant witch with the finger-waves stood with her arm hooked around a pair of skinny shoulders. Those shoulders belonged to Dominick. Dominick and Julian and Boris were having a conversation about gramophones.

I dropped my bag beside the counter and joined my dads, put my elbows on the ledge, and tried to look tough.

"Hello, lamby," said Julian without looking down.

"Lamby," Dominick repeated.

I shot a withering look up toward god.

"Busy day," Boris said, helpfully indicating the busyness with a wave of his hand.

"It's the warlock senate," I snapped. "The wizard committee wants things and stuff."

"Sustainable consumerism is *so* yummy," the fingerwaves *HOLY SHE* witch said. She looked perfect the whole time she said it. Like a mobster Betty Boop. "I had no idea there was such a charming antique store around here. Maurice kept this place hidden. Do you work here, Sideways?"

Julian and Boris both glanced at me. "Oh, do you know these people, Sideways?"

"That's why I made the sorcerer assembly joke," I said. "Yeah, I am known to these weirdos."

"I'm Inanna Blue, I'm a perfumer based in New Orleans," said fingerwaves with a wink. "This is Dominick. He's from Detroit."

Dominick scowled, or perhaps his face at rest was just like that. He slipped his hands in his back pockets. The padlock he wore like a pendant beneath his Adam's apple glinted as he spoke. "Is this where you work?"

"Yeah." I sniffed. I was going to die. "These are my dads."

That took him aback. Dominick looked stricken. He looked between Julian and Boris, the blood draining from his long, thin face. He looked at me. He looked at Inanna and said in tones sepulcher: "Love *does* win."

"Gay men are getting married and having lesbian punk children and running antique stores all over the place, Nicky baby." Inanna leaned her forehead against his. "Love wins, just not you."

Dominick—*Nicky baby*—took on a greenish tinge. He pursed his lips, and with a deliberate slowness that seemed to bring him a great and terrible pain, extended one hand across the counter for someone, a dad I'd guess, to shake. "Dominick Kozłowski. I'm the one who volunteered to teach Sideways how to stab people for a living. I assume they've told you that."

"Ah!" Boris clasped his hand and shook it with exuberance. The clap sound echoed around the rafters. Boris beamed with teeth, and Dominick shrank a little. "It's a pleasure. Yes, Sideways told me that they'd been offered an apprenticeship. I'd love a little gander through your portfolio."

"He'd love to show you." Inanna pouted her lips, cradled the side of Dominick's face like she was displaying him. Her nails, long and wicked purple, curled around the dome of his temple. Her knuckle tats made my stomach hurt. Together they read BABY DOLL. "Dominick is incredibly good at his craft, and I'm confident he can give you a full list of references to assuage any lingering fear over sending your little one off with a stranger. He did my hip dermals! Also, Dominick does jail support, he's a clinic escort, and he makes kolaczki for his local community pantry once a month. Everybody in this room could vouch for him."

Dominick closed his eyes. I thought he might be counting backwards in his head.

Boris released his hand, and I leaned back, put my shoulders against a stretch of wall that was minimally crusted with esoteric goods.

Julian was negotiating prices with someone who'd wandered up behind Inanna and Dominick. Noxious good-kid brain did somersaults, and I felt a compulsion to lean forward and help. I nearly did. There was a break in my instinct though, and after a moment of wheeling in circles, it occurred to me that I was looking directly into the face of a man who still wanted Madeline dead, and Madeline could very feasibly waltz right in at any minute. She could just strut on by, bump right into him.

I was not sure what would happen if she bumped right into him. She was hexed now, so like, bargain fulfilled, but the possible encounter seemed categorically bad. I could not text, my phone was a wreck. I could call though. That felt evil. Phone calls were so repugnant. But you know, what if he hit her with a skateboard! My monstrosity was justified here. I pulled out my phone and called her. Phone smashed like this meant I couldn't scroll up and torture myself with all the texts I'd sent her, which I still hadn't deleted for reasons beyond me. Technological decay meant character growth. Look at me go.

Miraculously, she picked up after the second tone.

She didn't say anything. Her silence felt accusatory.

"You upstairs?"

"Yeah."

"Don't come downstairs."

"Why."

"Dominick Kozłowski is trying to buy a . . ." I paused, tucked my phone against my chest. I glanced at Dominick, who had heard his name and was now peering at me with some pinched combination of confusion and scorn, and mouthed, *What are you buying?*

Without blinking, he set a candlestick on the counter—an angel's head bisected, yellow wax sprouting from its midbrain like a stalagmite, a congealed obelisk halo, a soft and squeezable tusk. It was a terrible object. It was categorically unwantable. It was made out of that figurine I'd taken from the church in the woods.

"He's trying to buy an abomination," my gut supplied. I frowned, rocked my head back. "So, just. Don't come down and create unnecessary drama, alright?"

"I won't." She paused. "Shiloh was asking for you. They said they've been texting you. Can you come up?"

"Are they dying? We're kind of slammed."

"They're casting."

"What?"

"Magic," she rasped. "Shiloh's cast a spell."

"That's . . ." *marvelous*, I was going to say. I grinned, struck with an overwhelming head-high of pride, but when I swung my jaw down my tongue just flopped around and I said nothing. I shut my mouth. I hung up. I put the phone in my pocket.

Julian was negotiating prices with one of the women I'd dined with on Saturday. She was a Pythoness, not one whose name I knew. She grinned at Julian with pinprick dimples. I felt so sure about Julian all of a sudden, a kick of loyalty that made me dizzy. I liked how delicately he moved his hands over his glasses as he polished them, I liked that he handled all objects like living things, that he gave gravity to moments that did not require it. Julian wasn't a witch. This room, his kingdom, was chock-full of witches, but Julian held himself with such wisdom and careful attention that he seemed dignified, powerful, in control of the chaos by virtue of accepting it and fostering it and settling it with the props it needed. I felt sure, somehow, that Julian was my family. Obviously he was my family, obviously my life would get bigger every day, but the magic that brought him to me was right. I did the right thing. I looked up from the creases in Julian's knobby knuckles, looked up at Lupe.

Lupe took off her designer sunglasses. She looked back at me.

I cleared my throat. "Is it time?"

Lupe glanced at Julian, chatting with her sister Pythoness, and Boris, with whom Inanna was discussing queercore bands they'd both apparently seen in the early aughts. "They look kind," she said. "I'm so glad." She shifted, tapped the edge of her purse. "You've still got a seat, if you want it. It doesn't have to be time."

"It does," I said. My ribs vised but I didn't cry, didn't double over and writhe and lash out at nothing. I stood there, breathing, feet shoulder's width apart. Hands at the ends of my wrists, knees beneath my hips, organs in their Jenga stack inside me. "I want this over with. I'll go get them."

She glanced around the bustling shop, through the witches, into the material edges of my world. I thought she was going to protest. She blinked fast, jerked her gaze down. "She was one hell of a witch. She'd be proud of you, of the coven you made. Tell me, Sideways—you're confident you've outgrown them?"

"No," I said. "I'm not. I'm a different kid than I was when I needed them, though."

"I'd say you are," she said. "Go fetch them."

I brushed past Boris. I wove through the shop, wove between its patrons, counted the steps to our apartment door. I unlocked it. I climbed the stairs and each step rang through me like a processional drumbeat, and I did not cry, I did not cry, I reached the top of the stairs and walked into my home without weeping. I crossed into my bedroom. I crossed to where the volumes rested, I knelt and picked them up, eased their combined weight into my lap.

My *Vade Mecvm Magici.*

They weren't mine anymore.

I folded, put my forehead on the leather. I rubbed my hands down the spines, the opposing deckled edges. I brushed my thumb along the pewter clasps, the clever, wicked indentation of their claws. I breathed in that pepper smell of them. They thrummed against my palms, nudged against the grooves of my fingerprints. My old lungs, my gills, my heavy parchment anchor. I breathed onto them. My belly expanded, pressed the books into my thighs, and I opened my mouth and said, "Thank you for Julian and Boris. Thank you for magic. Thank you for keeping me alive."

The cosmic power inside of them thinned and bled into my body, into the air that surrounded me. It was my body. It was the substance through which my body moved. I felt with hysterical clarity an ounce of its original shapelessness, the vastness from which all and no things could be made. It was void honey unclotted. It was indistinguishable from everything else, alive and not, material and not, real and not. It was, and I was, and I thought it meant I'd be alright.

I'd read the books and I was here. I'd still be here if they were elsewhere.

I stood up. I carried the books back downstairs.

Lupe stood with her Pythoness sisters, all of them in knee-length black dresses, all of them impossibly elegant. They were waiting around for me, one of them holding a wrapped parcel of something they must've bought from Julian, whispering to each other. When Lupe saw me, their heads turned in tandem. They watched me come close.

I held out the books.

Someone scooped them out of my arms.

"Reach out if ever you need us," Lupe said as she turned to leave. "Your friend was right. We owe it to each other to be present."

"Lupe, wait."

She paused midstep.

I took a step toward her, then another. I looked at her and she must've understood. She nodded, loosened her shoulders, and when I tossed my arms around her, she leaned in, returned the embrace with a hum.

"Give them to somebody else," I breathed. "Don't just shut them up in the Delacroix."

"I will," she said. "You have my word."

Then they left, and I closed my open hands and looked at them. Sound bustled around the shop and I understood none of it. It blurred together. Julian rang someone up, he murmured something about how to take care of top-grain leather, in what instances he'd recommend saddle soap, how to store things, how to make sure they're worn and lived in and a part of the world instead of some abstraction in storage. He wished the witch a good day. The line moved, customers advanced, and he straightened his fisherman's sweater. He inclined his head toward me and sighed. He said, "Care to get the next one?"

✳

Upstairs, in my bedroom, Shiloh showed me magic. They folded their hands over their eyes, and they murmured something full of slant rhymes and crisp, resonant consonants. Their dialect was a little thicker than mine, and they chewed it when they casted, drawled low and slow and sweet. Shiloh's hair fluttered around their cheeks, whirled and tossed in a breeze that existed for them alone, and color diffused in the air. They rocked forward, profile iridescent, then turned to look at me head-on. They uncovered their face, held out their hands as though they were offering them.

Even like this, even after everything, I still felt something clap inside me.

The scalding rat-poison blue was gone from their eyes. No white, no delineation of iris and pupil. Their eyes looked like mother-of-pearl. Acid pastels eddied and swirled. Their lashes were longer, thick and snowy white. They did not look like a human person. They looked, I thought, like a nymph. They grinned at me, actually grinned, like I'd never seen them grin before. "Well, then," they said. "Did it work?"

"It worked," I said. "It's beautiful. You're beautiful."

They grinned wider, then pressed their palms back over their eye sockets. They drummed their fingertips against their crown. They cast the spell again. This time, their eyes were pink.

Hours passed. Shiloh stretched across the foot of my bed. They whispered to the Scratch Book, I thought it'd be good for them, and murmured with a seriousness that kept me from eavesdropping. Periodically, they paused to place a blackberry on the page. Little ink tendrils crested from the pulp and sewed over the berry, dragged it downward, submerged it between jagged paragraph breaks.

"If you want him to be cool with you," I said, "feeding him's a good way."

"It makes me so itchy, calling this thing a devil," said Shiloh. "I am a proud exvangelical, I am not scared of devils, but I am still a little scared of devils." They gave Scratch another blackberry. "Less scary in the book than when he was in you."

"He's happier that way," I said. "Still plenty scary, though."

"Mm-hmm." They made a face. "I've got no idea what being a witch should mean for somebody with my history. I've got no idea what I'm doing. I grew up with that wounded spell book in our basement. I talked to it when I was a kid. I used to feed it like this."

"That does not sound like something a good little witchfinder should do."

"Elias did not let it go unpunished," they said with a frown. "I didn't attempt to do older sibling things often. I was avoidant whenever possible. David was Levi's baby, and he clearly preferred him, and I resented that when I was little. He thought it was funny when the book ate fruit though. I'd take him down into that room when I was eight and he was four, and we'd play 'pet book.' I told him it was a magic trick. In retrospect, no wonder that man was absolutely livid. It might've been the only good thing I did with my childhood, I think."

God, David's birthday. My guts tangled. I wasn't sure what to do, wasn't sure how to console them, or make things better, or even different. I was terrible at this. I felt a lurch of pain that I'd surrendered the *VMM*s. I'd outgrown them, but they had been such a material comfort for years. Answers to Shiloh's pain and our potential peril wouldn't be found in there. Scratch was a better bet, without a doubt. Still. Still. Selfish feelings scrambled my David ones. Did I even have David ones? I didn't feel guilty, but I did feel rancid. I thought about saying, *You've been a good sibling to me*, but that felt disastrous and I swallowed it before it could take proper shape in my mouth. Needed something different, something stupid. "Hey, Shiloh?"

"Hmm?"

"Are your eyes—are you just gonna keep them like that?"

"No," they drawled. "I am going to be horrifying and adorable in new, progressively worse ways every day from here on out. It's a good first spell, I think. A spell I made from me, through me, and not by carving up other beings."

"Yeah," I said. "It's pretty fucking good."

"Hey, Sideways?"

"Hmm?"

"Are you finished with Jing's book?"

"Why?" I cocked a brow.

"Because she texted me about an hour ago," they said. "To ask me if you had."

SEVENTEEN

LOVE AND LIGHT

I finished the book Thursday evening mid-shift. It was a slow day, the shop was empty of extraneous people, and it was just Yates and me behind the counter. She was perched in a folding chair, nursing a crossword puzzle she'd found half-finished. Julian loved to start crosswords but got anxious about them once he got more than seven answers in. She hummed along to a song on the record player.

I lay on my belly on the floor. I pinned the book open under my forearm and managed somehow not to cry all over it. I sucked my tears back into my ducts, made myself be cool. I was cool about this. My feelings made my face buzz.

Yates gently nudged my rib cage with her toe.

"Mmm," I managed.

"Are you alive?"

I opened my mouth to say something snider than yes, or maybe hiccup, but in the process I shifted, and I saw the paper's edge. It stuck out at an odd angle, misaligned with the bound pages. It had been tacked in the acknowledgments.

I pulled the paper out.

SIDEWAYS,

I LOVED THIS. I HOPE YOU DID, TOO. YOU MIGHT NOT REMEMBER, BUT YOU MADE ME A PLAYLIST A WHILE AGO, AND I LISTEN TO IT ALL THE TIME. IT'S NOT MY GENRE BUT NOW IT MIGHT BE. ANYWAY, IF YOU LOVED THIS AND YOU TRUST MY TASTE IN BOOKS, AND YOU WANT MORE OF THEM, HERE'S A LIST OF OTHER STORIES THAT MAKE ME THINK OF YOU. I ORGANIZED THEM PER TRACK ON THAT PLAY-LIST. IF ANY OF THEM SOUND LIKE THINGS YOU'D LIKE, I OWN A COPY OF ALL OF THESE, AND YOU CAN BORROW THEM WHENEVER YOU'D LIKE. WHATEVER YOU'D LIKE.

YOURS,

JING

The list was thirteen books long. There were elaborate notes beside each title, her reasons for each, bits of them she liked, fragments of prose she wanted me to see. She told me which ones had lesbians in them, which ones had magic that she thought I'd think was interesting, which ones had prose that reminded her of how a particular song felt. She drew little sigils along the edge of the page I didn't recognize. They'd been written in dark pink. A caption adjoining: *Stay stuck until Sideways grabs you.*

I rolled onto my back and stared at the ceiling. I pressed the note against my sternum.

"Sideways?"

"I'm in love with Jing."

"What!"

I shut my eyes. "I am in love with Jing Gao."

The chair screeched. I heard her descend, felt her lie on the floor beside me, position herself like me, unguarded, facing heaven. She took a breath. "Okay! What are you going to do about that?"

"I don't know." I screwed my brows up. "I don't know if I should tell her. I don't know if she'd want to know."

"I know Jing." She spoke just above a whisper. I could hear her smiling. It was high and windy on her voice. "She'll want to know. You need to tell her."

"She's brilliant," I said.

"She is."

"Should I—"

"When do you get off shift?" Yates rolled her head to the side. Dangly stars on her earring jingled. "Invite her over."

"Hmm." Terrifying. "Could you pass me my phone?"

She balanced it against the back of my hand, the one that rested on my chest. I breathed against it, then took it up, held it and the note in tandem. I pulled up her contact. I called her, cradled my phone to my ear.

She picked up immediately. "What's up?"

"Could you come over?"

"When?"

I took a moment, said, "As soon as you're free."

"Yes, of course. I just picked up my car. It's undead now and prettier than ever." She laughed once, as if to punctuate her sentence, and my gut tangled. "I can be over in an hour. Is everything alright? Are you okay?"

"I'm great," I said. "I just want to see you."

"I'll be there soon," she said, then hung up.

I put the phone back on my chest.

Yates pounced on me, giddy. "Oh, my goodness," she said. "Oh my god. I hope—I mean, what if . . ."

"No telling." I put a hand on her shoulder. My head swam and I felt for a moment that I was dying. It felt like there was a beehive under my skin. I was crawling, buzzing. I was rich and sweet and sticky gold. "I guess we'll find out soon."

✳

The hour came around fast. Yates clocked out, my dads resumed their post at the desk, and I waited for Jing around front. I flickered through a billion elaborate daydreams about her not coming, or her arriving and beholding me and changing her mind and leaving. I knew it was silly. I knew it was nerves. I could've misread things, I guess. I could've misconstrued the note to mean something it didn't, could've imbued my memories of rubbing blood from her hair with a false intimacy, could be relying too much on that time she'd asked me to kiss her and I hadn't.

I'd found a gift that I hoped she'd want among the shop's bookshelves, and it waited in my inherited leather jacket's breast pocket. My heart boxed with it. I waited but not for long.

A slap from heaven, her cherry convertible rolled up alongside my fathers' shop. She had the batwing roof drawn, a new necklace dangling over the dash. The trauma had been undone from the hood. New windshield, or else a supernaturally unshattered one. She was right. It looked better than it had before. There was a fine chromatic sheen to its paint job, unmarred and solid as hewn gemstone, and the red glowed as though there was metal melting inside of it, a factory furnace where the engine should be. Jing leaned her elbow out the window, slid her sunglasses down to the tip of her nose. She wore golden eyeshadow, a ghost of dark liner, circle lenses that made her eyes so rich and dark that they could've swallowed everything, the sky, the shop, my body, even the finest grains of light. She pouted her bottom lip, threatened a smile. "Pike."

I just nodded, dumbstruck.

"Do you want me to park, or do you just want to talk?"

I found myself, cleared my throat. "On the sidewalk?"

She wagged her slash-straight brows, revved her engine. "Come on, shotgun. Let me drive you around a little. I know cars can be hard, but—"

"It won't be a problem," I said. I didn't know that. It could've been. I hadn't had a full-blown car-based panic attack in months, not since right around Jing's birthday in

January, but it was possible. Maybe the car crash trauma would balance the kidnapping trauma, knock me back to normal. Definitely not. Still. For her, it was worth the risk. I rounded her car, opened the passenger's door, and as I eased myself down I felt like the coolest dyke in the world.

I leaned back. She switched gears, we pulled down the road, and I put her book between my knees, rubbed my thumb over the place where I'd bashed my head in. There was a scuff in the leather. I'd left a mark. My blood was gone, though, and the break I'd made was shallow. I skimmed the edge of my nail there. I tried to make myself breathe. We rumbled down the main commercial thoroughfare of Sycamore Gorge, pulled between a line of brick businesses, places that could be bought out by megacorporations but hadn't been yet, places where hornet-yellow apartment buildings could be constructed but hadn't been yet. Sycamore Gorge, for all the violence it'd brought me, was pretty in its way. It was heavy with lichen-kissed trees. Statuary dotted the sidewalk, the bodies of dead men, local corpses, lounging griffins. A pair of rottweilers played in the sallow grass. Kids streaked by on roller skates, lassoed one another with Hula-Hoops they'd made into apprehension devices. Flowers pushed up like limp zombie wrists.

She turned a corner, then another. The road's texture changed underneath us. Things felt rougher, looser. I pulled my hand off the dash, covered my mouth. I felt along the grooves of my lips, prodded myself, pinched the place where the feeling changed. There was something in this silence that

I didn't dare break yet. My music, my playlist, the one I'd made her that she'd built an archive around, droned quietly, whispered at us. I listened to it more actively than I usually did. I knew these songs inside out, but I wanted to hear them like she heard them. I wanted to know what they sounded like outside of my head.

We passed a field that looked like an upturned catacomb. We passed leggy corn silos, sprawls of church and gas station and Waffle House and rotting Victorian mansions. She turned a corner. Soybean flats peeled out around us; with my eyes half shut they looked like stretches of water. She took me in a direction I hadn't gone much, not intentionally. There wasn't anything I knew about in this area. This was farmland, and not the farms that carved mazes into their crops or passed around baby mammals for little kids to cradle in their palms. Rotting barns, patchy fields, gnarly elms ripe with chattering birds.

Jing turned into a cluster of limby trees. The road sloped down, snaked like a fishhook, and waiting in a clearing amid the knock-kneed woods was a sprawling concrete monster. It was a warehouse, I thought, maybe the remains of a mill. Outside Sycamore Gorge in any direction was a veritable elephant graveyard of dead manufacturing sites, and I'd done stupid things aplenty, but I felt sure I hadn't seen this one before. Its windows looked like insect eyes, bottle-green tiles that repeated endlessly along the building's face. Little for a warehouse, enormous for a place to stumble upon randomly. Its loading dock was open. I could see inside, and inside was nothing—a cavern emptied of its vital devices, tattooed with graffiti, dusted with fallen leaves, and faded trash, some stranger's sneakers. Silent, restful, lovely. I rolled the window down and the air on my tongue had a sweetness like Jing's perfume and vegetal decay, the cold crispiness of old concrete, fresh honeysuckle, the warm of the leather I wore and the leather underneath me.

She pulled in through the loading dock, parked on the empty warehouse floor. She pushed some button and the roof of her car retracted, made a humming sound. I thought about umbrellas closing. A white bird cooed and whirled between a pair of rafters. Wind breathed through the windows, wrung a song out of the structure that made my palms itch. I rubbed them against my jeans. I tingled all over. Jing pulled off her sunglasses. I watched her fold their plastic legs against the lenses of their body.

"How did you find this place?"

"Same way I found that house where we threw the first Scapegracers scare party." She craned her neck, examined the ribbed ceiling with a focus half-critical, half-reverent. It was like there was a gilded fresco waiting up there beyond the cobweb shrouds. The line of her throat stretched forever. I was overwhelmed by the length of it, so I looked up with her, peered up at nature's encroachment upon this Rust Belt mausoleum. My music fell away, was absorbed into the space even as it kept playing. "I like wandering."

"I like it here," I breathed. Light lanced through the leftward windows, shafted verdant over us like strands of mermaid hair. I drank in air, I brimmed with building magic. No invocation, no sigil to bind the cosmos to my will, just the raw, foaming jitters. The universe fell through me, flowed through my bone marrow, bled through the soles of my boots. I didn't find my voice. "Find" felt wrong. It came up on its own, it *happened*, curled between my lips like smoke after a hit, an unstoppable physiological effect of being here like this, with her like this. Aimless incantation. I said, "I like being alone with you."

She stretched her hands over her head. I watched her wrists float higher. "I've wanted to be alone with you like this for a while. I haven't shown anybody else this place. I don't know many people who'd like it like I thought you'd like it. You're good at seeing pretty where pretty doesn't belong."

"I finished your book," I said.

"I figured." She splayed her fingers above her. They cast odd shadows on her face. "Are you planning on telling me what you thought?"

"I loved it." I swallowed. I unbuckled, twisted to face her properly, murmured the shape of my meaty specific book feelings, then said, "I want to read everything you share with me, Jing, I meant it when I told you that. I want more stories with you. You know me, I trust you to show me things I'll like, or that I'll hate on purpose. I'd eat up anything you put in my hands. You know, I—I got you something." I reached in my jacket, fished the volume from its resting place near my breastbone. "We bought a bunch of old magazines and pulp novels at an estate sale a little while ago. Nobody from that list you wrote in the Scratch Book, but when I was reading up on those poets, I came across this name. I read through it. Some of it's over my head, I think. You'll have to talk me through it." I lowered my eyes. "It felt like your voice. I'd like to hear it in your voice."

She was quiet for a moment.

Leaves shivered on the edges of the floor.

Jing pulled the book from my hands with deliberate slowness. She fanned the pages with her thumb, tested the edge for sharpness, then laid it on the dashboard between us. I watched her hands, not breathing. She unbuckled herself. The belt shimmied back into its slit with a plasticky hiss. Tracks changed, and the song slicked through me. It'd been risky, putting it on the playlist. Earnest of me. I'd played my hand before I'd even had a proper look at the cards. Jing braced one hand beside the steering wheel. She lifted herself up, brought herself over the gearshift, placed her knees at either side of my hips. Her skirt pleated like a saw blade, it rumpled against my belly. She swayed above me. She was the whole world all at once. She caught her fingertips under my jaw and each point of contact felt electric. She tilted my chin up. I put my hands on the backs of her thighs, just above the seams of her knees.

She came down over me and my eyes fluttered shut. Jing's nose brushed mine. She pressed her hipbones against my solar plexus, bowed her head, covered us both with a swish of her snowy hair. She swayed her weight against me. I tripped my fingertips up and down her skin. She was a prickling sort of soft. Vitality hummed off her like static off an old TV. It made my nailbeds sing. The world beyond Jing's car spiraled kaleidoscopically. She kissed me. Jing kissed me. She kissed the stupid grin off me. She moved with the song's current, lips pressing with the song's offbeat, and I kissed her like it was spell casting, like kissing her could knead the cosmos into something we could take together and stretch like hot sugar between us, like it'd endow us both with deathless power, make transuniversal conduits of us, change something material about the way we were.

I kissed her. I kissed the hollow under her jaw, down the line of her throat. Her perfume fell over me, the rosewater and rich cream, and the cut of her nail polish, her salt sweat, her picked-scab acridity, the ghost of peppermint bubblegum. I leaned my forehead against the crook of her neck, and I sank. She hooked her hands under her jumper. She tugged upwards, revealed a stretch of skin, and I ghosted my hands up to help her. We pulled it over her head. I put my hands on her waist, kissed her belly. She smoothed a hand down the back of my neck. She touched my knobby vertebrae, caught the neckline of my shirt. She curled her finger in the collar. My face felt hot. I pressed it against her sternum, my lips above a lace clasp, and I let her push the leather off my shoulders, let her pull the shirt up and over me. I lifted my arms for her, then wrapped one around her middle when I was free of it. She was warm, I leaned into her. Chill air pricked down my back. I kissed her breastbone. I bit her nearby. She had a birthmark on a floating rib where I could fit my thumbprint.

She tripped her palm around my buzz cut. I wondered if she could scry on me, if the dome of my head was like crystal. She whispered my name, whispered instructions. I moved my hands for her. She clutched me tighter, took a tone with me that made my chest ache. Songs bled by. Light around us shifted. Her nails mapped my back, left raised pink sketches between my shoulder blades. I coaxed a sound out of her and she seethed, softened, I told her that I adored her, I told her again and again. I got greedy. I got the car door open, somehow, and I spilled out of it, put my shins on the broken factory floor. Weeds bloomed near my ankles. When I pulled her by the back of the knees to the edge of the seat, she laughed and I never wanted her to stop laughing. Laughter made her shake all over. In her lap she traced figure eights over my occipital bone until she couldn't take it anymore. Her rhythm came undone, she folded over me. She tried to catch herself, told me how beautiful I was, told me things that washed over me, that I felt more than I understood. She hauled me up after. Her strength was impossible. She spilled me across the backseat of her car, and she crawled over me, and she kissed me and she kissed me and stretched her chest over mine, raked her nails down my chest and yanked my jeans down.

We must have run out of playlist somewhere along the way. We flickered through the algorithm's stream of consciousness, glided down music unknown to us, songs I hadn't heard before now, that'd be marked forever as being a part of this, a part of us. They all flowed together. Everything did.

The same song played twice, and neither of us tore our hands away to change it.

✳

When the music stopped altogether, it was nearly too dark to read. I was in the driver's seat, Jing in my lap, the volume of poetry that I'd brought her in her hands. She held it open with a lazy grace, read them aloud to me, her voice raw, two steps down from where it usually rested in her register. I mostly paid attention. I had her close, had both my arms roped around her, and was preoccupied somewhat with how our skin felt, flush like this. What a miraculous organ skin was. I resented it for being a barrier, I resented any edge between us, but god it had its perks. I felt like a struck bell. I kissed the back of her neck, bit her shoulder mostly gently. She grinned when I bit her. I'd do anything to make her grin like that, but this I would've done just for me.

"Sideways," she said. She leaned her head back, lolled it onto my shoulder.

"Hmm?"

"Look at me."

I did, as much as I could. My eyelashes brushed her cheek. The light inside our warehouse was like that at the bottom of a lake. It made her hair look silver, her roots the most spectacular black. I tapped a dimple on her hip with my thumb.

"What do you want this to mean?"

I pulled her a little closer. She'd sanded off my jagged bits, I had no snide left in me. "I want to be your girlfriend. If you want it, I'd be your girlfriend in a heartbeat. Or boyfriend. I don't care."

"Of course I want it." She stretched, caught me in a kiss. She put the book on the passenger's seat, put her hands on either side of my head. "I wish we'd done this sooner."

"I don't think I was ready yet." I furrowed my brow. "Do you know what you're doing come fall? You shrug it off when it comes up. Talk to me."

"Hmm. I'm unenthusiastic about college." She hummed a note in the back of her throat. "I thought about taking a gap year abroad. My parents weren't thrilled. I've got options, there are schools that took me that I'd be able to afford, considerable but normalish debt notwithstanding. Some of them sound alright. I might want to do some of it, just to give it a try. Here's the thing, Sideways—I am utterly uninterested in a Real Job. Boomer-starred careers feel largely either evil or impossibly cutthroat. Do you know what I've been daydreaming about?" She drummed her fingertips on my nape. "Venues. The Delacroix House is one of a kind, but there are lots of small little witch harbors all across the country, that's what the Dagger Hearts were telling me. Imagine this—there's a dark bar with a stage, mirrored walls, tin panel ceiling. Boarding rooms upstairs, grimoire storage in the basement. A place for witches to come when they need a place to stay. Touring musicians could perform there, crash there. There could be dancing, good music, maybe halfway decent food. There could be a book club during the morning for sober queers. Benefits could be held there. It could moonlight as a testing facility if it's in a space that needs one. It could hold clothing drives or whatever. It could be good fun and *good fun*. A pocket dimension for everlasting parties. Our own little sanctuary.

"I've been thinking about it since you took me to Dorothy's the first time. Planning parties, you know that's what I love doing. Helping people as a Scapegracer and entertaining big crowds, that's the shit that makes me feel alive, Sideways. Most witches aren't rich by any stretch, but from what I gather, they're good at pooling resources to make community spaces come to fruition. I think I'd run a damn good establishment, one that'd be a place for normies, too. People who aren't witches but could be. Anybody who needs it. I might want to get an associate's or a bachelor's, I guess, just for the sake of bookkeeping and so on—but I'd be able to wrangle the funding to open it, I'm confident of that. I think I'd be great at this. I think I'd be helpful for people like us, that I could do something for people that'd make a difference in our communities that's still well within my skill set. I'm not Yatesy. I don't think I'd survive in a nonprofit. That's what she wants to do. Daisy wants to legally skewer abusers for a living, and I think she'll kill it, but I'm not so sure about whether I think prison's justice, and besides that, holy shit do I think I'd die if I did that much school. I am so sick of school. I'm sick of being on other people's schedules. I want to explore, and I want to find the perfect spot for a Scapegracers bar, and I want to run the big magic homo lighthouse of my dreams."

I gazed at her for a moment, just beheld her.

"You are," I breathed, "the coolest person I have ever fucking met."

"Yes, I am." She folded her hair over her shoulder, flicked it by my ear. "Right now, the point is—I don't know where I'll be for sure in the fall. I've got decisions to make. I want whatever we decide now to be about now, and not about then. I get that we might be in physically different spots, soon. I know you'll be traveling around with that Sister Corbie." She paused. "You as a piercer. God, that's hot. When you get good, if you could pierce anywhere on me, where would you do it?"

"There's a thought." I put a hand over my face. "A tongue ring, I think. It'd be elegant on you." Also, the thought of the whole ritual—Jing opened wide, her tongue in my forceps pulled as long as it could go, a needle in my hand, a needle through her tongue, adornment through the hole I'd made in her—it had an appeal, that's all.

"That's a selfish answer. I like it." She snickered and if doing so wouldn't have broken my heart, I would've shoved her off me for that. She cozied up a little more. Kissed the knuckles I hid behind. "It'd be a fucking honor to have you as my girlfriend, or my boyfriend. As my partner. I'd like to be your girlfriend back. If we'll be in different places in a few months, we can regroup and negotiate what that looks like when the time comes. I'm not worried. The future isn't real. This"—she brushed her lips over my browbone—"is real."

"Okay." I put my arm back around her, squeezed her against me. "Holy fuck."

"Yeah?"

"You're my girlfriend."

"You're keeping up." She yawned. "Do I need to be jealous of Madeline?"

"No," I said simply. "We had things to work out, and they're worked out. I'm not jealous of Yates or Daze."

"Good. It'd be silly if you were. I want that song, the one that's . . ."

"Which song?"

"My battery died."

I blinked, not understanding in this moment what those words meant in that order.

"Well, I'll be damned. I put this car through so much." Jing broke into a laugh, swore a string of things in god's name that must've made him blush. "Alright, let's place a bet. Who do you think shows up to give us a jump first, Lila, Daze, or Shiloh?"

"Money's on Yates," I said.

"Really! Fascinating. Say more. Why Yates?"

"Because I told her that I was in love with you about an hour before we came here, and I bet you anything she's texted me upwards of fifty times asking me how things went." I took a moment, drank in our sacred nearness, wary of the fact that I'd have to slither back into my T-shirt soon, find the boot that I'd kicked out of the car. I ran a hand over her, closed my hand someplace soft. "Are we telling people? Look, it's okay if you're worried about being visible. If you'd rather keep things quiet, I—"

"Oh, no. I'm claiming you." She smiled at me all crooked. "You're mine and I've got no intentions of being shy about it. My parents—ostensibly I'm out to them, I've told them maybe six times now and it hasn't really stuck, but they're not going to give me problems about it, and I'm not worried about anybody else. I'm not, I mean it. I'm proud of you, and I'm incredibly excited to lord you over people and kiss you in public until we drive our friends insane."

I shut my eyes, bit back the first few things that nearly came out of my mouth—surely, one could only tell a girl they adore her so many times in one night, yes? Would it dilute with repetition? I shook my head. Screw it, god is dead and we have killed him, there were no rules and I adored her. I'd say it until I couldn't speak, I'd mean it more every time. "I absolutely fucking adore you, you know that? I adore you."

"I've heard it around." She beamed. She reached for her phone, shot Yates a text. The screen illuminated her face like a kid telling ghost stories with a flashlight under their chin. I felt a little woozy. I traced the indentations her bra band had left in her side, followed the grooves around to her diaphragm. "Mm-hmm. You were right. Extremely excited, downright stoked. She's at Daisy's, and they'll pick up a battery and be here in maybe an hour, I'd guess."

"Thank god."

"I know," she said. "We're saved."

"Sure," I said. "Very thankful for Yates and Daisy, awfully glad that they're willing to go on a mini-quest to get us car power and find our hiding place in an abandoned warehouse on the side of some country road. We're saved. We're not gonna die here. Hey, Jing?"

"Mm?"

I put a hand above her knee, ghosted a kiss over the pulse point in her throat. Her heartbeat sped up under my lips. I felt like a vampire—now that was a thought. I kissed a little higher, kissed the hinge of her jaw, the place where it met her ear. I dropped my voice to just above a whisper. I'd laughed too much. My voice was ragged. It sounded like I'd been eating sand, which was funny. I smothered a half-formed pearl diving joke and I murmured against her, "Sounds like we've got an hour. Wanna pretend like we're gonna die here?"

EIGHTEEN

WHAT GOES AROUND

At lunch Daisy regaled with zealousness: "So we hauled our asses out to the middle of absolute nowhere and like, lo and behold, they'd made a flat-out horror movie–haunted warehouse nightmare building into their own personal scissor citadel . . ."

Yates dabbed her mouth primly and nodded at key moments of the story, added to Monique that it'd seemed very romantic to her mind, but she personally would've been afraid of bugs or serial killers in such a place under such circumstances. That she was happy that we were happy.

Monique and Alexis and Sheridan made for incredibly active listeners. They hung on Daisy's every nasal word. They all had a secondhand excellent time.

I was mortified in a way I liked. It made me grin, made my insides warm. Cut me and I'd ooze like a lava cake. I held Jing's hand over the table, where anyone could see it, shared the black cherries Julian had packed for me with her. I wore one of her AirPods. There was a pop single that'd just been released that morning, and she adored it.

I listened with great interest, nodded along while Daisy explained about how the four of us had gone to a diner afterwards, how we'd mixed all our milkshakes together into a single evil ubershake, and why that's why we'd never get to heaven. I murmured something about the ubershake being the second best thing I'd tasted that night. I let Yates kick my shins.

✳

In Jing's room, on Jing's shag carpet, I spoke with my sibling over the phone. *Ghastly* was available for streaming now, and it roared on-screen while I listened to them crying. Yates watched from between splayed fingers, jumped even though she'd seen it at least four times before. Daisy teased her for it. She cackled when blood sprinkled. Jing told her to shut the fuck up, shoved her, then broke her own rules and whispered at the killer girl cult on-screen, coached them through the massacre, tried to convince them to choose a different course of action like they'd hear her and react.

I squeezed my eyes shut. I pressed my forehead into the carpet's fluff. I spoke softly, said nothing with content, tried my best just to make sounds to affirm that I was listening, that I heard them, that I understood.

"I won't go far. We're looking at a motel a little outside of town. It's the only one that isn't fucking full. We're getting different rooms. I need to be alone for a night or two. She's going to leave right after, she's bought a plane ticket, but we're—we've got something we need to do, the two of us. I know tomorrow might be a lot for you. I know that the woman who I—I know that the survivor is coming to town tomorrow, to the Delacroix. I know she'll be getting her specter back. I wish I could be there when you come home so you can tell me, but I can't, Sideways. With David's birthday, I think I should have space to do—to be insane by myself. I'll be safe. I'll write down the address so if you need me, you can come get me. I'll have my phone on me. I don't think I'll text though, and I don't think I'll be online."

"That's alright," I said. "That's okay."

"Do you want to try and say goodbye to Madeline?"

"No," I lied. "I think we've said all there is to say."

"I didn't think I'd be so upset. I'd barely felt anything about it. I'd smothered it and now it's here and I feel like I'm drowning." They made a harsh, low sound. I couldn't tell if it was a chuckle or if they'd swallowed a sob. "I'll be fine. It will be fine."

"Call me if you need me, Shi." On-screen, somebody screamed bloody murder, and Daisy clapped her hands. I clenched my jaw. "Are you sure that you want to be with her for this?"

"With the girl who killed him on his birthday?" They made that sound again. "I've got my reasons, Sideways. I'll tell you about it, I promise."

"Okay." I didn't get it but I didn't press. Shiloh didn't take well to pressing and this wasn't about me. "I care about you. So we're clear."

"Ew." They coughed. "You are forbidden from being soft at me until I've regained stasis from this crisis. I will shatter if you tap me wrong."

"Aye-aye," I said.

"I love you, Sideways." They hung up on me.

Yates squeaked, tossed a fistful of popcorn at the screen. "That's terrible, oh my god, what a terrible thing to do to a person. Me, the person is me. Why would they do this to me?"

"Because you're cute when you squeal," Daisy said. She licked her chops like the big bad wolf. "Horror movies are made to make girls like you squirm, babes."

"Daisy, you are the worst person I've ever met," Yates said. She batted her lashes and scooted closer to her, uncrossed her ankles. "Just terrible."

I needed some air.

I heaved myself off the floor, shook out my wrists, wandered in the hallway's direction. There were eyes on me, but only briefly. I could very feasibly just need water or whatever. I waved two fingers at the Scapegracers behind me, left the door ajar. The phantom faux fur feeling prickled the skin of my face. I scrubbed a hand over it.

I walked through Jing's kitchen, crossed her ever yachty living room. Her mom passed me as I went, gave me a smile and a little half-nod, commented abstractly about my sweatshirt and how she thought it looked cool. I murmured something like a thank you. She was nice, had a benevolent normcore sort of vibe. Light-wash jeans and a white button-up, a navy blazer, a string of freshwater pearls. Polka-dotted house slippers. I wasn't sure if she knew about Jing and me. If she did, she didn't make a show of it. I passed her, made for the double doors. I crossed the threshold, stepped onto the deck, closed the door behind me.

The sun had set but it didn't feel dark yet. Ambient dolphin-colored light hung over me without an obvious source. No shadows. The flamingos in Jing's yard took on a lavender, frostbitten tinge. They slumped on each other, turned up the earth as their carousel impalement poles slanted. I tapped a vinyl lawn chair as I passed it. I walked across the yard, walked until I reached the pool's edge. It wasn't lit tonight. It was just a crater. I sat down, hooked my knees over the lip, dangled my ankles down in the darkness. I leaned back on my elbows. I lolled my head back.

No stars. Horizon to horizon, just a milky bruise.

I tried to focus on breathing. When I was little and just out of foster care, Julian and Boris had put me in counseling for a year or two to make the adjustment easier. It'd mostly worked great, aside from never having done jack shit about my propensity for violence and my inability to think before acting rashly. I summoned up a memory: a fat pretty white lady in horn-rimmed glasses with her elbows on an oak desk, telling me to close my eyes and pretend I was sitting on a hardwood floor. The grain flowed around me, looked like the cinnamon swirls in that raisin bread I loved back then. It smelled warm, spiced. The floor was pleasantly cold and crucially, the floor was flat. Its flatness formed an infinite plane. If I was to lie down, there would be enough room to accommodate my whole body, even if I stretched my arms above my head and reached as far as I could. If I wanted to run, I could run, and there would be hardwood floor under my feet forever. I would not fall through space. The surface would hold me. That being said, I was encouraged not to run. I simply sat. Any thought that wasn't about the never-ending potential of a flat plane without walls magically shrunk here to the size of a marble. Marbles might roll past me. That was alright. I didn't need to worry about that. I kept my hands in my lap, or pressed my hands to the eyes in the wood grain, and I watched my thoughts as glass orbs skittered all around me, never touching me, fast but without friction.

I searched around the sky for the moon but couldn't find it.

The concrete was not flat under my palms. It was dimpled, coarse to the touch. It felt cold. I pressed on it and my bones mashed closer to my skin. There were no eyes to trace. My thoughts were not marbles.

Why weren't my thoughts marbles?

What was I forgetting?

"Hey."

I lolled my head farther still, and upside down, I saw shins. Higher, over knees and thighs and torso and shoulders, Jing came nearer to me, her head the only brightness in sight. She came by the pool's edge, paused by my side. She stayed standing. She ghosted a fingertip over the back of my skull, mussed the dark artichoke fluff of my hair.

"Hey," I echoed. I craned my neck to look at her. Mostly I caught a glimpse of the inside of her wrist.

"Are you alright?" She traced a shape. I thought it might be a sigil. I wondered, should I be right, if it'd work, and what it'd do. "You left before your favorite part."

"Yeah, I'm fine. I'll be fine." I sighed, felt flush. "I dunno. I'm worried about Shiloh."

"Tomorrow's gonna be a hard day for them." She shifted, stood slightly closer. I leaned my temple above the side of her knee. "We should do something for them when they get back. Make a big dinner or something. Do you think they'd like that?"

"Probably." I shut my eyes. "Am I a bad person, Jing?"

"That's a hell of a question. In what respect?"

"David Chantry."

Her fingertip paused dead center at the top of my head. "No. I wouldn't say so. It's a grim accident if you ask me. We tried to save everyone. Ripping the house up, we did that so that everyone could escape. He didn't. That's not on us."

"I don't feel bad about it. I don't feel guilty. Lots of shit keeps me up at night, but not him. Shiloh is my sibling and I love them and I've never lost a wink of sleep about David Chantry's death." My jaw clenched, I made myself unclench it. "He was a kid. He was a shitty little freshman. A *boy*. He was awful to me but it's not like he knew better. Or maybe he would've grown up and been Levi or Abel and still would've been gleeful about the prospect of vivisecting me. I don't know. He was a person. He's dead and you'd think I felt anything about that. I don't. When I think about him, I feel nothing at all."

"Would anything materially change if you felt a different way?"

I glanced up at her. She seemed so far above me, more than was possible. "What do you mean?"

"Feelings have weight. Magic is just feelings with force, anyway. But I'm little convinced of feelings as an action on their own, and I don't want you to beat yourself up for feeling wrong. You can't help how you feel, and what you feel matters less than what you *do*. I mean, what about Sheriff Chantry? From what I've heard about the guy, he's a genuine zealot and he really, truly believes in that shriveled little desiccated husk of a heart of his that he's helping people when he rips the specter from their bodies. He probably feels good. He might feel concern for witches. He might feel helpful when he's maiming them, or righteous, or kind. Wild how little any of that shit matters. If he didn't believe any of those things and ripped your specter out, your specter would still be out, and nothing would change. See what I mean? Feelings that manifest in you making choices are what's important. If you felt horrible about David Chantry and you went into a full murder-guilt-grief spiral, I've got no idea what that'd do about the fact that David is dead, and that Shiloh is hurting. Feels selfish, if anything. Self-centered, anyway. You love Shiloh. You demonstrate that every day. They believe it, they believe in you, and so do I. You've chosen to be a good sibling to them. You've chosen to respect their boundaries and to check in with them, and to put energy toward caring for them. That's what pressing here, if you ask me."

My brows came together. I bit my lip. I nodded.

"Tomorrow's gonna be stressful for us as well. Last Saturday was one of the longest days of my life, and we're imminently facing another long Delacroix witch drama session, so god knows what that'll be like. You're worried for good reason. Stressful shit is happening and people you love are in peril. It checks out that you'd be edgy about things. Sideways—are *you* alright?"

"Well." I swallowed. "I'm in love with you. I know that much."

"I'm in love with you, too." She drummed her nails on my scalp. "Do you want to come inside? It's cold out here."

"Yeah." I peeled my hands off the ground, rubbed them on my canvas overalls. My fingers felt stiff. She was right. It was colder than I realized. I took another glance down at the pool, empty of dead animals and uncannily normal, and pulled myself up, put my feet underneath me. I stood. My head rushed. I put an arm around her shoulders, pressed my nose against her hairline. "Let's get back. I wanna see the end."

✶

Destiny illuminated us. We woke up at a reasonable time. None of us were hungover or on the edge of serotonin syndrome, and while we might've felt foggy, none of us had a hard time finding ourselves within ourselves enough to set our bodies vertical and in motion. If any of us did, we kept it to ourselves. I kept it to myself. We had resolved to look cooler than we had the previous time, as though a certain degree of hotness alone could confer power. We were not witches with which to be fucked. Yates crown-braided her hair and donned a marigold jumpsuit. She had a little leather backpack, just big enough to carry the Scratch Book inside. Daisy slithered into a milky satin minidress that ought to have been counted as a controlled substance. Jing wore a black turtleneck and houndstooth slacks, slicked her hair over her skull and pinned it in a bun above her atlas. She painted her lips a rich, gory purple. For my part, I found a sport coat. I wore it with a tank and Dickies but listen: I tried.

Jing pulled me aside before we left. "I know you're nervous."

I nodded, sucked my cheeks in.

She snorted, jerked her mouth up in a lopsided smile. Murmured something under her breath. I leaned close, inclined my head to listen, but she grabbed me by the sport coat lapels and yanked down with such force I thought that I'd fall over. She murmured against my hairline, then kissed me square in the middle of my forehead. She released me, smoothed my lapels.

My head swam. Tinsel pompoms thrashed behind my eyes. I blinked, woozy, and she laughed and took my wrist. "You'll be fine," she said. "Nobody fucks with my baby. Whatever's stressing you out, it won't lay a finger on you, understand?"

"I understand," I lied.

The four of us left her house.

We wanted to make a day of it. We'd be in a better head-space when we arrived at the Delacroix. We walked from Jing's to a little café. It was one of the sweeter spots in Syca-more Gorge, a smidgen more twee than a twenty-four-hour diner, but only just. They offered a brunch menu, and alcohol that we considered but ultimately decided against. It was an aesthetic objection over a moral one. If we had mimosas in our bloodstream, that might give off disconcertingly Star Thief energy, and none of us were particularly thrilled about that.

Yates and Daisy discussed the implications of their favorite makeup brand changing some primary ingredient in their lipstick formula. The consensus: this change was weird and for the worst, and they were fascinated about how it'd come to pass and what goal the manufacturers had in mind for it. They speculated about larger market implications, whether it'd be noticed by the beauty community, whether the change would be lauded because this new ingredient was "organic" where the old had been "synthetic" and supposedly was better on that virtue alone. Evidently Yates' theory was that the lipstick stain on my forehead—allegedly it was remarkably intact—was a consequence of this formula shift, which made excessive transfer inevitable.

Not a revelation, but nevertheless: my friends were brilliant. I did not know what any of this meant. I felt sick in love with them. Sick in general.

I smoothed my hands against the booth vinyl. My thoughts were an overturned fishbowl of marbles. They rained like hail around me, like bullet shells. They plinked and rolled in high speeds. Rolling was fine. I was fine. The vinyl surface was flat, and it held me. The tiles held the rubber teeth of my boots. I was fine. A waiter swung by and asked us something, I nodded and somehow he wrote the nod down. I blinked and asked for coffee. I didn't remember to thank him. I bore my incisors down on the inside of my lip, shredded the weird skin there. It hurt a little. That was a feeling, so be it. Flat plane, rolling marbles. I glanced around for stimuli that might be causing the low-grade panic attack but all my thoughts seized up, shrank, dropped off the table and clattered across the checkerboard floor. I was in god's grip for no reason. I needed my head on my shoulders. This hardly seemed fair.

Jing put her hand on my hand under the table.

I shivered. I rubbed my thumb over her knuckles. I held my breath, but it didn't seem to have an effect on my lungs, they kept moving despite my intentions to the contrary. I couldn't feel the air but it must've flowed anyway. I focused on Jing's touch. She was here, corporeal, present and alive and warm.

She hooked her ankle around mine.

My mouth curled up at one corner. It twitched but still, an expression. My sickness ebbed but didn't vanish. I liked the thought of my combat boots and her platform heels. It felt like lighting a whole box of sparklers at once. Chemicals flowered in my head. I shifted, rubbed against her. Friction was good. Feeling was good.

She squeezed my hand tighter. She rested it above her knee.

My food arrived. Apparently I'd ordered food? With my nondominant hand, I sliced open a pair of poached eggs. The yolks bled gold over either half of an English muffin, swirled with the hollandaise, bright and garish as punctured suns. I managed to hack off a bite-sized portion with my fork alone. I stabbed it, put it in my mouth. It burned me, but it still managed deliciousness and its taste sank into my sinuses, coated the back of my throat. My stomach roiled. I thought for a moment I might be legitimately sick, but the moment passed and I swallowed without incident. I drank water. Water made my teeth hurt. I tried coffee and wondered if coffee alone might be the move.

My other hand stayed under the table. It was still, idle shifting aside.

Jing made some proclamation about how she thought that the workers who mined mica should have a direct share in makeup sales and that she thought that ambiguity around ingredients, alongside positing potential health risks and what have you, obscured exactly where and by whom component parts of makeup were made.

I nodded. I mumbled something about unions.

A song played in the café from some unseen radio. Oldies, classics, jazz standards.

This was Madeline's Delacroix song.

I sipped my coffee. It tasted burned, which perversely I preferred. I drank it black and as slowly as was possible. I felt bad about my eggs. They looked gorgeous. They smelled gorgeous. I thought that if I ate much more, I'd die.

"Like, I mean a little bit of transparency about the . . ."

Something clattered. It was a tinny, brittle sound.

"Jing?"

I snapped my head up.

Across from me, Daisy and Yates both stared unblinking across the booth, eyes fixed beside me. Daisy's brows pulled down, Yates' shot up. They flickered through different gradients of confused and concerned too fast for me to track.

I turned my head. Gave Jing's knee a squeeze.

She sat with her lips parted. She'd stopped midsentence, hadn't moved, hadn't blinked since then. Her face had a waxen sheen. There was a point of tension between her brows, under her eyes, in her chin. She'd dropped her fork, it'd smacked the plate beside her breakfast. Her hand hovered in midair. Her fingers held stress. They were poised to still be holding an object.

Jing didn't blink. Her hand under the table felt clammy on mine.

"Jing," Yates said again.

"Babe," I said. I swept my thumb over her carpals. "Hey, what's going on?"

Jing stood up. She banged the table on her way up and all the plates jumped, clinked so loud I thought the ceiling might split and rain dust on us. She dropped my hand. The hand that had been holding my fork fell limp at her side. She shivered hard. Sweat beaded at her brow. I opened my mouth to ask her if she was feeling sick when she changed. Her lips screwed up, her eyes shot wide, and she slammed her hands on the table with a snarl. She curled her fingers around the table's edge. She gripped it. The veins on the backs of her hands wormed out in high relief. Her shoulders shook. The look on her face tightened, compressed into screaming deep concentration.

"Hey," I breathed. I scooted closer, braced a hand on the back of the booth. "Hey, what's wrong? What's going on?"

She rolled her eyes to look at me. Her head didn't swivel on her neck. Just her eyes. She looked—wrong, something was extremely wrong.

She squeezed the table and took a step to the side. She yanked the table with her. It let out an animal screech. She pulled it another few inches to the right, and Daisy seized it, held it steady, leaned forward and hissed, "What fucking gives?"

Jing's hands jerked loose. They floated in space in front of her, clawed at nothing.

She staggered toward the café's glass door and collided with it. She pushed it open with her shoulder. The hanging bells sang, and I watched her body take a sharp turn, stumble out of sight outside.

Daisy and Yates and I looked at each other.

Daze slapped down a hundred-dollar bill and we peeled out of the booth in a tangle.

I was at the door first, I pushed it wide and Yates and

Daisy spilled through it. Adrenaline and caffeine slammed through me, but cognition hadn't caught up. I whipped my head around, then spotted her. Jing had moved *fast*. She loped in the opposite direction from her house, moved with a jittery, off-kilter gait. She looked like a marionette. It was spiderier than running. She kept catching her hands on things, making grappling strangle hands at the necks of streetlamps and stop signs, but they slipped through her fingers and her body barreled on.

Jing normally moved slowly, walked with weight and cocky determination.

This was not how she moved.

Daisy took off after her like a dart. She shot down the block and in an instant she was on Jing, had circled around her, positioned her body in front of Jing's and stuck her arms out wide to block her.

Jing caught Daisy around the waist. She clung to her, twisted around her. She tried to pull her along.

Yates and I caught up. Yates looped her arms around the two of them, angled them both against me. I rooted my heels. Jing shoved me, swiped her feet against the sidewalk, but I was impassable. I couldn't breathe. Jing tore Daisy's shoulders to ribbons. She gasped, trembled all over, her complexion tinged a horrible, cadaverous gray. Yates cooed at her, whispered broken phrases to soothe and console her, the edges of questions that didn't need asking. I kept expecting her to go slack, but she never did. She writhed against me, against Daisy and Yates.

"What's happening?" Yates breathed. "Jing, sweetheart, you've got to talk to us. Tell us what's going on, what's wrong."

Daisy flared her nostrils. Jing was hurting her, and it was starting to show on Daze's face.

I took a breath, hissed an apology, and pulled Jing from Daisy's arms. I swept her up, held her against my chest. She pitched in my arms. "I'll put you down if—"

"Don't," Jing spat. "Don't put me down, don't let me go."

Yates' eyes popped wide. "It's magic, then. How? Why?"

Daisy touched the back of her shoulder. Her eye twitched. She brought her hand back around and examined her fingertips. They'd come away wet and red.

Marbles clattering around in my head. Richard Corey pressed to death under the weight of a trillion marbles. A red marble screaming in a dead fawn's mouth. A lilac marble alive inside a raccoon.

Jing thrashed in my arms and a sound of pain tore out of her.

I'd forgotten about her mimic.

She'd given me her mimic when she'd given me her book. I'd given her the malt and I put the mimic in my pocket. I saw Tatum Jenkins. I dragged Tatum Jenkins behind the gas station because I hated him for being alive and I'd mashed his face against the bricks. I'd rolled around the grass with him. He'd torn at my jacket. He'd knocked his hands down my front.

He'd taken her mimic off me. He'd pulled it from my pocket or he'd gone back, found it in the grass. He had it. He had the fruit of the spell he'd set on that roadside. He had a mirror of Jing's magic.

She wouldn't stop thrashing until she was near it or it was deactivated.

This was all my fucking fault.

"Jing, I'm sorry," I breathed. "I'm so fucking sorry."

She didn't say anything. I wasn't sure if she heard me. Her spine contorted and she nearly broke free of my hold on her. I needed to fix this. I'd done this. I had done this to her.

"Jing, I'm about to make decisions on your behalf, sorry—"

"I do *not* care," she snarled. "I just want to *stop*."

"Daisy, Yates." I held her closer. I was afraid of hurting her, tried to keep my arms roped around her in such a way that I lacked hard edges. I couldn't blink. I spoke without moving my jaw. "It is *imperative* that you don't let her go. I'm going to go get Shiloh, they'll know what to do." Would they? Why would they? They'd been a witchfinder. They would know, they had to know something.

"So be it," Yates said. She took Jing from me, staggered under her weight. I thought Jing would bowl her over, but Daisy lurched and seized her around the waist, and the two of them pinned Jing upright.

Jing caught her arms around their necks. She murmured something I didn't catch. I think it might've been addressed to god or something like it. Holding still made her quake so hard I worried about her brain.

"Be fast," Daisy hissed.

"I will be."

We split in opposite directions.

I took off. Phone out of my pocket, phone against my ear, the sad little sliver of visibility left of my screen a vibrant green. They didn't pick up. I tried again, called them again, they didn't pick up. My lungs burned. I tried a third time. Their inbox was full. I could walk to their motel, it was only about two miles out of town, or I could hitch a ride, could steal a bike, but two miles was so far away from here and I remembered how the mimic had made my body feel. I remembered walking over glass for it, remembered grinding the glass into my calluses, stomping down those frigid porch steps and thinking that I was going to die. I hadn't been able to pry my jaws apart to scream then. Not even in the face of the Chantry family witchfinders. Not as they explained my evil to me and packed me into the back of their car or carried me inside.

Jing had spoken. She'd fought against it.

A sixth time and they didn't pick up.

I put my phone in my pocket.

I did this. This was my fault. I'd do it myself. If I could get the mimic in my hands, I could figure it out. I could smash it to dust, surely that'd make it stop. I needed it. I needed to go get it. Without a doubt in my mind, I knew where it was.

I knew how to get there.

NINETEEN

ALL-AMERICAN BREAKFAST

On foot it must've taken longer than biking, but I didn't feel it. I beat my soles on the pavement and buildings rolled around me, skittered and crashed around my head. My shins howled, I pictured them splitting like pencils. My ribs closed on my lungs like fingers on a fist. My body moved. My head was a kinetic firestorm and I thought everything at once, I made a palimpsest of my own consciousness, I couldn't parse anything, I just pressed forward. Sycamore Gorge was so little. Three gasps and the commercial row was gone, the residential sprawl was gone, the air cloyed with the sweet reek of thawing cornstalks and I found myself alone. More cars than usual on the road, which meant there were cars in general on the road. I sank my ring and middle fingers into my jugular. I counted the flutters. I wasn't sure if I was having a panic attack. My stomach hurt and I wheezed a laugh, squeezed tears back, sprinted on.

Fucking sport coat wasn't warm enough.

The long Candy Land squiggle road to our local palace of evil shaved a line through the trees. Knuckled branches bore down at my shoulders. Undergrowth vanished, left the gnarly root tangles exposed to the chill, wet air. No acid dewdrop baby leaves like had been cropping up closer to town. Nature was an ugly concrete sepia. No life, no growth, no wildness.

I hadn't gone to the Chantry house since right before Christmas.

The sigils Madeline cut into these trees had made me so ill I'd nearly crashed and died then. They'd hurt me because they were and were not me, because they'd been carved with magic that'd flowed through my specter displaced in Madeline's mouth. It'd been stolen. It'd fritzed me out because it was wrong. My specter was in me, now. I wasn't sure if the sigils were still active. I didn't know if they'd been discovered since then, slashed through, rendered useless. Madeline didn't know about Tatum, or at least didn't know enough that the tripwire had caught Jing's car—could I extrapolate that she couldn't spy with these marks anymore? Would they still make me glitch out now that my specter lived where it belonged?

I didn't know. I had no idea. Yates had the Scratch Book so I couldn't ask him.

I'd cover my face with the blazer if it came down to it. Fuck it.

I shivered hard and put my hands in my pockets. There was no wind. The stillness stifled me. I felt like I might smother if a breeze didn't pick up and put a current around me soon.

Rumbling on the ground. The gravel trembled, the trees groaned and bowed away from the road, roots creaking, threatening to break. That sound made my gut drop. I slammed my palms over my ears, forced the sour back down my throat.

There was a car coming. I was so fucked.

It crept closer. A bass line thundered, disrupted my shimmering watery kidnapping flashbacks. I knew this song. This song had played at least five times at every single fucking party anybody threw two years ago. Rowdy lo-fi rap track. It'd been extremely popular for like a month and I hadn't heard it since. When I was lacerated with tin-can shrapnel at a farm party, this song had been playing. It sounded like being catastrophically crossfaded. I'm talking damn near death's door.

I put my hands down and turned on my heel, bewildered.

A black BMW crawled down the dirt road like an overgrown caterpillar hunter. I could've outpaced it. It had tinted windows, East Coast plates. I stayed still, put my legs shoulder-width apart, jerked my chin back.

I'd kill them. They could smear me into the dirt under their tires but barring that, if they got out of this car, whoever they were, I'd wreck them. I'd break something. I wanted to bolt, animal brain wanted me rocketing back in the rotten chapel's direction deep in the tree line, my heart and gut wanted me careening head-on to the witchfinders' estate.

My knees buckled.

I grimaced at myself. Ground my molars to dust.

The BMW eased to a halt. The passenger's side window rolled down and a girl spilled out of it, all smiles. She dipped her elbows out of the car, stuck her whole head out the window to look at me properly. Older than me, but barely. I'd put her in her early twenties. White girl, pretty in a way that made her look uncomfortably Daisy-ish. Longer nose, maybe. Beachy ombré-streaked hair. She waved a few fingers. "Hey," she started, then mouthed something else. I couldn't hear her over the bass. I leaned in and she must've caught on—her smile cut down and she frowned with teeth, like a wolffish, her eyes enormous and smoggy, noxious gray. She twisted in her seat, kicked the driver, barked an order with her lip curled up to her nose. The driver—her brother? her boyfriend?—turned down the music. Then she looked back at me with a *humph*, beaming sunshine again. She rested her cheek on one fist. "Hey, cutie. Are you going to the memorial?"

I stared at her.

"Gosh, Leighton, he looks really upset." The girl pouted her bottom lip in a cartoonish show of sympathy. "Really gruesome, isn't it? It's nice to see somebody who's actually being thoughtful about poor David. It's just awful. Like, I think about Grace and my heart just shatters. He was her *baby*. It feels like everybody's forgotten about him in all the excitement, you know?"

From inside the car, voice flat: "Reason for the season."

Holy fuck. Holy shit.

I nodded, a single jerk of my chin.

"Do you want a ride back up to the house?" The girl batted her lashes at me.

Again, another nod. I kept my jaws glued together. I did not breathe.

"Hop in," she said with a wink. She slipped back into her seat, slung one foot up on the dashboard. She wore red-bottomed heels.

I moved mechanically. Whatever ancestral knowledge with which my body was endowed shrieked in lurid detail in the back of my head about how terrible of an idea it was, willfully putting myself in a situation like this, in the back of a witchfinder's car on the way to a witchfinder's house for *a memorial party*.

But they thought I was one of them.

I was not about to out myself as being otherwise.

I heaved the car door open, shut it behind me. I crawled to the middle seat. It had a heavy leather plastic musk to it, smelled new and expensive and disgusting. Plush cushions, suspiciously clean. My stomach roiled. Electricity shot up and down my arms and I felt the hysteria bubble in the back of my throat. I hated cars. I hated the backs of cars, I hated cars on dirt roads, I hated this dirt road, I hated witchfinders, I hated them, I hated them. I felt like I was dying. I was dying. I blinked back tears and sat perfectly still, with mimic spell stiffness.

"Jesus, didn't need to slam it," said the boy, who looked, to my mind, like someone had superimposed Abel Chantry's face onto Tatum Jenkins' face and given the outcome scream-ing ginger hair for spice. He glanced at me in the rearview mirror, sniffed. "Who the fuck are you?"

"I hate you, you're such an asshole," the girl snapped. She looked back at me, rocked her cheek against the edge of her seat. "Don't mind Leighton. He's being crabby for no reason. I'm McKenna, McKenna Bailey—are you local Brethren?"

I jerked my chin down. There was a metal screeching sound in my head.

It was really bothering me that I couldn't tell if they were siblings or a couple.

The meaty ginger, Leighton—he did not look impressed. He wore a baseball cap, and he took one hand off the wheel, put it on the brim. "Who are you with?"

"This isn't a fucking frat party, a child has fucking died. Let the poor guy be pensive."

"Are you gonna suck his cock right here, or should I pull off into the trees or something?"

"I hate you," she said, grinning again. She shoved Leigh-ton so hard the car swerved.

I stared straight ahead and did not throw up. Improv camp memories spasmed inside me. Scene: I was in the car with witchfinders of some relation named *Leighton* and *McKenna* on my way to a memorial for an evil kid whom I had a hand in manslaughtering. Character: I was a morose witchfinder cis boy and McKenna wanted—McKenna was making passes at me. I was a hot sad villain on the way to a villain jamboree.

Thank god this sport coat was too big for me.

"Did you know David?" McKenna reached back, put a hand on my knee. "I never met him, but you know, I've heard he was such a little rascal. Like the most adorable little boy in the whole state."

"David was a fucking dickhead," Leighton said.

"I will literally strangle you," McKenna said. "Oh my god, he was a kid!"

"I was on a hunting trip with the Chantrys and the Shaws two years back," Leighton said. "Stag hunting for haruspicy. One of the first times David had ever been out. You know what he did, McKenna? He fucked up and shot a squirrel. It would've been fine, you know, a teachable moment about not dicking around with guns or at least not being wasteful, but before we could show him how to make the incisions and read with it, he fucking stomped it. He stomped a squirrel he shot because he was pissed that he shot it. Serial killer shit. Brutal."

"Oh, whatever." McKenna yawned. She glanced at me. "The mood is pretty grim inside, just a heads-up. Elias has been crying *all day*. Abel's stepped up, he's doing most of Elias' duties around hosting and looking after Grace and Levi. I mean I suppose I get it, but it's a little—it's a little *off*, don't you think? If you ask me, he ought to be thinking about his family and our community. Showing a little strength. How is he supposed to be Grace's rock if he's blubbering on and on like that? It's emasculating."

At the tip of my tongue: *Is it gay to mourn your child?*

Could they drive even *slightly* fucking faster?

"Abel's having the time of his life if you ask me. Think he's gonna give us a sermon?" Leighton grimaced. "His ego was bad enough before all this. He's gonna be insufferable."

I made a sound in my throat.

Leighton flicked his eyes up at me. Apparently, that was the right sound to have made. He sucked his teeth, turned the volume up a little. "Kennie, roll for him."

She patted her hair and pulled a grinder from the glove box.

"Pass," I said as low in my voice as I could. It came out all gravel. I grimaced, covered my mouth.

Leighton and McKenna looked at each other.

Both of them looked back at me.

Barely above a whisper: "It's inappropriate."

"Aw." She chunked the grinder back and slammed the compartment shut.

Leighton shook his head. "Suit yourself. You've got something on your forehead, by the way. Just so you know." He smoothed his hand over the wheel, and the Chantry family plantation rose from the earth before us.

My dread spiked before I even got a proper look at it.

The space between me and the manor was absolutely caked with cars. Cars parked on the lawn in rows before a festival, cars that cost more than the impossible tuition gate between myself and higher education. The driveway was congested to the point where I thought it must've been a mirage, that my trauma had unwound my ability to perceive numbers and that I was being compelled by extravagant hallucinations. No. Leighton wove through them, swore about what he'd do if he scraped his paint job. They were real. I wasn't sure how many—maybe seventy-five vehicles?

Witchfinders were into tradition, weren't they?

Was there a *whole family* with each car?

Leighton parked between two Range Rovers. He climbed out, closed his door with a deliberate gentleness that I thought might've been passive aggression. He gestured at McKenna and me to follow him.

McKenna winked at me before she climbed out.

I got the fuck out of there and did not follow them up to the porch.

I peeled around the side.

The ground felt unsteady underfoot. I stumbled forward, and my knees went to jelly. It felt like stepping too suddenly would bust through the surface tension and I'd hurtle down toward the core of the earth. I made my way through the cars. I kept my head down, hunched my shoulders. The cars stretched all the way around the house's flank. They kept fucking going. I felt like I was wading through a herd of sleeping cattle. If I made a sound, they'd wake up and stampede me. I needed to focus. My inclination was that Jing's mimic would be in that room in the basement, the one where the specters had been stashed. I'd check there first.

I rounded the corner.

A few dudes were grilling—grilling!—in the backyard.

They didn't look up at me when I stomped by, laughed together, nodded exuberantly at each other's jokes.

The back door had been propped open with a little wooden wedge.

Inside, four men lounged around a metal table. Their shadows looked bruisy on the sunflower wallpaper, their complexions ghoulish in the mildew-tinted overhead light. Faintly, I heard music—Frank Sinatra, maybe, or somebody who might as well have been Frank Sinatra. "Love and Marriage." I took a step inside. My chin trembled. I pressed myself against the wall, edged along as quietly as I could muster.

The men ignored me. One of them whistled along.

A doe lay on its back on the table. Still, so dead, I told myself. Its fur was the color of Daisy's hair. One man held her front hooves in one hand, held a glass of wine in the other. The man nearest the door tossed a bowie knife in the air and caught it, waggled his eyebrows at his boys, who made sounds like, *Haha, very cool, asshole.*

I stepped out of the room just as I heard him cut her open.

Before I shut the door, one of the men said to me: "The luncheon starts in a half an hour, heads up. Abel pushed the timeline forward."

"Got it," I said.

"Are you—are you Nash's kid?" There was a wet sound as the deer's guts slopped on the floor. "Pardon me, but I'm not sure I recall your name."

I shut the door behind me before I could think of an answer. Bile hit my teeth. I swallowed hard. It was dark. This was the frat house sprawl, I knew that much. I remembered. I could smell it. I moved before my eyes adjusted, darted through the dark, made for that skinny, body-stained hallway. I reached a hand in front of me, pawed around the air for a vertical surface. I kicked a table, crunched a bottle, stomped something slippery that might've been fabric. The air here was animal sour, mired with processed-snack rot and expensive cologne, sloshed liquor, the ambient sweet dankness of weed. It burned my eyes.

I brushed something cold with the back of my hand.

It was a metal curve. Clammy, solid, fluted pointlessly. A little exploratory fondling and it occurred to me that it was a sconce. I was in the hallway with the shitty corrugated flower sconces. I crept farther down, felt along the wall with the pads of my fingers.

The texture under my hands went from powdery to lacquered.

I felt lower, found the doorknob.

One jiggle and the door swung wide, compelled to fly from my fist by some unseen force. It smacked the opposing wall. I jumped, whirled around once, but the darkness was unbroken. The music played faintly, near indiscernibly, just loud enough to make the shadows lilt. I stepped inside, closed the door behind me. The darkness was absolute here. It pressed on my nose and mouth. I pawed around the wall for a switch and I found one.

Dingy fluorescence bathed the room in sallow, skim-milk light.

The witch profiles I'd taken down from the twine had been replaced. The candids clustered to each string shone with glossy newness, had an astringent smell. I beheld for a moment with a smile on my mouth—I recognized faces, now, I'd seen these people at dinner, seen them lounging in hallways and smoking and laughing. I saw Inanna under a different name, a person who might've been Andy in another life. I saw Dominick. I saw my fathers. Jacques, Pearl, Maurice, and Jupiter. A teacher I'd had in middle school. People I'd knocked shoulders with in the hallway of the Delacroix. I'd torn all this down. I'd ruined their progress. I'd protected witches from witchfinders, we'd done this, Shiloh and I, at great personal risk.

I hadn't done anything.

Hadn't prevented jack shit.

I grinned wider, clapped my hands over my stomach. The futility rocked me. My face split. My head swam off my shoulders, my blood gushed so fast I thought it'd kill me. I stood there, petrified and hysterical, clutching myself, grinding my heart between my teeth. What good was my rage, then? I'd torn this room open with it. I'd torn open Tatum's face with it. The line was restrung with pictures and Jing was thrashing in the arms of our girls because if she didn't, she'd be here. *Here.*

I peeled my eyes off the pictures. I took a few steps deeper into the room.

That scab spell book lay on the sewn swan altar. Green cover, slack and unmarked. Baby Shiloh had fed it blackberries. Hard to think of a kid in here.

I shook myself. I shook without shaking myself. My skeleton thrummed inside me. My long bones moved like plucked strings. I swiveled my gaze back and forth across the room, overwhelmed by the sheer number of eyes on me, and then I caught a glimpse of a teacup on a countertop.

The contents of the teacup glinted. It looked, from this angle, like glow-stick juice.

I staggered to the counter and seized the teacup, held it close to my face. I peered down into its depths. There, at the teacup's bottom, a lavender marble put off light like a distant star. I wasn't sure what the liquid was that it rested in. Water? It was clear, but it sloshed oddly when I twisted my wrist. Rubbing alcohol? Vodka? Some magic witchfinding corrosive acid?

Fuck it, this was for Jing. I dove my ring and middle fingers into the cup, fished the marble out. The liquid was frigid but didn't hurt. I slammed the cup down, held the wet mimic in my hands. I rubbed it between my palms, let out a shuddering breath. Maybe I'd fucked up, maybe I hadn't helped where I thought I had—but I had this, and I'd fix things with it. I'd make things okay.

What the fuck was I supposed to do with it?

Did it have an off button or something?

"How do I," I mumbled, whipping my gaze around the room. Surely in this literal torture chamber there was a meat tenderizer or something I could crush it with. Should I just stomp on it? Or would stomping on it make it worse?

There was a soft sound beside me, like a pigeon fluffing and flying overhead. Out of the corner of my eye, I saw it—the book with a green leather cover opening over the swan mouths. Its pages turned softly, gracefully. I thought of pirouettes. It landed on a blank page. Ink bloomed inside, stabbed up in pinprick dots that stitched together and formed phrases. The book read: *Blow on it.*

I stared at the book. My throat clapped.

I cupped the mimic in my hands, held it like I was cupping water for drinking. I brought it close to my mouth. I imagined it was a birthday candle. I filled my lungs and blew.

The lavender trickled out of the marble and vanished through my fingertips. The light extinguished inside of it. It was a marble. Mundane, nondescript. It could've been a chunk of ice.

I dropped it back in the teacup and sighed, scrubbed one of my hands over my head. Jing would be fine, now. She'd have autonomy over her body. She'd be able to move or stay as she pleased, and she wouldn't be coming here. She wouldn't be dragged to this, subjected to this, pried open on the countertop and robbed of her specter.

I turned on my heel to go.

I did not take a forward step.

Grace Chantry stood before me wearing lace gloves and a smile. She held a rifle in her hands. She cocked her head to the side, popped a vertebra in her neck. Her blond curls bounced. She lifted her gun up. She jabbed the muzzle between my eyes.

I stared at her finger on the trigger. Little white flowers. I went cross-eyed. My jaw slackened and I did not swallow. I held up my hands, stretched my fingers apart.

"You know what," she dripped in that mid-Atlantic voice of hers. She gave me a slow appraisal, recurled her grip on her weapon. Little white flowers danced on the trigger. Caterpillar on a hook. "You've got some nerve coming down here alone, sweetheart."

My chin trembled but I didn't cry. I didn't blink. I couldn't look away from her finger.

Grace strode forward.

The gun between my eyes drove my head. I took a backwards step, then another.

My back clapped the wall.

My knees buckled. I thought I'd faint. The world got blurry. It was hard to see her finger. The flowers bled together. It looked like she was gloved with foam.

"Name your coven," she said.

My mouth twitched.

She tsked. "Oh, I wouldn't toy with me. You're an intruder. I'm the lady of the house. Stand your ground laws aside," she purred, "do you really think anybody would ever know what happened to you? My husband's force is eating finger sandwiches on the veranda. Speak up. Your coven?"

"Don't have one," I lied.

"Look at that." She smiled a little wider. Her teeth were

terrible, preternaturally even and scalding white. "A *girl*! Here I'd thought you were a boy witch—boy witches are useless, so I'm not sure why I'm surprised. Anyway. You're a liar. You just blew that mimic out. Someone from your coven has had a terrible morning, haven't they? Those are no fun. Awfully gallant of you, coming down here to save her. You've dashed her invitation to my soiree. A sister? A girlfriend? And they say romance is dead."

I breathed in and in and in.

"Say." She squinted at me. "You look awfully familiar."

In and *in* and *in* and *in*.

Recognition sparked. Her face lit up, went rosy. "Why, you're that bitch who slithered out of my window last October, aren't you? That's it! You must be the stupidest girl alive, having made it out of this house once and returning of your own volition."

A manic grin cracked over me. My eyes brimmed. "You got me there."

"I'm not in the mood to save anybody." She licked her teeth. "You picked a sorry day for heroism. May God forgive the mess."

I knew what that meant.

I knew it. I felt it.

I jerked my chin up and met her gaze.

Grace Chantry pulled the trigger. Lace grub thrashed hard on its hook.

Click.

Something flashed, then a silence passed between us.

Inside it, I did not die. A bullet did not obliterate my face and the brain behind it. I stood with a gun to my head, she stood with a gun in her hands, and neither of us had been changed.

Grace's smile froze. She pulled the trigger again, then again.

Bruisy light burst in front of my eyes. Lilac sparks, then stillness.

One of her lacy hands flew over the magazine, still pregnant and prone. Her smile fell. She pulled the gun off my brow, twirled it like a majorette's baton, and lunged at me, angled the rifle's butt at the bridge of my nose. If she couldn't execute me like a soldier, she'd beat me to death like a dog.

The gun skittered off nothing. It struck a flash of light, rebounded.

She wound back and struck again. Harder, more frantic. Two of her hairpins clattered to the floor. She cracked the butt of the rifle over my crown and struck light again. She contorted her pink pout into a snarl. Tears welled at the corners of her eyes. They spilled with abandon. "This isn't *fair*," she gasped. "I can't believe this, why would you do this to me, why won't you . . ."

The light that surrounded, that shielded my head, was the same color the mimic had been. Jing's magic—this was Jing's magic, my lungs filled to bursting and I gasped, broke into a grin that nearly broke me.

She'd kissed my forehead this morning. She'd murmured

against my hairline and she'd marked my brow with her lipstick. The spell she'd done driving, the one that'd fed the mimic, she'd used her kiss mark as a sigil.

Jing's kiss was a mark of Cain.

Jing loved me and I was unkillable.

I grinned like an idiot. I curled my lip. I watched Grace Chantry batter against the open air, watched her crack her weapon again and again, and then watching got harder. A tear dripped off my jaw and splashed the floor between my boots. "Give it a rest, Mrs. Chantry." I licked my bottom lip. My voice was thick, raw, and awful. "You'll pull something."

Something came over her. Her face was dry at once. She took the rifle in both hands and shoved it against my collarbone, against my windpipe. She leaned her weight against it. "If you think that sigil will hold forever," she sneered, "you've got a new thing coming, baby doll."

I spat at her.

It sparked on her cheek like more lace.

Grace's brows shot up. She puckered her lips in a perfect peony O. She shifted, edged me a little to the left. She opened her mouth and whispered. Her whispering sped up, I couldn't track the consonants as they fell out of her mouth. They reached a fever pitch—her tongue moved so fast between her teeth that she could've lit a match with the friction.

I heard that dove sound again. The rustling.

Something snaked around my thighs.

I glanced down and my smirk plunged.

The swan taxidermy altar wasn't as dead as it had been before. The birds twisted up my body, coiled their necks around my legs, my hips. Their wide bodies braced my shins. They stretched their wings with a vile, creaking sound, twined them around the meat of my torso. The swans moved with stop-motion uneasy smoothness, disjointed and deliberate, a way that no animal could ever muster on their own. Their fake, glass eyes sparkled under the hanging lamp.

I wish I'd kicked. I wished I wrenched and fought like Jing had against the mimic. I wish I'd been stronger, sturdier, but fuck, with taxidermy swans surrounding me it took all I had in me not to scream bloody murder and piss myself. A beak needled under my arm and cemented there. The tears fell faster. I sputtered, froze like if I moved they'd maul me.

They couldn't maul me.

The birds weren't alive to maul me.

I looked up and Grace leaned against a nearby countertop. She'd set the rifle down, drummed her French nails on the green leather grimoire's spine. She glanced around the room, hummed along to the song that bled under the door. Her eyes fixed on a twine strand hung across the room. She extended a finger. "Eloise Pike," she said. She glanced at me. "That's you, hmm?"

I bit my bottom lip.

"Eloise," she pronounced slowly, drawing out the syllables like *elle, oh, wheeze.* "Pike's an interesting surname. I knew a witch called Pike a few years ago—my, more than a few, now. I age myself." She chuckled. "Anyway, she was a mean one. Brassy, independent. I liked her. Lenora was her name. A grand old Pythoness. She had a brat who'd be about your age."

No.

"Here's the thing about this whole witchfinder business: you can't pull a specter out of somebody with a stock sigil. It must be drawn by the witch herself. Forcing people to draw one, that doesn't usually work. So, we coax. I am a great believer in women's power. I like seeing us climb ladders. I like seeing us win. Elias, bless his heart, usually appeals to holy morality. He's so cheesy with all that. See, I appeal to money. Access, connection, status. If you make a deal with me, sign your specter over, I can see to it that you marry rich." Grace shook a hand through her hair. She smoothed it behind her ear, collected herself. "Mm, take this one girl. Trailer trash, nasty disposition. Easy. Liked rough boys. Her sister had real artistic talent, though, and she adored her sister more than anything else in the world. So, I took this little witch, and I told her that if she gave me her soul I'd give her a man with a big house and three cars, and I'd see to it that the right people saw her sister's work. I'm a woman of my word. Why, this dress is a Chelsea Stringer original. I bought it off the runway last spring. Isn't it lovely?"

I thought about Daisy Brink and Jing Gao as little girls finding Daisy Stringer's body in their garden. In my head Daisy Stringer and Daisy Brink looked just the same. She'd quit her coven. She'd lasted—she'd survived—without her specter for nearly a decade. I glitched, I shifted. The birds constricted when I moved. They squeezed me tighter. Circulation felt fuzzy in my legs.

"Now, Lenora . . ."

My breathing went ragged.

Grace Chantry smiled at me. She pursed her lips, cocked a brow. "Oh, sugar. So, she *was* your mother. Well, you'll be pleased to know that she was the most stubborn bitch I'd ever met and she wouldn't budge for anything. She was more than content to keep you in that shithole flat you shared forever. Nothing swayed her. She was incorrigible and proud to death of being a witch." She clicked her tongue. "Which of course is why I hexed her brakes."

A sound cut out of me. I thrashed against the swans, I kicked and howled and howled and howled, my mouth opened wide and sound spilled from it. They held me back. They held me when I beat my fists against the wall and held me when I went slack. I heaved. I shook my head, my jaw unhinged, I choked and coughed and spluttered. I said mother, mother, but my lips didn't move. It was a single, jagged note. It unfurled forever. Inside I was nothing. Everything I was degraded, and I was just the sound. My throat split. The pitch changed, went ragged. My hands dangled limp behind dead white feathers.

My mother's murderer fanned a hand over her heart. "I can't kill you, so I'm going to give you a choice now, Eloise. Here it is: if you draw a pretty sigil for me, give your soul to me, I'll let you go. You can limp to your friends. You can give them a running start. Or, you can stay right here, your specter intact inside your body, and when we're done with the raid I'll come back and tell you all about it." She smiled serenely. "It's been a hundred years since there's been a real witchfinding total war. The Honeyeaters' Theater—gosh, legendary. It's going to be my pleasure, watching the Delacroix go up in flames. So. What will it be, sweetie?"

My shoulders jerked. I looked up at her. I said, my voice in ribbons: "I am my mother's child."

"I thought you'd say something like that." She rolled her eyes, turned away from me. She took a few steps toward the door, took her time. Fit her hands around her waist. "It's for the best. I've got no idea what I'd do with a mannish lesbian. Pretty witches are the only ones that last."

"How could you be like this?" I shook my head. "What is there to gain?"

She laughed at that, really laughed. She laughed like an ingenue. She gave her green spell book a kiss, took up her rifle and rested it against her shoulder. "Are you kidding me? I'm the witch who married the witchfinder general. I've got earrings made from the souls of bitches who wronged me. I am the queen of the world. I'm the future, baby. You're going to wish you were me. Talk soon, okay?"

Her heels tapped across the floor. She turned out the light. She bathed me in darkness and the door closed with a click.

IT'S OKAY

I wailed in the dark forever. Every moment spiraled in on itself. Time crushed, and inside its oils every splinter of a second was infinite. I kicked but I couldn't get traction. The swans didn't budge. Straining made things worse. I couldn't get out of this on my own. I couldn't reach my phone when it rang, and it rang more than once. Help sang at my hip and I couldn't reach it.

Slime slugged down the back of my throat. I couldn't breathe. I felt like I was dying.

I hadn't made peace with the accident. I'd found a brittle dry point that let me grow up, but I hadn't moved on, and my ability to move through space in a linear fashion in the wake of *an accident* was already tenuous at best. It'd been an act of god. It'd been a freak happenstance. It'd been a newspaper horror story for twenty-four hours. It had not been okay. I haven't been okay.

Ha, but murder?

My mother's murderer was a witch. A witch blithely awaiting the time to come when her soiree took up arms to murder all the witches in the Delacroix House. She hadn't mentioned David. She hadn't spoken his name even for a moment of indulgent self-victimization. She'd cried because she was angry that she couldn't put wet lead in her wall.

They were going to march on the Delacroix. I thought about the survivor, who'd be arriving in the house around now with the intention to swallow the soul that'd been stolen from her. My phone rang again, and I couldn't tell them, I couldn't pick up and warn them to run, to scatter.

The Honeyeaters' Theater.

I needed Mr. Scratch.

I needed my girls, I needed my fathers, I needed to collapse on the floor, a drink of water, a miracle, a crowbar.

I kept thinking I'd hit a wall where I wouldn't be able to cry anymore. I thought I'd burn through all my energy reserves and pass out. I didn't. I felt every gooey breath through my teeth, I felt every twitch and shudder my body made. Trauma churned in my gut like a furnace and generated enough heat that I thought I'd die before I was emptied of it.

I couldn't tell if my eyes were open or shut.

In the darkness something moved.

It was the door swinging open.

The light flipped on and I recoiled from it, spat and hissed like a cat splashed with water.

"Oh my god—oh, Sideways."

My eyes adjusted.

Levi Chantry stood in the doorway. He wore his school uniform, button-down and blazer, pressed gray slacks and argyle socks. His face was screwed up, his eyes enormous. He covered his mouth with his hand.

"*You,*" I growled.

"One moment," Levi said. He rushed into the room, hands fluttering in midair, and stood beside the swan trap. He kept glancing around, between my face and the tangled taxidermy and the endless drawers. He was so infuriatingly, insipidly preppy-looking. I wanted to do him real harm. I wanted to go beyond a Chett hex. For Madeline, for myself, I wanted to tear this *Dead Poets Society* jackass clean in half. "Oh!"

I blinked, bewildered.

Levi flew to a nearby drawer and pulled it open wide, dove a hand inside it. He reached inside quickly, but with a nervous, steely deliberateness. He withdrew an ancient-looking knife. It curved at the tip. It was made, without a doubt in my mind, for slicing open meat.

He turned to me, knife in hand, and swayed close.

I thrashed and snarled and spat at him.

"Please be still," he breathed, "I don't want to slip."

"What are you *doing?*"

He sliced off the head of a swan. It fell to the floor. Thoughtfully, Levi put the knife in his teeth, and he wrapped his hand around the decapitated swan body, jerked it backwards. Its body went stiff with normal corpse inanimateness. It came away from my body and he tossed it aside. It landed like a beach ball, lighter than it should've been.

I looked between the headless swan and Levi Chantry, confused beyond speech.

Levi shook his head, mumbled around the knife, pressed his hands to his eyes. His hair stood up on end, grew longer, softer, fell around his jaw. His skin rippled. Bones shifted, elided. Levi Chantry pulled his—their—hands back, and at once they were Shiloh again, under their glamour, their face wan with naked dread.

I let out a whimper and heaved forward. I had one arm free, now. I hooked it around their chest, risked slicing myself open on that knife in their teeth to press my face into their shoulder.

They murmured something, took the knife up. "Sideways, I cannot describe to you how fucking terrified I was when Yates called me, said you were coming to get me and you never showed up. I—I'm sorry I missed your calls, and livid, *livid* you came here alone. It's a miracle you're alive."

It literally was.

"I didn't know what else to do. I had to get Jing's specter—it was all my fault that Tatum had it," I said. My voice was hoarse as hell. I wasn't sure if I was understandable. "I shouldn't have mugged him, I—"

They snapped their head up. "You *mugged Tatum?* Beg fucking pardon?"

"It felt righteous at the time," I said. "I don't know, it was stupid, and he got the mimic off me. I didn't know what else to do other than come here. I knew it'd be in this room."

"There's no way to deactivate them without having the physical object," they breathed. "You—you did not make the right call, you absolutely should've gotten me before you did this, you should never come anywhere near this house but particularly with how many witchfinders are here, holy shit. I've never seen so many in one place."

"They're going to the Delacroix House," I said.

They paused right before they beheaded a second swan.

"They're going to the Delacroix House to kill everybody inside. Like the Honeyeaters' Theater. Grace told me."

The swan head smacked the floor with a *thunk*.

"We've got to warn them. We've got to get you out," they said, "and we've got to get out of town, Sideways."

"We're going to the Delacroix House," I said.

They sucked their cheeks in.

"Shiloh, we can't run away from this. I can't. I have to be there for whatever happens. I'm not going to run away." I felt my own breathing. I felt like I'd been running. I rested my free hand on their shoulder. "Are you going to come with me or not?"

"With you." They nodded once. "No question."

"Thank you." I shivered. "God, are you alright? Were you alright going through that crowd?"

"So long as I don't run into the real Levi, I'll be fine." They frowned and put the knife against the final swan throat. "I can't do clothes, just faces. Faces is literally the full extent of my magical practice now. I'm just feeling grateful that Levi is a fucking loser who would wear his school uniform around on a weekend just to suggest that he's studious. I don't have any clothes he'd wear otherwise." They furrowed their brow. "What are we going to do about you?"

"I don't know." Some of them knew my face—Grace and Abel and Levi and Elias, at the very least. "I had a bandanna over my nose when I mugged Tatum and the witchfinders who gave me a ride here thought I was a cis boy."

Shiloh choked. "I'm sorry, the what who gave you a what thought you were a what?"

"I know!" I didn't get it. I mean, I was incredibly cool with the prospect of looking androgynous, but full-on boy energy was not the desired look at all. I grimaced. My whole face hurt from bawling. "McKenna and Leighton." I blinked. "McKenna hit on me. Like, very unsubtly hit on me."

Shiloh peeled away the last swan body and I was free. I stood there for a moment, just feeling out what it was like to support my own weight. Meanwhile, Shiloh looked haunted. I took a step toward them, hooked an arm around their neck. I pressed my forehead to their forehead.

They looked at me and said thinly, "McKenna Bailey is my ex-girlfriend."

If there had been water in my mouth I'd have sprayed it.

"You know, if you and I are her taste in men," they murmured, "questions raise themselves. Not that it'd matter. McKenna Bailey is a spectacularly terrible person and if she were gay she'd just be a spectacularly terrible gay person."

"I mean, she's a witchfinder. That tracks."

Shiloh made a face. "Kennie made herself the main antagonist of bible camp for years, Sideways. Years."

"Bible camp," I said. I scraped my tongue with my teeth. "We need to get out of here. We need to move fast."

"Agreed." They put their hands back on their face, breathed their incantation, and my sibling warped into a nightmare person. Miraculous what a few months of HRT could do. They looked wholly separate now and I looked at their Levi-mask and found it nearly impossible to see the Shiloh there. They looked at me with their evil brother's evil face and frowned. "I've never done it on anybody else. I do not know how. The whole gimmick is that I am my own sigil, and—"

"It's cool, I'll keep my head down and we'll walk fast." I shook my head. "It's beautiful magic, Shi. You're beautiful. Just not right now."

"I know." They rolled their eyes. "I feel so tacky."

Hand in hand, the two of us peeled out of my dungeon and into the frat den beyond.

Boys played pool there. They chatted idly, glanced at the two of us as we passed.

"Levi," one of the boys said as another sank the eight. "You alright?"

Shiloh waved a hand and pressed forward.

"You holding hands with guys, now?"

"Sure am," Shiloh said as they dragged me toward the door into the cooler room.

No men in there anymore, but the hollow doe remained

on the table. I gave her a glance as we barreled through, said a little prayer for her sake. I wasn't religious. I was wildly ambivalent about the idea of intelligent design and the whole concept felt flimsy seeing as I knew how cosmic power functioned on the ground. Still. Still.

I told her that I was sorry.

Shiloh pulled me outside.

No more grilling dudes. I pointed at the spot where they'd been and I said aloud, "Dudes were grilling there. Just casually grilling."

"I don't know how to explain to you that most witchfinders are white barbecue dads," they hissed. "Alright, plan: we steal somebody's car."

"Cool," I said. "Good plan."

We rounded the corner of the house.

Tables spilled from the veranda onto the opposing edge of the yard. Families clustered around them and ate merrily. The tablecloths were nice. A school picture of David sat beside the flower arrangement in the middle of each table.

I gave Shiloh's hand a squeeze.

They shook their head, sucked in hard. "I'll be fine. Later."

"Got it." I scanned the crowd, searching for Grace. I didn't see her. I saw Elias folded over a different woman's lap, trembling all over, the woman scratching little circles on his back while he wept and wept and wept. At the edge of the veranda, with a microphone, I saw Abel. Beside Abel, mayday—Levi prime.

Fuck. No veranda for us. I whipped my head around the

lawn seats and my eyes caught the odd couple themselves. I stabbed a finger in Leighton and McKenna's direction. "Them," I hissed.

"The Baileys." They frowned. "You really want me to rob my terrible ex-girlfriend."

"No, I want to rob your terrible ex-girlfriend and I want you to be backup. Leighton—boyfriend or brother?"

"Brother," they said wearily. "I don't like that it was posed as a question."

"Their vibes were ambiguous," I said. I took a deep breath, lugged the dregs of my mostly dormant drama skill set from the pit of my soul to the surface. "Play along and act like we're friends, alright?"

"We're friends, that shouldn't be hard." They sniffed. "Does cis boy witchfinder Sideways have a name?"

I shook my head. Fuck, what was a good yuppie WASP boy name? I was blanking. "Chett. My name is Chett."

"You're naming yourself after your archetypal asshole."

"Yup." I cracked my knuckles. "Can you tell I've been crying?"

"Oh, totally." They paused. "On the plus side, your voice is very husky right now. I would say that you're adequately twink-passing in the voice department. Maybe a bit hunkier than your average twink, as a matter of fact. Chett the butchqueen."

"Wild," I said. "Never been a queen before."

"So, are you just gonna stroll up and ask for their keys?"

"Just watch, baby." I shook my hands out, hunched my shoulders forward. I wove between tables. I'd cried so much that I didn't have to work hard to simulate not being nervous. My body was no longer capable of flinching. We'd sunken far past that point of despair and were now hemming on enlightenment.

I strode up to the Baileys' table and cleared my throat.

Leighton and McKenna looked up from their plates of coleslaw and fruit salad. McKenna grinned. Leighton did not. I did my best to look at neither of them, stared at the ground we triangulated instead. It was a super fucking boring stretch of ground. Just grass. No weeds. Unseasonably green, which made me think that the Chantry family, on top of their other myriad crimes, also did water crimes. I hated them. I cleared my throat and rasped, "Changed my mind. It's fucking rough, all of this. Can I take you up on that weed?"

Shiloh beside me made an expression that made me nearly forget that this was Shiloh, a person I love, and not Levi, the most effortlessly patronizing dickhead in the world. They hadn't even said anything. It was just the vibe.

"Of course," McKenna said. She shoved her brother, glowered at him. "Hey asshole, go fetch . . ."

"This is Chett," Shiloh said.

My neck tingled, that lick of Madeline's hex on my skin suddenly squirmy. I fought the urge to glance at Shiloh's neck. I was curious if the Chett hex choker was still visible with their glamour spell. I resisted successfully. I was Chett the morose cis boy witchfinder, and I did not glance at my wretched preppy friends.

"Of course. My apologies. Go roll Chett the fattest blunt the world has ever seen, will you?" McKenna stared daggers at her brother, and meanwhile, as if of its own accord, her hand snaked up and grasped mine.

Shiloh looked at it.

I looked at it.

She looked at me with sparkles radiant in her eyes. Her winged eyeliner was impressive, I'd give her that. She flashed her teeth. "I know today has been hard on all of us."

Weird, I thought, that she was comforting Chett and not Levi. It'd been Levi's brother, after all, and from what I understood, Levi and David had been close.

I'd never been to bible camp.

Somehow I felt in that moment the gravity of Shiloh's earlier truth.

Leighton sighed, pushed his plate of beige sides away from him, and moved to stand.

"No," I said. I clapped him on the shoulder. "I don't want to make you get up. Look, if you hand me your keys I'll be back in a minute."

Leighton eyed me.

Underneath the table, McKenna inflicted some minor violence upon him.

He took the Lord's name in vain and slammed the keys on the table, mouthed something at McKenna that, again, felt like a slightly weird thing to say to a sister. I mean, I'd never had a sister, but—but surely calling one's sister a slut was kind of weird, yeah?

Whatever. I took the keys and jerked my chin up. I winked at McKenna for sauce.

I turned around, strode toward the endless spill of vehicles that passed for a parking lot, and did my best to keep my pace even. I wanted to run. I wanted to seize Shiloh's hand and bolt like a rabbit. I kept my shoulders hunched, kept my head down, willed attention off of me. I had a goddamned sigil for this, and it was not on my body. Figures!

"Fuck, you're good," Shiloh hissed.

"Thank you." Why did I lose my virginity at improv camp? Because I'm good at this shit. Girls love a bit.

We edged around a table and walked directly, square on, chest smacking chest, into a tall broad bronzy shell for violence. I blinked, stunned. I peered at the man.

The man, Tatum Jenkins, peered back at me.

"I know you," he said.

"Duh," Shiloh said. "This is Chett Smith. He was at Thanksgiving."

Chett Smith. Oh my god.

"No," Tatum said after a moment. He looked at my eyes, searched with an acute hunger. His temple was purple and algae green. His mouth, when he spoke, was missing pieces. It was a nice thought that he hadn't burned through some specter to heal up his face. It was even better that the curse Daisy and I had placed on him had *worked.* It almost made up for the fact that it was instantly clear that Tatum Jenkins was not stupid. He looked between the two of us and said, "Levi, explain some shit to me."

"There's no need to be vulgar," Shiloh said.

"Sure there is." Tatum smiled. A canine sprang free and fell to the grass. Blood oozed immediately, drooled down the cleft of his chin. He did not even flinch. "How is it that you're down here," they said, stabbing a finger toward the veranda, "when I just saw you up there with your mother?"

"Hmm," Shi said. "Fuck."

I put my fist in Shi's lapel and bolted.

Tatum was after us. Me and Shiloh wove between tables, I shoved one when I didn't clear it cleanly. Blond wet potato chips fluttered to the ground. Wine sloshed. We'd broken concord and people were looking at us, looking between Shiloh as Levi and me, a stranger, and Tatum with muddled bafflement and contempt. Like, how dare we break the solemnity of their pre-massacre misery luncheon. I shoulder checked the senator, Tatum's father, as I passed him. His cabernet made a ruby arc in the air and stained a nearby ivory dress.

Boys stood from their tables. People around our age. Runners.

They peeled after us like hunting dogs, concerned more with catching and trapping than cause. There was a chase to be had, so they were on it. They were on us. Their tongues lolled when they ran.

I felt fingers swipe the back of my neck.

I gripped the keys in my hand so hard I thought I'd crush

them. Thumb battered the buttons without looking or intention, I just needed the car unlocked, I didn't care, I couldn't think.

The alarm went off.

All eyes on us, every long pale face on long pale necks swiveled to follow our flight. More people stood, buttoned their blazers. They pushed their chairs in. Murmured to their dates. Big smiles all around us, an endlessly elaborating display of shark mouth dentistry.

We'd reached the start of the endless cars.

Leighton's BMW, screaming rhythmically, waited impossibly far away.

"Eloise," a voice called, and as we skirted around glossy hoods and behind knife's-edge exhaust pipes, instinct caught me and I looked up.

Grace Chantry stood atop a table. Miss Patience. Her sons stood on the ground at either side of her, Abel livid, Levi forlorn. She'd kicked the flower arrangement aside, crushed baby-blue carnations beneath her kitten heel. Water dripped from the table's edge. David's picture fell and nobody rescued it. She had her sights on us. Her rifle followed us, followed— not me, it was not following me. It was following my unkissed accomplice, the imposter Levi.

She adjusted her grip and aimed at Shiloh's head.

I shoved the keys in Shi's hands, twisted my body around them. I stumbled backwards. I kept my spine against their body, my shoulders squared, never more grateful for my broad and brawny fatness. I covered them and they pulled me onward. The car stopped screeching. I heard it unlock behind me.

I wasn't sure if Shiloh knew and I did not think to ask them.

Grace pulled the trigger.

The sound punched through everything and the world clapped scalding lavender bright.

The bullet ricocheted, was lost in the belly of a peach-colored Lexus.

Grace held up a hand and cut the whispering. She slung a strap over her shoulder, held her weapon at parade rest. She jutted out her chin.

Silence pulsed. No one spoke and no verbal orders were given. Save for some far speaker, blurring a Frank and Nancy duet, the world itself ceased sound-making friction. Everyone stood now. They faced us, watched us with expressions inscrutable. The runners had stopped, Tatum had stopped. He stood beside his father. They all just watched us.

Shiloh detached from me, got the door to the driver's side open and got their body inside. The ignition fired. The engine whirred, it sounded like a plague of locusts. I bolted around the hood, scrambled over shotgun. Shiloh was pulling out by the time I slammed the door shut.

We sped down the driveway so fast I thought the car would roll. I twisted, looked behind us, but the witchfinders did not pursue us. They stayed on their feet, watching, expressions neutral, their feet shoulder's width apart. They looked like a choir. We turned and I lost sight of Grace Chantry, her Chelsea Stringer A-line original drifting around her knees. Our Chett hex was imperfect, I felt with a twinge. We'd been so quick to decide who was hurting who. We hadn't thought about collaboration. We hadn't braced for Grace.

I panted. I gnawed the lining of my cheeks. "Why aren't they chasing us?"

"They can guess where we'll be going," Shi said. "They'll see us soon enough."

"She's a witch," I said.

Shiloh didn't say anything. They skimmed their tongue over their Levi-shaped teeth.

"She killed my mom," I said.

"God. I'm sorry." They shook their head. "I hate my mom."

"Ditto, solidarity." I jerked my phone out of my pocket, tried to get my heart rate under control and failed. Screen crushed as it was, I couldn't see who'd called me. I just called Yates. I squeezed my eyes shut, chanted, *Pick up pick up pick up pick up*, and heaven help me, she did. "Lila," I breathed.

"Sideways thank goodness holy shit I—"

"Jing, how's Jing."

"Strung out but fine, we drove her to the Delacroix. She's not fighting the spell anymore. It stopped. The mimic stopped. Madeline's with us. She says that Shiloh went to the Chantry house to find you, Sideways, tell me that they didn't—"

"They sure fucking did," I said. "We're on our way. Yates, I need you to tell everybody to get the fuck out of there. I— there are a thousand goddamned witchfinders congregating and they're all planning on going to the Delacroix. They're going to raze it. Salt and burn it."

Silence, shuffling.

A different, lower voice. "Sideways?"

I shook my head. "Is this—is this Maurice?"

"I understand that there are witchfinders on the way to my house."

"Yessir."

"I'll let the relevant parties know." He paused, murmured something to somebody who must've stood nearby. He sighed, then. Chuckled once. "I will not be evacuating, and I can tell you that a number of covens won't, either. Witches hardly have homes, but this is one. We won't be abandoning it. Will you be coming along?"

I nodded, and then found the breath to say, "Yessir."

"I'll see you soon, then."

I hung up. I stared out the window. "Can I borrow your phone?"

"In my left pocket."

I reached over, fished it from its ugly blazer confines.

"The password's my birthday."

"That's secure." A nervous cackle creaked out of me. My thumbs flew over the screen.

"What are you doing?"

"Can you turn on some music?"

They turned on some music. "That wasn't an answer."

I slipped their phone back in their pocket. "Texted Boris and Julian that I love them."

"Mm." They cocked their head to the side. "Did you include me in this?"

"Of course."

"Good," they said.

I turned the volume up.

TWENTY-ONE

LOUDEST BRIGHTEST

Half as many cars in the Delacroix lot as there had been last weekend. Half was more than I was expecting. Half meant some of us got out no matter what and that was a relief. Half meant that we were about to be hilariously outnumbered.

All at once it was a gorgeous spring afternoon. The clouds in the sky hopped like rabbits.

Shiloh and I got out of the car. I held their hand, led them up the steps to the long walkway. Light gleamed orange and alive inside the Delacroix, and I set my teeth on edge, squeezed Shi's hand so tight I couldn't feel it.

They squeezed back harder.

The door opened for us. Inanna and another Dagger Heart whose name I didn't know ushered us in, peered out at the blue sky behind us, closed the door once we'd stumbled inside. Shiloh put their hands on their face and rippled the them-ness back over them, albeit a them with longer, pinker eyelashes.

I eyed them, panting.

"I'd like to die cute."

"You're always cute." I whipped my head around, drank

in the crowd accumulated in the foyer. Maurice and Jupiter's lot, all the Dagger Hearts, Dominick and people whose raw out-of-pocket intensity meant they were probably Sisters Corbie, Blair and some hardy-looking Anti-Edonists, Guadalupe, a Star Thief who hurt Daisy's feelings. A man with long locs paced and prayed and tossed a little fire between his fingertips. Twin women with long red braids smoked together and peered into a looking glass that swirled with oil-slick colors. Lupe and Blair stared at each other from opposite sides of the room.

I took a few steps deeper in. I swiveled my head around, Shiloh close behind me.

I needed my girls.

Where the fuck were my girls?

Dominick had a hand on someone's shoulder—Madeline, she wore a *(my?)* beanie and I hadn't recognized her—and the two of them said little but kept their eyes locked and I made myself look away from them. I knew she wasn't supposed to be here and that was theoretically my problem. Maurice was also in the room and didn't seem upset and holy shit, I could die.

I could die.

Or actually—every other person could die. I'd be alive. I'd stay alive.

I needed Mr. Scratch.

I took a few steps deeper and then I couldn't breathe. My lungs constricted, my vision twinged black. I huffed. I screwed my face up, baffled, adrenaline blazing the Fourth of July above the bridge of my nose. My eyes lined up the stimuli in front of me but I didn't need it. I caught the edge of her perfume.

Jing.

I threw my arms around her and pulled her hard against me, pressed my face in her hair, and convulsed. She breathed, her ribs filled under my hands, and I focused on the texture of her turtleneck, the texture of her hair on my cheek. In her platforms we were the same height. I bowed my head, put my brow in the crook of her neck and gasped, "I'm sorry, I'm so sorry."

"Shut the fuck up," she said. "Holy shit, you went to the Chantry house? The godforsaken Chantry house? Why do you always go there? You have worms in your brain."

I laughed and it hurt. I kissed her neck, her cheek. I put her face in my hands, the tip of my nose against hers. "You saved my life."

She looked at me, black eyes expanding forever, back and back and back.

"Your spell. When you kissed me. You saved my life. I'm bulletproof, Jing."

"I'm a very good witch," she said with a little smile. "Figures."

A sound came out of my throat and I kissed her.

Daisy bowled into us and almost knocked us flat.

I let go of Jing and kissed stupid Daisy on her stupid forehead, then whipped my head around, searched for Yates. She was nearby, whispering to Shiloh with the Scratch Book in her arms, cradled against her chest. She stroked its spine.

She nodded at something they said, murmured something back with a gesture in Inanna's direction.

"The Dagger Hearts are the only ones who've really done much battle magic." Daisy sniffed. She wormed out of my hands, bounced on her toes. Her silky little dress felt egregiously impractical now. The scratches Jing had torn into her shoulders flashed hot pink. Angel amputation scars. Daisy bit a bit of skin beside her thumbnail. "Not on this scale, either. None of these covens have ever really shared spell notes so everybody's freaking the fuck out to the point where they've circled around to chill. You know it took your asses like forty-five minutes to drive here? You should've seen us a half hour ago. Exciting stuff. We hid poor Molly in the basement. She's chain-smoking and watching TV I think. She thinks this is hilarious. What a legend."

I snorted. "Think we can reasonably Chett like two hundred people at once?"

"Maybe if Mattel decides to sponsor us." She snickered.

Jing made a face. "The Anti-Edonists have experience holding off strikebreakers and cops, but they've got a whole thing about not being aggressive and it's left some mighty big holes in their strategy. Plus, all of their spells—fucking all of them—straight-up bible quotes. The Anti-Edonist grimoire is literally a book of prayers. They wrote a gospel with an ink devil. Anyway, their shit is all predicated on belief, and I'm pretty goddamn sure they're the only ones who are Jesus enough to be able to hold it."

"Fuck that." I shook my hands out. "Lila?"

She looked up, eyes glassy. "I'm glad you're okay."

I nodded, took a few strides toward her. "Can I see Scratch?"

"Of course," she said. She handed him to me. "I accepted Yale, just so you know. It was like, ten minutes ago. Just in case."

"I am so fucking proud of you," I said as I opened the book wide. Yates stood beside me, and I felt Jing and Daisy circle around, Shiloh as well, knees against knees, our toe tips the prongs of a five-pointed star. "Scratch," I said.

He slithered back and forth in big, erratic splotches.

"Scratch, what should we do?"

HONEYEATERS HONEYEATERS HONE-YEATERS HONEYEATERS

THEY CAME AND KILLED MY HONEYEATERS
MY DAUGHERS ARE DEAD NOW
MY DAUGHTERS WILL DIE

"Scratch," I breathed. I felt the first real vine of it unfurl in my gut, then—fear, real fear. I grinned like an idiot. I'd cried so hard that my sinuses felt like stones under my skin. "Scratch, you've got to help us out, here."

I AM SO AFRAID OF FIRE

I AM SO AFRAID OF YOU DYING

I WANT TO EAT THEM I WANT TO EAT THEM ALIVE

I WANT TO PULL THEM APART AND CRUSH THEM INTO INK

"Please." I tightened my grip on the cover. "We need weapons, we need a plan—"

"Holy fuck," Andy said. "There they are. They're pulling in."

The stillness broke and everybody churned around us. Witches swarmed and rearranged themselves. Eyeliner ran, sequined shoulders squared. Dagger Hearts staged themselves around the room and chanted rhythmically, and whatever they casted raised the hair on the back of my neck. Blair strode across the room and caught Lupe's shoulders, said with her voice high in her throat, "Goddamn it, Guadalupe. For ten years I've loved you, and I will until my last. I didn't think you'd stay but you stayed. I'm so glad you stayed. I'm so proud to know you. It'll be an honor to defend this place with you."

"Blair," she breathed. She curled her fingers around her lapel. "You idiot."

Her face fell.

She swayed into her. Her hair spilled black and starlight down her back. She kissed Blair openmouthed, and she put a hand at the small of her back, kissed her deeper.

I could hear it outside. I could hear cars parking, could hear doors slamming.

Scratch fritzed. He repeated the same fistful of phrases over and over again, churned them and rearranged them. I flipped pages but our sigils were gone. Every page was his weeping. If I turned too fast he'd goo between slices of paper, ooze like strands of honey, stretch and break and fall into more gnarls of anguish.

"He wants to eat the ones who burned him," Yates said. Her head snapped up.

Oh, shit. I looked up at her, and Jing at Daisy. Resonant and ringing, I felt the idea pop up to the surface. It was shared between the four of us. A pulse rang through me. Shiloh shifted like they could tell we'd struck something, but they were not a Scapegracer, and they looked between the four of us with their eyes rimmed red. They looked behind us, out a window. A vein flashed in their jaw.

"Madeline," I called.

She was at our side in an instant. "Please say you've got a fucking plan."

"Storage," Jing said.

"Upstairs," Yates said.

"The room with all the random magic junk," Daisy said.

"What?" Shiloh rubbed their hands together. "Whatever you're talking about we need to do it now."

Latticework rainbows weaved over the foyer, made a wall—a ward, an honest to god ward spell. Four Dagger Hearts locked elbows in front of the door. Their spell fell out of their mouths with a syncopated beat. I felt my heartbeat adjust to it.

The door pounded. It warped in its frame.

The Dagger Hearts chanted faster.

"Got it," Madeline said. She peeled off toward the dining room and I careened after her, my Scapegracers and my sibling beside me. Yates pulled Scratch from my arms and shoved him in her backpack.

Bright bass clattering—the witchfinders rammed against the door.

We tore through the dining room. It was still impossible, still pressed past physics to accommodate spare seating. Without bodies it felt like a cave. The candles jutted up from their tables unburning like so many stalagmites. The stage was empty, the grand piano's keys covered, strings exposed.

A scream tore out in the foyer behind us.

I heard the door burst open, heard boots pound inside.

We rounded a corner I'd forgotten about on the far side of the stage. It looked different than I'd remembered it, the brocade wallpaper was a different color and the pattern was larger, clawed around like the legs on harpy eagles. The hallway hadn't been here last time. It'd been somewhere else. I shook that off.

There was a door marked EMPLOYEES ONLY and Madeline jerked it open. She held it, and Yates ran through first, then Jing, Daisy, Shiloh, me. Madeline dropped the door behind us.

Spindly terrible staircase. It looked like a Nephil's spine. Twiggy, delicate rods of metal helixed up to drill through heaven, and I hated it as much as I had that first time. Yates was already halfway up. My girls bounded up, wound around and around. Winged seeds from sycamore trees falling in reverse. I put my hand on the rail and I ran. I climbed, I put my boots on each step and vaulted upwards. My stomach flipped. I glanced down, saw through the steps, saw the bones of the screw stairs and the floor far beneath me.

I saw Levi Chantry at the stair's bottom.

He started climbing.

Shiloh put a hand on my back and I kept going. Dizziness rocked me. My core burned. I felt like I'd guzzled oil and my insides were slippery with it.

"Come on," Yates called above me. She'd gotten the door open, she held it for the rest of us. Without looking up I felt somehow when Jing passed through, felt Daisy follow through in her wake. Another coil, Shiloh's hand never leaving me, and finally the door was upon me and I spilled through it with sea legs, shins aching, lungs on fire.

Shiloh walked in backwards.

"It's not too late, Addie. It's not too late for you or"—*deadname*—"if you just come down with me. I can get you out of here, this doesn't have to end like this, why won't you hold still and listen to me you little—"

I could see Madeline round the stair's top loop.

Levi crept behind her, blue eyes as big as tennis balls, veined like licorice, unblinking, near bursting. He had a gun slung over his blue cardigan. He looked at her beseechingly, looked in, beheld Shiloh. He panted like a dog. His shoulders rose and fell, made the gun sway.

Madeline whirled around to face him.

She slammed her sneaker against his sternum.

He windmilled his arms, mouth popped wide, brows up to his hairline. His tailbone smacked the railing. He pitched backwards, hips over ribs. I saw his ankles fly up, hit the place where his face had been a moment before.

His body slipped out of sight.

I heard the smack a moment later.

Madeline sprinted through the door and Yates shut it. They both flew away from it, backed up, stood behind Shi and me, stood with Jing and Daisy.

Shiloh walked toward the door. They pressed their palms against it.

"Shi," I said.

"I'll keep it closed." They didn't look up. "Do whatever you need to do. Be fast."

"Don't do any stupid shit, I swear to god."

"I won't," they breathed. "Fucking *move*."

We moved.

The storeroom had shifted slightly from the last time I'd been inside it. The rows were skinnier, there were more of them. Portraits that'd been downstairs at some point lay in stacks, wrapped in brown paper. Astrolabes slumped against busts. Books hummed. Jewelry stands, boxes upon boxes upon boxes, shipping crates that looked like something that might've fallen out of a Victorian freighter, filing cabinets, lavish displays of cutlery. I picked an aisle and peeled down it, scanned like mad. I knew I'd found Scratch by the grimoires, but where were the fucking grimoires?

I sprinted. No vases on either side of me, just wet samples of pickled baby mammals, hand mirrors, a bunch of porcelain dolls that I hated very fucking much. My head rushed. All this arcane shit and none of it useful to me. I tore a white sheet off a rocking horse. I kept running.

I hit the end of the aisle and ran into Jing. She took my hands, pulled me down the row and then up along to another. We caught sight of Madeline, who'd partnered up with Daisy.

"Have you—"

"No, not yet."

"Guys!"

Yates' voice sounded from a few aisles down.

We split, ran in that direction.

She stood with her back to a perilously tall bookshelf. Her yellow romper shone like a beacon, we flew to it, to her. She had her hands looped around the straps of her backpack, the place where Mr. Scratch lay. She looked at an industrial-looking metal set of shelves.

The shelves held urns and tall-necked amphorae, flower vases, covered jars.

I seized a porcelain one with blue winding flowers.

I lifted it above my head and hurled it to the floor.

It shattered into a billion pieces with a spectacular hyperpop clatter sound. Porcelain splinters flew in every direction, splashed my work pants. Amid the wreckage, bubbling and churning, was a glob of angry ink.

I slapped my hands on my thighs. "Come on, little fucker. Hitch a ride on me, I've got a job for you."

The ink devil rolled in on itself. It looked like a nosebleed clot. Its movements were weak, and if it spoke, I couldn't hear it. Still, it squelched over to me, gushed over my boot and climbed, crept up my pant leg. It slithered through the fibers, coursed over my kneecaps, the lines of my femurs, my belly, my chest. Faintly, its voice from nowhere and everywhere at once: *Good morning little sorcerer I am alive I squirm I brim with hate.*

Fuck, I love book devils.

Jing seized another urn and everything devolved. Madeline stomped a jar under her heel, Yates cracked a flower vase by knocking it against the blunt edge of a shelf. Daisy whammed them on the floor two at a time. The ink smell slit through the dust and the amber. It cloyed, electric and alive. Three book devils coiled around my body, clung to me, tendrils of their living murk swishing wild around my upper arms. I couldn't see it on Jing, couldn't see it on Madeline— their clothing was dark enough to obscure their seething disembodied fugitives. Yates and Daisy looked like they'd rolled in paint. Yates seemed vaguely discomforted but nevertheless determined. Daisy was a kid with a fistful of tickets at the county fair.

"Ladies," Shiloh shouted. I could hear them, could feel them grit their teeth. "With speed, if you please."

Jing ran. She and Madeline shot forward, Daisy and Yates close at their heels. I came up behind. The ink devils writhed against me, spiraled around me, circled my limbs and my neck. The wet snail feeling rocked a sick nostalgia through me. They felt like Mr. Scratch.

I could see Shiloh, now. They'd braced the door with a grandfather clock and an upturned table, slammed their shoulder into it to boot. They looked up, glanced between us, searching, desperate. They saw the splotches on Yates and Daze. They moved their mouth. I wondered if they were casting.

"How many witchfinders are out there?" Jing jerked her chin out.

"More than one," Shi hissed.

I passed a suit of armor and something shiny caught my eye. Book devils against me made me bold, the ink spell made me feel salty and brutal and sparkling with life. My gums thrummed. The suit of armor had a magnificent peacock-plumed helmet, a face like a beak. There was a pole-axe in its hollow grip.

I slid it from its hands.

The poleaxe was heavy, handled like a Louisiana slugger. Black handle, then the head: gibbous moon blade on one side, a hammer on the other, a prickly spike peaking up top. It was heavy, grounding. I spun the handle in my hands, looked up at Shiloh.

"I'll go out first," I said.

They looked between me and my stupid decision. They shook their head, exasperated. They nodded and Daisy and Madeline pulled the table aside, lugged the grandfather clock out of the way.

Shiloh let go, leaped aside.

The door flung open and three identical witchfinder boys loomed on the other side, one grinning, two grim-faced. Grim boys in jerseys, grinning one with his shirt unbuttoned, a gleaming crucifix pearly at his throat.

My life was a Hammer horror flick.

I opened my jaws and yelled. The scream tapered into a laugh, my lungs seizing, my diaphragm throwing a rave. I lunged; I reared the poleaxe back. I flew through the doorway. I did not blink. My heart swelled ripe with love. I slammed into the smiley boy with my full weight behind the metal edge and something broke on him. I knocked him back into his boys. His chest opened—shallow, but fuck did blood fall fast. He blinked, bewildered, down at his chest. It looked like he was wearing a pageant sash. It smelled like sucking a fistful of coins. Like Tang and ink.

A devil burst forth from the folds of my clothes.

They were drawn to the blood. They needed little encouragement. They squelched from one boy to the next and it was like acid had fallen from the sky. The devil whirred around them, dissolved them. I thought about the formaldehyde sheep's eye on my tongue, about how it'd felt when Scratch had devoured it.

The tops of their heads were gone.

Jaws slack, bodies still upright through some force unknown to me. Shock, maybe. They did not move but I did not know if these men knew that they had died. The devil ate fast. It unknit them bloodlessly, their upper limits dissolving, gushing black and happy. They were neck, shoulders. Hilariously, with a sound that would give me nightmares for the rest of my life, the devil noshed past their arm sockets, and their arms thunked on the floor.

"Fuck," I said. "Oh fuck, holy shit."

Screaming from the dining room.

I flew down the stairs three at a time. There were two devils on me, I trusted them to keep me upright, I was humming past the point of comprehending fear again. I felt like I'd eaten the sun. There was a nuclear reactor behind my face. I kneecapped a witchfinder girl as I passed her, and the devil above us oozed through the floor grate, done with those three boys, to drizzle over her shoulders and melt the dome of her head.

My heart in my stomach went *bambambam!*

I reached the floor. I stepped over Levi Chantry, yanked the door open.

There was violence in the dining room. Pearl and Jacques crouched behind the grand piano, clutching each other's shoulders. They levitated chairs. The chairs soared through the air, crashed into fifteen—fucking fifteen—guys. It was like a fucking pledge night invasion. They were armed, there were splintering holes in the lip of the stage, but I figured it was hard to take aim when one was pelted endlessly with heavy wingback armchairs. One dude was flat-out horizontal, howling beneath one that'd landed on his leg. Knee at a funny angle. Knees shouldn't bend that way.

I pointed the point of my poleaxe at the crowd.

A book devil leaped from the back of my knee, flowed around my hips, over my shoulder, down the inside of my arm and then out. It glided off the poleaxe's handle. It sprang from the spike, torqued, unfurled in midair like an octopus. Its appendages laced together. It fell like a net over their shoulders.

Madeline went for the stage. She jumped up, threw her arms around Jacques and Pearl. She held them a moment, then the three of them rose.

The rest of us kept running.

Daisy Brink dove through the double doors into the bloodshed like it was a mosh pit. It *looked* like a mosh pit—magic swept in aurora LED bursts, fists flew, bodies slammed bodies and elbows clattered into ribs, knives made arcs through the air like slung jewelry. I wondered about the lack of bullets and decided to stop wondering. Blair and the Anti-Edonists held off cops, yeah? These were cops and mayors and dentists and whatever. Same skill set.

Daisy raked her nails up her satiny sides and tossed her head back, basked. Ink tendrils shot from her, shimmered through the air, glommed onto bodies in motion. It looked like she was a mushroom bloom. Daisy had broken so many urns—there had been so many urns, there were so many burned books that had been stored upstairs, there were so many dead witches, these books had lost so many witches— and I kept waiting for her to stop sprinkling devil juice, but she didn't. Yates and Jing, hand in hand, darted beside her, pushed out into the foyer. Shiloh snaked out with them but peeled off from us, knelt where Andy lay on the floor, spitting blood. Jing looked back at me.

I rolled the handle over the back of my hand and caught it, then set it down. I followed after her empty-handed. I knew that they were all I'd need.

The Scapegracers marched through the foyer and out the front doors. We walked in lockstep, bubbling with broken, livid things. Jing took my hand and when I felt her brush by me, I took Daisy's. Jing murmured something. It was what she'd murmured against my hairline this morning, and I heard it clearly now—*nobody touches the ones I love, nothing can hurt my beloveds*. She whispered it again, again. My forehead tingled, and the feeling washed through me, made a circuit through my body and bled out through my hands. The spell extended, cloaked us, illuminated us with a veil of lavender light.

There were a hundred-some witchfinders waiting outside. They stood politely, hands clasped, murmuring among themselves, pretending to laugh at small talk. Red-beaked canisters of gasoline waited between their ankles. Someone checked their watch. Someone answered a business call. Elias Chantry had a hand over his heart like he was at his brat's recital.

Grace stood atop a Range Rover.

She looked down at us. She snapped one hand.

Muzzles raised.

"Us Scapegracers forever," Daisy said.

It sounded like a thunderstorm and all I saw was light. Ink lifted from our shoulders, surged from us, I felt it rush around me. The light filled my nose and mouth, it tasted sweet and clean. I tipped my head back. I felt like I stood in a river, fully submerged, water above my head. It swept around me, churned circuits, stole the sound out of my head. My clothes billowed around me. I could feel my girls, I could feel their hands and the heartbeat we shared, but I couldn't feel the porch under my feet. The light vibrated. It scintillated; I saw infinite color fractals unfurl in space. I was plunged into opalescent milk. I had red gills. I did not drown. My ankles hung limp, I was suspended in light, the boards of the porch were far below me, the porch did not exist. More ink fell from us, through us, from behind us. I heard a voice like Mr. Scratch's, but it was not Mr. Scratch's. It was not a voice at all. It said,

WHAT DO YOU WANT?

I couldn't speak, the light was in my mouth, but I felt: *I want safety for these witches. I want my friends and me to live. I want to grow up. I am so in love.*

THERE IS NOT ENOUGH CONSOLIDATION OF THE POTENTIAL THAT COULD BE US TO CONSUME ALL THAT MIGHT HARM YOU HERE. THERE ARE DEVILS WHO HAVE BEEN KNEADED INTO BEING THAT FEAST BUT THEY ARE NOT ENOUGH. THEY WILL NOT BE ENOUGH.

In my stomach, in my spleen: *If they are not enough, can we make more?*

WITCHES CAN ALWAYS MAKE MORE. MAKE US BE, AND WE WILL BE. WE WILL BECOME BEINGS. WE WILL BE THE SUBSTANCE FROM WHICH BOOKS MIGHT BE BOUND. WE WILL EAT FOR YOU WHEN WE ARE. THROUGH THE CIRCUIT OF YOUR BODIES AND INTO EARTHLY AIR: DO YOU SCULPT THIS INTO US?

All of us, from the seams of our folded hands: *We do.*

The void slithered in through our ears and climbed out of our mouths.

My boots landed softly on the porch.

TWENTY-TWO

HELLO MARY LOU

Molly the survivor sat on the stage without a specter inside her. She was middle-aged, wore thick-rimmed glasses and a vile grandpa sweater. She thumbed through a comic book. We all stood around her.

"It wasn't there?"

"It wasn't there." She held the floppy closer to her nose. "This letterer sucks."

"I'm so sorry," someone said.

"I'm so sorry," said Shiloh from under my arm.

"Mm-hmm." She sniffed. She rolled the comic up and slapped it against her opposing palm. "Those boys made a real mess of your restaurant, Maurice."

"Mendable damage," he said. "I wish I could say otherwise for you."

Outside, Inanna and Dominick and Lupe and Blair were crafting a spell together. It was intricate work, a cover-up this big, but witchfinders did this shit all the time. It's not like there were bodies to hide. Whatever organic material had once been assigned to the powers who'd brought violence here was gone, undone, consumed by wet book globs. No trace. Not a hair.

Jing kissed my knuckles, smeared purple over the cracks.

"What now?" Molly frowned. "Am I just supposed to die, or . . . ?"

I cleared my throat. I didn't step forward. I was not confident that I wouldn't collapse.

Molly nodded at me.

"We kneaded a fresh devil," I said. "We've made a being. When Madeline Kline took my specter from me, I held a devil inside me, and he kept me alive like a specter might. This devil's new. It hasn't been anything but fed yet. It can be yours."

I felt Daisy looking at me, but she didn't protest.

"I've never had a book devil. I've never done the coven thing." She gave me a long look, then stood. She stepped before me, tucked her comic book under her arm. She took off her glasses. She smacked her lips. "But I like the sound of new. Where is it?"

I shifted.

Yates put her face in her hands.

"You might wanna," I said, "you might wanna just cup your hands."

She looked skeptical but did as I suggested. She held her hands between us.

I spat the baby devil into her palms.

✳

For the life of me, I couldn't figure out a Windsor knot. I tried, I fumbled my hands up and down the length of my crimson tie and fashioned all manner of stupid lumps, but none of it had the intended dapper effect. I stared in the mirror.

The Sideways across from me shifted their weight. They looked, I thought, like a forties mafioso. Were there lesbians in mobster movies? Didn't matter. Mirror Sideways' mirror girlfriend snaked arms around their waist and said, "My, do you look handsome."

"How the fuck do ties work?"

"Spin."

I spun.

Jing folded her hands on my shoulders. She smoothed her hands down my lapels, felt along the tailored lines, the planes over my body. "I've got excellent taste."

"In suits?"

"In butches."

I scraped a hand over my skull—red and purple and baby blue and gray again, vivid noxious zigzags—and grinned. Jing shifted her weight, popped a hip. The lavender sequins made light dance off her shape, and I thought back a few months, conjured the Delacroix porch in my mind.

She took either end of my crimson tie and performed some witchcraft still unknown to me, managed to smooth the lines together, make a knot. She put a hand beneath it. She slid it up until it kissed the hollow of my throat. "There," she said. "Perfect."

I shaped a thanks, moved to press it to the corner of her mouth, but a hairbrush soared through the air and collided with my chest. I coughed, furrowed my brow. Kicked the hairbrush aside with my shiny leather monk shoes.

"No kissing until we take pictures," Daisy said. She leaned against Yates, gunmetal glitter against sky-colored silk, and rocked her head back. She wagged her brows, shimmied her shoulders. "I forbid you from fucking up her lipstick until later."

"Oh boy," Yates said.

Jing turned her head, looked her over.

"Madeline's social media," Yates said. "She signed with a label."

"A label," Jing said.

"Indie label, but a legit one." Daisy read over Yates' shoulder. "A hundred dollars says that she releases at least one album about eating Sideways' soul."

"I double your wager," Jing said.

"I think that she will move on in healthy ways and not milk that trauma for art," Yates said.

I shook my head, whistled through my teeth. "I'm about to be broke as hell and I'm not gonna make wagers on whether or not I'm someone's muse."

"As someone who's going to be comparably broke with you," Jing said, "I am confident that I could steal cash somewhere along the way. I mean, we're only going to be in each city for what, two weeks? There are so many bridges ahead of me to burn. The world is my oyster. Madeline Kline is going to release an album about eating Sideways' soul and internet music critic bros will salivate over it and I'll buy it on vinyl and eat Sideways to it, and I am going to be rich. So motherfucking rich, I tell you."

I scrubbed a hand over my face.

It was stupid, how much I loved this girl.

I thought about the stack of notebooks under Jing's bed, alive with old demons, unwritten, not ours. It'd be a hell of a year, recruiting. Me being a diligent artisanal person stabber student, her seeking out people with specters inside them who have all the raw materials for magic but no devil to gird them. Dominick, suffering as we made out in the back of his van and so on. It'd been Jing's idea, one she'd worked out with Maurice and Jupiter, cosigned by members of all the covens present on that day at the beginning of April. There'd never be another devil burned then locked and bound in urns again. When we were hurt, we'd heal together. We'd make anew together. We'd share resources with one another where we could, help as we were able. It was incredibly kumbaya, and if you asked Shiloh, the right kind of leftist of us, but more so I think there was the double bind of realizing that we would've died—violently perished—without each other.

The Scapegracers had overseen the devouring of two

hundred–something people. Lots of politicians and lawyers and law enforcers gone, undone. The story crafted for us was elaborate, four covens together could make masterful lies, but if one of us cracked we'd all crumble. There were more witchfinders beyond Sycamore Gorge. There would always be more. The world is structured such that witchfinders reproducing themselves is easy.

New witches are harder.

But then, there has never been somebody quite like Jing.

Yates stood, spun around once, stretched her arms above her head. "It's seven," she said. "Two hours of pictures, then we can show up and it'll be ten minutes before they crown Monique and Sheridan."

"Battle time," Daisy said. "Move out."

Jing led me by the tie.

✳

It was dark and light shattered, pop music zinged huge and loud in the soles of my shoes. Plastic glitter streamers poured off the walls. Paper stars, drifting disco ball. A little platform where our lesbians would stand. In a matter of minutes, the popularity contest to end all others would be announced, and a teacher who'd been cruel to me would crown gays she hated with shimmering plastic. It'd be a first for Sycamore Gorge. I didn't know if that'd change anything. I didn't know if the dykes who came after me would look at them and feel warmer, feel better, like there was a horizon toward which they could walk. I didn't know if it'd make them have waking nightmares about being Carrie. I didn't know. I didn't think. When the names were called, the two of them in their matching gowns would hold hands and smile at our cohort. We, the Scapegracers, would hold hands nearby and chant.

Dual lesbian prom queens, fine and good.

But *floating* dual lesbian prom queens?

There was time left still between now and then, and more time between them and our elaborate and flamboyantly illegal after-party. There was time between then and graduation, when we'd go in different directions and space would stretch between our bodies, our love tested against distance and duration and experience. There was time until the heat death of the universe, climate catastrophe, nuclear warfare. There was time. There was a space I lived within, and I lived. I was here. I liked this song. Jing had shown it to me the first day we loved each other with language attached. It had a sparkly snare that made me feel good. I felt good.

I put my arms around Jing Gao. I swayed with her, my jaw to her cheekbone. We leaned against each other, we held each other up. This wasn't a slow song, we were the only kids not jumping, we'd jump later. I'd mosh later, fight later, be extravagantly stupid in an hour, give or take. My tie would be around my head. I'd be marvelous and out of control.

Not now.

She tipped her head back and the light caught her face. It hung around her, creamy with magic. She was lustrous, radiant. She smiled at me and she shut her eyes, and I bowed my head and kissed her. We moved slowly. My heart beat slowly. It was the easiest thing in the world.

THE END, BITCH

ACKNOWLEDGMENTS

I wrote *Feast Makers* during lockdown-era Big Covid. It was January and too cold to go outside, not that there was such a thing as outside. Somehow, I made innumerable friends during that time, all of whom indirectly contributed to this book by being persistently lovely and brilliant while it was being made, Em and Hannah chiefly among them. Thank you to Jenny for verifying my continued existence and being warm to the beast that is me when I'm drafting. Thank you to Sar and Sneha, robustly. Thank you to all the friends I've made since drafting this book, non-exhaustively Thomas, Christina, Cecily, Asya, Ada, and Benji, for having taught me things about storytelling and why we continue to write in the face of the unbearable. Thank you to Anita, cris, Patrick, Margaret, Steve, Rhonda, Jeremy, Sara, Hilary, and Bill, for mentorship that has made me better. Thank you to my mother and my little sister, forever.

Thank you to the Erewhon team, past and present, whose collective vision and labor has made material my nonsense, and for generally being exceptionally insightful and kind human persons. Thank you to Diana, who was given this project in its final instillation and immediately understood, to Viengsamai for exceptional insight, to Marty for persistence and kindness, Sarah for her leadership and vision, Leah and NaNá for keeping this manuscript on the rails, Cass for coordination and generosity, Anka and Dana and Samira for making these books so beautiful, Kasie for her warmth and organizational skills, and Liz for having initially taken the chance on *Scapegracers*. Thank you to Kiki, who is cool and signed on to be my agent at an odd moment in my career and has subsequently made it better and brighter. Thank you to all the workers who print, bind, transport, and distribute this book, whose labor is invaluable to the book's existence, thank you thank you thank you!

Thank you to every horror movie I saw in high school, particularly *The Craft*, *Ginger Snaps*, *Jennifer's Body*, *Fire Walk with Me*, *Jawbreaker*, *Heathers*, *A Nightmare on Elm Street 2*, *Hello Mary Lou: Prom Night II*, *American Mary*, *Carrie*, *Suspiria*, *All Cheerleaders Die*, and *It Follows*. Where would I be without you? Thank you to every fagdyke I know. Thank you to queer people who live long enough to be elders, thank you to random adult butches I'd glimpse when I was a kid, thank you to every single trans teenager alive, thank you to bad choices I made young. Thank you not to Ohio, but the memories I have of unstoppable happiness that happened there, like stone fruits and seances and smoker's alley, thank you to corn mazes and graveyards, thank you to coyotes at three a.m., thank you to the night when my friends and I snuck into a development plot where the houses hadn't been built yet where we, being idiots, screamed and danced and collapsed on the road gaping up at the big black sky, at which